BOOK OF THE JUST

Book Three of The Bohemian Trilogy

DANA CHAMBLEE CARPENTER

PEGASUS BOOKS
NEW YORK LONDON

BOOK OF THE JUST

Pegasus Books Ltd.
148 W 37th Street, 13th Floor
New York, NY 10018

First Pegasus Books edition October 2018

Interior design by Maria Fernandez

Library of Congress Cataloging-in-Publication Data is available.

ISBN: 978-1-68177-858-7

10 9 8 7 6 5 4 3 2 1

Printed in the United States of America
Distributed by W. W. Norton & Company

For the love of a dog:
Koko, Gracie, Philos, and Artemis

PROLOGUE

I t's time for bed, Luc," the young woman said.

"I don't want to go to bed." The heavy-lidded little boy tucked his arm under his head and sluggishly kicked at a stack of blocks, sending them tumbling to the rug.

The father leaned against the doorjamb of the nursery, smiling at his son's tantrum, curious to see if the boy would win this battle of wills against his orderly nanny. As the father watched, a snippet of a story came to him: "'Keep back, lady, no one is going to catch me and make me a man.'" The father, who never forgot anything, mentally flipped through the rest of Peter Pan's tale in search of parental insight and wondered if it was time to move his son into a room of his own, away from the babyish decor and the low toddler bed.

Based on the date of the boy's birth—and assuming a typical human calendar—Luc should have been celebrating his second birthday. But neither dates nor calendars were relevant to someone like Luc—or to his father. And since the boy had never celebrated a birthday, he didn't know to miss it.

In the first days of parenthood, Luc's father had meant to follow all the typical human customs and let his son grow up like any other boy. But then his patience had worn out. He wanted a son he could train, not one who needed diapers changed and lullabies sung. So the father had traveled the dark planes between place and time as only he could, his newborn son tucked against his chest. He'd pulled his cloak around them both and disappeared into the shadows, reappearing somewhere else with the newborn suddenly grown into an infant. Someday, when the boy reached maturity, the aging would stop altogether. But in the meantime, the father would manipulate his son's growth as it fit his need and whimsy.

He had tried again to care for his infant son, but it was not in his nature to handle teething well. He'd considered finding a foster family to care for the boy until he reached an age that would be less demanding, but the father had seen the consequences of letting someone else raise a child. He had lost his daughter forever because of it.

Determined, he had wrapped himself up once more and traveled again. The infant had become a toddler, and his father had managed as best he could, until he couldn't manage any longer. Father and son had taken one last trip though the dark planes. Now the toddler was a child, and they had been happy together for months. Luc was less focused on basic needs and far more interested in his desires. That was the fertile playground his father knew so well.

"I said I do not want to go to bed!" Luc sat up, yanking the zipper of his footed pajamas up and down as if he was ripping open his chest over and over again. Up and down. Up. Down.

"Little boys don't always get what they want," the woman answered as she sprayed lavender oil on the pillow.

With a growl, Luc grabbed a wooden train car from the floor and threw it at the nanny's head.

She crossed the room quickly and took the boy by the arm. "We do not throw things, Luc!"

"I don't like you anymore. I wish you were dead!" he screamed. "Die, nanny, die!"

Shock flashed across the young woman's face, her skin turned pasty like glue, her eyes vacant like those of the toy soldiers at war on the table behind her. The bottle of lavender slipped from the nanny's hand, shattering on the floor as she pitched forward like a puppet cut loose from its strings.

Luc backed away, wide-eyed, until he ran up against his father's legs. The boy gaped at the work of his words, his dead nanny lying among the disheveled blocks and train cars with a sickly sweet pool of lavender seeping into the floor. His eyes brimming with unshed tears, he turned to look up at his father.

Luc's father chuckled. "Did I ever tell you about a boy named Peter Pan? He killed people, too, but he didn't cry about it."

He patted his son on the head and led him out of the nursery.

PART ONE

It takes two people to make you, and one people to die. That's how the world is going to end.

—William Faulkner, *As I Lay Dying*

CHAPTER ONE

A dream for a dream," the old woman said to Mouse as the wails of the dingoes rose up from the dry riverbed below.

Mouse knelt on an outcropping in the hills above. The day's warmth, which was still trapped in the stone, seeped into her bared skin. She looked out over the wide Australian outback. The sun had sunk below the edge of the world, leaving only the thinnest line of light, like a last gasp, bloodred along the horizon.

"Are you ready, little one?" Ngara asked.

Mouse looked up into the old woman's round face, chiseled with lines, and nodded. "I am ready."

"Sisters, come." Ngara motioned with her hands, and a group of Martu women stepped out of the shadows cast by the fire at the side of the outcropping. Their bodies painted with bone-white dots, they looked like skeletons with gaping mouths. They encircled Mouse, each of them laying hands on her, touching her head or back or arms in blessing, a community of women giving her strength for what was to come. Not long ago, Mouse would have shunned such contact. But love changed a person, even someone who had lived as long as Mouse. So did dying.

Ngara took Mouse's face gently between her calloused hands and drew her fingers across her forehead, leaving behind streaks of white and black paint. The women started to dance, the gentle slaps of their feet on the stone beating out a hypnotic rhythm.

"Give us your dream and we show you ours," Ngara said. "Something that was and is. Something that will be."

Mouse sat back against her heels, a thrill of anticipation running through her. The women's ceremonies were intimate and private, closed even to the Martu men. To be invited to join was like being asked to be part of the family. Mouse had always longed for a family.

But Ngara wasn't asking for any normal dream. For the Martu, the Dreaming, or what they called the *Jukurppa*, was Truth—the secrets of the gods and the ancestors wrapped up in stories. These stories didn't just tell what once was. Sometimes the stories showed the dreamer what was coming. Ngara was asking Mouse to tell them a story that gave away a secret. Mouse wasn't used to sharing such private details with anyone because her secrets—her truths—were dangerous.

"It will be well," Ngara whispered to her as she painted lines down Mouse's neck and then thrust them across her collarbone and around her breasts. "Do not be afraid."

Mouse took in a deep breath filled with the sweet scent of an herb the women had put on the fire. She would have to be careful to give Ngara what she wanted, but not give away too much. She nodded to herself as she settled on the story she would tell, one that would give the women the truth they most needed to hear.

She closed her eyes and surrendered to the beat of the women dancing and to the song of the dingoes and the patterns Ngara continued to paint on her naked body. And Mouse let a dream come.

"I am a little girl," she said. Her voice sounded far away, like an echo calling back. "I am walking in the Mary Garden with Father Lucas. He is a wise man. He loves me." She smiled as the image came to her, more memory than dream, just as she intended. "We are alone because the others are afraid of me." Mouse's smile slipped as she carefully turned her thoughts. "Father Lucas and I are talking about a book, and I am not watching the path. I fall and cut my leg on a rock. The sharp edge of it slices me to the bone. I bleed. Father Lucas pulls me to him and tears a bit of cloth from his habit, then presses it against my wound."

Mouse had an unnatural and perfect recall, a consequence of being her father's daughter. She never forgot anything. She remembered exactly what had happened all those years ago with Father Lucas—which birds had been singing, where the sun had been in the sky, what flowers had been in bloom. But as Ngara started to sing, a deep, vibrating hum without words, Mouse felt the memory change and her control slip away. All those details in her mind scattered like dried leaves on the wind. Pushed by Ngara's incessant humming, the remembered sun spun and danced across the sky, the delicate lilies of the valley turned their heads up, stretching into roses, and ran crimson red. The twitter of the garden finches grew shrill and sharp, like the bark of jays. All of it had gone wrong somehow.

Mouse shook her head slowly, trying to get control of her dream again. She knew the truth she wanted to give Ngara: a story of a man who had loved Mouse like a daughter and died because he knew her secrets. But the dream wasn't Mouse's anymore. It was a thing of its own, alive. And it was hunting for another secret to tell.

"The Father's hands are covered in my blood," Mouse continued. "I look up at him, frightened. I see worry in his eyes as he pulls the cloth back to study the wound." She could hear the fear in her voice as if it belonged to someone else. "He snatches his hand back, pushes away from me, and I look down to see what scared him."

Her mind screamed out that this had not happened. Father Lucas had never pulled away from her. He had not been afraid. Had he?

"I watch my skin knit itself back together—so smoothly there is no scar, no proof that it ever happened, except for the blood on Father Lucas's hands."

Ngara drew the paint down Mouse's arm and into her palm, letting it pool and swirl.

"Now Father Lucas is screaming. Why is he screaming?" Mouse tried to open her eyes but couldn't; she felt cut off from her body, paralyzed. "The blood is burning him. My blood is killing him! I wipe at it with my hands, with the cloth, but it only spreads. Please, make it stop." She tried to lift her hands to her face but was held still by Ngara's hum and the rhythm of the dancing women.

Tears streamed down Mouse's face. "Father Lucas is dead. He is on a stone table. I am washing his body for burial. I am a woman now." She rocked slowly to the beat of the women's song. Her jaw clenched. "There is another man in the room."

The dingoes howled out of time, a haunting countermelody to the women's music.

"It is my real father, the one who gave me life. I want to kill him." Mouse went still again. "He is standing over me. I see the stars behind him. He is laughing. He has a secret." Her breath came shallow and quick now. "I reach for him. He wraps me in the darkness of his cloak and I am gone."

The women danced fiercely, their feet pounding the stone as Ngara sang faster and louder, each note hitting Mouse like a torrent of rain. And then the old woman's hand slammed into Mouse's chest, and it was like someone had turned on a spotlight in her mind. Though her eyes were still closed, Mouse squeezed them tight against the brightness of the light. She didn't want to look. She didn't want to see the secret this dream had found.

But Mouse had no choice. "Someone is here, but it is hard to see," she said. "There is a shape, a hole in the light. I think it is my father." Her hands balled into fists, the paint oozing up between her fingers. "He is turning toward me. I am afraid." Her face tilted back like she was looking up.

"Oh, no."

Mouse's eyes snapped open. Her vision suddenly crowded with the brilliance of the Australian night sky, the Milky Way illuminated like a thunderous wave about to break against the earth. Disoriented, she threw her hands out to keep from falling into the stars.

Ngara caught her by the wrists, bringing Mouse's focus back to the rock, back to the women tightening the circle around her, their feet now still but their hands beating out rhythms on their thighs and chests. One of the women blew against a leaf at her lips and an eerie, rattling whistle played out into the night. The dingoes had gone quiet.

Mouse looked at Ngara. The old woman's eyes were wide with awe and fear.

"What was that? What did I—?" Mouse tried to ask, but the old woman laid her finger against Mouse's mouth, silencing her.

"You must see the *Jakulyukulyu* now. The dream of the Seven Sisters." She pulled Mouse's face back up to the stars with one hand and ran a stone knife quickly down Mouse's sternum with the other, making a long, shallow slice in the skin. Mouse gasped but did not look down at the cut, or at the blood she could feel seeping down her chest. She was caught by what she saw in the wide sky.

The stars were moving.

"This is the songline of the Seven Sisters, the first women, the women who dance in the night. Our sisters, and now yours." Ngara wove the tale into the new song the Martu women played.

"In the Jukurrpa, there were the first women and the first men. The women had their laws apart from the men. The women followed their own law." As Ngara spoke, Mouse watched the stars play out the story, dancing in a circle together. The high whistling seemed to come as much from above as beside Mouse.

"But then a man, Yurla, wanted one of the Seven Sisters. He did not care what the women wanted. He chased them through the land until he caught one to make his own."

In the sky, Mouse saw the Pleiades pull away from the larger group of dancing stars. Another star crept behind them, stalking them.

"But the Sisters would not leave the one. They tricked Yurla, made him think they would all stay. They made him happy."

The Pleiades circled around the lone star.

"When he grew complacent, they blinded him, snatched up their sister, and went to hide in the sky. Yurla searched all around him, but he could find nothing. He was lost. And the Sisters had their vengeance."

Ngara eased behind Mouse and crouched beside her, her mouth at Mouse's ear.

"Watch now," Ngara whispered as she pointed at the sky. "The Sisters show you what you want. Watch."

The Pleiades slid into their familiar, blurred cluster while the single star fell away, as if a string tying it to the universe had suddenly snapped. The star sank quickly at first and then slowed as it neared the horizon, the dark outline of the hills to the north made visible against the starlight. It hovered a moment above a single peak and then went dark.

"The Sisters' secret is now yours," Ngara said as she moved back in front of Mouse and laid her hands on either side of Mouse's face. "You understand?"

"No."

"The Sisters will give you something there in the cave of the *kurdaitcha*—the vengeance seekers."

"I don't want revenge," Mouse said, shaking.

The old woman shrugged her shoulders. "Dreams show only truth."

"And what about my dream?" Mouse asked.

Ngara took a step back.

"You saw everything I saw, didn't you?" Mouse didn't need the old woman's answer; she could see the truth in her face. "What did it mean?"

Some of it had made sense to Mouse—Father Lucas's love and Mouse's guilt over his death, in particular. And the vision of Mouse's father looking down on her, laughing, was also a real memory, though not one she had meant to show the old woman. That was the last time she'd seen her father, atop Megiddo in Israel two years ago, when her father had left her for dead. He had told her something important, but Mouse, who normally remembered every word she'd read, every place she'd been, every face she'd met, could not remember her father's last words to her. In the quiet of the night, Mouse sometimes thought she might capture that moment again, but the harder she tried, the further it seemed to slip away.

The one secret Mouse had pushed into the far shadows of her mind was the truth of who her father was. That was the secret the dream had gone hunting for—and found.

"What did you do to me?" she asked the old woman as the other Martu broke the circle and went back to the fire.

"I bring dreams."

Mouse narrowed her eyes, studying Ngara with a new awareness. "You've known since I got here, haven't you? Known what I am?"

Again, Ngara shrugged. "You walk long, like the ancestors. You are dusted with the First Dreaming. Part of the old ones, you are."

"You thought I was special and took me in." Sadness weighted Mouse's words.

"You are special."

Mouse shivered at the old woman's voice. In the year that Mouse had been living with the Martu, Ngara had always spoken to her like a grandmother. It hurt to think that from now on, her words would be laced with awe. But Mouse needed one more answer, an explanation for what had happened at the end of her dream.

"Special—maybe—but not in the way you imagined. Now you know the truth." Mouse again saw the image in her mind of the figure silhouetted in the bright light, turning toward her, but the face—it wasn't her father's. It was hers. She hesitated, but swallowed her fear. "Why did I become my father?"

"The truth is in the dream," Ngara said.

"No. You were shaping it, controlling it. I could feel it."

Ngara sighed. "I opened the doors for you to see what was and what is and what will be."

"Are you saying I'm going to turn into my father?" Mouse felt the power in her flare with a flash of anger.

"I say nothing. The truth is in the dream."

Angelo was waiting with the other men around the fire pit where the Martu shared their food and their stories. Savory scents of roasting lizard meat and roots greeted the women as they drove in from the surrounding darkness.

"How was it?" Angelo asked as he wrapped his arms around Mouse.

"Interesting," she replied, but the children were already tugging at her shirt, begging her to come dance with them to celebrate her initiation. Mouse bathed in the firelight and the warmth of inclusion. Her unnatural abilities and oddness had kept others at a distance during her childhood. Later, the knowledge of what she was—her father's daughter, an immortal, hunted prey—had kept her on the run and isolated. Angelo's love had driven away much of Mouse's loneliness, but being part of a community satisfied a hunger for belonging that was too big for one person to fill.

As she spun with the children around the fire, their feet keeping time with the clack of the rhythm sticks and the shifting vibrations of the didgeridoo, Mouse stole a glance at Ngara. The old woman seemed as she always had. She caught Mouse's eye and smiled, her face lit with an easy delight.

By the time Angelo slipped his hand in Mouse's and pulled her away from the fire toward the little shed that served as their home among the Martu, the chants of welcome, Ngara's ease, and the children's joy had driven away Mouse's worry about the Dreaming and what it meant. But when she told Angelo about her first vision, the flutters of foreboding came back.

"It wasn't real," she said, as much to herself as to Angelo. She pushed against the reawakened disquiet. "The music and the paint and whatever that herb was, it all played against my mind. Made me vulnerable."

"You, vulnerable? To what?" Angelo asked.

"What's the one thing that's been driving me all my life? My fear that I'd end up like my father. It's no wonder that's what my mind showed me."

She was working hard to believe her own explanation and to dismiss the magic she'd felt in the moment. It was easy to do while standing in the clean, electric light, sheltered in the tidy, boxed-off shed. But the nerves pricking at the back of her neck pestered Mouse with the truth of what had happened out in the wild of the outback.

"It was all in my mind," she said.

"None of that matters, though, does it?" Angelo asked. "Ngara knows who you are—there's no way we can stay."

"Why not? She's known all along that I was something . . . odd. So nothing's really different, is it?" Mouse could hear the lie in her voice. She could tell from his face that Angelo had heard it, too. "Well, she seemed fine tonight. Let's just wait and see how it goes."

"That's the hundredth time you've said 'Let's wait' when I've mentioned leaving. What's—"

"Actually, it's only the eighth," she said playfully as she lay back on the bed. "The first time was—"

He pulled his shirt over his head and tossed it at her. "Quit showing off and stop dodging the question. Why don't you want to leave?"

They had come to Australia to hide—from her actual father and from Angelo's spiritual one, Bishop Sebastian. They'd spent nearly a year hopping from one country to another, trying to hide their trail. As hard as it had been on her, it had taken an even greater toll on Angelo. Mouse had seen the strain on his face morning and night. No routines. Never normal. Always afraid. When they fled Israel after she'd healed from what her father had done to her at Megiddo, Mouse had thought she and Angelo could be a home for each other, even on the run, but it was hard to make a home in the back of a bus, or on a train, or in some rent-by-the-hour motel at the end of a dark alley.

About a year ago, Mouse had known she had to do something. Angelo was wearing out. She needed to find someplace off the grid where they could settle for a few weeks, maybe even months, to let Angelo rest. She'd brought them to the outback, away from everything, and then pushed them even deeper into the desert, where they'd stumbled across a small Martu community at the borders of Karlamilyi Park. Mouse and Angelo had expected to stay only a few days and then move on, but the Martu people had taken them in as if they'd been stray dogs wandering in from the desert. They fed them, gave them a home, and made them part of the community. Mouse worked at the clinic helping the *ngang-kari*, the native healers, tend the sick and elderly. Angelo helped with the endless labor it took to survive in the desert, constantly hunting food or water. It had been a blessing, a type of sanctuary Mouse had never thought to find.

And she didn't want to leave.

"I like it here," she said. "We're safe."

"No, we're not."

"As safe as anywhere."

"You told me that the only safe place was on the run. What's changed?"

She couldn't tell him that *he* was what had changed. At first, having him running with her had made everything easier. She had someone else to keep watch while she slept, someone to help her strategize the next move, someone to talk to. Someone to love.

But that last had made it harder, too. She couldn't stand seeing his eyes dark, watching all of his curiosity and wonder at the world turn into fearful scrutiny and suspicion. Everyone was a potential threat, an agent of Bishop Sebastian's Novus Rishi or a puppet controlled by her father. Angelo had become obsessed with her father—she supposed it was born from seeing what he had done to Mouse at Megiddo. Enraged by her empathy, her father had unraveled her like a yarn doll and left her, not to die, but dead already. Dead in a way that she had never really believed possible for an immortal. Angelo had sat beside her broken, bloodless corpse for three days, refusing to mourn. His faith had called her back.

Ever since, he talked constantly of finding a way to protect them. A year ago, he had started having bad dreams and had grown quick-tempered in his exhaustion. That was when Mouse knew she needed to find someplace where they could at least pretend that life was stable and safe, somewhere they could play at being normal.

And he *had* gotten better since they'd settled in the shed out in the middle of nowhere with people who accepted them as they were. He wasn't quite the playful, ever-hopeful Angelo he had been, but Mouse wasn't ready to give up the idea that with a little more rest he could be—that time could undo the taint Mouse's life had left on him.

"It's me, isn't it?" he asked her now. "You think I can't handle it on the run."

"It's just . . . I like how we are here, Angelo. It feels like a real life—simple, but happy. Normal. I've never had that." She sat up with a smile and pulled him down onto the bed with her. "Don't you like how we are here?" She slipped her leg into the gap between his.

"I like you wherever we are." He bent down to kiss her. "I just want us to be safe. And I don't want you making a decision that puts us at risk because you think I'm too weak to handle it. I know I'm not as good at running as you are, but you've had lots more experience than I have."

"Are you calling me old?"

"If the *poulaine* fits." He ran his finger along the painted patterns on her face and down her neck. "What are these?"

"Ngara painted them. They're part of the ceremony."

"From the Dreaming?" His fingers kept playing along the lines and swirls, making her skin quiver, her body moving to meet his.

"Some from the one I called up. Others belong to the dream they gave me."

"They gave you a dream?" Angelo lowered his mouth to kiss the bare skin between the patterns, a creamy contrast to the black and white paint.

"About the Seven Sisters, the Pleiades," she said, her voice soft.

"Do these patterns run over your whole body?"

Mouse laughed. "Yes, they do. See?" She pulled her shirt over her head, exposing the painted Dreaming that crisscrossed her chest and abdomen. "They even go around to the back." She turned and stretched out across the bed. Angelo traced the set of zigzagged stripes along her shoulder blades, and Mouse moaned softly.

"Tell me about these Seven Sisters," he said.

As with her own Dreaming, the story lost some of the magic in the retelling—partially because they were in a metal shed on a squeaky bed and not under the stars. But also because Mouse wanted it that way. If she accepted truth in the dream of the Seven Sisters, she had to accept the truth in her own dream as well.

She told Angelo about her second vision but kept her voice soft with seduction and her focus on his hands as they trailed along her skin. When she explained what Ngara said about how the star descending at the end was meant to show Mouse where to find the Sisters' secret, Angelo's hands stilled.

"Ngara thinks there's something in that cave that can help us?" he asked.

"Help us get revenge. You have someone in mind?" Mouse asked, teasing.

But Angelo's mood had shifted. "I don't care what it's meant for, Mouse. If there's a chance there's something in that cave to help protect us—something we can use against your father—"

"Or yours." Mouse pushed herself up.

"They're not the same. The Bishop and his group are powerful, but they're only human. The only resources they have are money and influence and—"

"Eyes and ears everywhere."

"As long as we stay off the grid, they probably aren't going to find us. What's stopping your father?"

Mouse knew he was right. Bishop Sebastian and the Novus Rishi were driven by an obsession to fight evil, a battle they understood to be real and immediate, and one they were prepared to win at any cost. They wanted Mouse to help them do it—whether she wanted to be an Armageddon warrior or not. But the Novus Rishi were merely flesh and blood. Staying ahead of them was only difficult, not impossible. She couldn't say the same about her father. If he decided he wanted Mouse, he could take her any time, in any place, and there was little she or Angelo could do to stop it.

"We don't even know there's anything out in that cave, Angelo. It's just a story an old woman told around a campfire."

"You said you saw the stars move."

Mouse looked away.

"Do you think it was just a story?" he pressed.

She wanted to say yes. She wanted to laugh at all of it—her dream, their story. She didn't want any of it to matter. Because she didn't want anything to change. But she couldn't silence the caterwaul of warning—her seven-hundred-year-old instinct told her that something was coming.

"Ngara said it was for revenge," Mouse said sadly. "I don't want revenge. Do you?"

When he finally answered, there was a steeliness in Angelo's voice. "I'll do anything to keep us safe."

"Seeking vengeance isn't—"

"Even if it was meant for revenge, Mouse, that doesn't mean we have to use it that way," he said. "Besides, the story you just told me suggests that maybe this secret the Sisters are giving you is the same thing they used to get rid of a predator. I'd sure love to have something that could do that, wouldn't you? Something we could use to shake off the people hunting us?"

"Yes, but—"

"Then let's go find it."

"We don't even know what we're looking for."

"We'll figure it out. We're good at this stuff. And I'm tired of just waiting for the next crisis—I want to *do* something to be ready."

Mouse chewed at her lip.

"It'll be fun, anyway," he said, his tone lighter with the assurance that he'd won her over. "Going on a quest. In a cave."

"In the dark. With bugs."

"Come on, where's my adventurous Mouse? My mighty—"

"Don't you do it!" she half shouted, half laughed, as she threw a pillow at him. He caught it and tossed it back at her. She pulled it to her chest and sighed. "Okay. We'll go tomorrow."

He leaned over and kissed her. "Now let's get back to finding out where those patterns go," he said, tugging at the top of her shorts.

Mouse stilled his hand. "How about we wash them off instead? They itch."

The truth was she wanted to be free of the dreams, as if pretending they hadn't happened would silence the foreboding.

"I'll see if there's any water," Angelo said with a twinkle in his eye. The outstation had an old cattle bore where they could draw water, though the quantity and quality depended on how long it had been since the rainy season.

He came back a few minutes later to find Mouse pacing. "I warmed it at the fire," he said, putting the bucket down and dipping a rag in the water.

"It smells good." Mouse unfastened her shorts, let them fall, and then kicked them over to where her shirt lay crumpled on the bed. "Desert oak needles, right?" They were floating in the warm water and sending up a musky, woodsy scent.

"You're showing off again," he said.

She took the rag from him and squeezed the water over her leg, making rivers of gray as the black and white streaks melted into each other. The murky water ran onto the floor and disappeared between the wood slats. While she wiped away the pictures, Mouse's perfect memory played out the ceremony in detail, her mind trying again to make sense of it all.

"Stop worrying," Angelo said softly as he took the rag and ran it across her back. He lifted her hair and let the warm water trickle over her neck. "That's the last of it. You're clean."

In her mind, Mouse had worked her way back to the moment in her dream when she had become her father. She felt the flare of anger again. No matter what Ngara thought, no matter what truth was in

the dream, no matter what happened, Mouse would never let herself
be like her father.

She turned and pulled Angelo's face down to hers, her kiss filled with
urgency, not just for passion but escape. Mouse's mind normally worked
on countless levels at the same time—a buzz of problem solving, floods
of faces and words, a salvo of sounds and smells all accosting her at
the same time. Even now, she could hear the didgeridoo still rattling
by the fire at the heart of the outstation. A dog had leaned up against
the side of the shed and was scratching at fleas. A camel off in the far
distance brayed, and Angelo's heart thrummed against hers. She was
used to her mind being so full, but sometimes it became too much. Like
now. She needed the images from the dreams to go away. She needed
to hold fast to the happiness of life here in this moment.

Angelo had an uncanny knack for driving out all that mental noise.
It was quiet with him. Calm. He knew what Mouse wanted, and he gave
it to her. He wrapped his arms around her waist, her skin still wet, and
pulled her down to the bed.

Later, when Angelo had gone to sleep, Mouse lay in the silence, letting
her fingers play along her chest. The paint was gone, but she could feel
the patterns on her skin as if they were still there, undulating and warm
to the touch. As she traced the pictures, she let her mind rest in the fog
of half-sleep. She was back atop Megiddo, her father looking down on
her as she died. He was laughing. The stars were laughing behind him.
And then he was telling her something. In her memory-dream, she would
always see his mouth moving, but she could never hear his words.

Until tonight.

Mouse sat up, suddenly awake. Ngara was right. The truth was in
the dream.

There is good news, Mouse could hear her father saying in her mind,
the memory clear now. *It seems I finally have what I want. And you have
a brother.*

As she shivered with the excitement of remembering and the fear of
knowing, Mouse put her hand on Angelo's shoulder to wake him. But

then her mind tossed all the pieces into place at once. Angelo would understand how dangerous this was—Armageddon-level dangerous. He would call Bishop Sebastian. Bishop Sebastian would want Mouse more than ever. He saw her only as a weapon, a weapon he meant to use against her father. Mouse didn't want to be used as a weapon.

She pulled her hand back. She couldn't tell Angelo about her brother until she had a plan. The guilt of keeping yet another secret from him lodged like a brick in her chest. She rolled away from him and found herself face-to-face with a little lizard that clung to the side of the crate-turned-bedside-table. The lizard blinked slowly at her in the glow of the camp lantern.

"I have a brother," Mouse whispered to the little lizard. Despite her worry at what it all meant, the words spread like sunshine through her. She wasn't alone in the world anymore. She had a brother, someone just like her.

Mouse closed her eyes and with a soft, happy sigh drifted off to sleep.

CHAPTER TWO

A wash of wildflowers spilled out over the ridge, the purples too soft and yellows too inviting for the harsh outback. But it wasn't the sudden beauty that made Mouse sigh. It was the dozens of dead camels scattered across the valley, their bloated bellies rising like islands among the sea of flowers.

"I wish they wouldn't kill them."

"The camels don't belong here," Angelo said. He'd gone out with the Martu men once for a culling, chasing down the herds, guns popping and echoing against the hills as the beasts toppled into the dust. The camels were invasive, brought in by white colonists a century ago, and killing them was an act of survival and stewardship for the Martu. Not for Angelo, though. He'd stayed home at the next slaughter.

"We don't belong here either," Mouse tossed back.

"But we're not feral."

Mouse turned to look at him, her eyebrow raised. Her hair was matted with sweat and tangled by the wind, and she had smears of red desert dirt on her face. They'd driven an hour from the outstation and then left the jeep miles back at the end of the rutted path. Angelo looked just as wild as she did.

He laughed. "Well, at least we don't eat everything in sight." He wrapped his arm around her waist and pulled her to him. "And we aren't likely to fall into the watering hole, die, and contaminate the only drinking water for miles."

"There has to be another way."

"This isn't our problem to fix, Mouse. Like you said, we don't belong here. We're just guests." He took her hand. "And we have our own problems to work out."

Mouse almost said, "More than you know," but she stopped the words at the back of her throat. Since last night, she hadn't been able to think about anything but her little brother, somewhere out in the world. Her mind kept sketching scenarios, an invisible doodle of what-ifs. Some conjured up a wave of wonder at what might be, the promise of finally having someone who shared in the uniqueness of being both human and not, someone who understood her. Her heart filled with unbearable joy at such imagined companionship. But other scenarios, far more likely, ended in terror: her brother at her father's side, waging war on innocents, Mouse facing off against them, and rings of death and destruction rippling out from them like shock waves from a dropped bomb.

Despite her unnatural gifts and lifetimes of experience, Mouse could find no clear path forward. There were too many variables. She knew what she wanted, but she wasn't sure it was the right thing to do. And she was pretty sure Angelo wouldn't go along with it.

That thought brought her to the more immediate problem she had to solve—how and when to tell him she had a brother. When they'd fled Israel together, Mouse had promised Angelo three things: She would never shield him from the dangers of being on the run, she would never sacrifice herself to protect him, and she would keep no more secrets.

But a little boy's life hung in the balance, and Mouse couldn't take the risk that Angelo would call the Bishop.

Angelo had severed ties with his mentor when he'd made the choice to come with Mouse. He hadn't been happy about it, but he had understood that they needed to fall completely off the grid to have any hope of escaping the Novus Rishi, with their long reach and pervasive power.

Disappearing took planning. Over her long lifetime, one of the rules Mouse had learned was to be prepared for anything. She had squirreled away cash, gold, birth certificates, passports, and credit cards all over the world in places that were good at keeping secrets—home bases in her centuries-old game of hide-and-seek.

Angelo had fed the Bishop lies, calling with regular updates as they moved around Europe and gathered what they needed. Then they'd made an indirect path toward the Ukraine, one of the best places in the world to get lost. Angelo had kept the Bishop on the hook, deceiving the man who had once given his life purpose. When they crossed the border, Mouse and Angelo had disappeared like a blip on the radar gone suddenly dark.

"Hey, where'd you go?" Angelo whispered at her ear, his breath on her skin a cool contrast to the sweltering desert air.

"Sorry, got lost in my head." She leaned back against his chest.

"Well, it *is* kind of big, so—"

Mouse goosed him in the side and then pointed over the sea of flowers and camel corpses to the ridge of hills on the other side. "The mountain we're looking for is that tall peak to the right. That's where Ngara said the secret of the Seven Sisters will be. Ready?" She pulled away from him, antsy with guilt and worry.

"I want you to try something first," Angelo said, tugging at Mouse's hand.

She sighed. "Not again."

He pointed at a patch of thick green shrub dotted with yellow flowers that looked like melting butter, lit by the low outback sun. "Burn that one," he said.

Mouse scoffed. "Aren't burning bushes a God thing?"

"Come on, just try."

Angelo had been pushing Mouse for months to test her abilities. Her immortality, heightened senses, and mental acuity were all part of her birthright, but that inheritance also gifted her with darker abilities, powers she had spent seven hundred years trying to escape. Angelo believed she ought to embrace that power and learn to control it. He wanted her ready to face her father when the time came. He also argued that they had the perfect training ground—one of the most remote places in the world. He reasoned that it was as safe as taking a new driver to practice in an empty parking lot.

Mouse wasn't convinced. Besides, she didn't want to play with her power. She didn't want to use it as a weapon. She shook her head as she stared at the bush.

"Fine. If you don't want to burn something, why not make it rain?" Angelo asked, running his sleeve across the sweat on his face. "You know, Jesus calmed the storms. Can't you manage a light shower to drive off some of this heat?"

"Haven't you ever read the fairytales where some well-meaning witch called for rain in a drought?" Mouse kept her tone light, attempting to tease him out of his frustration, but she was really afraid.

She had kept her power tethered her whole life—until two years ago when she'd had to unleash it. She had joined with it, let it become fully part of her, so she could save Angelo from a mob of demons in a Norwegian church when they'd opened the Devil's Bible. Since then, the power had been surprisingly docile. It didn't surge uncontrollably when she got angry or sad. It didn't jump to lace her words with the power to compel a person to do her will. It didn't feel like an enemy anymore. Mouse could still feel it inside her, tickling, dancing, but it seemed content now. Or was it just waiting for a chance for something more?

"If I ask it to rain," Mouse said, "one of two things will likely happen: nothing, or it starts to rain and never stops, and Australia becomes an ocean again."

"Well then, you know what Yeats said."

"What?"

"Surely Ms. Perfect Memory has Yeats stored away up in that big head somewhere." Angelo kissed her on the cheek. "'Education is not the filling of a pail but—'"

"'The lighting of a fire.'" Mouse shoved him away. "You should never be allowed to make jokes."

Angelo kicked the shrub again, laughing. "Come on, try. But this time, don't ask it. *Tell* it to burn. And really try this time, Mouse."

With a sigh, she squatted beside the shrub. She felt the purr of power at the back of her throat. Angelo hovered over her.

"Can you move over there?" She nodded to a spot a few feet away. "I like you uncooked."

As Angelo stepped away, she bent close to the bush and pulled a branch toward her. "Burn," she whispered.

A gust of wind whipped up over the edge of the ridge and carried the word away, but the shrub did not burn. And Mouse was glad.

"Sorry," she said, shrugging at Angelo. He pressed his lips into a disapproving line, but before he could say anything, she led him down the hill into the swath of purples and yellows. "Let's find that cave before we lose what's left of the sunlight."

<hr>

The shallow entrance to the cave was marked with Aboriginal rock art, but there was no sign of anything that might be the secret the Seven Sisters meant for Mouse to find. She and Angelo kept moving farther back into the cave. Sometimes they had room to walk, and other times they crawled, squeezing through cobwebbed crevices down into the mountain.

Hours into the search, one of the cramped tunnels unexpectedly opened onto a massive chamber with huge columns of stone erupting to touch the high, curved ceiling. The room looked like the sanctuary of a forgotten cathedral. But it was the image painted on the side wall that took their breath away. "It's huge," Angelo whispered. The lights strapped to their hard hats oscillated wildly with each turn of their heads, but Mouse and Angelo used the narrower beams from their handheld flashlights to follow the lines of the picture, as if they were tracing it for an art class. It was a snake, rearing high up to the towering ceiling, then twisting down to the floor and back into the shadows at the far end of the space.

"It's beautiful," Mouse said. Unlike most of the cave art they'd seen, this painting was still vivid, brilliant and sharp under the glare of the flashlights, as if it had been painted just that morning. The ochre stood out, bright red-orange, against the dark cave wall, and was patterned with blacks and whites that seemed to writhe under the light, as if the snake were alive.

"Do you think this might be what the Dreaming wanted you to find?" Angelo asked.

"Maybe," Mouse mumbled as her fingers hovered above the image, almost but not quite touching it.

"Look at its eyes."

Mouse swung her light up to where the wall curved into the chamber ceiling. Enormous, pupil-less white eyes, framed with wavering circles of black, looked down on her. They were spirited, wise, and full of life. Mouse shivered.

"It's the Rainbow Serpent," she said, her voice full of awe. "One of the beings in the Martu creation story, one of their most sacred figures."

The painting seemed more sacrament than art, an act of worship or penance. Mouse knew about those, too. That's what the Devil's Bible had been for her—an illuminated manuscript filled with her penitence and sorrow.

Angelo made the sign of the cross. "It has a lot of teeth."

The serpent's mouth was open, and long white fangs curved down around its jaw, glowing eerily in the scattered light. Mouse snatched her hand back from the wall.

"This is it," she said, peering toward the darker end of the cave.

"I sure as hell hope so," Angelo said. "I don't think my legs can take much more."

"No, I mean the chamber. It stops. There's nowhere else to go." She shined her light against the flat back wall.

"Come out, come out wherever you are," Angelo sang as he moved along the wall away from Mouse, searching.

She moved along the wall in the other direction. They swept their flashlights into nooks and crevices along the sides of the cave. As they searched, their boots crunched bits of loose rock against the floor, which echoed through the chamber and sounded like hundreds of invisible creatures gnawing and smacking at some bony meal.

"There's nothing here," Angelo said when they met again in front of the Rainbow Serpent. "I guess it *was* just a story. Sorry to make you go through all this for nothing. At least there weren't any bugs."

"None that we saw," Mouse said playfully, and then she caught the disappointment on his face. "It was a long shot, Angelo. And we don't really need some magic weapon anyway."

"Yeah, you say that. But what if your father shows up? You refuse to work on using your power, and I—"

"He's not coming. I doubt he even cares about *me* anymore."

"What's that supposed to mean?" Angelo asked.

Mouse opened her mouth, ready to confess about her brother and explain that her father would surely have no use for her now that he had a son. But fear choked her words. "It's been so long. Two years," she said instead. "If he wanted me, he would've come and gotten me, right?"

She kept her face turned away, pretending to scan the long wall under the Rainbow Serpent, running her light around the seams where stone met stone. She let out a small yelp and jumped back as a fist-sized spider scuttled out from underneath the snake.

Mouse punched Angelo in the arm. "I told you there'd be bugs," she said.

"Just so I'm prepared—are you going to hit me every time we see a spider?"

"Yes."

The spider disappeared through the tunnel, and Mouse stepped closer to the wall again, searching the place where it had crawled out—just where the painted snake's belly slipped down to touch the floor. She looked back at Angelo with a twinkle in her eye. "There's a gap! And it's big—more like a small opening. It's hard to see because it blends in with the painting."

Angelo grabbed her hand. "No, Mouse," he said. "You're not going in there."

Mouse spun around, ready to argue, but the panic on Angelo's face silenced her. He was afraid not of what might happen here in this cave but of what *had* happened. His panic was a ghost from when Mouse had been trapped in the collapsing ruins of the monastery at Podlažice, the place where she had once written the Devil's Bible. She and Angelo had crawled into the decaying structure looking for the lost pages of the book, which her father had hidden like bait in his Mouse-trap. He had meant to bury her beneath the ruins, but Angelo had been there to pull her out.

"It's okay," she said, stepping close and wrapping her arms around him. She wanted to convince him to stay here, safe, and let her take the risk, but she had promised she wouldn't play the hero anymore. "You want to go first?" she asked. "It's big enough for either of us."

Angelo looked down at the opening. "You think?"

"All we can do is try. Or we can leave." She shrugged.

Angelo blew out a sigh. "No, we've come this far." He crouched, shining his light down into the gap. "Yeah, I think it opens up below."

"How far down is the drop?"

"Let's see." He put his flashlight in his mouth, slid his legs into the gap, and eased himself down.

As he slipped farther into the dark, Mouse laid her own flashlight on the cave floor and grabbed his arms, bracing her feet against the wall and having second thoughts about letting him take the risk.

"Angelo, how about you—"

"There! I've got footing on something—a ledge or the floor, I can't tell. But you can let go now."

Slowly, her heart pounding, Mouse let go of one arm and then the other. Angelo disappeared.

"It's another chamber, not as big," he said, his voice hollow and faint. "There are several large formations jutting along the edges and then it smooths out. I can't see the bottom."

"Is there room for me?"

"Just a minute."

She heard the scuffling of boots sliding against rock.

"Okay, you can come through now," he said, "but take it slow. The ledge here is fairly narrow. I wish we'd brought better equipment."

"Yeah, what were we thinking, leaving that hoard of spelunking supplies at the outstation?"

"Smart-ass."

She chuckled as she shoved her flashlight in the neck of her shirt and then slipped her legs through the gap, reaching out with her foot to feel for the ledge. Mouse was shorter than Angelo, and the ledge was too far down for her. She'd have to let go and trust she'd land in the right place.

As she loosened her grip, she felt Angelo's hand slide around her waist. "If you go, I go," he said.

Mouse dropped and caught the ledge with the edge of her foot, but it kept sliding on the loose rubble, off the rock and into nothingness. Angelo jerked back as he caught her weight, his knee slamming down onto the ledge as her hip scraped the stone. Panting, he pulled her up against the rock wall.

Mouse twisted toward him and shoved his hands away. "Don't ever do that again! If I fall, I get broken, but I get put back together again," she said. "You don't!"

"I guess that makes me Humpty Dumpty, huh?"

"It's not funny!" The light from the flashlight shining up from her shirt cut her face into odd angles, a chiaroscuro jigsaw of anger and fear.

"What was I supposed to do? Just let you fall?"

"Yes."

"I can't do that."

"You have to learn."

As the panic of the moment faded, so did Mouse's anger. For so long, she'd been focused on hating her immortality. She'd never realized how comfortably she wore it, how cavalier and invincible it made her feel—until she'd met Angelo, who was not invincible, but who was every bit as cavalier. Mouse pressed her lips into a hard line as she watched him rubbing at his knee, sweat beaded on his forehead. If Angelo wanted her to respect his right to make his own choices and take his own risks, he needed to acknowledge that those risks were far costlier for him than they were for her.

But she knew that now wasn't the time for that discussion. "Let's go see if there's anything to find and then get out of here," she said as she pulled her flashlight free and pointed it down into the dark chamber.

They inched their way down the rocky ledge until it feathered back into the wall, where they were forced to jump to a nearby rock jutting up from below. Carefully leapfrogging their way from rock to rock, they moved down into the chamber. The air changed the farther down they went—it grew colder and charged with energy. It tasted like magic.

"I hear water," Mouse said.

"Can you see where it's coming from?"

She leaned past him, looking down. "I see the glint of the light against something shiny. It might be water. And there's an odd glow coming from the other side of that jagged rock there."

"I don't see any glow."

"Turn your lights off."

The cave went pitch black for a moment.

"I see it! Like a blue haze," Angelo said. "Maybe that's it."

He led them on until finally they could see over the edge of the last craggy stone and down to a small ledge hanging over a river several feet below. The ledge was scattered with shards of obsidian, glistening under the beams of light like exploding stars. The source of the blue glow rested on top of what looked like an altar—a black stone table erupting from the back wall, as flat and smooth as if carved. In the center was a long, iridescent sliver of something that pulsed with a pale blue light.

"What is that?" Angelo whispered.

"I'd guess the secret of the Seven Sisters."

"But what is it?"

"A bone? Though the way it's curved, it looks like a fang."

"Like on the painting of the snake back there?" Angelo spun around to look at her.

She nodded. "The Rainbow Serpent."

"Did Ngara mention it in the story she told you?"

"No. That Dreaming was just about one moment in the Sisters' song-line. I learned about the Rainbow Serpent when I was here before, a—"

"A long time ago," Angelo said, chuckling.

"Yes, my young Padawan," Mouse shot back in her best Yoda voice. "Most of the indigenous people here believe that the Rainbow Serpent formed the land, diving deep and pushing up the mountains, cutting the rivers and streams, shaping the dunes as she moved across the world. And when her work was done, she went underground to stay. Her spirit lives there still." Mouse shrugged. "Nobody says what happened to her body. Maybe she left bits and pieces of it here and there to feed the land with her magic. Maybe this belongs to her."

Angelo stared at the pulsing blue light. "Given everything I've seen since I met you, I'm not about to question a story that's been passed down for millennia. And it makes sense that if that bone," he nodded down to the shining altar, "came from her, it's got power. Maybe enough power to beat your father."

Mouse went still. "We're just looking for something to protect ourselves, not a weapon to win a war. Right?"

Angelo didn't answer. Instead, he scooted farther down the side of the rock, looking for a path to the bone. Mouse followed until he stopped at the edge.

"This next one's going to be too far for you to jump," he said, handing her his flashlight. "I'll go down and get the bone and bring it back up."

She grabbed his sleeve at the shoulder. "Absolutely not."

"My legs are longer than yours. It's simple physics. You can't make it, and I can."

"None of that looks stable, Angelo." She looked down at the scattered black stone. "And what did we just say about weighing risks? You're Humpty, remember?"

"To hell with that," he said, and he jumped.

He landed solidly on the rock nearest the obsidian ledge. Mouse coiled herself, ready to jump after him, but she could see that he was right. She'd never make it; it was too far.

"Be careful," she spat.

Angelo eased off the rock and onto the black ledge. He crossed to the altar in two strides, reached down, grabbed the bone, and turned to smile at Mouse, his arm raised in triumph.

And the ledge fell out from under him.

Angelo caught the corner of the altar with his free hand as shards of obsidian fell like arrows into the river, which was much wider and deeper than it had first seemed. Mouse cried out, but her uncanny mind was already racing to juggle the pieces—how long could Angelo hold on, how long would the fragile stone support his weight, how far was the drop, and how could she get to him?

With a squeal, the stone altar cracked along its base at the wall. Angelo looked up at it and then over at Mouse. She saw the fear and resignation in his face.

"Catch."

She was shaking her head, opening her mouth to argue, but he didn't give her time. He threw the sliver of bone over to her. She caught it on instinct, dropping the flashlights, which pinged on the rock and plummeted into the dark. She shoved the bone inside her shirt at the same moment she leapt toward the jagged rock, toward Angelo.

Her body missed the rock by more than a foot, but her hand caught one of the serrated edges of stone, spearing it through her palm and anchoring her as she swung her legs up to the flat front of the rock. She was still too far away to reach Angelo, and they'd run out of time.

The obsidian shelf broke away from the wall, tumbling down into the abyss and taking Angelo with it.

Mouse jumped, too, but her hand was still hooked on the stone, which snagged against the bones of her knuckles. She fell back to the rock face, blind with panic, but her mind grasped at the sound of water. *The river.* The river would save him from the fall. But then it would sweep him away from her. Drown him.

Peace, be still, something inside her whispered almost teasingly.

"Be still," Mouse said, her head full of her failure to make the bush burn just hours ago. She looked down at the river, her eyes fierce with determination. "Be still!"

She didn't yell, but the command sank like a stone down the depths of the chamber and into the water. The words were charged with the full force of her power and driven by desperation.

She held her breath, listening until the echo of her voice finally died. In the silence, Mouse could no longer hear the sound of running water. All was still.

She turned to pull her hand free of the jagged rock and jumped. The water stung like thousands of biting ants, cold and hot at the same time. She sank until her feet jammed into the river bottom, and she pushed up, breaking the surface of the water like a shot. She spun, looking for Angelo, the light on her headlamp swirling in the dark.

"I'm here," he called out. He had his arm wrapped over a rounded bit of stone protruding from the cave wall.

Mouse swam through the still water toward him. "Are you hurt?"

"I don't think so. Just cut up a little from all the rocks. You?"

She shook her head. "Can you move?"

"I just said I wasn't—"

"I need to see you move." He seemed unhurt, but Mouse had another fear she needed to quiet. Every other time she'd laced her words with her power to command something, it had gone terribly wrong. She needed to know that her order to "be still" had commanded only the water. "Angelo, please, just do it."

Angelo let go of his handhold on the stone and treaded water, waving his hands in the air. Mouse put her arms around his neck and kissed him.

"Let's get out of here," she said.

"There's no place to climb out. It's too steep. We could just let the river—" Angelo looked down at the water, then squinted as he studied where the river rested against the rock. "It's not moving."

He looked at Mouse, his eyes lighting up with awareness. "You did it! Didn't you?" He laughed. "'Peace, be still'? And you said the burning bush was cliché." He swooped his arms around her, splashing water on her face. "You did it, Mouse! I knew you could." He kissed her. "Can you undo it?"

She leaned down to the river, her breath making tiny ripples in the water. "Thank you," she whispered as she imagined a ghostly echo of the Rainbow Serpent undulating just beneath the surface. "I release you."

The river rolled forward once more. The water dancing around the stone and slapping the rock wall sounded like someone laughing as the river carried Mouse and Angelo away.

They weren't in the water long before the river widened and grew shallow. Mouse and Angelo let their bodies float behind them as they dug their hands into the silt of the riverbed and pulled themselves along. They slipped out from under an overhang, the mountains birthing them back into the world. Exhausted, they dragged themselves up the creek bank. They lay panting, Mouse watching the hazy cluster of the Pleiades make a slow slide down the night sky, a silent prayer of thanksgiving running through her mind. She reached into her shirt and pulled out the bone. It was as long as her forearm and about as thick at its widest end, but it tapered to a fine point, fine enough that it had pierced Mouse's side when she'd jammed it into her shirt. A thin streak of red, mixed with river water, ran down the iridescent tip.

"It's not glowing anymore," Angelo said, pushing himself upright.

"Guess it doesn't need to, now that we've found it."

"I'm glad. Explaining why you've got a bone shard seems tricky enough. Can't imagine what we'd say if it was a *glowing* bone shard." Angelo ran his hand through his hair, raking out some of the water. "What do you think it does?"

"I have no idea. But I bet Ngara will."

"I guess we know our next stop then. You ready?"

"My body's not."

"It's just a few hours' hike through the desert and then an hour's drive back to the outstation. You getting old or something?" He was chuckling before he even got the words out.

Mouse shoved him back down. "What did I tell you about not making any more jokes? You're just bad at it." She curled her leg over his, bent down and kissed him, then laid her head on his chest. He played with her wet hair.

"Thank you," he said quietly after a few moments.

"For?" But she already knew.

"Keeping your promise."

"Thank you," she said in answer.

"For?"

"Not dying."

CHAPTER THREE

Jack Gray loved a good hotel. This one, replete with all the modern luxuries and draped in the old-world exterior of a sprawling baroque palace, exceeded even his extravagant desires. He stood on the terrace, watching the sun spread behind the spires of Prague, and basked in his good fortune. The clean, bright chime of bells called the city to life. He looked down to the streets and watched the people come and go, marveling at how simple they looked from such a height—circles of heads and lines of bodies.

"Jack!" a voice called through the door.

Sighing, Jack turned back toward the penthouse suite. "You need something, sir?" He measured his tone carefully, keeping it professionally detached but bright enough to sound eager to please. Feigned affability was part of the game he had to play when he traveled with his new patron. The Reverend liked smiles and efficient service.

Jack ran his hand over the back of one of the soft velvet dining chairs as he stepped into the room, the bells of Prague still ringing behind him. He figured a little kowtowing and a few "yes sirs" were worth this kind of payoff. Exotic locations and luxury hotels certainly fit Jack's expectations more than the tiny office in the basement of a yeshiva in Jerusalem, where he'd spent the better part of the past two years. His previous benefactor, Rabbi Asher Ben-Yair, had kept Jack under the glare of a computer screen, sifting through databases. An old man, the Rabbi cared more about comfort than luxury, and his idea of comfortable was a little too sedate for Jack.

But the Reverend liked nice things as much as Jack did, and the Reverend wanted to go places. So did Jack.

"Son, I've got something on my lucky tie," the Reverend said as he came through the bedroom door, his broad Southern drawl drooling over the vowels. He stopped beside the fireplace that divided the living area from the dining room. He wore a crisp pair of suit pants, which rested perfectly against his shined shoes, but he was bare chested, his heavy belly bulging out over his waistband and pulling his shoulders down. "Our bodies are a temple," he had once said to Jack when he'd caught him looking at his stomach. "Mine's round and robust," he'd said, laughing as he slapped at the mound of fat. Then he'd yanked Jack's shirt up, exposing his slender frame. "You, however, are weak. Pretty and weak." After traveling with him these past few months, Jack had learned to keep his eyes on the Reverend's face.

"Kitty's in here getting her hair done for her women's meeting, and I'm late to the breakfast. Can you take care of this?" He tossed the tie to Jack and spun back into the bedroom, not waiting for an answer.

Jack snatched the tie from the air, studied it a moment, then headed to his own room on the other side of the living area. He shoved his hand in the outer pocket of his leather laptop bag and pulled out a package of alcohol wipes, specially designed for cleaning silk ties. The Reverend's various appetites often resulted in stains left for Jack to clean up—some easy, like a spot on a tie, others not so much. Jack liked being prepared, not from a Boy Scout sense of readiness but in a calculated way. He'd always been a good student, in school and in life, though he didn't really care about learning. He cared about success. He could game any system, figure out what hoops needed jumping in order to get what he wanted, and he had a gift for pleasing the people who could help him the most.

That knack had drawn Jack to the woman who had set him on the path that led him here. He'd known her as Dr. Emma Nicholas, a history professor who accidentally introduced him to the Devil's Bible. Despite his careful efforts, Jack could never get her to eat out of his hand like he did his other teachers. When he learned from the Rabbi that "Emma Nicholas" was a sham, a false identity, Jack had almost laughed with relief, pleased to have proof that he hadn't lost his touch. He had just been naïve in taking the woman at face value. He'd been trying to read the mask rather than the person.

He still didn't know her real name; no one did, as far as he could tell. Not that it mattered—she would always be "Dr. Em" to him. Jack had much to thank her for. She had inadvertently launched his career when his work with the medieval codex known as the Devil's Bible had drawn the attention of the Rabbi, one of the leaders of the Novus Rishi. And it had been the crazy two days Jack had spent with Dr. Em in Nashville a couple of years ago that had secured his position among the powerful group. They seemed obsessed with his former teacher, though he still didn't know why. All he knew was that they wanted him because he knew her.

Jack opened the package of cleaning wipes and started to work on the Reverend's tie under the bathroom's too-bright lights. *That's just the way the world works,* he thought as he smiled and gave himself a little nod. *Who you know is always more important than what you know.*

The Rabbi, for instance, armed himself with knowledge, and he got nowhere. But the Reverend was a people person, and he was on the move. Unlike his fellow members of the Novus Rishi's inner council, Reverend Kevin Ayres lived loud. Modestly wealthy from oil on his side, the Reverend had married "up" and into one of the richest tech dynasties in the world. His wife brought all the cash; the Reverend brought all the charm. Together, they had cofounded the Global Council on Righteousness more than ten years ago, achieving instant celebrity among the worldwide evangelical Christian community. The Reverend and Mrs. Ayres had the best of all worlds—they played among the international social elite, pulled politicians' strings with the power of their religious empire, and, apparently, had God's ear by command.

Jack reached for the hair dryer and shot the first warm gust at his own thick, wavy hair. He stole an approving glance at the tousled brown locks in the mirror and then bent back to the Reverend's tie, sweeping the air back and forth to dry the alcohol. He had been satisfied with the perks of living in the Reverend's orbit, but sometimes he felt like a tethered dog, expected to jump at his master's command. Technically, he still worked for the Rabbi. The trips he'd taken with the Reverend had also been missions to collect books and artifacts the Rabbi wanted, items the Rabbi felt would be instrumental in the Novus Rishi's efforts. No one actually told Jack what those efforts were, but he'd pieced enough together to know that it *all* had to do with Dr. Em. The Rabbi had plans for her, and Jack was beginning to suspect that the Reverend did, too—though not necessarily the same as the Rabbi's.

The Rabbi was old and recently in ill health and could no longer travel, so he had sent Jack to collect the things he wanted. Most of the books and artifacts were held in museums or private libraries, but Jack wasn't sent to make copies. He was sent to acquire the originals, whether the owners wished to relinquish them or not—which is where the Reverend came into play. The Reverend's primary function in the Novus Rishi was to covertly provide the money and influence they needed to grease the wheels of their expansive machine. And if money and power failed to achieve the desired ends, the Reverend seemed willing to do anything to advance the Novus Rishi's cause. He seemed especially eager to help Jack.

Jack looked up at his reflection in the bathroom mirror, squinting and leaning in as he studied himself. He looked tired, worry weighing on him. There was a little more gray peeking out at the temples of his thick brown hair. He needed a trim. The Reverend didn't seem to mind that Jack let his hair grow long, almost but not quite touching the tops of his shoulders, but if it strayed just a bit too far, Mrs. Ayres was quick to share her disapproval. In tandem, the two of them ruled as if they had a mandate from God that let them righteously judge everything and everyone.

Sit, stay, heel, Jack thought bitterly.

"Where's my tie, son?"

Jack startled at the sudden appearance of a now-shirted Reverend. As Jack turned, the Reverend pulled the tie out of his hand and leaned past him toward the mirror, tying and adjusting in sharp, sure motions.

"The place you're going this morning for the Rabbi . . ." the Reverend said, his tone flat, the drawl nearly gone.

"Yes, sir?" Jack's eyes shot up to meet the Reverend's in the mirror. They were flat and cold, too.

"Don't go inside. I have someone who will meet you at the back and take you where you need to go."

"Yes, sir."

The Reverend slid his tie tight, the knot biting into his neck and pushing the excess flesh of his jowls up and over the starched collar. Then he turned to Jack and leaned back on the marble countertop. "I want you to fetch whatever's there and bring it to me before the others get here."

Jack knew he meant the rest of the inner council, which was scheduled to meet in the Reverend's suite once he was finished wining and dining his horde of evangelical foot soldiers. The closing event of the annual conference for the Global Council on Righteousness was a fundraising gala, which would be held that evening in the hotel's garden.

"Sir, you understand that there's likely nothing there, and, if there is, it's almost certainly useless." A bit of leftover belligerence dusted Jack's tone. He sounded almost patronizing. "Of all the books and artifacts I've researched and gathered for the Rabbi, not one of them has—"

"This one's different."

The Reverend reached down and yanked at his belt buckle.

"Why is this one different?" Jack asked as he sat down on the edge of the tub. He tried to purge the skepticism from his voice, but he'd heard the Rabbi and Bishop Sebastian say the same thing about other long-sought-after treasures. Each one was going to be *different*. Yet all the discoveries ended up the same—powerless old relics and shams. Jack had tried to convince them to go after the Devil's Bible, the one ancient book he knew held the power they were looking for, because he himself had felt it, had touched it. But the Bishop and the Rabbi were too afraid of it. The book belonged to the enemy, had too much power, was too dark. Jack thought those were just excuses, but he hadn't had the courage to make the same suggestion to the Reverend. There was something still unpredictable about him, something Jack hadn't yet figured out.

"Don't question me, son," the Reverend said as he unzipped his pants and stepped up to the toilet. "I know there's something there. And I want it."

"But the Rabbi will expect me to—" Jack was turning to avert his eyes when a shock of wet, sour-smelling urine struck his face. "God damn it!" he yelled, falling back into the tub, wiping his face with his shirtsleeve and trying to get his feet under him again.

The Reverend was suddenly on him, pressing him back against the tile. "You don't question me—ever. Now go fetch the thing and bring it to me. And you say nothing to the Rabbi, you understand?"

"Yes, sir." Jack kept his eyes down, his face flushed with shame. The Reverend zipped his pants.

"Kevin, you should wash your hands." Jack spun to see Mrs. Ayres just outside the door. He couldn't tell from her face whether or not she'd seen anything. "We need to go," she said. "We're both already late."

"Yes, ma'am," the Reverend said, his drawl oozing out once more as he ran his hands under the faucet. "Thank you for the tie, son." He took his wife's hand.

Smiling back over her shoulder, Mrs. Ayres said, "You should get cleaned up. And Jack? Don't take the Lord's name in vain."

Jack sagged back against the wall, his hair still dripping piss.

Jack passed by a passel of tourists waiting for the Old New Synagogue to open. He turned onto an empty, narrow lane that ran alongside the medieval building.

He had decided to walk from the hotel, hoping the fresh air would clear his head of the lingering humiliation. He pushed his normally brisk pace into something fierce, which set his calves burning and matched his temper. He was angry with the Reverend, of course, but more with himself. Why hadn't he done anything? He could have shoved the bloated whale back against the toilet. He could have slammed his pompous face into the mirror. At the very least, Jack should've grabbed his stuff and walked out. But he just took it like a helpless puppy.

And now he had to worry about what would happen if he came back empty-handed. Despite the Reverend's certainty that there was something of value to find at the synagogue, Jack knew better. He'd gone on the same pointless quest too many times. On the upside, if Jack found nothing, he wouldn't be caught up in a tangle of allegiances and betrayal by keeping it from the Rabbi. But he was more afraid of what would happen if he didn't have something to give the Reverend. Jack gritted his teeth, swearing to himself that he would not suffer such humiliation again, whatever the cost.

He slipped around the corner to the back of the building as the Reverend had instructed. The person waiting for him wasn't what he expected. She was leaning against the iron railing that separated the synagogue's tiny back terrace from the city sidewalk elevated behind it.

"You Jack?" she asked in nearly pristine English. She wore a ragged army jacket and black jeans. Her hair, dyed a brilliant purple except for a long, thin streak of white, spilled out over her shoulders. She had a motorcycle helmet tucked under her arm. She certainly wasn't the sort of person Mrs. Ayres would want associating with the Reverend.

Cautiously, Jack nodded. "And you are?"

"The person who gets you where you want to go." She dug her hand down the front of her shirt and pulled a cord from around her neck. At the end of the cord hung a key. She scanned the street quickly, then stepped down into an alcove and emerged just a few seconds later lugging a ladder with her.

"What's this?" Jack asked.

"Your way in." She nodded upward. Jack looked up, too. Several feet above him were metal rebars cemented into the back wall of the synagogue. They formed a crooked line of hand- and footholds that rose up to a small gable with an iron door, the Star of David soldered on the front.

The girl propped the ladder against the wall. It was the perfect height to meet the lowest of the rungs.

"I have to go up there?" Jack asked.

"Yes."

"I thought maybe it would be in the library."

"Nope."

Jack lowered his gaze to look at her. She was still looking up at the attic door, and Jack saw fear in her eyes. A shiver of dread ran through him.

Through his study of the Devil's Bible, he knew the history of this synagogue, built just a few years before the book was written. Ottakar, the Golden and Iron King of Bohemia, had ordered a new convent built for his aunt, a nun who would later become Saint Agnes. He had told the stonemasons building the convent to also construct the new synagogue. Rumor said that angels brought stones from the destroyed Temple in Jerusalem to serve as the foundation of the synagogue in Prague. The most famous legend swirling around the Old New Synagogue was about the Golem—a monster made of clay by the Rabbi Judah Loew ben Bezalel to protect Prague's Jews in the 16th century. But when the Golem turned violent, the Rabbi took from its mouth the bit of parchment that held the magic spell that had given the creature life. The legend also said that the sleeping Golem still lived in the attic of the synagogue, waiting to be awoken once more.

Jack sighed with resignation. He'd assumed that the artifact Rabbi Ben-Yair had sent him to collect was connected to the legend of the Golem. But over the years, a handful of scholars had been granted permission to study the legend and the attic, and they had found nothing. That was why he'd been confident in suggesting to the Reverend that there was nothing to find. The fear in the girl's eyes shook Jack's confidence a little.

"You'd tell me if there's a Golem waiting for me up there, wouldn't you?" he asked, straining to make it sound like a joke.

She didn't laugh or answer.

He put his foot on the first rung but paused and asked over his shoulder, "Can you at least tell me what I'm looking for? Do you know?"

She kicked at a piece of loose stone with her heavy boots, her hair hanging across her face as she looked away. "I don't know what it is." She looked past him, up at the attic door again. "But it should be in the far corner to your right. That's where . . . that's where you should look."

As he climbed another rung, the ladder shook, and he threw his arms out to balance against the wall.

"Go on. I'll hold it for you." The girl pressed her weight against the bottom of the ladder, stabilizing it.

He was a few steps up when she called out, "You'll need these." She stood on tiptoe and held up a flashlight and the cord with the key on it. Her hand was shaking, the fear still naked in her face, but as their eyes met, Jack realized her fear wasn't about whatever was in the attic—her fear was for him.

After a few more steps, he reached the lowest of the bars jutting out from the wall. The iron cut into Jack's hands as he climbed. He looked down when he got to the top. The girl was pulling the ladder away.

"Wait! Where're you going?"

"No one's supposed to be up there. The ladder's a bit of a giveaway."

"How will I get down?"

"I'll be close, watching. Close the door behind you, then open it a crack when you're ready to leave. I'll come with the ladder."

"What if I need to get out in a hurry?"

She held his gaze for a moment. "You scream."

"Great," Jack muttered.

He stretched his leg out to plant his foot on a stone ledge on the other side of the attic's iron door. He put the flashlight in his mouth, wrinkling his nose at the taste of rubber and trying not to think about germs. He gripped the rebar tightly with one hand and reached around with the other to put the key into the lock of the door. A part of him was disappointed when it slid in smoothly and clicked open with ease. With a last look down, Jack swung himself up across the threshold and into the attic.

Sunlight pressed past him, casting a dim light on the space. This also wasn't what he'd expected. He'd thought he'd be exploring a larger version of his grandmother's attic, crammed with the detritus of life, but this place seemed to be empty. Large rafters crisscrossed the space, and mounds of earth or stone rose up all across the floor. Jack thought they looked like the tops of hobbit houses. He crouched and carefully pressed against the mound nearest him, expecting his hand to sink into heaped ash or dust, but the top of the mound was solid, made of cement or rock. Thick chains ran from some of the beams down through the attic floor, and suddenly Jack realized what he was looking at—these mounds were actually the rounded domes of the arched ceilings from the chapel below, and the chains anchored the huge chandeliers that hung there.

Confident that the floor could support his weight, Jack shoved himself upright. But his foot, which had still been hanging over the threshold, nudged the door against the wall with a crash. A family of wrens went flurrying, their panicked churring like a clock being overwound. Jack ducked as a bird whirred past his head and out into the blue morning.

Turning on the flashlight, Jack reached back and reluctantly closed the iron door behind him. The dark changed everything—the mounds now looked like graves, the deep valleys between them buried in blackness. Jack edged out into the attic, heading for the far corner as the girl had said. He eased over the first mound, shining the light down into the valley. It was filled with dry dirt or dust and bird droppings. Grimacing, he watched his twelve-hundred-dollar Berluti calfskin shoes disappear beneath the filth until he finally felt the rock floor once more. By the time he'd crept his way across the attic to the corner, anger had driven away his fear. Jack just wanted to find the damn thing or not, get back to the hotel, and take a long shower. The Reverend owed him a new pair of shoes.

Spurred by a childish hope that he wouldn't have to get his hands dirty, Jack carefully checked all of the hard surfaces in the corner first— the wood beams overhead, the tops of the mounds, the bit of framing along the edge of the wall—but he found nothing.

"Of course not," he spat as he looked down at the heaps of filth. He shoved his hand down into the dirt circled by the flashlight. The material felt silky, like ash, but heavier. The layer was almost elbow-high—a lot of dirt to collect in an attic, even one that was seven hundred years old. Tiny clumps of it crawled up his shirtsleeve as if drawn by static.

Jack pulled his arm back, frantically raking it against his pants leg, though it was covered in dirt, too. He spun the flashlight around the attic, studying the valleys filled with the dry soil. Add a little water and it would make clay. *Enough clay to build a Golem*, Jack thought. A few years ago, he would have laughed at such a thought, but after those two days in Nashville with Dr. Em, Jack knew well enough that there were things in the world he didn't understand. Things he would just as soon not know about.

But he did know. A slender thread of sweat inched down his neck, and he lowered his hand to the dirt as if he expected a snake to strike. He moved methodically through the valleys in the corner. When his fingers brushed up against something cold and hard, he yanked his hand back like he'd been bitten.

"Shit," he muttered as he sat back on his heels, his instincts and his wants at war. He wanted to get out of here, but he was scared to touch the thing buried in what he was now convinced were the remains of a monster.

"I'm a scholar. This is research," he said, trying to bolster his confidence. "Other scholars have been up here. No one died. I'm a scholar."

He held his breath and rammed his fist down in the spot he'd kept marked with the flashlight.

His fingers closed around something metal and cylindrical. It was so cold on contact that it almost felt like a shock of electricity pierced him and ran along his hand and up his arm and neck and head, tingling like bugs swarming over his scalp. When he pulled the object out, a fine shower of dirt rained from it, glistening in the light as the individual grains fell back to join the multitudes. Jack knew instantly what it was—an amulet, and an old one by the looks of the tarnished silver. He pulled it close to his face, squinting against the bright light of the flashlight he held against the amulet's dull surface. Decorative swirls had been etched along the round sides of the cylinder, and on the bottom, a Star of David. When he turned the amulet, Jack felt something shift. He lifted it to his ear and carefully shook it, listening to the muffled rattle. There was something inside.

Jack put the flashlight in his mouth again to free his other hand, pressing and prying as he tried to open the amulet. He didn't see the displaced wren squeeze in through a tiny gap along a slender window nearby until it zipped past him so close that he felt the rush of air from the whirr of its wings. Startled, he dropped the flashlight into the valley of dust. The shrieking bird zoomed in tight circles around the attic. Unnerved, Jack scrambled back over the mounds toward the door. The bird wanted him out. Jack wanted out, too. He could wait to explore the amulet back in the comfort of the hotel. After his shower.

As instructed, Jack pushed the door open a crack and waited, watching a handful of tourists or shoppers meander up the lane. The girl came from underneath a yellow table umbrella at the edge of the canopy of trees on the other side of the street. She didn't look up. She disappeared from Jack's line of sight as she neared the synagogue. A few moments later, he heard the clank of the metal ladder against the stone beneath him. Sliding the amulet into his pants pocket and pulling out the key from around his neck, Jack eased out onto the stone ledge, grabbing hold of the protruding rebars. He saw more wrens returning home as he closed the iron door.

Climbing down was harder than going up, especially because he was trying to hurry to avoid being seen. Sighing with relief as he felt his foot land on the wide stone surface of the sidewalk, Jack turned to find the girl gaping at him—but not him exactly. She was looking just above his face.

"What is it?" he asked, his voice high with panic. "A spider?" Jack slapped at his head. A cloud of dust erupted from his filthy shirt, and he bent over, coughing. When he righted himself, a piece of his hair hung loose across his face. It, too, seemed caked in dirt, the brown made ashen. He looked at the girl again. Her eyes were still wide, her mouth hanging open.

"It's just a little dirt," Jack said.

"Did you touch it?"

"The dirt? How could I not—it's everywhere up there."

"No. Did you touch *it*?"

"The amulet?" He could make no sense of the horror in her voice. The danger was over, his mission accomplished. "Yeah, see?" He pulled the amulet out of his pocket.

The girl gasped and hit his hand, sending the amulet flying to the sidewalk, where it pinged and rolled to a stop.

"What'd you do that for? That thing is old and priceless!" He bent to pick it up, but she grabbed his hand.

"Don't touch it!"

"Why not?"

"There's something wrong with it." Her voice was shaking, but her eyes were fierce and her grip on Jack's arm tight. "I went up there—a couple of years ago, when my dad was a rabbi here. I stole his key. I wanted to read the books they wouldn't let the girls read." She lifted her chin defiantly. "I thought there might be more books in the attic. When I was looking, I saw something shine in the sun. I picked it up, for just a second." She shuddered. "Did you not feel it? Something coming out of it—something wrong."

She looked at Jack's eyes, almost pleading, and then she shook her head. "I threw it away from me as fast as I could and it still . . ."

"What did it do?" Jack was scared again.

The girl's answer was to pull him through the door from where she'd gotten the ladder. The narrow doorway opened into a cramped, dark hallway with two doors on opposite walls. One door stood open, revealing a utility closet filled with buckets and brooms and mops. The girl yanked on the other door and shoved Jack into a tiny bathroom crowded with just a toilet and small sink. She pushed him toward the mirror over the sink.

Jack stared at his reflection for a moment, then jammed his head under the faucet and turned it on. Icy water shot out over his hair, and he raked his fingers through it violently. He could see rivulets of cloudy water running down the drain, and he stood, expecting to see his thick brown hair, sopping wet but otherwise just as it had been that morning at the hotel.

It wasn't.

Jack gripped the sink and studied his reflection. His hair had gone completely white.

CHAPTER FOUR

Mouse and Angelo drove up the track to the outstation just a few hours before dawn, exhausted from their cave adventure. They were surprised to see the hearth fire still burning and a dozen Martu sitting around it.

"The desert caught fire," one of the children announced as she ran up to greet them. "Between here and the Canning Stock Route."

Mouse looked sharply at Angelo. That was not far west of where they had crested the hill of wildflowers and dead camels, not far downwind from where Mouse had commanded the bush to burn. Angelo was already shaking his head, but Mouse turned back to the girl.

"Was anyone hurt, Paya?" she asked as she looked over at the group around the fire.

"No," the girl said. "We set a cool fire to catch the hot one, the wild one. The cool fire ate the other and now we will have good hunting when the grass grows back. I get to go this time!" And she took off running back to the others.

"See?" Angelo said to Mouse.

"See what? It doesn't matter that they stopped it or that no one got hurt. What matters is if I started it." Mouse spun away and headed to their shed, just beyond the glow of firelight. "I can't control it."

"But you can, Mouse. You did it with the river in the cave. You just have to want to do it. Right now, you're so scared of it that you—"

"I should be scared of it. Look what almost happened." She flung her hand back toward the Martu and then swung open the door.

Angelo followed her inside. "You have no idea whether or not you started that fire. How many times since we've been here have there been wildfires out in the bush?" He threw himself onto the bed, his body covered in scrapes and bruises. "Besides, no one got hurt."

"But they could have. I can't take that risk."

"Then we'll find another way for you to practice using your power, a way that doesn't put anyone at risk. But for now, can we just go to bed?" His words were already slurring as sleep settled on him.

Mouse was tired, too. Her body hurt, and she wanted to crawl up beside Angelo and sleep for days. But she couldn't shake a growing uneasiness. She slumped into the chair at the far wall, rolling the bone shard in her hands and looking out at the starry sky. How was a magic bone supposed to protect them? But then Mouse corrected herself—Ngara had never said it was meant to keep them safe. She'd said it was meant for revenge.

Mouse didn't want revenge against anyone. She just wanted to be left alone. And for all his talk about defeating her father, Angelo wasn't vengeful either. Then again, Ngara had said that the Dreaming not only showed visions of what was and is but also of "something that will be." Were the Seven Sisters giving them a gift for the future?

Mouse put the bone on the crate beside the bed and gently eased down beside Angelo, curling toward him and putting her hand against his arm. The warmth of his skin reminded her that she was not alone. They would figure this out together. And tomorrow she would find Ngara and, hopefully, some answers, too.

"Where've you been?" Mouse asked as Angelo came in through the back door of the little shed. She was stirring oatmeal in a pot on the hot plate that served as their kitchen. "You left so early. I thought we might sleep in—let me tend to all your scrapes and bruises." She lifted her eyebrows at him suggestively, but her playfulness vanished when she saw the bone shard in his hand. "What are you doing with that?"

"Trying it out. I wanted to see what it could do."

"And?" She turned back to the oatmeal.

"Nothing."

She turned off the hot plate and grabbed a spoon. "It didn't do anything? You couldn't feel any power coming from it?"

"Not that I could tell." She could hear the twang of bitterness in his voice. He tossed the bone on the bed and threw himself down beside it. "Maybe it's only meant for you."

Mouse leaned against the wall, blowing on a spoonful of oatmeal. "Maybe. You want some breakfast?"

"It's almost noon."

"Did you eat already?"

"I'm not hungry."

With her heightened senses and seven hundred years of experience, Mouse usually read people easily. She could pinpoint the subtle differences between guilt and shame, or between someone lying and someone simply hiding a truth. She could even anticipate what they would say or do. But Mouse had never been able to read Angelo that way. It was one of the things she loved about him—he was unpredictable. He made everything feel new, which was quite a challenge for someone as old as Mouse. But like any normal couple, Mouse and Angelo had learned each other's norms—a preferred side of the bed, cream or sugar in their coffee, pleasure spots, trigger points. Mouse could tell that something was very off with him.

"What's going on?" she asked.

He shot upright like he'd been waiting for the question. "What's going on is that your father's coming and we're not ready."

Mouse finished chewing, refusing to take his bait and let her temper rise. "Okay. But that's no different than yesterday or—"

"Or the day before that or the month before that or this whole damn year," Angelo said. "Which is what I've been telling you. We have to stop pretending that everything's fine, Mouse."

"Where's this coming from? We've talked about this. Where else—"

"You've talked but you haven't listened."

"I'm listening now. Why are you so angry?"

He held the bone up. "God or the Seven Sisters or the Rainbow Serpent—whatever the hell it was—sent us a weapon. We have to learn to use it."

"Eventually."

"Now." He stood up.

"Why's everything suddenly so urgent?" She couldn't make sense of his panic or his anger.

"It's not! I've been telling you for months that we need to learn how to use your power to fight your father, but you've refused. Always pushing it off until later. You want to go play doctor. You want us to play house. Now we have a—"

"I'm not playing. I *am* a healer, and I thought we were a family." Mouse tossed the bowl of oatmeal on the table with a clang. She blew out a breath and counted Angelo's heartbeats, then tried a different approach. "Why'd you go out so early?"

"I couldn't sleep."

"Another nightmare? You haven't had one of those in—"

"This isn't about me." But Mouse could hear the confirmation in his voice.

"Why didn't you wake me up?"

"I'm not a child, Mouse! I can handle a bad dream without mollycoddling."

Mouse let the silence hang for just a moment. "How many times have you held me while I trembled and wept after a bad dream? I didn't realize I was being childish when I let you help me."

"It's different." He sank back onto the bed.

"Why? Because you're a man and I'm a—"

"No! Because I'm already useless." He sighed and buried his head in his hands.

Mouse sat down beside him. "You're not useless, Angelo. You give me—"

He shook his head, cutting her off. "I know you've kept us here because I couldn't handle the pressure of being on the run. And I know there's nothing . . ." He rubbed at his eyes. "When your father comes back—I can't handle watching him do what he did to you at Megiddo." His jaw clenched and his hands balled into fists. "But there's nothing I can do to stop it. I thought maybe this—" He picked up the bone shard.

"You had another dream about Megiddo?"

"Not really—this was different. Your father was there. He was doing something . . . terrible. I was trying to stop him, but I couldn't get to him. My legs wouldn't work for some reason." He pressed his hand down like a vise on his thigh. "And there was another man there—someone I knew but I can't think of who it was. He was covered in tattoos. I'm not even sure it was a man. His face was full of a terrible sadness. I couldn't bear to look."

"Where was I?" Usually when he had dreams about Megiddo, Mouse was in the dirt, dead or dying.

"You were . . ." He looked away. "You were with him."

"The other man?"

"No. You were with your father."

"What do you mean?"

He shrugged. "You were beside him—with him. You were together. You were wearing a cloak like his."

"What was I doing?" Mouse's skin prickled with dread.

Angelo shook his head. "Nothing. Not that I remember. You were just there. You had the bone we found in the cave." He looked over at her. "You were wearing a mask with feathers or hair—something wild."

"Then how do you know it was me?" The anxiety that had been crawling all over Angelo seemed to be creeping into her now.

"I could see the eyes behind the mask. They were green, like yours." Angelo looked back down at his hands.

"Your mind is just cramming what I told you about my vision into your old nightmare about Megiddo. It was just a dream, Angelo. I would never join my father."

"I know." An airy thread of doubt ran through his words.

Mouse swallowed. "I would die before—"

"You can't die."

"You know what I mean."

"I know it was just a dream—but I'm tired of being afraid all the time." Sadness spilled over Mouse like oil on water. "I know."

"And I'm tired of being the weak one. I don't have your power, and this thing's obviously not going to work for me." He handed her the bone shard. "So the only thing I can do is make you ready. I need to know that we're doing something to get ready, Mouse. Because he's coming, sooner or later, and you know it."

The squeals of the Martu children sifted into the silence. Mouse pushed up from the bed and went to the chair beside the window to watch them play. It took her a few minutes to find the courage she needed.

"There's something I want to tell you." Her voice was shaking. "I didn't tell you before because I didn't know . . . I still don't know what it means."

"Another secret?" It was more accusation than question.

"No. Just something I needed to figure out before I—it doesn't matter. I'm sorry I didn't tell you sooner." She took a deep breath, forcing herself to slow down. She needed to be calm so he would be. "I remembered something that night after the ceremony with Ngara."

Mouse was afraid of the consequences of what she was about to confess, but she wanted Angelo to stop living in dread, certain that the worst was coming today or tomorrow. She knew what living in the shadows did to a person—dried up their joy, turned them bitter and hard. Maybe the truth would loosen the grip of fear just a little.

"My father's not coming. Not now. Maybe not ever."

"Why?"

"Because he has someone else to give him what he wants. I . . . I have a brother. That's what I couldn't remember that my father told me at Megiddo. The Dreaming ceremony must have helped my memory and—" If she kept talking, maybe Angelo would stop looking at her that way. But suddenly she had no more words. "I have a brother," she mumbled again.

"How could you not tell me about this?"

"I was afraid of what you might do." She whispered it so quietly he didn't hear.

"What?" he asked.

"Nothing. I should have told you. I just wanted to figure out what it might mean first. For us, I mean."

"It means I need to call the Bishop."

Mouse stiffened. "And that's why I didn't tell you."

"They have to know."

"Why?"

"So they can get ready."

"For?"

"Whatever your father's planning to do now that he has a—"

"A child, Angelo. We're talking about a child."

"No. We're talking about something like you."

Mouse sat back hard like she'd been hit.

"I didn't mean it like—" Angelo walked over to her. "I'm sorry. That came out wrong. But Mouse, we need to—"

She shook her head, biting into her lip. "I can't talk about this right now." She stood and moved past him to the door. "I'm going to the clinic, and I need you to leave me alone."

She grabbed her shoes and ran barefoot across the red, dusty earth toward the laughing children.

❀

Sweat ran down Mouse's neck after an hour of hunting shells and tossing spears with the children. It felt clean, ordinary, and human—everything she needed to wipe away the sting of Angelo's words, which had brought back a torrent of nasty taunts from her own childhood. *Odd*, they'd called her. *Witch. Demon. Outcast.* The slurs still hurt even after seven hundred years. Playing with the Martu children had served as a joyful antidote until Mouse's questions sent her in search of Ngara and answers.

Normally Mouse loved a good puzzle—figuring out how the pieces fit together and what picture they made. But when the pieces came in bits of dreams or visions shrouded in myth, how was she supposed to see the edges clearly? And how was she supposed to understand whether the picture they made was of something that had happened, would happen, or might happen? She hated the uncertainty, but it was the idea that she and Angelo were being played with that turned Mouse's steps away from the clinic, where she'd meant to spend the afternoon, and sent her storming toward the community house, where she knew she would find Ngara.

A suffocating wave of claustrophobia stopped Mouse at the threshold. The old woman sat on the floor, crouched over a large square of linen canvas with shallow bowls of paint lined up at its edges. Mouse's memory sucked her back seven hundred years to a tiny cell in the monastery at Podlažice where she, too, had hunched over parchment, lined by jars of ink and scattered quills, as she had painted the elaborate illuminations in the Devil's Bible.

Ngara's work was elaborate, too, though in a different way, more abstract but with fine detail. She had started at the corner with a small brush, pressing dots of color in intricate patterns that erupted as she moved across the canvas. With shifts of pressure, she controlled the shape and shade of each dot so that the image seemed to emerge completely alive in its making, not like conventional painting that started with sketches and layers that were flat and dead until the artist refined the work, finally bringing the picture to life.

Ngara's work was already alive, as if she was simply revealing it to the world.

Mouse took a step into the room and dropped cross-legged onto the floor near the open door. She took full, slow breaths to drive away the feeling of being trapped. Ngara silently worked on.

"It's powerful," Mouse finally said. Watching the old woman paint seemed to siphon off Mouse's anxiety. "It's beautiful."

"Yes. And terrible."

"Why terrible?"

"It is Kumpupirntily," Ngara answered as she looked over her shoulder at Mouse. "The Lake of Disappointment."

"That's the salt lake near here, right?"

Ngara nodded.

"The children say no one goes there."

"Because the *Nyayurnangalku* live there."

With her unnatural abilities, Mouse had been able to pick up several of the Martu dialects quickly, but the proper nouns, many ancient in their origin, did not translate easily.

Ngara saw the question in Mouse's face. "It's the name of the beings that live under the lake."

"Beings?"

"Like people, but not. Devils. Long, sharp claws to grab you with. Long, sharp teeth to eat you with."

Mouse half expected the old woman to smile, like a grandmother telling a fairytale, but Ngara did not smile. Her face stayed stony in its warning. "The children know the truth. No one goes to the lake except when the wind blows. When there is wind, the *Nyayurnangalku* are away, asleep. When there is no wind, they come hunting."

Mouse shivered. She knew enough of the darkness in the world to believe there was probably some truth to the story. She watched Ngara's brush trail a long line of black like a maze around the haunting white of Lake Disappointment.

"We found something in the cave," Mouse finally said. The brush stopped.

"A bone?" the old woman asked.

"How did you know?"

"It's for the pointing. For the *kurdaitcha*."

"The vengeance seeker?"

"Yes."

"It was deep in the cave beside a river. Angelo nearly—"

"A special bone, then," Ngara interrupted. "To be so deep inside the land."

"It was glowing."

"Ah." She pushed back to rest on her heels, her hands pressed against her thighs, the black paint dripping from her brush to the floor.

"What does it mean?" Mouse asked.

"A very special bone. From the old ones. For you." She turned to look at Mouse again, her eyes alit with awe.

"I don't want it."

"What you want does not matter. What is coming will come."

"I don't care what's coming. I don't have to do anything I don't want to do." Mouse felt her anger rising, and the general uneasiness that had been haunting her since the Dreaming hardened into an ominous foreboding that sank deep into her bones. Instinctively, she looked out at the sky, searching for the oncoming storm. With a twinge of regret, she realized that this was what Angelo had been trying to tell her. He'd felt it already. And he was right—Mouse had been hiding from it in a land of make-believe.

The old woman shrugged. "The old ones do what the old ones do. I cannot change it." Ngara pressed her lips together, then added, "You cannot change it."

"I will," Mouse answered defiantly as she stood. "I'll take the bone back, bury it deep in that damn cave, and then Angelo and I will leave."

She hadn't made the decision until she said it, but now that the words had been let loose, they also unleashed an urgency in Mouse, the feeling that she and Angelo were racing against something—and that they were already behind.

Ngara turned back to her painting, pressing red dots into the rivers of black. "What is coming will come. You will not change it."

"Watch me."

Mouse fought a panicked impulse to run as she went to find Angelo. He wasn't at their shed or anywhere around the outstation. Finally, one of the children told her that he'd gone with some others to Parngurr to pick up supplies. Frustrated, Mouse headed to the clinic.

The trapped, hot air in the small room pushed against her like stale breath. She opened a window and turned on the fan that rested on her desk in the corner. She stood in front of it, letting the oscillating air cool her off and quell the seething rebellion inside her. It didn't matter what Ngara said. It didn't matter what the Seven Sisters meant with their bone gift. No one had the power to say what was meant to be for Angelo and Mouse except the two of them. And only the two of them. To hell with everyone else.

Mouse shoved the hair out of her face and headed into the tiny, windowless room at the back of the clinic to inventory supplies, thinking about what she needed to restock before she and Angelo left. She knelt before a small refrigerator that took up half the room. It was the only appliance at the outstation with its own designated generator. It stored insulin and other medicines that would spoil in the scorching heat of the desert. As she opened the door, light and cold air rushed out, washing over her. It was as if someone had pulled a curtain back, exposing what was on the other side, and Mouse suddenly realized why Angelo had gone to Parngurr with the others.

She closed the refrigerator door and sat on the floor in the darkness.

Mouse and Angelo had ditched their phones when they'd gone off the grid in the Ukraine. No phone and no credit cards meant they were virtually untraceable. As long as they were together, they didn't need a phone anyway. Mouse literally had no friends and no family—besides her father—and Angelo had turned his back on all of that when he'd decided to go on the run with her.

The Martu outstation had only one phone line, for emergencies, but it was unreliable at best and certainly not an option for an international call. But Parngurr was. Hosting a larger community of the Martu,

Parngurr also served tourists who came for a rugged outback experience. The small town had a store and a gas station and a laundry—and reliable phone service. Including burner phones in the store and a satellite signal.

It's where Angelo would go to call the Bishop.

Mouse waited for the flash of temper or rush of panic. She felt empty instead, her mind methodically working through the problem. How much time did they have before the Bishop's Novus Rishi descended on them? Given the remoteness and difficult terrain, it would likely be days. But Mouse didn't want to bring that kind of trouble to the Martu. She and Angelo could leave tomorrow and have time to get to—where? Port Hedland, maybe. They could call the Bishop again from there, draw him away from the outstation, and then get on a boat going somewhere else.

She sat back and pulled her knees to her chest. She'd already decided they needed to leave, she reasoned. Angelo calling the Bishop just made it all messier and faster. But the word *betrayal* sifted into the conversation in her mind.

Mouse pushed herself up and busied herself with counting needles and bandages and making itemized lists of what Ngara would need to order for the clinic over the next six months. A few hours later, one of the children came to fetch her. Ngara, the other adults, and older children were going out to hunt, and Mouse was needed to watch after the little ones. She spent the last of the daylight painting with the children, and then, as darkness fell, they moved out to the hearth fire to tell stories while they waited for the hunters to bring home supper.

The children drew close, a couple of them climbing into her lap as they sat on the ground. The snaps and crackles of the fire drove away the chill that settled quickly in the desert at sunset, and Mouse's heart grew heavy with the good-byes she couldn't say.

"Tell us the story about the wolf in the woods," one of the children said. It was a tale Mouse had told many times.

"Once upon a time in the Sumava forest," she began.

"A forest has many trees," a little boy added.

"Juniper and oak and lindenwood," they all shouted out. They liked hearing about the mountains covered in trees and the wide, rushing rivers and the deep lakes and snow—all impossible pieces of a world they would likely never see. They begged her to draw patterns of snowflakes in the dry dirt.

"And once," Mouse continued, "a young girl ran away to hide in this forest."

The children knew the story so well, they took it from her.

"The girl met a wolf," one of them said. "His name was Bohdan."

All the children said the name. They held the long vowel, their mouths perfect circles as their tongues played with the unfamiliar sound and then slid over the *d* and clipped the *n* at the end.

"The girl saved him because she was *ngangkari*, a healer," a boy said.

"And they were friends, the wolf and the healer," another child added.

"But she was sick, too. Her *kurunpa* was dark and sad. Her spirit did not live in her heart. It clung to her back and whispered wrong things."

"It told her she was bad. Broken. No good." The words, high and bright in the voice of innocents, pierced Mouse like daggers.

"Bohdan saw the dark *kurunpa*, and he drove it away."

"How?" one of the littlest ones, new to the story, asked.

Mouse answered this time. "He taught her love—for others and for herself."

"Then the *Mamu* came." The little girl's eyes were wide and full of the firelight. "They were evil and hungry, and they took the body of Bohdan, and he was gone."

"But his *kurunpa*, bright and strong, would not leave. He went inside the girl, the *ngangkari*, and became her *mapanpa*, her magic healing, her love."

"And she was saved!"

"Saved," they all echoed.

Mouse saw the lights of the jeep far off in the distance—Angelo had come home from Parngurr.

CHAPTER FIVE

Jack Gray stared at himself in the mirror of his hotel bathroom. Steam from the shower still fogged the glass, but his stark white hair cut through the haze.

After several more attempts to wash it out in the tiny sink at the synagogue, he had finally accepted that it wasn't just dirt from the attic. Something had happened to him. And then the fear set in. *What* had happened? And was it still happening? Was the spell slowly draining him of life? Was he going to die?

The girl—he'd never asked her name—had stayed with him as he panicked. She assured him he would be fine. She had touched the amulet, too. It seemed that touching it was the trigger to set off the spell. Once a person let go, the spell stopped. The girl had touched it only for a moment and had a single streak of white in her hair as proof. Jack had held the amulet for much longer.

Once he'd calmed down, he and the girl had gone back outside the synagogue. The amulet still lay on the sidewalk where the girl had flung it. She went back to the utility closet where she'd stored the ladder and came out with a wad of thick rags covered in splotches of different colored paints. She shoved the rags into Jack's hand. Shaking, he knelt and carefully gathered the amulet in the rags, cocooning it in the thick cloth. When he stood up, the girl was gone.

He had walked back to the hotel holding the rag away from him like it was a snake. Once he was inside the suite, he'd run to the bathroom, tossed the rag and amulet on the counter, and sobbed with relief when he saw that he was still himself, skin still young, eyes still vibrant and dark—all normal except for the shock of white hair. He'd stepped into the shower with one last, desperate hope.

But now the truth was staring back at him from the mirror, inescapable and blinding like snow.

Jack shuddered, a chill running through him as it dawned on him that the girl had probably told the Reverend what had happened to her. That was why he'd been so sure this wasn't just another of the Rabbi's pointless quests. The Reverend had known there was something of real power in the Golem's attic. That was why he wanted Jack to bring it to him and not tell the Rabbi. The Reverend knew the thing was dangerous. He knew—and he hadn't warned Jack.

Jack slammed his fist into his reflection in the mirror. Cracks erupted like a spider's web out and around where his knuckles hit the glass. He jumped back, surprised at what he'd done.

"Good Lord, what happened to you?" Kitty Ayres stood in the doorway gaping at Jack, naked and now dripping blood on the bathroom floor.

He snatched at a hand towel and wrapped it around his bleeding hand. "I slipped on the wet floor and slammed into the mirror," he lied. He stood a little taller, not at all embarrassed as Mrs. Ayres ran her eyes over every part of him and then took a step closer.

"No, I meant this," she lifted a wet lock of white that clung to the top of his shoulder.

Jack's eyes darted to the amulet, which had slipped out from the bundle of rags where he'd tossed it on the counter. Mrs. Ayres turned to look, too.

"What's this?" she asked as she reached for it.

"Don't touch it!"

She snatched her hand back and looked up at Jack in the shattered mirror. "Why not?" she asked, her face sharp with anger.

"*That's* what happened to me."

She bent closer to examine the silver amulet. "What is it?"

Jack wasn't sure how much Mrs. Ayres knew about her husband's non-evangelical alliances with the Novus Rishi, but right now he didn't give a damn about what he was supposed to say or not. "An amulet."

"How did it do that to your hair?"

"Magic."

She turned to look at him over her shoulder, a slow smile stretching across her face. She pulled her cell phone out of her blazer pocket. "Where are you?" she asked after a moment. "He got it. You need to come see."

"So you knew, too," Jack said as she put the phone away.

"Honey, I know everything the Reverend knows."

"Why didn't either of you warn me?"

"Bless your heart, Jack. We needed to know if the girl was telling the truth. That's a lot of money we paid her—a person might say and do anything to get their hands on that kind of money." She laid her hand against his bare back. "Now, we need to get you some clothes on before the Reverend gets here." She looked Jack over once more before she stepped out into the bedroom. "And bandages for that hand," she called back.

Jack's anger was dwindling into defeat. He'd been used. But what could he do about it?

"I need new shoes."

Kitty Ayres came back in through the door with a pair of pants and a shirt she'd pulled from the closet. "Don't you worry. I'll go pick you out something myself this afternoon." She started to close the bathroom door but paused and nodded to the amulet on the counter. "Be sure to bring that when you come out."

Jack sank onto the toilet, his head in his hands.

He entered the suite's sitting area several minutes later, dressed, hand bandaged, hair dry and coiffed, the amulet again wrapped in rags. He held it carefully in front of him and then laid it on the marble coffee table. The Reverend was sitting on the couch, stretched back with his jacket open and his belly spread out over his lap. He chuckled and shook his head when he saw Jack's hair.

"You okay, son?"

"Sure." In addition to the fresh clothes, Jack wore a cloak of indifference. He knew not to expect any remorse; the Reverend never apologized for anything. All Jack could do was move forward, a little more wise and a little more wary. It was another gift he prided himself on—his ability to cut his losses and start looking for the next open door of opportunity.

Mrs. Ayres came around the room divider from the kitchenette with a cup of coffee in her hand. "Here you go, honey. You could probably use a pick-me-up." She handed the cup to Jack and then settled onto the couch beside her husband.

"Well, sit and tell me about it," the Reverend said.

Jack sat on the black leather stool beside the coffee table across from them. He told them a truncated version of what had happened and then waited for questions.

"Since you're the scholar here, what do you think it is, *Dr. Gray?*" the Reverend asked, leaning forward and peeling back the rags to expose the silver cylinder.

"It's an amulet, usually worn for protection." Jack mimicked the dusty tone of one of his least favorite history professors. "Typically, a spell or good omen is engraved along the surface, but this one only has decorative markings." A small sigh slipped past his stiff lip; he knew where his next words would take him. "There's something inside."

"How do you know?" Mrs. Ayres asked.

"Sometimes the amulets were made to carry the spell or a protective talisman inside. And . . . I heard something rattle when I was examining it in the attic." Jack pulled at the back of his neck as a little shiver ran up his spine.

"Well, open it up and let's see," said the Reverend.

Jack swallowed. "After what it did to me already, I'm not touching it again."

"How'd it do that to your hair?" Mrs. Ayres asked, her voice charged with curiosity as she leaned even closer to the amulet. "You said it was magic. How does that work?"

"I'm a historian, I don't know anything about these kinds of—"

"Let's be honest, son. You're not a historian. The only thing you're really a scholar of is your own ambition." The Reverend chuckled. "Now, I don't see that as a bad thing, but you're young still, which means you've got a lot of ladder left to climb. And what that means is when I tell you to open it, the only answer I'm looking for is 'Yes, sir.'"

Jack held the Reverend's gaze, testing his own courage. And then he blinked. "Yes, sir." He looked down at the amulet, his face hot with shame. "I'll need a pair of tweezers."

Without a word, Kitty Ayres got up and came back with a pair of gold tweezers in her hand. "Here you go, honey."

Jack bunched the rags up around one end of the amulet and held it tightly while he used the tweezers to tug at the other end. It took several minutes to scratch through the corrosion and then even longer to use the tweezers as a pry bar to ease the silver lid from the cylinder. At last, it popped free like the cork from a wine bottle.

As Jack tilted the amulet, the Reverend and Mrs. Ayres leaned in close to watch a rolled scroll of silver slide out. Jack moved toward the scroll with the tweezers, ready to unroll it and read the spell.

"Stop." Surprisingly, the command came from Kitty Ayres rather than the Reverend. "We'll take care of it from here. We just wanted to be sure there was something in there."

"Don't you want to know what it says?" Jack asked.

"We'll know soon enough," she answered as she wrapped the rags around the amulet and scroll.

"But I—"

"I think you need to be gone before the others get here," the Reverend said.

"What do you mean?"

"You've met Bishop Sebastian," the Reverend answered.

Jack looked at him, confused.

"Your hair," Mrs. Ayres said.

"Ah." Jack leaned back as he began to understand. "And the Rabbi will be joining by video. He'll want to know what happened to my hair. He'll ask me about—wait, did he know the amulet was dangerous?" Jack wanted a full lay of the land. He needed to know where the mines were hidden if he hoped to get out intact. "Did he know it could—"

"He didn't know about the amulet. He thought he was sending you to find a bit of parchment with the spell that other old rabbi used to give the Golem life," Mrs. Ayres said. "Our Rabbi thinks if you put that spell in the mouth of something already alive, it'll have the opposite effect—regardless of whether it's human or immortal."

"Does the Rabbi want to kill someone?" Jack asked, though pieces of what he knew were starting to fall into place on their own. All the research he'd been doing for the Rabbi—combing through ancient texts for references to immortal beings, collecting variations on the Book of Enoch, picking through spells and magic artifacts purported to be weapons against evil, trying to track down the legendary, lost Book of the Just—it all added to what he knew about his old mentor. Even as Dr. Em's student, Jack had known her to be odd, but during the two days he'd spent with her in Nashville, he'd learned that she had the power to control people, that she was connected in some visceral way to the Devil's Bible—which meant that she was also very old. Maybe immortal. It didn't take a keen analytical mind to connect the dots—the Rabbi wanted the Golem spell so he could kill Dr. Em.

"Not some *one*. Some *thing*, more like," Mrs. Ayres said. "An abomination before the Lord."

Jack could've sworn the Reverend rolled his eyes at his wife before he muttered, "He's an old fool looking a gift horse in the mouth. And that's enough talk, Kitty."

Jack nodded to the scroll that had been hidden in the amulet. "Is that the spell? The one that gave life to the Golem?"

"I honestly couldn't say, son."

"Are you going to give it to the Rabbi?"

"I've got someone who can tell me what it says. And until I know what it is, I don't want anyone else, including any of the Novus Rishi, to know I've got it. Do you understand?"

"Yes, sir."

Kitty Ayres gasped. "Oh, Reverend! We should send Jack to *The Redeemed*."

"What?" Jack asked, leaning back. He didn't like any of the scenarios his mind was playing out.

"It's our boat," she said.

"Yacht," the Reverend corrected as he pulled out his buzzing phone, a smile playing at his lips while he read the lit-up screen.

Mrs. Ayres sighed. "Jack would be out of the way until we figure out what to do about his hair. No one from the Novus Rishi would know where he was to ask him any pesky questions. He could just—"

"Our boy will be leaving in the morning to do another chore for me," the Reverend said.

"Well, I'm at least going to go get you some new shoes, and then we're going to send you out on the town for the night. I think you've earned it." Mrs. Ayres got up and headed toward the door, ruffling Jack's hair as she went. "Oh my, that's soft as lambswool. And it'll be striking against dark clothes. Just you wait and see—you're going to be a girl magnet, honey."

"I'll walk down with you, sweetheart. I've got to get back to my Righteousness meetings." The Reverend bent to collect the rag-wrapped amulet and scroll and put them in a pocket inside his briefcase. "Have fun tonight, but get back to the hotel first thing in the morning," he said to Jack as he lifted his belly to button his suit.

"Yes, sir."

⚬━┿━⚬

Days later, Jack was still living on the decadent indulgence of that last night in Prague while he watched a foreman rake mud from the legs of his overalls, sending chunks of it splattering down to the ground. "You can't go in yet. It's not safe."

"Why not?" Shaking a piece of mud from his otherwise clean boots, Jack Gray stepped back, his own bright orange overalls, still pristine, glaring as he moved into a patch of sunlight.

"Need to finish with the hydraulic supports and clear away a bit more of the overhead debris," the man said. He turned and pointed behind him at a tangled mess of toppled trees and sunken earth. "There's some crawl space down there, but it gets tight. Seems pretty settled—looks like the structure collapsed maybe a year or so back—but I want to be sure before I send people down there."

Jack would have been happy to wait. He would have been happy to never come out to the Czechia backwoods or coop himself up in a tiny hotel in quiet little Chrudim for a whole damn week, watching men in overalls play in the dirt. And he would certainly be happy to never climb down into that muddy rubble and take the risk that it would all come crashing down on him. But it wasn't his decision to make. The Reverend was already impatient. He wanted to know if there was anything to find in the ruins of the monastery at Podlažice.

"I can't wait any longer," Jack said as he shoved past the man toward the gaping hole, the roots of the upturned trees hanging low across it like a rope curtain.

"Hey!" the man yelled. "You die, it's on you. At least take this."

Jack Gray turned around, throwing his hands up just quickly enough to catch the hard hat the man had tossed to him. As Jack lifted it to his head, he pushed back long locks of white hair that fell across his eyes. He was getting used to it now, and Mrs. Ayres had been right—it made quite a statement when he wore dark clothes. Black was Jack's new favorite color.

Of course, none of that did him any good out here in the muck in the middle of nowhere, but the Reverend had given him no choice. Excavation crews had been at work on the ruins for a couple of months, but the site had only recently been identified as the Podlažice monastery, long believed to be the birthplace of the Devil's Bible. The Reverend had confirmed the news the same day Jack found the amulet and had immediately started pulling strings to acquire private access to the site before a cadre of scholars and preservationists took over. The Reverend wanted Jack on hand to make sure the excavation crew was careful not to destroy anything that might be useful to the Novus Rishi. He wanted Jack to be the first to search the site. But in a few days, the scholars would descend.

Jack knelt, parted the curtain of roots, and crawled into the dark, pausing to turn on the light on his hard hat. Several hydraulic jacks lined the crawl space, their bottoms sinking into the soil as their tops pressed against the upper shelf of debris. The sour smell of the mud made it hard to breathe, and the sharp edges of exposed stone cut into Jack's knees as he snaked his way lower into the monastery ruins. There were a few short tunnels peeling off from the main pathway that had been cleared, and Jack shined his light back into each of them, searching for signs of anything interesting. It all looked like rubble to him.

"If there's anything here," he muttered to himself, "no one's going to find it for years." But he kept crawling forward anyway. He wanted to sound convincing when he told the Reverend he'd searched as well as he could.

Nearly two hours later, he pulled himself past another hydraulic jack and twisted to look down another dead end, swearing that this would be his last—he'd look here, then crawl out, call the Reverend, and head back to the hotel at Prague.

But as he inched his way farther into the deep nook, something almost familiar tickled his senses, like a smell triggering a memory. Jack took a deep sniff of air, but it was all mud and dirt and made him sneeze. He realized it wasn't really a smell that had caught his attention. It was a feeling—like the wind before a storm, charged with some mysterious energy.

Where had he felt that before?

And then his mouth dropped open and his eyes grew wide. He crawled farther into the dark crevice, smiling, his heart thrumming with excitement and a little fear. When he could go no deeper, he tugged at the bulky steel-lined work gloves he wore. He had meant to take no more risks like he had with the amulet, but the power he sensed here wasn't unknown. He'd met it once before.

Jack Gray's work on the Devil's Bible had led him to a clinically clean room in the National Library of Sweden. The librarian had splayed open the book like it was a dead thing on an examination table. But Jack had felt how alive the book was, coursing with power. He'd been wearing gloves then, too—thin cotton museum gloves meant to protect the historic artifact, meant to shield the Devil's Bible from body oils and grime. But the Devil's Bible had called to Jack; it wanted to be touched by him, skin to parchment, just as whatever lurked in this dark crevice now called to him.

A lost ghost of Podlažice was aching to be found.

CHAPTER SIX

A ngelo climbed out of the jeep, laughing.

Mouse stood watching, half her face lit by the firelight. The other half stayed cool in the shadows. She waited as they unloaded supplies, and then Angelo made his way to her. She saw the levity slip from his face as he neared, but he kissed her on top of the head anyway.

"I missed you," he said.

Mouse felt the phone in his pocket when he hugged her.

She pulled away and headed back to their shed.

"You're still mad at me?" Angelo asked as he matched his step to hers.

"No." And she wasn't, but she realized that she'd held out some hope that she had been wrong—that Angelo had just gone to Parngurr with the guys to get away for a bit. The hard truth that he had indeed called the Bishop burrowed into Mouse's chest like some fat tick sucking away at her spirit. But she couldn't give in to it. If the Novus Rishi were on the way, she and Angelo needed to be ready to go at first light.

Mouse already had their backpacks on the bed waiting for them. Angelo followed her into the small room, but she said nothing. Instead, she moved quickly from the shelf full of trinkets the Martu children had given them to a pile of books by the bed to the stack of clothes in the corner, grabbing items here and there. After a year of calling the outstation home, they'd accumulated too much, and now she had to choose what to take and what to leave behind. Mouse hated choosing.

"What's going on?" Angelo asked as he saw the backpacks.

"You need to get your stuff packed. We're leaving in the morning."

"Why?"

"Angelo, don't."

"Don't what? What's happened? I have a right to know why we're—"

"You have a right?" Mouse scoffed and then turned to look at him. "Why'd you go to Parngurr?"

"I wanted to—"

"Call your Father?"

He sighed, dropped into the chair behind him, and closed his eyes. "I didn't do it, Mouse."

"Sure."

He pulled the phone from his pocket. "Check for yourself. No calls. No texts."

Mouse turned back to packing. "It doesn't matter. We need to go."

"Why?"

"The dreams, mine and yours, the bone—" She shoved a shirt into the backpack, shaking her head, not wanting to have this conversation. "It's just time to go."

"I already know that. I mean why doesn't it matter that I didn't call?"

"You went to call."

"Don't you want to know why I didn't?"

She shrugged.

"I realized it wasn't my decision to make. Not alone." He walked over to her, tried to put his hand on her back, but she pulled away to the other side of the bed.

"You're damn right it's not your decision to make."

"It's not yours either."

72

"He's my brother."

"You don't know what he is."

Mouse spun around, her eyes sparking and her mouth taut, ready to attack.

"No—wait. Listen." Angelo put his hands up and sat on the bed so he could look her in the face. "I am sorry I went to Parngurr. It was wrong. I was wrong." His eyes were fierce with regret, pleading for her to understand. "I don't want to fight. I want to talk—we need to talk, Mouse."

"No, we need to go, Angelo."

"Fine, let's deal with that first. Where? Where do you want to run this time?" Bitterness sharpened his tone.

"You just said you knew we needed to go. And you're the one who's been pushing for us to leave. Where were *you* planning to run?"

"I know we need to go—soon—but I haven't been pushing for us to leave, Mouse. I've been pushing for us to get ready. If we're finally going to do that, here is as good a place as any. Better than most because we're so isolated."

"The Martu aren't safe with us here. I see that now after Ngara said . . ." Mouse's earlier anger at the old woman had dissolved into sadness and shame. "It's like you said—I've been a fool, a child playing make-believe. I just thought we could be happy here."

"What did Ngara say?"

"That something's coming and . . . and that running won't change anything."

"She's right."

Mouse was shaking her head. "Being on the move, hiding, that's the only way to—"

"That might work for you, Mouse. But I think we both know it doesn't work for me."

She sucked in a breath, drawing courage with it. "You're right. You should stay here and figure out your next step. I'll go and draw the trouble with me." Mouse heard the whisper of Father Lucas at her ear: *Have you found trouble, little* andílek? She could hear her own voice, bright and innocent, answer: *It's found me, Father.* So it was again, she thought wearily. And so it would always be.

"That's not what I meant, Mouse. If you go, I go."

"Are you sure?" Her voice shook. "I know you love me—so surely that it sometimes feels like the only truth I can hold on to. But there was no way you could know what this kind of life is like. You think I do it better than you, but you've forgotten how you first found me. I was so tired of running and hiding, so broken and lost, that I was desperate to end it any way I could. I don't want that for you. And there's no shame in saying—"

"I've been an ass, Mouse," he interrupted. "Too afraid of being weak or useless instead of just doing whatever you need me to do. I won't lie—I wasn't prepared for being on the run. I overestimated what I could do and underestimated what you'd already been through. But, Mouse"—he took her hand in his—"I don't want any life that doesn't have you in it. I don't care whether we're running or hiding or living in an icy hole in the ground in Antarctica. I want to be by your side."

Mouse dropped the shirt she was folding, gratitude washing over her and resurrecting some hope as she bent and kissed him, hard and long. "So, sidekick," she said with a smile as she pulled back, "what do we do next?"

"I've been thinking about that on the ride back from Parngurr. If we let your cryptic vision or my fuzzy dream or some mythical gift from the gods set us off like a starter pistol, we're running blind—like Oedipus. We might think we're getting away, but what we're really doing is running headlong into trouble." Angelo sat up straighter. "So, we figure out what we can—how to use your power and how to use that bone. We come up with a battle plan, then we make a strategic decision about where to go—find high ground to make our stand."

Mouse looked toward the darkening window. "Ngara didn't say what was coming. It could be my father, but it could be—"

Angelo sighed. "Let's focus on what we know. The only thing that's new is that your father has what he's always wanted."

"Which means he might not want me anymore."

"Or that he'll want you even more, now that he's got his last piece in place. Or that his coming has nothing to do with you—he's just ready to make his move now that he has a powerful ally."

"That's still guessing—you said we needed to focus on what we know. We don't know what my father wants. But your Father's made it clear. He wants me, and nothing has happened that would change that. Maybe Ngara's warning was about Bishop Sebastian."

"I'm less worried about the Bishop and the Novus Rishi than I am about your father."

"Yeah, well, they don't want to turn you into some kind of Armageddon weapon, do they?" Mouse pushed away from the bed and started pacing, picking up items and cramming them into the backpacks.

"I wouldn't let the Bishop do anything to hurt you."

"You might not have a choice."

Angelo shook his head, dismissing her worry. "The Bishop cares about me. If I put myself between you and him—"

"I don't want that any more than you want me to protect you."

"I'm just saying we have some leverage there. But with your father . . ."

Mouse knew that what Angelo said was partly true. Her father didn't care about her. Especially now that he had a son, her only value to him, if any at all, was the same as the Novus Rishi's—as a possible weapon to use against his enemies.

"But this isn't just about me and my father now, Angelo. It's about my brother." Her voice grew quiet. "He's just a little boy."

Angelo lowered the backpacks to the floor. "When you imagine your brother, what do you see?"

Mouse stood in front of him, her eyes closed. Her face softened and a smile grew without reservation, full of joy.

"It's Nicholas you see, isn't it?" Angelo asked gently.

Mouse looked at him sharply, the smile gone. "What do you mean?" But the truth was already pricking at her eyes.

"You see golden hair and big blue eyes and tiny hands reaching for you. You hear a laugh you know well and a cry for Mama." Angelo pulled her down to the bed beside him. "But it's not your son we're talking about, Mouse. He's gone. This boy belongs to your father."

"He's still just a boy."

"But he isn't. Like you aren't just a girl."

Mouse kept her head down, the tears now blurring her vision.

"He'll probably have powers like you, won't he?"

She nodded.

"But he doesn't have a Father Lucas to teach him like you did—a loving and kind and good soul to guide him. To warn him about the dangers that come with that kind of power. To show him the beauty and love in the world. Where would you be without Father Lucas?"

Mouse ran her hand across her face, wiping at the tears.

"What will your father raise this boy to be?"

She turned to look at Angelo. "I don't know, but would you have your Bishop train his crosshairs on a little boy?"

Angelo stared at her for a moment, silenced, then shook his head. "No."

The buzzing hum of a didgeridoo vibrated though the night air as the Martu began to celebrate their hunt. Mouse looked down at the woven basket she held in one hand and a carved lizard in the other—both gifts from the children. How could she choose which to take and which to leave behind?

"What do we do?" Angelo asked.

"I don't know." Mouse lay back on the bed. "But even when I'd forgotten almost everything that happened on top of Megiddo after my father attacked me, the one thing that rang clear and true in my mind was that I had the power to choose what and who I was. And I chose, Angelo. I don't want to be anyone's weapon or warrior. Not even yours." She balled her hands into fists. "And I won't think about my brother that way either."

Angelo eased back beside her and was quiet for a long time. "You're right," he finally said. "We're talking about a boy, regardless of what your father means to do with him. You're also right about us needing to go.

My dream and yours—they sure seem like someone's trying to get our attention. If something's coming, I don't want to bring it down on the Martu. They don't deserve that."

"Do we go now? Or stay long enough to figure out our next move?"

"What move? I thought we were just running."

Mouse turned to him, tucking a bit of hair behind her ear. "No, you were right, too. We need a plan. I'd really like to not be Oedipus."

Angelo chuckled. "Well, I bought the phone with cash and haven't used it, so there's nothing there to trace. The Novus Rishi haven't found us out here yet, so there's no reason to assume they will now. A few more days won't hurt, right?"

Mouse lay there, silent. She had something else she wanted to say, an idea that had been growing despite her efforts to quell it. She knew it was impossible. "Since we're planning where to go next, I have something else I want to consider. It's complicated, and I don't even know where to start—"

"You want to go get your brother."

Mouse nodded, smiling at how well he knew her. "We could be his Father Lucas." Her voice cracked at the rush of emotion.

Angelo brought her head down to his chest. They lay listening to the didgeridoo.

"Let's do it," Angelo said. "Let's go get him and bring him home."

Mouse propped up on her elbows to look at him. "It's a crazy idea."

"Good thing we do crazy well." He smiled and she leaned down and kissed him, easing her knee between his as he ran his hand under her shirt at the small of her back, pressing her closer.

They took their time, letting each kiss, each soft touch, each sigh of pleasure wash away the residue of the day's anger and fear. Even the didgeridoo had gone silent when, later, Mouse found the courage to ask about the one worry their lovemaking couldn't erase.

"Angelo," she said, so softly it was like the beat of a moth's wings. "What if it's not your Father or mine that's the dark thing coming? The thing Ngara says we can't outrun?"

"What else would it be?"

"What if it's me?"

Mouse felt him go still beside her. "What do you mean?"

"In my dream, I became my father. In yours, I stood side by side with him."

"You wouldn't do that," Angelo said.

"But if these are prophecies . . ."

"Maybe they're warnings about what's at stake, inspiration so we keep fighting."

Mouse played with the thought for a few minutes—it didn't feel true to her. She wasn't inspired. She was afraid.

"Is God toying with us?" she asked as sleep curled around them.

"Something is."

<hr/>

They woke rested and eager.

"Any dreams?" Angelo asked.

"No. You?"

"Nope."

They settled on staying one more week so they could plan their next steps and wrap up loose ends at the outstation. Angelo had already promised to go to Newman with a couple of the men to get irrigation equipment that day and to help install it in the lot where the Martu were trying to grow a small garden. Mouse still had work to do to prepare the clinic before she left, but she was scheduled to spend the day with a *ngangkari*, a native healer, visiting Martu families who lived several miles out from the rest of the community.

Angelo was helping clean the breakfast dishes at the community house when Mouse came to say good-bye. "Tonight, we'll tell Ngara and the others that we're leaving, right?"

"That's the plan."

"I'll see you this afternoon," she said, leaning in to kiss him.

"Be careful."

"You, too."

"I love you."

"*Miluji tě*," she answered back in Czech. It was their ritual good-bye, a talisman of protection while they were away from each other.

Late that afternoon, Mouse got back to the outstation first. It was quiet, no children running free from shed to shed. Even the dogs seemed to be hiding.

She headed to the clinic to drop off the medical equipment she'd taken with her and to work on inventory. As she turned the corner of the small shed, she realized the door was ajar. She stepped cautiously over the threshold, and then she stopped.

There was a man sitting at her desk in the corner, his back to her. The fan was running. At every turn, it lifted the long locks of his white hair.

CHAPTER SEVEN

Mouse knew him by his smell. She watched him swiveling the desk chair gently from left to right, waiting, his back to the door. She could kill him with a word. He'd always been such a fool.

"What the hell happened to your hair, Jack?"

She sauntered into the clinic like she'd been expecting him. Fear ran over her like icy water, threatening to paralyze her, but she wouldn't let Jack see it. She needed to learn what she could from him while there was time. She wasn't really afraid of him—he was just a harbinger. She was scared of what would come in his wake. And of what she would have to do when it did.

He spun around in the chair, startled, and then stammered, "Hello, Dr. Em." He cocked his head and added, "Or whatever your name is."

Last time Mouse had seen Jack, he'd been sent by some mysterious benefactor to sniff around, looking for secrets about the Devil's Bible. Jack knew "Dr. Em" to be a typical, if enigmatic, college history professor who had information he needed. He'd tracked her to Nashville, then got caught in the nasty backwash when Mouse's father came looking for her. Mouse was sure that Jack had put the pieces together and figured out that she wasn't what she seemed, but before she could confirm her suspicions, she'd been forced to run. She hadn't given him much thought until she'd met Bishop Sebastian, Jack's presumed benefactor. She figured Jack knew everything the Bishop knew. And now he'd found them.

"Is this your first time in the outback?" she asked as she put the medical supplies she'd been carrying on the examination table.

He chuckled but didn't answer.

Mouse was considering her options. She could command him to go back to wherever he'd come from and forget he'd ever been here. She could make him forget his own name. She could send him walking out into the desert, and no one would ever see him again. But in the brutal and tender confrontation with her father at Megiddo, Mouse had finally accepted that she had the power to choose what she wanted to be. Until then, she'd always thought herself a victim of her birth, of her bloodline. She'd let others define her as her father's daughter. But no more. And in accepting her power to choose, Mouse swore she would never take that power away from anyone else—not even to protect Angelo. She would not compel Jack to do anything against his will.

"What brings you all the way out here?" she asked.

"You."

"Where's the Bishop?" She was trying to untangle another knot that was troubling her—*how* had the Novus Rishi found them? It seemed too much of a coincidence that Jack would show up only a day after Angelo claimed he hadn't called Bishop Sebastian, but Mouse didn't like where that thread took her.

"The Bishop?"

"No need to play games. I know your benefactor—Bishop Sebastian."

Jack raised his eyebrows, and a smile played at the corner of his mouth. "Bishop Sebastian's busy in Rome."

"I would have thought he'd be eager to see Angelo." She was trying to interpret Jack's odd demeanor—there was something here she hadn't figured out.

"Who's Angelo?" Jack's heartbeat, still racing a little from Mouse surprising him, stayed steady; he honestly didn't know who Angelo was.

The game shifted instantly.

If he didn't know about Angelo, Mouse had another play at hand, one that would keep Angelo safe. She could just leave with Jack now, before Angelo got back. She'd left Angelo behind once before to keep him safe, when she'd gone to face her father at Megiddo. Angelo had made her swear she would never do it again. If she broke that promise, she might lose him—but at least he'd be safe.

"A mutual friend the Bishop and I share," she answered.

"And he's here?" Jack looked nervously past her shoulder.

"No. It's just me." Mouse chewed at her lip. Something here didn't make sense. Why wouldn't the Bishop tell Jack about Angelo? The answer came quick on the heels of the question. Someone else must have sent Jack. "How about you? You got a traveling buddy?"

Jack smirked and shrugged his shoulders. But Mouse read the truth all over him.

"It was stupid to come here alone, Jack."

He held the smile but shifted in his seat, and Mouse heard his heart jump. He was scared of her. She played with the moment, stretching and leaning against the table, but she kept her eyes on Jack. The fan flipped his hair.

"What happened to you?" she asked again, leaning forward and tugging at a lock as it lifted in the blown air.

He flinched at the movement and pushed his chair back a little, but he never stopped smiling. "Do you like it?"

She shrugged. "Makes you look older."

"I guess you'd know, huh?"

She laughed. So he had learned some things in Nashville. But how much did he know? And if the Bishop wasn't his source, Mouse needed to know who was. "Did you figure that out all on your own? I mean, you were never the best student—"

"I knew there was something wrong about you when I left Nashville." He cocked his head and waited a beat. "The Rabbi filled in most of the rest."

Mouse took his bait. "The Rabbi?"

Jack leaned forward, elbows on his knees and chin in hand, his face dripping with smugness. "My benefactor."

"Ah," she said. She lifted her eyebrows and then shrugged. "You got me. Even the worst students do something right now and then. So, is that why you're here? Did the Rabbi send you to find me again?"

Jack looked down at something he held in his hand. "It wasn't easy."

"How'd you do it?"

"We've been looking for over a year."

"Why? I don't have any secret notes on the Devil's Bible. I'm happy to talk to your Rabbi about my theories, but—"

He looked up and smirked. "You said no games, Dr. Em. You know I'm not here about the Devil's Bible."

Mouse sighed and nodded. There was nothing to gain from playing dumb about the Novus Rishi—Jack had been the first one to tell her about them, even if he hadn't called them by name. "Okay. So you're working with the Novus Rishi, and they sent you to find me. How'd you do it?"

"Hard work and sacrifice, as any good research project demands, just like you taught me." He leaned back in his chair. "Don't you want to sit down?"

"Don't you want to tell me about your hard work and sacrifice?"

"I do, actually. But I want you to be comfortable."

"You think you have the upper hand here, Jack, but you don't. Your masters sent you out here by yourself, and they clearly didn't arm you well with all the information you need. I know you're a little scared of me, but a little scared isn't nearly enough."

He held her gaze, but she could hear the blood rushing through his veins and see the goose bumps rise on his skin.

"Knowing how I found you isn't going to help you, Dr. Em," he said and crossed his arms. "I'll skip over the boring parts, but just know I did my groundwork. You'd be proud of my research—a year's worth of tedium, panning through so much shit while I was looking for gold.

But then I found it—silver, not gold—in the Golem's attic of the old synagogue in Prague."

"What did you find?"

"An amulet."

"With a spell inside?"

"The professor gets an A."

"The spell was to give the Golem life?" Mouse, of course, knew the story well.

Jack laughed. "Uh-oh. Lost a point on that one. I thought the same thing. But turns out, it was a locator spell so the rabbi who made the Golem—"

"Rabbi Judah Loew ben Bezalel," Mouse said.

"No one cares how smart you are."

Mouse snapped her eyes toward him. He didn't sound like himself.

"Anyway, the spell was so the rabbi could find the Golem if he lost control of it and it ran away," Jack said, his voice suddenly light and conversational again.

Like the fan in the corner, Mouse's mind swiveled from one problem to the next. She worked to estimate Angelo's return and set a mental clock ticking down the minutes—less than an hour, she guessed. She was also trying to anticipate the Novus Rishi's next move. Were they on the way? How would Jack have contacted them from out here to let them know he'd found her? Was he supposed to bring Mouse back alone? How did he think he would manage that? And what the hell was wrong with him? She needed him to keep talking.

"Why would a location spell turn your hair white?" she asked.

"It didn't. The curse the rabbi laid on the amulet did."

Mouse nodded. "That way, the rabbi would know if someone else was trying to find the Golem, to steal it or use it for their own purpose."

"The Reverend said it was like the dye pack that explodes if someone steals money from a bank."

"The Reverend?"

Mouse's heightened senses were focused on reading Jack. He'd intentionally mentioned the Rabbi earlier to show Mouse she didn't understand the game at play, trying to make her second-guess her options. But this name-dropping had been a mistake—just the mention of the Reverend sent Jack's heart skipping. He was terrified.

"We have a Bishop, a Rabbi, and now a Reverend. Sounds like you're setting me up for a joke, Jack."

"Yeah, well this one's not funny," he spat back.

Mouse studied him. Jack had always been arrogant and cowardly, but now he seemed erratic, swinging from overt confidence to palpable fear like he was hanging on by a thread. He clearly wasn't himself. "This isn't funny to me either," she said softly. "You seem like you're in trouble. Let me help you."

He burst out laughing. "I think you're the one in trouble, Dr. Em. Me? I'm golden. I found you."

"Let's finish that story. You got zapped by a curse but discovered a locator spell for your trouble. That wouldn't have been enough to find me. Spells don't work just because someone reads them out loud."

He stood up. "God, it's hot in here!" He put the thing he was holding down on the desk and tugged at the sleeve of his jacket, peeling it off and exposing a sweat-soaked T-shirt underneath.

"Maybe wearing all black in the middle of the desert wasn't a great idea," Mouse said, but she was looking at the thing he dropped on the desk. It was rolling gently back and forth.

"Shows off the hair," Jack replied as he reached over and closed his hand around the tiny wooden mouse on the desk.

"That's mine," she said.

Angelo had given it to her in the airport in Prague. She'd carried it with her when she'd gone to confront her father at Megiddo. She'd pulled it out of her pocket and clung to it when she was dying. She had been alone and wanted a reminder that someone in the world loved her, thought her good. She'd assumed that the tiny, battered mouse still lay among the rubble of a millennium's worth of human destruction atop the place many believed would be the site of the final war, of Armageddon. To know that her little mouse was in enemy hands ignited her anger.

"I want it back."

"Sure. I don't need it now." Jack tossed it to her and leaned his fore-arms against the back of the chair.

As she caught it, Mouse saw that it was stained with her blood, and her anger shifted to fear as the pieces fell into place. A spell to locate something. Her blood. There was only one element missing—power to fuel the spell. She reached out with her uncanny senses, searching.

"What's in your pocket?" she asked, already knowing.

"The last part of the puzzle you're trying to work out." He looked over at her, grinning, his eyes alive with something that didn't belong to him. "My treasure—and I had to sift through actual rubble for this one-of-a-kind nugget."

As he pulled it from his pocket, Mouse shuddered. He held a shard of stone between his middle finger and thumb, the point of it driving into the rounded flesh of his fingertips. It was dull and flaky on one side, but the other was vividly painted with a piece of a portrait.

Mouse knew the source. She was looking at a rendering of her own brilliant, green eye, with just the beginning curve of her nose at the edge where the stone had broken. It was her father's work, a shattered remnant of his portrait of her from the walls of her cell in the monastery at Podlažice. And it was charged with his power just as it had been when that power had poured into her, tempting her with all her wants, filling her with desire, searing her with ambition until she thought she would explode.

"That's not treasure, Jack. It's a bomb."

He laughed again. "I've had this for weeks. Nothing's happened."

"It has. It's changed you."

"Made me stronger maybe, but—"

"Do you remember what you felt when you touched the Devil's Bible?"

"Exactly—power. And now I have a piece of it all my own."

The same energy that her father had poured into the Devil's Bible had fueled the traps he'd left for Mouse in the ruins of the monastery. Echoes of it dusted the piece of stone in Jack's hand. That malevolent energy twisted a person's mind, made them do things.

"You don't want that, Jack," she said, her voice filled with the concern of a teacher for her student.

"The hell I don't."

"Did you ever read about what happened to some of the people who worked with the Devil's Bible? They went mad." She shook her head. "Please, I know . . . I know what it can do to you. It feels good at first, but then it claims you, twists your mind—"

"You scared I might use it against you?"

Mouse couldn't stop a laugh from barking out and bouncing around the tiny clinic, but it made her feel sick. "Do you even know why the Novus Rishi sent you to find me?"

"The Rabbi wants you dead."

Mouse paused. It was new information but not that surprising. The Bishop had made it clear that if she would not fight for the Novus Rishi, they would do whatever they had to do to take her out of the game.

"Why does he want me dead? What am I to the Novus Rishi?" She already knew, but she wanted to make Jack understand.

"A threat."

"Exactly. Have you asked yourself why?"

He just looked at her.

"Because I'm dangerous, Jack. The power you hold in your palm can do nothing to me. Its source is my source. That same power runs through my veins but a hundred times stronger than your little sliver of it."

She took a step toward him. He clenched his fist around the stone in his hand and shoved himself back into his chair. And then Mouse heard what she'd been waiting for—the distant whine of an engine, one she knew. Angelo was home.

She rammed the chair back against the wall, the wooden legs squealing against the concrete floor. Jack threw his hands up, instinctively, and Mouse's painted eye fell to the floor, staring up at her. She scooped it up with one hand and grabbed Jack's wrist with the other as she rushed up beside him, twisting his arm to his side and up his back.

She shoved him out of the chair and pressed the sharp point of the shard against his carotid artery.

"You're alive because I want you that way, Jack," she said, her voice cool and matter-of-fact. "You fight me, and the sharp edge of your *treasure* gets jammed into your artery and you die."

She sounded convincing even to her own ears, though she knew she would never kill him. Mouse meant for there to be no more deaths weighing on her soul.

"We're going out the door and across the yard," she continued. "You're probably thinking about how much bigger you are, how easy it would be to take me. Just remember—your friends know I'm so dangerous they want me dead."

She pushed him through the still-open door and out into the torrid heat toward the community house. She saw Jack's four-wheel drive parked behind the long, low building. The caterpillar cloud of dust signaling Angelo's return moved steadily closer along the horizon. Ngara and several other women came out of the community house carrying hunting spears and circled around Mouse and Jack.

"This is not your friend," Ngara said. "He lies."

Mouse let loose of Jack's arm and kicked him at the back of the knees, making him drop into the dirt as the women closed ranks, dozens of spearheads pointing at his head and chest.

She pocketed the piece of painting and stepped back to speak to Ngara. "Angelo and I need to leave."

"Where will you go, little one?"

The tenderness of Ngara's voice pulled at a sharp thread of sadness running through Mouse's fear and anger. She didn't want to say good-bye this way. "I don't want to tell you anything that might put you and the others in more danger. I've already brought you much trouble. This man is only the lightning strike, Ngara. The bush fire is coming."

"How soon?" The old woman squinted as she scanned the land behind the community house.

"I don't know. But you must be ready."

"They will want our stories . . . of you."

"Yes. And you should tell them whatever they need to hear. It's the only thing that will keep you safe."

"We will not give away our stories. They are our treasure."

"They won't ask, Ngara. They will take them from you."

"We will hide our stories and ourselves out on the land. We have tricked the *whitefella* before." She turned and said something to one of the women. The woman stepped out of the circle guarding Jack and went back into the community house. Mouse could hear her giving instructions to the children still inside, and then the roar of the engine drowned her out.

Angelo was climbing out of the jeep before it even stopped. "What happened?" As the women parted, exposing Jack at their center, Angelo asked, "Who's this?"

"Jack Gray," Mouse answered. She'd already told Angelo all about Jack.

"You okay?" he asked.

Mouse nodded. "But we need to—"

"I'll get the bags." He started off toward their shed.

"Angelo, don't forget the thing on the table beside the bed."

Mouse hadn't been able to make herself pack the bone the Seven Sisters had given her. If she took it, she felt that she was accepting the future the Sisters had laid out for her in the Dreaming. The bone shard made it all feel true in a way that terrified Mouse.

Angelo turned to look at her, knowing. "You sure?"

"We might need it."

Her stomach twisted when she saw the fear in his eyes as he nodded and took off again toward the shed, but she clenched her jaw at the hot bile climbing up her throat. She turned back to Jack. "You were stalling earlier, so I know someone's on the way. How'd you contact them? How close are they?"

Jack just looked at her, blankly.

She slammed her knee into his face. Blood spewed from his nose and splattered his white hair.

He spat. "Give me my stone, and I'll tell you."

But Angelo was already back with the bags, pulling open the hatch on Jack's four-wheel drive. "Mouse."

She looked over at him and didn't like what she read on his face. She peered into the back of the vehicle where Angelo pointed. "Is that a—" he started to ask.

"Sat-com device or signal booster of some kind—yeah. Like the military uses." Mouse turned back to Jack. "Who the hell is coming?"

He turned his face up to her and smiled, blood pooling between his teeth and stretching like string between his lips. "The Reverend."

CHAPTER EIGHT

A storm of dirt and stone swirled around the SUV as Mouse and Angelo raced across the outback. Jack bounced against the back seat of the car, his hands tied with the jumper cables and his hair clinging to the drying blood on his face. They were headed south—away from the outstation. The Martu had crammed as many people as they could into their two jeeps and headed north to hide in the hills along the Rudall River. Those who couldn't fit in the jeeps gathered supplies and walked out into the desert. They were the old ones led by Ngara.

Mouse looked out her window into the sky where she knew the Pleiades would be if only she could see past the late afternoon sun. Silently, she asked the Seven Sisters to hide Ngara and the others as they had once hidden their sister.

When Mouse had seen the communications device, her mind had worked out the rest of the strategy. They'd thrown Jack into the car and said a hasty good-bye. Even with a device like that, communication would be limited by distance, and whomever the Reverend had at the ready would need to be close enough to act on any information Jack sent them. They had to be close, but close in the wide expanse of the outback was a relative term. Best bet for their base of operation was Port Hedland.

That was three hundred miles across impossible terrain. Ngara had told her that Jack had been waiting for about three hours. That still gave Mouse and Angelo plenty of time to draw the Novus Rishi away from the Martu and then make a run for it themselves. They kept Jack's phone and the com device active, hoping that whoever was coming after them would follow the signal and bypass the outstation. Mouse meant to dump the electronics at Lake Disappointment and then turn west. They'd leave Jack at Newman and move on toward the coast, staying clear of the Great Northern Highway, where they would be easy to spot.

But Mouse knew she'd built the plan on too many ifs.

She turned and looked back as a jolt sent Jack slamming into the door. "Who is this Reverend?" she asked.

"Give me my stone," he said.

"What stone?" Angelo asked, his arms jerking as he wrestled the tug of the steering wheel.

"He has a piece of one of the murals from Podlažice."

Angelo glanced at her sharply and then back out the window as he navigated the rugged terrain.

She understood his concern. "It only has a ghost of power left in it—barely enough to make the locator spell work and mess with Jack's head. It's not a danger to me."

Her father's power, concentrated and potent in the undiscovered ruins of the monastery, had twisted Mouse's mind when she and Angelo had gone looking for the missing pages of the Devil's Bible. That tainted power had nearly driven her insane.

"It's not affecting me," she reassured Angelo. "I'm in control, okay?"

"Since you're in control," Jack said snidely, "would you mind turning up the AC? It's stuffy back here."

Angelo flashed his eyes up to the rearview mirror. "Will it draw your father?" he asked, ignoring Jack.

Mouse laughed. "I've been trying to tell you—the way I am now, it's not like it was before. The power's just a part of me. I can't turn it off even if I'm not using it. It's like I'm a perpetually running lighthouse. My father could've found me any time he wanted over the past two years. And this?" She dug the piece of painting out of her pocket. "There's so little power left that I didn't even know it was there until I went looking for it."

Jack lurched forward, trying to get at the shard in Mouse's palm. She had anticipated the move and jammed her other hand against his throat and shoved him into the back floorboard.

She held the painted eye close to his face. "You want it? Fine. I need to know what's coming. Tell me who the Reverend is."

"Just make him tell you, Mouse!" Angelo shouted as he fought to control the car.

She jerked back, her face inches from Angelo's, and saw the sweat running under the edge of his hair, his jaw twitching as he clenched it. He was terrified.

"I won't force my will on someone."

"It would be so much easier."

"No, it wouldn't." She turned to look out the window to hide her despair. In the struggle to work out the right and wrong of what she *could* do and what she *shouldn't*, Mouse had held to two rules—no killing and no compelling another person. She had done both in her long life, some by accident, some with intent. All of it hung on her conscience. In her mind, those two rules defined her goodness and proved that she had a soul, even if she couldn't see it.

"Look." She pointed out the window to where a line of white grew against the horizon. "It's Lake Disappointment. We're almost there."

"Wait," Jack said from the back. "Your name is *Mouse*?"

"Nice to meet you." She sneered. "You said the Rabbi wanted me dead. Does he know that I'm . . ."

"Old?" Jack offered.

"Immortal."

"Bishop Sebastian said you were, but the Rabbi thinks he knows a way to do it." Jack pushed himself back up onto the seat.

"I thought the Novus Rishi wanted her to work for them. Why would this Rabbi want her dead?" Angelo asked.

Jack lifted his shoulders and his eyebrows at the same time. "It's all politics to me."

"Is this Rabbi here, too? Is he coming?" Angelo asked.

"Just the Reverend," said Jack, all the levity gone from his voice.

Mouse twisted around to look him in the eye. She'd heard his fear, could feel it rolling off him even through the mental fog caused by the portrait shard.

"You mean the Bishop's not here either?" Angelo asked, a new tremor of worry in his voice.

"Just the Reverend," Jack said again, holding Mouse's gaze, unblinking, almost as if he were pleading with her.

She reached her hand back and laid it gently on his knee. She was scared, too. "What does the Reverend want?"

There was a flicker of the old Jack behind the terror in his eyes—the student giving his former mentor a warning. "Only you."

Mouse felt it settle in her chest like the Delphic oracle's omen to Oedipus: *Who seeks shall find.*

Angelo stopped the car. Mouse was still staring at Jack.

"We're here," Angelo said. "Let's toss the stuff and get going."

Mouse climbed out as if sleepwalking. Angelo opened the back hatch and hauled out the com device, then carried it over to the edge of the salt lake. There was no water anywhere to be seen, only a wide expanse of white that butted up against the red dirt and stretched out until it touched the indigo blue of the horizon.

"Is the wind blowing?" Mouse asked, her voice hollow.

"What?" Angelo turned to look at her.

"It's safe if the wind is blowing, Ngara said. It means the *Nyayurnangalku* aren't here."

"The what?"

"Monsters. Demons. They live under the salt surface." She was looking out over the lake.

"Toss me the phone and we can go."

"No." It poured from her mouth, more a moan than a word.

"Mouse?"

"We have to hide." She spun around, looking for an outcropping or a ravine—anything that would provide some kind of shelter or camouflage. The flat land knotted with clumps of spinifex grass mocked her.

"What is it?"

"From that direction." She pointed back the way they'd come. "Helicopters. I can't see them yet, but I can hear them."

Angelo ran to the back of the car. "Bags?"

Mouse nodded, still squinting as she scanned the sky. "If we get away, we'll need the water."

Angelo slung one of the bags over his shoulder and handed the other to Mouse. "And Jack?"

"Leave him. He's safer here and we're quicker without him."

"Which way?"

"There's nowhere, Angelo." She knew it. There was nowhere to hide and no way for them to escape what was coming.

He put his hand under her chin and lifted it gently. She could see that he knew, too. "Which way?"

"Across the lake. Maybe . . ."

He grabbed her hand and started jogging into the white salt and sand.

"Good-bye, Jack," Mouse called over her shoulder.

They ran for about fifteen minutes before coming to the first lift of land, a small hill of dirt in the wash of salt. It would've been a tiny island had there been water. It wasn't enough, but it was all they had.

Mouse and Angelo threw themselves behind the back edge of the rise, the twang of salt filling the air. The car was a small speck of reflected sun in the distance. Two helicopters crawled across the far sky until they reached the car. They circled like vultures.

Mouse counted one breath, then two.

The helicopters turned and headed out over the lakebed toward them.

Angelo turned to look at her, his mouth open as if to speak, but a wave of blown salt and sand crashed into them, stinging their skin. They both threw their hands up instinctively to shield their eyes. Jack's sliver of painted stone fell to the ground. Mouse watched it disappear and reappear in the swirling salt.

She pushed herself up to her knees and spread her arms. "Blow wind!" she commanded, and a tempest began to twist around them, pushing outward and driving the debris away from them and toward the helicopters. But Mouse had gotten salt in her eyes, sharp grains scratching against her eyelids, tears pouring down her face. She couldn't see, but she heard the helicopter pilots yelling and the chopping rap of the blades moving away.

"They're leaving!" Angelo yelled over the torrent of engines and wind.

But Mouse was shaking her head. She'd heard the crunch of the landing skids raking across the salt surface. "They're landing," she said, but she wasn't sure if Angelo had heard her. She reached her hand out for him. He wasn't there.

She heard his footsteps moving away from her. She jumped up, lurching in the direction of his sound, and slammed into the backpack he was still wearing. He had his hands up and to the side.

"We surrender!" he shouted. "We surrender!"

Mouse's vision was clearing. She could make out a dozen or so men dressed in sand-colored armor, carrying guns. Some stood a few yards away. Others crouched under the rotating blades of the landed helicopters. A couple were half in and half out of the fuselage. Mouse's tempest still whipped away the airborne sand and pushed against the armed men. Each gust lifted her hair, the strands undulating as if she were a snakeless Medusa. Her eyes met those of a man in one of the cockpits, seated beside the pilot. He was the only man not wearing armor. He wore a business suit, gray with a thin silver stripe. There was a pin on his lapel—a cross made of swords. The Reverend. He was smiling.

Mouse watched his lips move as he spoke into the mic of the headset that bulged out behind his fat cheeks. She read his lips, but too late. *Take the girl down. The priest doesn't matter. Kill him.*

She jerked when the first shot rang out. Jerked when Angelo did. Jerked when it tore through his stomach and out of the backpack, spraying her with shrapnel and his blood. Jerked when more rounds slammed into him and when they hit her in the legs and arms. Jerked when she tried to catch him as he fell back.

She knew then why she'd had them run out across the lake. Her subconscious mind had been giving her a choice—one she had shut away until now because it crossed a line. Mouse didn't care about lines anymore.

Her face was buried in the salt beside Angelo's—hers down, his up. The blood had splattered everywhere against the white salt. It looked like one of Ngara's paintings.

Mouse mouthed the word "Come," her lips digging into the bloody salt, and though no sound came out, she knew she'd been heard when the air went instantly and completely still.

The men stopped shooting.

And the *Nyayurnangalku* came.

They broke through the crusty salt like roots erupting from the earth, driving upward, long clawed hands ripping at the white soil until they birthed themselves in the empty air. Tall and wiry, so thin their joints jutted out from taut skin, they reached out and wrapped their long, spindly fingers and claws around the nearest man. They reeled the men into mouths crammed with jagged fangs, teeth sinking into necks and abdomens, yanking off flesh in chunks and crunching bones. The creatures devoured their prey as if they'd been hungry for millennia.

The helicopters lifted off again, men hanging from the skids with one hand and firing their guns with the other. Bullets fell like hail in random bursts. Mouse coiled herself around Angelo's head, trying to protect him. She closed her eyes and searched desperately for proof that he was still alive. She saw the brightness of his glow and opened her eyes again, scanning the scene, looking for a way out.

The demons had pulled down one of the helicopters. The other had pulled back behind the cloud of debris. Most of the men who'd been on the ground had been eaten. Some of the creatures were still feeding on what was left. Someone in the helicopter was still firing.

Mouse opened her mouth, ready to do whatever she must to get Angelo out, to save him. Her power coursed through her. She heard the whirr of a bullet. It sounded so much like the whistle of an arrow that for a moment Mouse forgot where and when she was.

The bullet ricocheted off the ground in front of her and shred her throat. Blood and cartilage shot out from her neck and her head dropped. She could feel the darkness closing on her like the coming night. She closed her eyes, searching for Angelo again.

Her heart broke. The glow of him, his soul, was slowly slipping past his body, down and up, like she'd seen so many times over her long life with other bodies on other battlefields and in hospitals and bedrooms through the ages.

Not this one, she begged. *Not this one.* She tried to make her hand move to cover his mouth, to hold his life in his body.

She had no air to make the words. To make him live. To tell him she loved him. To tell him good-bye.

She had one last choice as the darkness fell.

Not a word, but a calling out in her mind: "Father."

PART TWO

For the first time in her life she thought,
might the same wonders never come again?
                    —Eudora Welty, "The Winds"

CHAPTER NINE

Who is she?"

The high, bright voice of a child filled the chamber.

"Your sister."

"What's her name?"

"Mouse."

Giggling trickled around the white stone walls and floor. "That's not a real name."

"It's the only name she has."

"She looks dead."

"She is."

"Will she stay that way?"

"That depends on you, Luc."

"Why me, Father?"

"You get to choose. We can make it so she stays dead, or we can let her be and she will heal and wake up again."

"Wouldn't she be sad to stay dead?"

His father was quiet for a moment. "I think she will be very sad when she wakes and remembers what happened."

"What happened?"

"Someone she loves is gone."

"Oh." Luc stepped close to the table. Mouse's shorts and shirt were soaked with blood. Small and large holes dotted both her legs and arms—entrance and exit wounds. Her throat was splayed open, exposing raw, red tissue and white specks of cartilage and bone.

"She looks gross," Luc said.

His father chuckled. "Yes, but that will heal."

"But she would still be sad."

"Her heart would be broken."

"Can that heal, too?"

"Sometimes. But it's much harder."

Luc stood on tiptoe to press his face close to Mouse's. Her eyes were open and vacant. "She has pretty eyes."

"Yes, she does."

"Is she nice?"

His father knelt beside him, his arm draped over the small shoulders. "I think you would like her very much."

"Is that why you brought her here?"

"Yes. And she can teach you things I can't."

"Like what?"

"Human things."

"Why would I want to learn those?"

"Because you are also human."

"But you're not. How am I?"

"Your mother was human."

"I think I remember her. She screamed a lot." He clasped his hands behind his back and looked over at his father. "Is human a good thing?"

"It's neither good nor bad, Luc. It's just what you are."

The boy squinted at dead Mouse. "And she is also human, like me?"

"Yes. The two of you are very special. There are none other like you."

"And she can teach me things?"

"Yes."

"Then I don't want her to stay dead, Father."

⚬——⚬

"The holes are gone," Luc said. "It's been forever."

"Yes."

"How long is forever, Father?"

"In this case, about two months."

"When will she wake up?"

"It won't be much longer."

"I want her to play."

"You must remember that she will be very sad and maybe very angry, so she may not want to play at first."

"Why will she be angry?"

"She doesn't like me very much."

"Why?"

"I was a little mean to her the last time we met."

The boy wondered what it would be like if his father were mean to *him*. He shivered a little and didn't want to think about that anymore. Instead, he said, "She will be sad because her heart is broken like her body was?"

"That's right."

Luc blew out a sigh. "But you said it takes even longer for a heart to heal than a body," he whined. "I'm tired of waiting." He scowled and crossed his arms. "I think you're wrong. I think she'll be all better when she meets me."

"Why?"

"Because I want her to be."

"I see."

"And because I'm pretty. She's pretty again now, too. Just like you said."

"You are pretty."

"Were you pretty once, Father?"

"Yes, I was."

Luc studied his father's disfigured face. "Will I look like you when I grow up?"

"Look at your sister, Luc." He pointed to where Mouse still lay in the same position, in the same bloody clothes that now reeked of rot. They had closed her eyes, and the wounds had healed. She looked like she was sleeping. "She's all grown up. Did you know she's more than seven hundred years old?"

Luc leaned toward his sister's face with wonder-filled eyes. He ran his small hand gently over her cheek. "She's soft," he said as he turned and smiled at his father.

"Yes. And you will be like her. I'm counting on it." He sighed, full of hope. "A long time ago, I was pretty, too, like you and your sister. And then I . . . I had an accident that scarred me and made me look like this."

Worry creased the little forehead. "I might have an accident, too."

His father's face grew grim as he stared at his son while images of what might be eroded his hopes. The whole point of the tedious journey into parenthood had been to give himself the same advantage his adversary had claimed—an ally that could bridge the gap between the divine and human, someone in touch with his own humanity, someone who could use that shared humanity to compel the masses, to command an endless army of converts. What the boy said held some truth. If Luc grew to be just like his father, would not the same weakness, the same limitations, and perhaps the same fate cling to him?

And then he looked back to his sleeping daughter, and he hung his hopes on her. Mouse would make Luc more than just his father's son. He ran his fingers softly across her lips. "I think your sister will help us keep you safe," he answered Luc.

"I wish she would wake up."

"Me, too."

"You must eat something, Mouse."

It wasn't the first time her father had visited her since she'd woken, but she had no concept of time here—not when it was day, nor when it was night. Not that it mattered to her, anyway.

She lay on the floor against the back wall of the circular room. It was all white and empty but for the table in the center. She was curled around her backpack, her face resting against a small, unzipped section at the top. The air inside the bag still smelled like Angelo and their life at the outstation.

"It has been months, Mouse. He's gone. Accept it and move on."

Mouse slowly pushed herself up. Her knees bulged out from her ema-ciated legs like burls on a spindly tree. "Get out." They were the only words she'd spoken. Her body had come back to life, but the rest of her remained dead to the world.

"You've been through this before, after Marchfeld. Should I bring you paper and inks? Set you a task where you can work out your guilt for not calling me soon enough, for not using your power, for letting yet another of your beloveds die?" He was trying to trigger her temper, anything to evoke a reaction from her, anything that might give spark to a renewed life. Nothing he'd tried had worked so far.

She pulled the backpack closer, lay down on her other side, and curled up around it once more.

"Get out," she said.

"Maybe we should kill her after all," Luc said.

"You think so?"

"She's been like this forever. If she can't play, I don't want her."

"You must be patient, Luc."

"You said I don't have to do anything I don't want to do."

"Yes. But sometimes we have to be patient to get what we want."

"How much longer?"

"I don't know. She won't listen to me."

"I'd make her listen."

His father looked down at him from where they stood near the door to Mouse's chamber. "Do you want to meet her?"

Luc crossed one leg behind the other and swung his arms side to side. "I'm scared of her, Father."

"Why?"

"She never smiles. She only stares. She looks mean."

"She's not."

"She won't hurt me?"

"Not ever." An unfamiliar longing pulled at his chest, but he couldn't understand it and so smothered it with his expectations. "She will love you."

Luc put his foot down and finally said, "Okay, Father. Will you go with me?"

"I think it's better if you go alone. She's mad at me."

"Because of when you were mean to her before on that mountain?"

"Megiddo? Yes, but I think she also blames me for what happened to her friend."

"Oh. Was that your fault?"

"Not really."

Luc waited just a moment more, then stepped forward and through the door. He turned and walked around the curve of the wall, his hand skimming its surface as he took oversized steps toward Mouse.

"Hello!"

She opened her eyes but didn't move.

He came around and crouched in front of her face. "I'm Luc." He reached out and put his hand on her forehead. "I'm your brother."

She met his gaze. His eyes were big and green, like hers.

"I want you to play."

Mouse sat up, leaning heavily against the wall, her breath fast and shallow from the exertion. Her thin, dehydrated skin stretched taut over her bones as she spoke. "Go away, please, Luc."

He sat down criss-cross applesauce in front of her, their knees almost touching.

"You're my sister. My sister Mouse. And I want you to get better so you can play with me. I'm bored. Father says you know all sorts of games. He says I would like you. But right now you are scary and gross." He pinched his nose. "And you smell bad."

"I don't want to play, Luc."

"Because you're sad? Because your friend is gone?"

Mouse didn't answer.

"Father says you're also mad. Are you more mad or sad?" His voice was too loud for the room.

Mouse turned her face up to look at the dark silhouette of her father standing just beyond the door. "Mad is easier than sad."

"Is it? I've been mad once. I didn't like it. I don't think I've ever been sad. I mostly get what I want."

"Lucky boy."

"I suppose." The boy scowled. "You aren't lucky though."

"No."

"Father told me about the guns and the helicopters and the blood and the demons that were eating people out in the desert." His eyes grew wide. "He said you and your friend were all shot up and then you called for him. He came, just like you asked."

"Did he?"

"Yup. He saved you. He picked you up and wrapped you in his cloak and brought you home. But he thinks you're mad at him, so he won't come talk to you now."

"I don't want to talk. I just want to be left alone."

"Are you mad at him?"

"Yes."

"But you can't be!"

"Yes, I can."

"No, you can't! He didn't do anything to your friend! Father came when you called. He saved you."

Luc was getting angry, but Mouse didn't care. "It happened because of him." She sounded like a machine.

"That's not true! That's stupid! You should be mad at the people who did it! That's what I would do. I'd make them sorry for what they did."

Mouse leaned her head back against the wall and closed her eyes. Something lurking in the dark abyss of her started to wake. Like a thirsty animal coming to a watering hole, it drank in Luc's words.

I'd make them sorry for what they did.

"What's your friend's name?" he asked.

"Angelo." Mouse waited for the paralyzing grief to rise again, but the words—*make them sorry*—filled her up with a new purpose and left no room for anything else.

"Angelo's a real name . . . right?"

"How old are you, Luc?"

The boy didn't look like just a boy. He seemed pinched, his shoulders hunched, his face unnaturally serious except for an unnerving spark of curiosity—like he'd be willing to do anything to get the answers he wanted.

"I don't know," he said. "I'll live forever. What does it matter how old I am?"

"You're very smart."

"I know." He sat up taller, smiling. "My father told me I have gifts."

Mouse snapped her head up again to look at her father, who had now come into the room. "Yeah? Me, too."

"Oh? What can you do?" Luc challenged.

"You first," she said.

"I can hear everything and see everything and I know things and . . . I never forget." His brow furrowed.

"Me, too."

"It's like I'm a big empty hole sucking up everything around me. But, Mouse?"

"Yes?"

"I don't understand most of it. Do you?"

"Not always." She felt a tiny flicker of pity for the boy but not enough to escape her apathy.

"I can also make people do things." He picked at a piece of skin on his thumbnail. "I told my nanny once to—"

"That's enough, Luc." Her father put a plate of food on the stone table in the center of the room. "Your sister needs to eat and get her strength back."

"He's further along with his . . . gifts than I was at his age. Your doing?" she asked her father.

He shrugged. "He learns quickly."

"Father said you could teach me things he can't," Luc added.

"Why should I do anything for you?" Mouse asked.

Luc sucked in an angry breath, but calmed when he saw that his sister was speaking to their father.

"I saved you," their father answered.

"But not Angelo."

"You called me too late."

She swallowed. "You killed me at Megiddo," she said, but with no hint of accusation, no touch of feeling at all. She felt like dead wood.

"I left you dying. I didn't kill you," he replied.

"First lesson, Luc. Never trust our father."

"Why?"

"He will only ever tell you the part of the truth he wants you to hear."

"Why?"

"He likes the power it gives him. But if you learn to ask just the right questions and listen very hard, you can hear when he's hiding something." Mouse let her head drop back against the wall. "Ask him if he knew I would come back to life when he left me at Megiddo."

"Father, did you?"

"I guessed. That's as good as knowing for us, isn't it?" He chuckled.

"Did you hear it, Luc?" Mouse asked.

"I think so. Can we try again?"

"Sure. Ask him why he brought me here."

"Father, why did you—"

"Because you needed me. And I'm your father, so I came."

"I heard it that time! For sure!" Luc said excitedly.

"Good boy," Mouse replied, indifferent. "The trick is to figure out what he's hiding."

Luc threw his arms around Mouse. "I like you! Will you teach me more?"

She sat limp in the circle of his small arms. "Sure," she answered and then turned to her father. "But I have something I need to do, and I need our father to teach me a few tricks, as well."

"What do you have to do?" Luc asked, already impatient.

"What you told me I should do—make those people sorry for what they did." She reached for her father's outstretched hand. "Will you help me?"

Her father pulled her up and caught her around the waist when she faltered. "I've been waiting seven hundred years for you to ask."

CHAPTER TEN

W hy don't you stay here with Luc and let me go? It would be much easier and faster," he said, days later, as Mouse tugged a cloak around her shoulders. He had made it for her, tearing a piece from his own black cloak and shaking it once with a snap, like a magician on a stage. A full cloak had grown from the piece of cloth in his hand. It looked just like his, but smaller, tailored precisely to Mouse's measurements.

"I told you," Mouse answered blankly. "I have to do this myself, and I want to do it alone. All I need you to do is teach me your trick."

"Fine," he sighed. "Let's try again. Picture the place you want to be."

Mouse took up the edge of her new cloak and wrapped it around herself, filling her mind with the image of where she wanted to go. She opened her eyes.

Her father was leaning against the wall, his arms crossed, shaking his head.

Mouse tossed the cloak back angrily. Anger seemed to be the only emotion she could feel anymore, but it was different than any anger she'd felt before—this was detached, devoid of the other emotions that often polluted her wrath. There was no sorrow or guilt. This anger was pure and ruthless, and she had given herself to it. She dressed in black, which she had decided was the color of rage. Red was too bright. Black ate everything.

"What place are you thinking of?" her father asked.

But she didn't have to answer. He sighed again. "Going there is fine, but it can't be about him. This power is driven only by your want. Any other emotion weakens it."

He'd been trying to teach her the skill of folding herself in her cloak to travel the dark planes between space and time. It would give her the power to go where she wanted, when she wanted, like her father. Learning this was the first step in her plan.

"Rest for a moment and then try again," he said. "And remember, it's about you, not him."

Mouse pulled herself up to the table in the white marble room, her legs dangling in the dark of the hanging cloak. "Why don't you wear your human face around Luc?" she asked, wanting to change the subject. She did not care to talk about Angelo with her father.

"I want my son to know me as I am. This—" He motioned to his demonic form, burn scars twisting his skin and muscles, knobs jutting out beneath his shoulder blades where his wings had once been, making him appear hunchbacked. "This is all he's ever known, so he is not afraid. I'd like at least one of my children to not be afraid of me."

"I'm not afraid of you."

"You were."

"Not anymore."

He smiled. "I don't think you are afraid of anything anymore. Not even of losing that soul you fought so hard to prove you had."

She held his gaze placidly. No bait would draw her out. She fingered the bone shard strapped to her thigh and rationed her rage for the vengeance she meant to claim. Nothing else mattered. "Have you noticed how much Luc looks like you?"

"That's as it should be, isn't it? He's my son."

"I don't mean his features. I mean how he holds himself." Mouse saw the flicker of wounded temper in her father's eyes, but she couldn't summon enough empathy to care. "You've said you want him to be normal, to understand his humanity. You want me to teach him how to accept himself as he is, as both human and not."

"And?"

"Have you looked at him?" She pointed toward the hall where Luc sat reading. "He's freakish. His shoulders are hunched like yours are now. He even moves like you—pinched and twisted."

Her father shoved himself away from the table.

"Your son is more demon than boy," Mouse continued.

Anger rolled off him as he took a step toward her, but then he spun back to the door and leaned against the frame, watching Luc for a few minutes. He bowed his head and spoke softly over his shoulder. "Fix it then."

"Put your pretty face on," Mouse shot back.

Her father walked back toward her, little flecks of shimmering blackness falling all around him as he transformed into his human visage, pale skin framed with dark hair that was thick and carefully messy, a scruffy goatee setting off his eyes, which were so black they looked pupil-less. "Satisfied?" he asked.

She nodded. "It's a start," she said and fiddled with the edge of her cloak. But she had one more dig to get in. "You say you want him to know the real you—are you going to show him the real you on the inside, too? Because that's the part that's likely to scare him off. Are you going to tell him about all the things you've done?"

"Someday."

"I bet," she scoffed. "Why would you?"

"Because I need him to trust me. And trust is built on truth. But all in good time."

A tickle of warning played at the edge of Mouse's indifference, but she didn't care enough to chase it. She hopped off the table. "Let's give this another go."

"Focus on what you want." He put his hands on her shoulders as she bowed her head.

Mouse's frame had started to fill out again, but she still looked starved of light and care, and she had shaved her head—nothing soft belonged to her. She was a furnace full of ashes, dead and cold except when Luc's words stoked her rage. She used them now to fuel her want and her power. *Make them sorry for what they did.*

She pulled the cloak around her once more and let the words drive out everything else. When she opened her eyes, she was somewhere else.

The white salt-sand of Lake Disappointment stretched out around her, tiny sparks twinkling like diamonds under the rising moon that hung low in the sky. There was no sign of the attack—no bullet casings, no crimson stains, no charred remains of the helicopter that had been pulled down. All was as it had been, as it should be. Her father said it had been over a year. For her, it felt like only days or a handful of weeks since she was last here.

Mouse knelt on the little rise that had sheltered her and Angelo. She let her eyes slip out of focus, and her perfect memory played out the scene. She fought the urge to duck and cover her head. She swallowed the bitter taste of adrenaline. She let herself feel it all for the first time—the fear and the guilt about what she could have done differently, about all the things she might have done to save Angelo. She let the emotions come, but she would not allow her body to react to them. No racing heart. No jolt of the body when she remembered too perfectly the sound of the bullets firing.

No tears when Angelo fell.

She let all that raw emotion build until she thought she would rupture, flinging pieces of her among the salt crystals, and then Mouse fed it all to her rage as she replayed the scene once more in her mind. She focused on the faces of the soldiers, slowed down the action so she could keep count of who had died at the hands of the demons and who had lived.

Four men.

They went on a list in her mind. She closed her eyes and filtered through the smells—fuel and oil from the helicopters, the dry saltiness of the swirling soil, a sulfuric rottenness from the demons, the metallic twang of the flying bullets, her sweat, Angelo's—and she pushed them all aside until she could zero in on the unique scents of the four surviving soldiers.

Citrus. Musk. Bay rum. Cedar.

Then she added another name to her list. She didn't need to smell him. His face stayed in her mind always. It had driven out even Angelo's. She focused on that face behind the windshield of the helicopter and read the words as his lips formed them. She'd repeated them so often they'd drowned out Angelo's last pleas of surrender.

"Take the girl down. The priest doesn't matter. Kill him," the Reverend had said.

The Reverend.

He made five. Five targets . . . for a start.

Mouse stood, the outback wind whipping her cloak behind her, and she looked up to the massive spread of star-filled sky. All her life she had craved the light.

Andílek, remember that "the light shines in the darkness, and the darkness has not overcome it." Through seven hundred years and beyond the grave, Father Lucas could still call to her conscience. He had fed her on the idea that she could be the light in the darkness. Mouse had chased that dream like a moth, incessantly fluttering around the flame that would inevitably sear away the gossamer wings and send it crashing down into the fire.

Just as it had her father. Just as it had her.

She would chase the light no more, she swore. She would exorcise her conscience. She would sacrifice her soul—completely, irrevocably. And she knew the first step for such a ritual. Like the medieval Christians of her childhood, she would undertake a pilgrimage, an unholy pilgrimage to strangle what was left of her hope and goodness so she could do what she needed to do.

Mouse lifted her face to stare boldly up at the heavens once more. But her eyes weren't drawn to the stars this time. Instead, she drank in the empty darkness between the light.

———

Mouse lifted her eyes to the chandelier. The empty sockets of a hundred human skulls stared back at her. Rows of femurs dangled below twisted vertebrae like ashen pendalogues. She imagined the heavy clunk they would make in a breeze—such a dull contrast to the delicate tinkling of their more traditional crystal counterparts.

The flash of a camera blinded her for a second, and she spun toward the handful of tourists gawking at the bone chandelier or oohing and aahing at the skull bunting draped between rafters in the Sedlec Ossuary.

"The church is closed. Get out," Mouse commanded with a flick of her hand.

The tourists turned on their heels and walked without a word to the large oak doors, bent their heads against the bright sunlight, and left Mouse alone in the bone church.

A feather of guilt tickled at Mouse's conscience. But that would be gone soon enough, she thought as she looked down at the items clutched against her chest. Despite having lived so long, Mouse had little to show for it. A woman on the run couldn't carry much. She'd learned a long time ago to let go of things. Most things.

Through all her comings and goings, she had held tight to the stone angel Father Lucas had given her as a christening gift when she was a little girl, full of hope. She had left it with Angelo before Megiddo, a token for him to remember her by when she was so sure she would never come back. But Mouse had kept a handful of other objects, too, items binding her to people she had loved, people who had loved her. She had always thought of them as anchors to her humanity, to all that had been right in her life—all that had been good in her.

She had no use for any of that now.

Her boots clacked against the stone floor in the empty church as she marched toward one of four large pyramids built from a thousand bones. She knelt at the iron gate that kept visitors an arm's length from the pyramid, and she unburdened herself of the objects she was carrying. The Sedlec Ossuary wasn't her first stop. It was her last.

Mouse had gone to her conventional hidey-holes first—a smattering of the world's oldest and most secure banks, places she hadn't even taken Angelo. She had gathered up all her nests of false identities, closing off her escape routes into a new life. Mouse was done pretending to be something she wasn't. She knew, now, what she really was. Not good. Not a teacher. Not a healer. Not a girl, nor a woman either. Not human. Not loved. She was her father's daughter, immortal, a demon. And the world could accept her or not—she didn't care anymore.

She'd also gone to the mountaintops around Devil's Lake in the Sumava forest in Bohemia—*Czechia*, she reminded herself. A giant sycamore stood in the place where once another had been. The remembered one had been struck by lightning and carved by a young Mouse into the angel Raphael more than seven hundred years ago. Mouse had burned that statue as it held the body of her beloved Bohdan when she sent him to heaven, where he belonged. Another sycamore had grown from the ashes of the dead one. Even the new one was old and sick now.

Mouse had no sorrow to shed for it.

She had knelt at the base of the tree, taken a nearby fallen branch, and gouged it into her palm, tearing at the flesh. She whispered the words of a revealing spell as her blood dripped against the weathered, peeling bark of the tree. The dirt around the trunk had bubbled and buckled, as if a large mole were tunneling upward, and then a small glass jar rolled to the surface. The glass was a beautiful, deep lapis blue with an intricate overlay of silver scrollwork. Inside, distorted by the old, wavy glass, was a tuft of wolf's fur.

Mouse had snatched the jar and pulled the cloak around her once more.

When she'd stepped out of the dark a second time, Mouse had still been surrounded by trees, but the earthy scents of the mountain spruce gave way to the sweeter linden tree and the sharp twang of wildflowers. They grew hip high and twisted in and about the dozens of headstones scattered around Mouse. The sun was in the same low spot against the horizon—Teplá wasn't far from the Sumava.

Many of the markers were broken and overgrown, but Mouse wasn't looking for names or a date. She knew where she needed to go. At the far back, nearest the tree line that inched ever closer to the neglected cemetery, were the oldest graves. Mother Kazi, the woman who had helped to raise Mouse at the abbey in Teplá, the woman who had trained Mouse as a healer, the woman who was the closest Mouse ever had to a real mother, lay buried under seven centuries of dirt at Mouse's feet. An obscure nun with no family beyond her Norbertine brothers and sisters, Mother Kazi was remembered by no one except Mouse. She had only a flat stone to mark her remains—a stone carved with a bellflower that Mouse had laid herself as she wept for her lost Mother.

Mouse had no more tears to give.

The stone had sunk beneath the onslaught of time, but Mouse knew it was there, waiting for her. She stretched her hand wide to open the wound so the blood would flow again. When she called to the stone, the stone rose to answer her. Beneath it, wrapped in the gauzy glow of Mouse's protection spell, was Mother Kazi's old satchel, filled with the tools of her healer's trade. Tools she had passed down to Mouse. Tools Mouse had treasured as a reminder that she was a healer before she was her father's daughter.

Mouse pulled the satchel free of the spell and the invading roots and held it to her chest. Then she tugged at the cloak again.

The air had become instantly musty and thick at her third destination, and her eyes had needed a moment to adjust to the dim light. She had peered out of a small square window that looked down to the Vltava River. Tourists milled about the base of the tower, but no one was allowed into the seven-hundred-year-old structure. Mouse spun on her heel and up the aged stone steps, higher and higher, past landings with doors that opened onto rounded rooms. They were empty now, but in her memory, she saw them as they were when she lived here at Rozemberk Castle.

Those had been dark days but for the singular shining joy of her son, Nicholas. As she had rounded the last of the steps and entered the top room nestled under the cone roof, Mouse had sunk to her knees, no longer able to keep the ghosts at bay. She had shared this room with her son centuries ago, though she could still smell the flowers they had gathered together in the gardens, could hear the happy crackle of a fire in the hearth. She could feel the weight of her baby's head resting on her shoulder as she sang to him, could hear his coos and cries in her mind as if they were real again.

Joy and loss burned in her chest, but Mouse would not grant them release.

She squeezed her fists until her nails cut into her skin. She walked the width of the room to a bracing rafter that swept up from the stone wall to join the beams of the roof. Her hand was already bleeding. She laid it against the dusty wood and whispered the words of her spell, her voice throaty and dark from fighting the growing sorrow. A panel of wood slid back to expose a hidden compartment that held a wooden statue of a mother holding her infant son, nursing him as she sang the words of a lullaby carved at the base: *You are loved, little one, you are loved.*

Mouse had gripped the statue like a club. She had closed her eyes, too weak in her newborn indifference to withstand the powerful feelings this place evoked. She couldn't pull the cloak around her quickly enough.

And now she'd come to the last and holiest place of her pilgrimage: the monastery where Father Lucas had died protecting her, where she had washed his tortured body, where she had been good and kind and left him dead, in peace, on the stone table and then watched the monks take his body and boil the flesh from his bones so they could use them in their grisly sanctuary.

Mouse knelt beside her reclaimed treasures in the Sedlec Ossuary and looked up at the mountain of bones before her. Lost among the thousands were those of Father Lucas. But she hadn't come for bones. Mouse had come for her soul.

She gripped the iron bars of the gate and started climbing. As she reached the opening at the top, a stripe of sunlight crawled across the floor under the chandelier as someone opened the door.

"I said get out!" Mouse ordered, her power filling the words with her will.

The door snapped shut, and Mouse climbed over the top railing and dropped down to the platform beside the bone pyramid. She crouched near an opening on the facing wall. Dozens of coins from different countries lay scattered among the skulls at the opening. Tourists had tossed tokens to the dead. For what? Mouse wondered. What fortune did they expect from a wishing well of dismantled skeletons?

She thrust her hand into the opening, her palm still oozing blood, and said her spell. The book dropped from somewhere higher on the inside of the bone structure. She caught it and pulled it out. Her hand was shaking. The small leather book felt like the weight of the world to Mouse.

Father Lucas's breviary.

The backs of the pages of his most cherished psalms were covered with his notes. Mouse had read them many times over the years before she had decided it wasn't safe to carry her treasures with her and had hidden them. She hadn't seen the familiar sweep and scroll of his hand-writing with her own eyes in hundreds of years. She knew the words of his notes by heart, not only because of her perfect memory but because she had heard them so many times, read them so many times, recited them to herself in times of darkness.

His notes were for her. They spoke of goodness and perseverance. They spoke of mercy and forgiveness. They spoke of love.

Mouse hardened herself like armor against each of them.

She slid the book into the waistband at her back and climbed out of the enclosure. She gathered up the souvenirs of her journey and wrapped the cloak around her a final time.

"Where've you been?" Luc asked as she materialized beside the table in the circular white marble room of her father's house.

"Were you waiting on me?"

"Yes. I cut my thumb." The boy was sitting in the doorway holding up a bandaged finger.

"Do you need for me to look at it?" she asked as she put her things on the table.

"You were gone so long it's all better now." He stood and came close to the table. "What are those things?"

"Things that don't belong to me anymore." She walked to the rounded wall behind the table where she still slept on the floor, her backpack a pillow, and dug her hand into the front pocket of the bag. She turned back to the table.

"What are you going to do with them?" Luc was eyeing the pile of papers, jar, satchel, statue, and book as any child might—with a gleam of desire.

As answer to his question, Mouse put her hand over the pile. "Burn," she commanded.

The papers and passports took fire immediately, as did Father Lucas's breviary. A tiny ghost of her little-girl-self cried out as she watched the leather shrivel and melt—*Oh, God, what have I done.*

The new, hard Mouse eviscerated that ancient, naïve one with the other truth she knew was tucked into the binding at the back of the breviary—a letter written just before Father Lucas's death, telling Mouse who her real father was. Mouse had worked hard all her life to believe as Father Lucas believed—that she was not simply her father's daughter. That she had the same capacity for goodness and evil as any person. That she had the power to choose.

But Mouse didn't want to choose anymore. Not what she ate or where she slept or what she wore or whether or not she lived. The only choice that mattered was the one that had peeled her up off the floor and gave her a singular purpose—vengeance. And she didn't care if it was right or wrong. She didn't care if she was good or not.

She bent her head as Father Lucas's voice filled her mind, unwanted. *You turn the knife on those who hurt you. But I have taught you to do better.*

Mouse gritted her teeth against the memory and held her hand out over the flame to drop a last object on the funeral pyre of her old self. It was all she had left of the life she'd lived before Lake Disappointment. She told her hand to open and drop the little wooden mouse in the fire. Her hand trembled but held tight to the last remaining bit of her life with Angelo. Mouse held her arm over the flame until the heat started to blister her skin, bubbling at the wrist. She looked up to see Luc watching her, his face full of wonder.

Furious at her weakness, she pivoted away from him, pulling the cloak around her as she spun.

⚬━┼━⚬

The music was loud, but not loud enough for Mouse. She needed to drive out what was left of the voices in her head.

She wove between people on the crowded dance floor to get closer to the band. The walls of the underground tunnel flashed with neon pink and red lights. Grainy images of an old Tod Browning movie about carnival sideshow performers flickered against the curved roof of the tunnel. Posters for the headlining techno group plastered the wall behind them, declaring WE'RE ALL FREAKS HERE! The pub at Forte Prenestino was known for attracting the best of the fringe bands.

Mouse and Angelo had lived at the Forte for a couple of weeks during their wandering year after fleeing Israel. Coming back to Rome had been Mouse's idea—a strategic one. She'd figured Rome would be the last place Bishop Sebastian would think to look for his prodigal son on the run. They had returned to the city in the back of a cargo truck and come to the Forte—an actual military fort abandoned decades earlier and co-opted by the counterculture, many of them members of the local arts community, many young, all of them people who had been shunned by the wealthier pockets of Rome. They had repurposed the buildings,

turned underground barracks into homes for the homeless and the tunnels and courtyards into event spaces where they hosted festivals and
concerts to raise money to support the growing community of people
living off the grid. Mouse and Angelo had only been two more in the midst
of hundreds of displaced people.

She knew it had been the happiest two weeks Angelo had spent
during that year of relentless running. *Compassion, understanding, har-
mony,* she could hear him say in her head—his priestly idea of God's
vision for the world and what he thought the community at the Forte
strived to achieve. He said it gave him hope.

Mouse had come here to purge Angelo's hope from her head. He
was dead. And she had no use for hope anymore. She gripped the little
wooden mouse in her hand so hard it cut into her palm as she shoved it
into her pocket, and then she wove herself into the crowd.

"Dance with me," she said to a man standing beside her, her power
pressing easily against each word like it belonged there. *Oh, andílek,* the
ghost of Father Lucas chastised her as the stranger turned his back on his
partner and stepped close to Mouse. A spicy, rich butterscotch smell from
the beer in his hand encircled her as he leaned down and asked her name.

"Mouse," she said, her chin lifted defiantly.

His mouth curled into a crooked grin, but he said nothing as his
eyes slid over her body. He put his free hand around her waist and they
swayed and bounced to the hypnotic rhythm of the music.

Mouse looked into the stranger's face, but as the neon lights flashed
from pinks and reds to yellows and oranges, her mind twisted the man's
features into Angelo's, morphed the sweetness of his cologne into the
smells of coffee and linen and olive oil—Angelo's scent.

She shook her head angrily and pulled away from the strange arm
holding her. The man kept dancing beside her. She turned to the woman
on her left.

"Dance with me," Mouse said.

The woman ran her hand over Mouse's shaved head and down her
neck as she rolled her hips, her other arm raised and twisting in time

to the beats playing against the tinny thwang of an oud. Her breasts bobbed up and down. Mouse waited for the music to penetrate her, to fill her mind. The beat was hard, strong. But it wasn't enough.

For my sake, little andílek, be strong and believe in your goodness as I do, Father Lucas whispered.

"Louder," she cried out to the band.

The drum machines and synthesizers surged, pounding the walls and low ceiling.

Mouse waited. She felt Angelo's lips on her neck, his hand at the small of her back, and she turned, a smile almost pulling at her mouth until she saw the stranger bent over her.

"Louder!" she commanded, the smile twisting to a sneer. "Dance harder," she said to the man and woman. Their faces lost any signs of life. They stared back, blank and empty, as they moved frantically to the music.

Come now, another voice echoed in her mind. *You're playing dress up—wearing dark clothes, torching your toys, fondling one or two souls.* Mouse could feel her father chuckle in her head. *If you're really trying to cauterize your conscience and sear away those virtuous voices, it takes more than a sizzle. It takes an inferno.*

People at the back of the pub were covering their ears and complaining about the noise, and some started to leave. Mouse shoved her way through the crowd.

"Stay. Dance," she ordered, her voice quiet, but the fierceness of her intent drove the command outward. The people dropped their hands from their ears and started to dance.

Mouse used a chair to step up onto the bar so she could look down on the scene. The lights flashed, the movie ran fast-forward—images of a clown and conjoined twins and little people blurring into one another. Legless, armless torsos. Bald, childlike giants. Mouse closed her eyes.

There was no Angelo. No vision of him in her head, no remembered smells or touch. He was finally gone.

With a sigh of relief, she opened her eyes.

I beg you, andílek, do not turn your back on what is right and good.

Mouse growled and sucked in a breath. Father Lucas was with her still. Always Father Lucas. She threw her hands up to her shaved head, squeezing at the sides as if she would crush it—anything to rid herself of his tender voice.

"Louder!" she yelled. The repetitive synthesizer notes now screamed like air-raid sirens, the heavy base dropping on the crowd like bombs and sending a concussive wave shuddering through the tunnel. Mouse felt her eardrum pop, needles of pain shooting into her head and down her neck. Some of the people screamed and pulled at their ears.

"Dance!" she yelled.

And they did—frantic, erratic movements no longer connected to the music, which was now only noise.

Mouse waited a heartbeat and a breath. No voices came to her. No visions of the dead. No pangs of conscience. No ache of remorse. Her mind and soul were void.

Coldly, she looked down on the writhing people, some with thin threads of blood trickling down bare necks. She put her hand in her pocket, pulled out the little wooden mouse, and flung it into the crowd.

"Stop dancing. Stop playing," she said impassively.

The room went quiet and still. She stood in the silence, nodding to herself. She was finally ready for the hunt. Mouse had people to kill.

CHAPTER ELEVEN

Ready or not, here I come!" Luc called out.

Mouse held her breath and braced herself against the branches inside the yew tree. Luc was on the other side of the yard, turning around the corner of the Austrian chalet that had just become their new home. They'd moved a few days after Mouse had come back from her pilgrimage. Loosed from the anchors to her humanity, Mouse had found herself antsy, unsettled. The eerie stillness of her father's house had felt claustrophobic. Playing on her promise to "fix" Luc, she had convinced her father that the boy needed a change of scenery and some fresh air and sunshine.

There had been nothing fresh or sunny about her father's house—if it was a house. It felt like another world or no place at all, a pocket stitched into that shadowy no-man's-land between time and space that Mouse had learned to travel. Maybe it was hell. But it was no place for a Pinocchio boy trying to be human.

The round white marble room that she had come to think of as hers had opened into a seemingly endless string of other rooms in her father's house, mostly empty but for a few exceptions. Luc's room had a bed but no toys, no books. There was a sparse bathroom that stank of soured urine and a room that seemed to be covered in blood splatter—some of it black and cracking with age, some still moist and thick like glue. Another room might have been a display in a museum, various devices set up around the walls—a Judas chair still encrusted with evidence of its victims, a rack, and a table lined with smaller torture tools like the Pear of Anguish. Shoved back against the side wall was a small metal box with a tiny slot closed off by an iron grille. Mouse's first love, Ottakar, had nearly lost his life and his mind in such a box. Wearing her new indifference, she had shrugged off the memory and moved on.

The adjacent room had been covered with mirrors, every inch of the wall and ceiling glistening with reflective glass, some old and wavy, some perfectly clear. Four ornate, freestanding floor-length mirrors stood in the corners. Even the floor was a polished silver. Mirrors inside mirrors inside mirrors, and all of them showing her herself. Mouse hadn't gone back in that room.

The most ordinary room Mouse had found in her father's abode held a discordant collection of furniture—a few couches, ranging in style from Victorian to art deco, along with chairs, a wicker bird cage filled with dried flowers and the desiccated remains of a blue bird, and a tin lantern with punched holes in the shape of a rainbow between clouds, the candle inside still burning. Mouse had moved a couple of couches into a larger, open space to create a makeshift family room where they had spent most of their time—when she wasn't out hunting.

Even with her efforts to make it more human for Luc, her father's home still felt like a place crafted outside of time. Or a prison. Mouse had found no windows and no way out. There were no sounds of birdsong or traffic or wind or rain. She also never found her father's room.

Despite the inhuman surroundings, Mouse's influence had evoked dramatic changes in Luc. Though he never said anything about it, he was clearly more relaxed when his father wore his human form. Luc stood taller himself and walked with more natural ease. His father noticed, so when Mouse had suggested that Luc needed room to run and play in order to be less demon and more boy, her father had whisked them to this little village just outside Innsbruck, Austria, to the chalet, which was warm and cozy and everything normal, everything her father's place was not.

The afternoon sun now filtered down from a sky that was robin's-egg blue. Luc paused at the backyard swings, the mountains sitting like waiting giants behind him. The boy lowered his head a moment and then lifted it, smiling, and walked in a direct line toward the yew tree and Mouse.

"Found you!" He reached in and grabbed her leg.

An image of herself hugging him and laughing at his cleverness darted into her mind. Some remnant of the old Mouse knew it was what she ought to do, what she wanted to do, but the void inside her now swallowed it up before it could take hold. "How'd you find me so quickly?" she asked vacantly as she climbed down.

"I listened like you taught me. I heard your heartbeat."

"Well done. Now it's your turn to hide."

His face beamed with joy. "I like this game. I'm good at it."

"I'll count to a hundred."

"No peeking!"

"I promise."

Mouse sat in the swing and closed her eyes. She'd been spending most of her days with Luc, teaching him, playing with him, listening to him. But she spent her nights searching for the first four people on her list—citrus, musk, bay rum, and cedar.

She didn't sleep.

"Ready or not, here I come." Despite the change in location and the cozy comfort of the new home her father filled with the trappings of a normal life, despite the bright sun on her face, Mouse still felt like a stranger to herself, her voice dull and dead like sounds underwater.

She walked barefoot through the grass, listening for a breath or a heartbeat or a giggle. Luc had given himself away more than once because he couldn't stop laughing when she got close. He didn't seem bothered by Mouse's robotic nature. He liked her anyway.

She cocked her head, listening harder, but there was no sound of him. Mouse walked around the corner toward the front of the house. She searched the front yard, all the trees and the bushes. She went back into the house.

"Luc!" she called. The house was empty. Her father was gone.

Mouse walked out onto the patio. "Luc! You win. Come out now!"

Her mouth went dry. She strained her ears, filtering out the hum of the ski lift a mile or so behind the house. A copse of evergreens stood between the house and ski slope. Mouse took off for the trees, calling, "Luc!"

As she broke through into the shadows and saw the thick underbrush, she recognized a twinge of panic. She couldn't hear him or see him anywhere. She closed her eyes and used her power, searching for a glow. But Mouse had never bothered to check to see if Luc had the soft wash of light that she'd come to understand was a person's soul. She had only ever seen a flicker of her own, once, when she was dying at Megiddo. Would Luc have one?

A murky darkness playing against the back of her eyelids seemed to be her answer until she saw a faint shimmer deep in the thicket at the base of a giant sequoia. Mouse ran.

He wasn't breathing. His heart wasn't beating. But as she came closer, the glow of him grew fuller and brighter. Luc's collarbone jutted up like a knot under the skin above the neck of his tangled shirt, and he had sequoia needles in his hair.

She dropped down beside his little body. "Breathe," she commanded. Nothing happened.

Mouse lowered her mouth to his and pushed her own air into his lungs. She pressed down on his chest, pumping his heart. It only took a little encouragement for it to start beating again on its own. Luc sucked in a gaspy breath and then screamed in pain.

Resurrecting her healer's skills, Mouse quickly set the bone back in place, bent his arm at the elbow, and held it still as she helped him sit up. "I know it hurts, Luc. But we need to get back to the house so I can wrap your arm to keep it stable. It will hurt less then, and it will all be well by tomorrow. I promise. Can you stand?"

He nodded and let her lift him up to his feet.

"I can carry you, but I'm afraid it will jostle the bone you've broken and make it hurt worse. Can you walk?"

"I think so," he said through his tears.

Back in the chalet, Mouse took only minutes to wrap his arm and settle him with pillows and a fuzzy blanket on the couch watching cartoons. She sat with his feet in her lap. He liked having his feet rubbed.

The moment of panic gone, Mouse felt herself fall back into the empty chasm she'd built. "Can you tell me what happened, Luc?"

"I climbed the tree, like you did. And I held my breath, but I knew you'd hear my heartbeat just like I did yours. So I told my heart to be still and quiet. I watched you walk to the front of the house, and I almost laughed, but then everything went blurry and I was falling." His eyes grew wide. "And then you were there."

"I'm sorry, Luc." She sounded anesthetized, remote.

"Why? It wasn't your fault."

"I should have been more careful. I should have warned you not to try to make your heart stop. I did it once, too."

"What happened?"

"Like you, I passed out and fell, but I was only hiding behind a wall. I just hit my head on a stone."

"Did it hurt?"

"Nothing like yours. You were very brave."

He smiled and looked past her toward the television, but then asked, "Did someone help you?"

"Yes." She had to make herself breathe.

"Who?"

"No one important."

"I can tell you're lying. I can hear it in your voice."

"Just someone who . . . loved me. But that was a long time ago."

"Can I meet him?"

"He's dead."

"You couldn't fix him?"

"No." She closed her eyes. She needed him to stop asking questions.

"But he fixed you?"

She nodded.

"What was his name?"

"Father Lucas."

"Thank you, Mouse."

"For?" She rubbed at his foot.

"Fixing me."

Something stirred softly in Mouse's chest. She counted the grains in the wood of the fireplace mantel until it grew silent once more.

◦━✦━◦

Hours later, after her father had come back and night had fallen, Mouse took up her cloak and went hunting. On previous outings, she'd gone looking for the four men at Port Hedland, where she assumed they had been recruited by the Reverend. She'd moved from there to various military sites around Australia, but she'd had no luck.

Tonight, she meant to try a different strategy—rather than hunt prey, Mouse would look for bread crumbs. She held the place she meant to go in her mind as she pulled the cloak around her, but then she paused. Part of her didn't want to go there at all. She had to let the part of her that was hungry for revenge consume her doubt before the rush of air sent her spiraling through black emptiness and deposited her on familiar ground. She heard the crack and pop of the fire and smelled the roasting lizard, and she let her cloak fall away to reveal the Martu outstation.

The Martu were gathered around the fire, but no one had seen her arrive. She was a black shadow against a black night, with only the glint of the bone shard strapped to her thigh to give her away. She picked her

131

way through heartbeats until she found the one she wanted, surprisingly not at the fire with the others but shut away in the community house. Silently, Mouse made her way across the dirt courtyard, her cloak hanging loose around her ankles.

She found Ngara huddled under blankets on a low bed shoved against the back wall of the room she painted in, canvas and paints still scattered about the middle of the floor.

"Ah, finally you have come, little one." The old woman's voice was weak.

"I am not your little one."

"As I see," Ngara said.

"You are sick?" Mouse asked. If she was sad, she didn't let herself feel it.

"Old, is what I am. And ready. But I have been waiting for you."

"Why?"

"You have a question for me and I have a gift for you."

"What?"

"Ask me your question."

"Where did they go? The men who came after us."

"They were all gone by the time we came out of hiding. All but one."

Mouse's skin prickled. "Who?"

"The white-haired man."

"Jack's alive." Mouse had wondered if he'd been collateral damage or if the Reverend might have considered him a loose end to be rid of, but no, Jack lived. A sneer pulled at the corner of Mouse's mouth. She'd found her first bread crumb. "Anything else?"

"He took water and drove away."

"Thank you." Mouse turned to leave.

"Now you take my gift."

"I don't need anything from you."

The old woman grunted with pain but kept working her way over to the edge of the cot until she could snake her arm out of the blankets and grasp at something hiding in the dark under the bed. At first, Mouse thought it was one of the Martu's woven baskets, but as Ngara pulled it free, Mouse could see it was a mask. The base was made of braided spinifex grass, with loose strands erupting from the top like hair and long, wedgetail eagle feathers sticking up like a crown. Smaller, brilliant blue bee-eater feathers, wound in grass tethers, dangled from the sides of the mask. The woven spinifex stretched across the face, pulling the features down as if they were melting.

Mouse had never seen this mask, but she knew it all the same. Angelo had seen it in his dream. It was the mask she'd worn as she joined her father, who was doing terrible things to the people in the dream. But Angelo had been there in the dream, too.

Mouse no longer cared about dreams or visions—they were all lies. Angelo was dead. And it was she, not her father, who meant to exact a terrible vengeance. She bent and picked up Ngara's gift. This mask was terrifying. It might be helpful with Jack.

"I made it for you. You are *kurdaitcha* now." The old woman sank back onto her pillow, her energy spent. "Put it on."

Mouse slid the mask over her face. It fit perfectly.

"Vengeance seeker. You have the bone still?"

Mouse laid her hand against the bone shard at her thigh.

"Do you know how to use it?"

"Stab it in and yank it out."

Ngara shook her head. "It has the power of the old ones. Point it at those who have wronged you, and the bone will do the work." Ngara closed her eyes. "Go be *kurdaitcha*." Mouse walked out into the night, but she heard the old woman add, "Then you can be Mouse again."

Mouse stopped, her head half turned back and disfigured by the mask, her cloak swept out beside her. "Mouse is gone," she whispered.

But as she pulled the cloak around her again, she caught Ngara's last words. "What is coming will come. You cannot run away from it."

Mouse went looking for the Bishop first. He and his Novus Rishi bore as much responsibility for what had happened at Lake Disappointment as anyone. She meant to kill them all, but she would save the Bishop for next to last. The penultimate. She wanted him to know she was coming for him. She wanted him to be afraid. The only person she wanted to be more afraid was the Reverend. He would be the last. Mouse meant to savor him.

As she expected, the Bishop was still at the Vatican, but the nearly three years since she'd seen him last had not been kind. He looked old and broken. Night after night, she stalked him. He was always alone, walking the streets of Rome with his head down.

She thought she'd have to wait weeks, maybe even months, before the Bishop led her to Jack's mentor, the Rabbi. Mouse planned to use him to find Jack. But it was only her eighth night of hunting when the Bishop exited the offices at the back of the Vatican around nine to get dinner, as he had every night since Mouse had been watching him. Except this time, he was dressed in street clothes. His gray slacks and jacket and sweater vest put Mouse on edge—he looked like a ghost of himself, unfamiliar and strange, but he blended well with the rest of the Roman crowd. She wondered if that was the point, for the Bishop to be anonymous, unrecognizable. The thrill of expectation ran over Mouse's skin.

Something different was happening tonight.

She followed him to a little coffee shop nearby. He sat at an outside table at the far end of the walk behind a row of parked scooters along the side of the street. A waiter approached and took his order. There were a few other groups at tables along the walk but none near the Bishop. A black Vespa zoomed past where Mouse stood in the dark of a tree in the green space across from and a little behind the coffee shop. The Vespa pulled a U-turn in front of oncoming traffic and zipped into an empty parking spot. A car horn blared.

The rider, a tall man dressed in black, swung his leg over the Vespa and then reached up to take off his helmet. A wash of white hair cascaded down his shoulders.

Jack Gray.

Mouse moved a little farther back against the tree. This was unexpected.

"You have anything?" the Bishop asked as Jack sat down opposite him.

Jack shook his head but saved his explanation until after the waiter gave the Bishop his espresso and went back into the café. "There wasn't enough blood left for a real spell," Jack said softly. Mouse cocked her head, straining to hear with her unnatural senses. "And that was the last of it."

"We'll have to find more, then."

"What's the point? We've been looking for almost a year without a single sign from the locator spell. Because she's dead!" A couple farther up the sidewalk turned to look as he raised his voice. He leaned toward the Bishop, now whispering. "She's dead. They both are."

"She doesn't die."

"I saw the gunfire. And the demons. No one could live through that."

"No one human." The Bishop's voice was heavy with grief.

Jack took out a leather pouch and slid it across the table toward the Bishop. "Well, I'm done."

"What's this?" The Bishop tugged at the pouch string and slid his thumb and forefinger into the opening. He pulled out a small sliver of stone covered with a painted eye.

Mouse sucked in a breath at the tickle of power emanating from it. She had watched the portrait shard disappear in the swirl of salt and sand and had assumed that it had been consumed by the lake as the demons came and went. But Jack must have gone back for it. As the Bishop turned the stone, Mouse's painted eye looked up at the hanging lights overhead. Jack sat back in his chair, his heart skipping.

"If you find more of her blood, you'll need this to power the spell." Jack reached forward and pushed the Bishop's hand down so the stone disappeared back into the pouch. "But you're going to want to keep it sealed up when you're not using it."

"Why?"

"It messes with your head. But there's salt in the pouch that—"

"A protection spell, to counter the dark power? You are clever, Dr. Gray."

"The locator spell is on a piece of paper in the pouch, too. I'm sure you know how it works. Now, if you'll just give me my money, I'll let you get back to—"

"No."

Jack leaned back, sighing. "Come on, old man. This is pointless. She's dead. And I'm done with all this dark shit. I want a simple life, someplace sunny where I can forget what I've seen."

The Bishop took a sip of his espresso. Mouse braced herself against a press of memories: sitting across from Angelo while he did the same thing, making his espresso last until just the right moment, the final sip perfectly warm. She gripped the vengeance mask dangling from her fingers.

"I thought she was dead once before." The Bishop paused, and Mouse could see his jaw clench. He set his cup down on the table. "But Angelo taught me to have more faith."

"Well, I'm not a man of faith."

"You are also not a man with many resources."

"Which is why you need to give me my money."

"Let me see if I can find another sample of her blood. And we will try one more time, Dr. Gray." The Bishop pushed the pouch back across the table.

Jack just looked at it.

"I can make it very much worth your while," the Bishop said.

"Not if the Reverend's looking for her, too."

"I do not believe he is a man of faith, either, Dr. Gray. He seemed very angry at how things turned out at Lake Disappointment, very much like a man who had lost a highly coveted treasure. He thinks she's gone." The Bishop took out some cash and put it on the table beside his empty cup. "He blames you for that loss."

Jack pressed his lips together in a hard line, but his shoulders sagged. He knew he was beat. "So what do you want me to do now?"

"Wait. I will see if I can find another sample." He pushed back from the table and stood up. "I'll be in touch in a couple of weeks. Goodnight, Dr. Gray."

The Bishop's phone rang out as he walked away, a metallic crooning of Frank Sinatra's "Come Fly with Me." Jack watched the old man cross the street, snatched the bag from the table, and then got up, moving back toward his Vespa.

Mouse had crossed the street, too, and waited in the shadows against the building beyond the café lights, her cloak draped around her. She slipped the vengeance mask over her head and then took a single step forward. "Hello, Jack."

He spun around at his name, his eyes widening as he stared at the monstrous face. He jerked toward the Vespa, but Mouse had anticipated his move. She twisted her leg around his shin and yanked back, sending him down to the pavement as she grabbed his forearm with one hand and wrapped her cloak around him with the other.

Mouse had only ever traveled through the dark planes alone. She'd underestimated the additional energy it would take to transport another person. She landed hard on the white marble floor of her room in her father's abandoned house. Jack crumpled under his weight, and Mouse staggered backward into the wall.

When Jack looked up through the curtain of hair hanging in his face, he screamed and scrambled back, banging into the table. He reached up and grabbed the corner, pulling himself up and twisting toward the door, already half running. Urine trickled in a thin line behind him.

Mouse laughed. "Bathroom's first door on the left."

He yanked open the door of Mouse's room and ran out into the hall, trying to get away from her. He tried door after door, their metal handles slamming into the stone walls as he flung each one open only to find empty rooms with no windows and no way out. Mouse patiently followed him, her cloak skimming the glossy floors. She was still laughing at his panic, taking joy from his suffering as she thought of Angelo bleeding out in the salty soil at Lake Disappointment.

Jack made his way through the labyrinthine house until he came to the family room. Mouse had prepared the place for him. Her father had cleared out most of the furnishings when they'd relocated to Austria, but Mouse had kept a couch and table, a lamp, a trashcan, and some stocked supplies. Jack ran to the other side of the couch, crouching as he tried to hide.

Mouse's boots clacked against the stone floor as she came near him. "Please, please, don't . . ." he begged.

Mouse let her laughter die away. She lowered herself onto the couch and crossed her legs. Jack folded in on himself, weeping.

"Welcome to Hell, Jack."

He lifted his head to look at her, his face twisted in fear. "What are you?"

Mouse knew she could make it quick for him—command him to give her the answers she needed and then kill him. But the new Mouse, abandoning the light and listening to the seductive call of her dark rage, wanted to see him suffer more than she wanted information. He deserved to suffer.

His heart was beating so fast it was almost one long, continuous rushing. His pupils were dilated, and the stench of adrenaline and his soiled clothes saturated the air. Mouse had never seen someone die of fright. She watched him for a few more minutes, her head cocked in curiosity, and then she pulled the mask off. She needed Jack alive—for the moment.

"Calm down or you're going to give yourself a heart attack."

Jack sat up, his eyes moving from her shaved head down to her cold eyes. He shook his head. "You." Disbelief mingled with fear on Jack's face. "You're dead."

"Not so much." She reached around Jack to lay the mask on the table. She smirked when he flinched. "Stop crying and take a tissue." She nodded to the box beside the mask on the table behind him. He reached his arm over his shoulder groping for it, but he wouldn't take his eyes off Mouse.

"For God's sake, Jack!" She snaked her arm past his head, grabbed the tissues, and crammed them into his lap.

Jack wiped at his face and nose. "The Bishop said—"

"Yeah, he knows a thing or two. You've been looking for me?"

"The Bishop wants—"

Mouse's arm shot forward again, this time grabbing the back of Jack's head, twisting it toward the table and slamming it down on the stone surface. The bone and cartilage in his nose cracked and popped. Blood poured down his chin. It happened so fast that he didn't have time to cry out.

"Does it look like I care what the Bishop wants, Jack? We're talking about what I want now."

Jack's hands cradled his broken nose, blood seeping through his fingers.

"Take another tissue and clean yourself up. I need you to tell me some things." She waited as he wiped the blood from his face, then she picked up a couple of the used tissues and twisted them. "Here." She jammed the tissue up his nostrils. "It'll stop the bleeding and stabilize the bone," she said, almost as if she couldn't help it.

Jack looked up at her, confused, like a lost boy. "What do you want?"

Mouse leaned back on the couch. "I'm looking for someone, too. Well, some *ones*. And you seem to be good at finding things. It's your knack, Jack." She grinned.

"I didn't know what was going to happen when I found you. I swear, if I had, I wouldn't—"

"We'll talk about all that later. I promise. But what I want to know right now is where I can find the men who were in the desert."

Jack sagged against the couch. "I can tell you where they came from, but I don't know if they're still there."

"That'll do for now."

"There's a compound out in Texas, a few miles outside of a ghost town called Rosenfeld. It's one of the places where the Reverend trains his men."

"Heavily guarded?"

"Probably, but I've never been there." He pushed at one of the tissues hanging out of his nose.

Mouse slapped her hands against her thighs and stood up. "Thank you, Jack."

"I can go now?"

"No. I think you have more things to tell me. But I'm going to let you take care of your nose and get some rest." She bent close to his head as he bowed it. "I've left you some food over there," she pointed to boxes along the wall. "And bottled water. You're free to explore, but as you saw, there's nothing here. There's no way out. Except me."

"When will you come back?"

She chewed at her lip. "Not sure. I've got a bit more hunting to do."

"Are you going to kill me?"

"I haven't decided yet."

CHAPTER TWELVE

Mouse shed her cloak in the shadowy light of her bedroom in the chalet at Innsbruck. As it slid from her shoulders, the façade of bitter braggadocio she'd put on for Jack also slipped away, leaving her face blank once more, her eyes cold and dead. She hung Ngara's mask on a peg on the wall, unsheathed the bone shard strapped to her thigh, and took off the black clothes. She stood naked in the empty room, staring into the silent dark, waiting for instinct to tell her what to do next.

After several minutes, she turned and picked up an old T-shirt from the foot of the bed. She pulled it over her head and climbed under the covers. The shirt had been Angelo's. It didn't smell like him anymore. She ran the worn fabric between her fingers as she listened to the soft sounds of her brother breathing in his room down the hall. Her father was pacing downstairs.

In a few hours, it would be the middle of the night in Texas, and she would don the mask and cloak and bone once more and become the master hunter. But *this* was the moment of real danger for Mouse—the quiet of night when her mind was vulnerable and something still soft came creeping into her consciousness. She rolled over on her side and curled into a ball and imagined laying brick on brick as she walled up that softness and smothered it with her will.

"Mouse?"

She shot upright. She hadn't heard him coming.

"What's wrong, Luc?"

He'd been crying. "I had a bad dream."

"Just a dream?" Mouse had crafted protection spells around the border of Luc's room, remembering her own childhood full of nightmares, real with demons who came in the dead of night to play their terrifying games. She would not let her little brother be tormented so.

"I was falling."

"I see."

"And I—" He hid his face in his hands, crying again.

"It's okay, Luc. I know." She'd already smelled the sharp twang of urine.

"But I'm too big to do that."

"No one's too big to get scared, and your body just did what's natural when a person gets scared. Okay?"

He'd already stopped crying.

"Let's get you cleaned up and then you can sleep in here with me."

He smiled as she took his hand and led him to the bathroom.

A few minutes later, he was curled against Mouse and sound asleep. He smelled like lavender soap and clean linen. His mouth hung open a little and his hand rested under his chin. As he sighed in his sleep, Mouse felt the soft thing tug at her once more. She tried to summon the discipline to shove it back into the dark, but she couldn't, not while she was nestled against the rhythmic rise and fall of Luc's chest, his rapid heartbeat fluttering so close it danced with her own.

o———o

"I can't play right now, Luc, I'm sorry. I have to go."

"I want you to stay. I want you to play." He stood at the threshold of her door, the smells of biscuits and bacon wafting in behind him.

"Go eat your breakfast. I'll be back soon, and we can play then."

"Not unless you tell me where you're going, and why you're wearing that mask. I don't like it."

"I'm . . . playing a game with someone."

"You're lying." His head was cocked to the side.

"Not exactly. It's a very grown-up game, and I can't explain it to you."

"Is it fun?"

"No." She bent her head and slipped the mask into place.

"Then why do you play?"

"Because I have to."

"I don't have to do anything I don't want to do. Neither do you."

"I don't like playing the game, Luc, but I very much want to win it." In her mind, she flipped through the images of the men responsible for Angelo's death.

"Will you win?"

"I don't know." Her hand shook as she strapped the bone shard to her thigh.

"If you stay and play with me, I'll let you win."

Mouse looked down at him through the mask's eyeholes. It was the first time she'd heard him willing to give up something for someone else. She knelt and took his hand. "That's very kind of you, Luc. And I will come back just as soon as I can, and we'll play then."

"Please, don't go."

Mouse stood and grabbed the edge of her cloak. "I'll bring you something when I come back." And then she was gone.

○━━●

The rotting remains of a storefront were all that was left of Rosenfeld. The moon hung overhead like a broken fingernail in the Texas sky. Mouse took off toward the low hills where she knew she'd find the compound. She could already hear the deep rumble of generators.

A few minutes later, she dropped down against the hilltop looking over a shallow valley. The compound seemed deserted. No lights. No movement. But Mouse knew not to trust the appearance of a thing. She could hear the heartbeats of at least twenty people. All but one seemed to pulse in the slow rhythm of sleep.

A sign on the gate of the razor-wire fence read THE ARMY OF GOD.

Mouse assumed that the compound would be equipped with motion detectors, so she couldn't just waltz in and take what she wanted. Well, she could actually. She could kill them all with a word, be done with it and back home playing with Luc in a matter of minutes. But it would not satisfy her hunger. She needed to see the men afraid, needed to feel their lives in her hands before she claimed each one in payment for the life they had taken.

Mouse wrapped her hand around the bone the Seven Sisters had gifted her. She prowled the border of the compound slowly, sniffing out her prey. Citrus. Musk. Bay rum. Cedar. She found them clustered together in a barracks at the back of the compound—maybe they were all part of the same unit. She pulled her cloak tightly around her, focused her mind, and instantly found herself leaning against the wall of the barracks. She waited a moment for alarms. In the answering silence, she moved around the corner of the building.

Someone had left a window open to the cool night air. Mouse climbed through like a shadow. Her nostrils flared. Citrus was in the far corner. Musk and Bay Rum were in the beds on either side of her. Cedar was near the front door.

She pulled the bone out of the sheath.

Point it at those who have wronged you, and the bone will do the work, Ngara had said.

Mouse pointed the bone at Musk.

Nothing happened.

What else had the old woman said? *Be kurdaitcha.* Be the vengeance seeker. It was all a matter of intent. The bone held the magic. The bone did the work. But the vengeance seeker had to fuel it with a desire for revenge. Mouse had to want these men to die. And she did—in her head. She needed to feel it in her heart.

She gritted her teeth and pulled up the memory of Lake Disappointment. She let it come, strong and real, adrenaline flooding through her. In her mind, she zeroed in on Angelo, past the flying debris and the roar of the helicopters and the whipping wind and the wails of the men being eaten by the demons.

She heard Angelo begging for his life and hers—*We surrender.*

She slowed down the bullet that would first shatter his rib cage and come shooting out of his backpack. She followed the trajectory of that first bullet, followed it to the man who had fired the shot. He half hung off the fuselage of the lead helicopter. He stared at Angelo's raised hands. Mouse watched the man's face for any sign of compassion or regret. There was none. Not even a pause as he pulled the trigger.

In her perfect memory, Mouse isolated the man's scent. Bay Rum.

She turned to her left. The bone began to glow and grew warm in her hand. Her mind held the image of Angelo pleading, his body shredded by bullets, his glowing soul seeping out between her fingers and down into the desert sand as he left her. But when she started to point the bone at her first quarry, her hand shook violently.

I beg you, do not turn your back on what is right and good.

Mouse hissed. She thought she had purged Father Lucas's ghostly counsel, but he was with her still. She realized with disgust that she couldn't do it. She couldn't kill a sleeping man in cold blood—not yet, anyway. Her temper flared at her failure. Without warning, the bone surged with a brilliant blue as it had when she and Angelo had found it in the cave. It vibrated in her hand, full of the vengeance Mouse had already fed it.

And Bay Rum's heart stopped. Just like that.

She spun toward Musk and then moved across to Citrus. She felt them die at the moment her eyes rested on them. Panicking at the loss of control, she held the bone shard away from her, letting it roll passively in her palms, but it still glowed with the cold blue light. She heard Cedar cough. Instinctively, she turned to him and took a step closer. He was clutching at his chest, his eyes wide when he saw Mouse. She watched his pupils grow large—then empty.

Shocked at the suddenness of death, she looked down at her hands, horrified, as the bone's light died, too. *I will not kill anyone today.* The words came against her will. They had been the foundation of her humanity for seven hundred years. Her last thread to anything good in her. And she had just cut herself loose from it. What did that make her?

She kept blinking, trying to clear the fuzziness from her sight. It was only when she tasted the salt that she realized she was crying. Even as she acknowledged the tears and the shock at what she'd done, she couldn't feel anything but rage.

And that made her even angrier.

She snatched her cloak around her and caught her breath at the sudden change in the air. The cool Texas night evaporated instantly in the dry heat of the outback afternoon at the Martu outstation. Mouse heard a child scream behind her, but she didn't care to look. She stormed through the community house door. Ngara's art room was bare. No canvas or paint. No cot crammed into the corner.

Mouse had come to scream at the old woman, to demand to know who or what had twisted fate this way and set Mouse and Angelo on such a dark path. She wanted to know where they were so she could bring the fight to them, too. But Ngara was gone, and Mouse's rage swelled, nearly blinding her.

"What are you?" the Martu child asked as Mouse staggered back through the open door.

"Gone," she said.

She wasn't thinking of a destination when she swirled the cloak around her. Her anger drove her toward a target like a loosed arrow. Her feet slammed against the ground, and she crouched to balance herself. She knew where she was by the smells—different and yet still the same. The minerals lifted into the air from the steam drifting up off the river. The linden trees were in bloom.

Mouse had come home again to Teplá but not to the cemetery this time. She'd come to the root of her failure—to the abbey where her struggle with goodness had begun.

But it was all wrong. The trees were thinned out, the gardens gone. The abbey buildings sprawled out in different places, the Teplá River dammed. The stones of the church wall in front of her were too smooth and the scale of it all too grand.

Yet, here she was, in the same place where she'd spent her childhood—on the outside of the Church of the Annunciation of the Lord at Teplá. Always on the outside looking in, Mouse had spent her childhood wanting to belong to those who did not want her—the righteous, the blessed, the good. Why couldn't she turn her back on them the way they had always shunned her?

Mouse slammed her fist against the wall over and over, trying to beat out the residue of her longing until her knuckles shattered underneath her black glove. She leaned heavily into the stone, weeping as she slid down to her knees. She pulled the cloak up to hide her face but was surprised to find herself falling through the dark planes her father had taught her to use. She felt something pull at her like a magnet, and she landed softly on a cold stone floor.

She shook her head, sobbing, and curled her arms over her head. She never would have come here of her own will. Not now. This was not a place to feed her anger. This place conjured old yearnings.

Midmorning light bounced around cave walls still covered in Mouse's paintings. A fading image of a wolf took up much of the back wall. *Bohdan.* Her salvation when she'd gone wandering in the darkness once before. Bohdan had believed in her goodness and taught her to hope for it, too. He had guided her back to the light.

Mouse spun around and ran outside. "Not this time!" she yelled at the heavens. "I don't care anymore. Not about goodness. Not about my soul. Sure as hell not about you!" Her voice echoed around the mountains. "I have nothing! You keep taking it. You break me, over and over again. And then expect me to pull myself up and be your good little girl? Well fuck you!" Spit flew from her mouth.

She sank onto the ground where she'd once watched the sun rise and set over the mountains beside her gentle Bohdan, her hand sunk into his thick, warm fur, the weight of his head in her lap. Together they had watched the sometimes soft, sometimes radiant colors of the sky play along the still waters of the lake below like living art. And Mouse had believed again in the mercy and glory of a loving God.

And then Bohdan had been taken from her. And Ottakar. And Nicholas. And all those men at Marchfeld. And seven hundred years of any gentle touch or friendship or love. Until Angelo. And now he had been taken, too.

"I can't do it this time."

She pushed herself upright, no tears left. She went to wipe the snot and saliva from her chin and saw her torn leather glove, bits of her own skin and blood peeking out along the knuckles. Mouse stood, unnaturally calm now. She walked slowly along the familiar path that wasn't really a path anymore, eaten by brush and mountain grass, down to the lake. She knelt at its edge and leaned over the water like the pine and spruce trees that circled the shore. She plunged her hands into the cold water, gloves and all, until the blood was gone and the sting of her broken knuckles was soothed. She sat back, cross-legged, and looked out over the lake that glinted in the morning light like a pane of glass.

She felt sure something had drawn her here—God or the Seven Sisters or some unnamed thing playing with her fate. She didn't care to know anymore. She didn't care what their plan was or what they wanted from her, so she gave them an impossible ultimatum: "You give me Angelo back and I'll believe in goodness again. Until then, leave me alone."

She threw a stone into the lake and watched the ripples dance against the shore, and then Mouse drew the cloak around her and left the Sumava woods for the last time.

⸻

"Oh, I love her!" Luc squealed as Mouse put the puppy down on the kitchen floor.

"I told you I'd bring you something." She looked up to see her father standing stiffly in the hallway. "You okay with this?"

He shrugged. "I understand a person can learn a lot from having a dog."

"A person learns *from* the dog—not from having it. A dog can teach you unconditional love."

"Surely not me," her father said, his eyebrow raised.

"I meant 'you' universally."

"I see. How was Texas?"

Mouse looked down at Luc. She hadn't told her father where she was going or what her big-picture plan was, but then, she'd never been able to keep secrets from him. She didn't care to anymore, but she didn't want Luc to know.

Luc was letting the puppy lick his face. "Isn't she cute?"

"You might want to take her in the backyard. She might need to go to the bathroom."

Luc scooped up the puppy and ran out the patio doors.

"You haven't said anything to him, have you?" Mouse asked her father. "About what I'm doing when I'm gone?"

He pulled out a stool and sat down. "I didn't think you cared. About anything anymore."

"I don't. Tell him if you want. What I've done can't begin to compare to your sins."

"Well, everyone has to start somewhere." Her father picked at a bit of puppy hair on the cuff of his pants. "It went well, I take it?"

"Yeah."

He chuckled. "Then why is your face covered in shame?"

"Same reason yours is covered in scars. When we fall, we fall slow."

Luc came running back into the kitchen, the puppy at his heels.

"What are you going to name her?" Mouse asked.

"Mine."

CHAPTER THIRTEEN

After Mouse's mission to Texas, her father left for several days, entrusting Luc to her care. She spent her days playing and her nights preparing. She wanted her next hunt to be consummate and clinical. While Luc slept, Mouse sat stone still on the patio in the growing chill and imagined herself killing the Rabbi and the Reverend and the Bishop in a thousand possible ways. She conditioned her mind and body to act without thought or hesitation, allowing no chance for haunting whispers from Father Lucas to sabotage her revenge.

That pent-up fury burned hot behind her eyes when she finally went back to her father's realm to see Jack. He was looking worse for wear, strung out on the couch, his leg draped over the back. He was singing "Jingle Bells."

"Christmas is two months away," Mouse said.

He squealed in fright and jumped behind the couch, then made an attempt at bravery. "How the hell would I know? I don't even know what day of the week it is."

"Thursday."

"I don't know any other songs anyway."

"You only know one song and it's 'Jingle Bells'?"

He shrugged. "Never saw the point to music." He took another step away from her, his courage growing with the distance. "Until now. When I'm stuck here with nothing else to do." He raked his fingers through his greasy hair. "And where's the shampoo? Or a goddamn toothbrush? I've only got shitty chips and packaged crackers to eat, and my clothes stink." He pulled at the sleeve of his shirt, sniffing it and wrinkling his nose. "Where is this place anyway?"

"You're in Hell, Jack, not a hotel."

"That's what I'm saying!" He flung his arms out to the side. Bits of crumbs sprinkled onto the floor, which was littered with empty water bottles.

"Your comfort should be the least of your worries." Mouse slapped the mask dangling from her hand against her thigh.

"Please just let me go, Dr. Em."

Mouse's eyes snapped up to his. She didn't realize she'd been avoiding looking at his face until now. He didn't look like the student she remembered—this cowering, white-haired man with a week's patch of stubble along his jaw, his normally posh clothes unkempt, his eyes devoid of their usual swagger. The swelling in his nose had gone down, but a wash of black and purple swept out under his eyes. What was she teaching him now?

The guilt lasted only a second before her rage ate it. It was getting easier for her.

"Where can I find the Rabbi?" she asked.

Jack leaned forward on the back of the couch, his head in his hands. "If I tell you where to find them all, all the members of the inner council of the Novus Rishi, will you let me go?"

"I only asked for the Rabbi, Jack. I want to do this right—a nice, orderly progression. One at a time. And you will give me the answers I need when I ask for them. And only when I ask. Do you understand?"

When he looked up, his face was wet with tears. "What's wrong with you?"

"I am what I was made to be. Now, the Rabbi?"

"His name is Rabbi Asher Ben-Yair and his yeshiva is near the Old City in Jerusalem."

"Good boy. I'll bring you some figs when I come back."

Mouse roamed the empty campus of Rabbi Asher Ben-Yair's yeshiva, the bone shard at her hip and her mask dangling from her hand. At the third locked door, her wariness rose. It was the middle of the day, and the campus was empty, though the sounds of the busy city filtered in between the buildings and covered roads.

As she turned a last corner, about to give up the search and go back to get the Rabbi's home address from Jack, a young man came out of one of the doors.

"I am looking for Rabbi Asher Ben-Yair," she said in Hebrew as she whisked the mask behind her.

The man studied her a moment, taking in her black clothes and cloak. "Go down to this intersection," he pointed. "Turn right. His home is two streets over, a couple of houses back. You will see the people coming and going." He turned to leave but paused and said, "May God console you among the other mourners of Zion and Jerusalem."

Mouse fastened the mask to the belt loop at her back and let the cloak fall over it like a curtain. She walked the two streets with a cold assurance, knowing what she'd find, but she needed to see for herself.

The young man had been right—the people led her to the door. She fell in behind an old man wearing a black vest that was ripped on the right front, below another basted tear. She followed him up two flights of stairs and past a steady stream of mourners.

"The Master of Mercy will protect him forever, from behind the hiding of his wings, and will tie his soul with the rope of life," she heard from the inner room. She could see an older woman sitting on a low stool, but she couldn't see the singer of the mourning prayer. Mouse stood against the wall, head down, waiting for the afternoon prayers to end. She followed the bustle of people leaving and on the landing of the stairs reached out to grab the arm of a woman, who looked up, surprised.

"Do I know you?"

"Tell me how the Rabbi died," Mouse said with quiet command.

—⦁—

She pushed past her cloak into the room of her father's house once more and swept over the couch, where Jack was sprawled out again, munching chips.

"Did you bring me my—?" He cried out as Mouse suddenly pressed her knee down on his gut.

"The Rabbi was already dead."

"What?" He gasped, spewing chips from his mouth, and pushed against her knee so he could breathe.

"Did you know?"

"No!"

She listened for the lie, but he was telling the truth.

"He was old and in ill health," Jack said. "But I thought—"

"He was killed when a bomb went off at his favorite bookstore. It killed eleven people."

Jack tried to shrug. "That's life in the Middle East, I guess."

Mouse stepped back and started pacing the room. The Rabbi's death a coincidence? Not likely. A dark suspicion wormed its way into her mind.

"Who next then?" she muttered absently.

"What?"

"Give me another name."

"Dabir Al-Maslul."

"Muslim?"

Jack nodded.

"Good God, you people got a Catholic, a Jew, an Evangelical, and a Muslim to sit on the same council and agree?"

"Not me. And they don't always agree." Jack pushed himself upright, brushing chips off his chest. "There's a Hindu, too."

Mouse put her hand up. "Only when I ask. Where can I find the Muslim?"

"Morocco. There's a special library—"

"The al-Qarawiyyin in the old medina of Fez. Yes, I know it."

And then she was gone.

A couple of hours later, she was back.

"He's dead, too—choked on something."

Jack sat very still, staring at her, and then quietly said, "Swami Layak Chaudri. Anjar in Gujarat, India. The Hindu monastery."

Mouse disappeared.

Jack was sitting in the same place when she came back.

"Well, shit," he said.

Mouse stared at him, her arms crossed.

"That just leaves the Bishop and the Reverend." Jack's fear was palpable—he reeked of it.

"What's going on, Jack?"

"I don't know."

"Were they all alive when you met with the Bishop last?"

"As far as I know. He would've told me if he knew. He for sure thought the Rabbi was still alive, because he was planning to ask him for more of—"

"My blood."

Jack nodded.

"I already know where the Bishop is," Mouse said, "so the last thing you can tell me is where to find the Reverend." She took a step closer to him, her hand resting on the bone shard.

"I can't help you." He sounded resigned. "Because I don't know. But the Bishop might."

⊸—⊷

Mouse stood with her back against the brick wall of the same coffee shop where she'd abducted Jack Gray. Jack was sitting in a chair close to her. The wind was blowing his white hair across his mouth. He had his cell phone on the table in front of him. It buzzed.

"He's on his way," Jack said over his shoulder to Mouse. The waiter brought Jack a cappuccino and a pastry.

Mouse was listening for the Bishop. When she heard his heartbeat and hurried step, she sat down at the next table, her back to Jack and the oncoming Bishop. She didn't want him to see her and bolt, and she wanted the added advantage of observing how he reacted to the questions she'd instructed Jack to ask.

The Bishop pulled out the chair opposite Jack and sat down. Mouse could hear the nervous thrum of his heart even though his voice was steady.

"Where have you been?" the Bishop asked.

"Away."

"Where?"

"Somewhere. Do you know about the Rabbi?"

"Yes."

Mouse listened to the blood zoom through his veins. She didn't need to hear the Bishop's answer to Jack's next question.

"And the others?"

"Yes."

"The Reverend's doing?"

"Of course." Mouse heard a hiccup of fear in his heartbeat. The Bishop cleared his throat. "Have you come to kill me, Jack?"

"What?"

The Bishop leaned in against the table. "You disappeared. Maybe you decided it was in your best interest to switch allegiances again."

"The man left me in the damn desert to die. I would never—"

"Then where have you been, Jack?"

Mouse turned her chair around. "With me."

The Bishop jerked back in his seat, but it wasn't shock that ran over his face like water. It was rage. Mouse knew it well. She imagined her face mirrored his own.

"Where's the Reverend?" she asked. Her fingers played along the smooth shard of bone at her hip. Her hand shook a little—but not with hesitancy this time. Mouse didn't think she'd have any problem killing the Bishop. He'd been Angelo's friend, a father figure, and he'd betrayed that trust.

"Angelo's dead because of you," the Bishop said.

Mouse leaned forward, her eyes sparking with hate. "You had a little something to do with that, too. It was you and your puppet here"—she put her hand on Jack's shoulder, making him jump—"who tracked us down."

"He was working for the Reverend."

"The details don't matter. You were all looking for us—your whole damn army. It doesn't matter who found us. *You* set the wolves to hunt us, and it was *your* Novus Rishi who cornered us, *your* Reverend who gave the order to shoot."

"The Reverend said . . . " The Bishop pressed his hand against his mouth.

Mouse thought he was about to get sick, but he slammed his fist against the table instead and his other hand shot out, grabbing her around the wrist. "Tell me the truth. If you ever loved him, tell me the—" His voice broke.

Mouse was studying his face. "What did the Reverend tell you?" she asked, though she was beginning to figure it out on her own.

"He said you called demons up from the sand. His men opened fire on them. He said you—"

She snatched her hand free. "You thought I did it?"

"The Reverend said you used Angelo as a shield, that you were trying to save yourself. He said he saw the bullets tear through Angelo and then you, and then the demons took you. He said there wasn't even anything of my Angelo left to bury."

"I never knew you were a fool," Mouse spat. "But I guess it was easier to believe that I was responsible than admitting that your own man had—"

"The Reverend is not my man."

"I don't give a shit about the politics of your little band of Armageddon warriors, *Your Excellency*."

"You're telling me that the Reverend ordered—"

"*Take the girl down. The priest doesn't matter. Kill him.*" The muscles in her face twitched with rage even as she recited the words.

The Bishop's face went stone still as the truth set in.

Mouse couldn't tell if it was anger or grief or guilt that stole the Bishop's words. It all looked the same to her now. "It's my turn to ask the questions," she said. "I'll know if you're lying, so don't."

"I'm not afraid of you."

"You should be. I grew up in the Middle Ages. I've seen torture your pretty little civilized mind can't possibly imagine. I'm eager to see how quickly you break."

"What would our Angelo think about that?"

Mouse's jaw clenched and released, the only sign that the Bishop's salvo had hit its mark. "I'll worry about that tomorrow. Today is about vengeance."

He leaned heavily back in his chair. "Then we want the same thing."

"What do you mean?"

"I know you're going to kill me. I don't care." His hands balled into fists against the arms of his chair. "This charlatan has stolen my life's work, the army I built, my Novus Rishi. And he has taken my son from me—" He choked on the last words.

Mouse would let herself feel no sympathy for him. "Angelo was never your son, old man."

He snapped his eyes up to meet hers. "Think what you want. Kill me in whatever gruesome way you want. I have surely earned it. But make me one promise—I want to see the Reverend suffer and die first."

Mouse had never thought to find a kindred spirit in the Bishop. "I'll bring you the Reverend's head on a platter," she said. "And then I'll coat it in your blood when I slit your throat." She eased back in the chair. "Now tell me where to find him and what it is he wants."

"I would think the last was obvious—he wants you." The Bishop leaned forward against the table. "How did you get away, but Angelo—"

Mouse turned to look out across the street. "My father came."

"For you. But not for Angelo?" There was an impossible hope in his voice.

They sat in silence for several minutes.

"It wasn't my choice," she finally said.

The Bishop wiped the tears from his face. "Did the Reverend see your father?"

"How would I know? I was dead. Does it matter?"

Surprisingly, it was Jack who answered. "Very much."

"Why?" Mouse asked.

"Because he won't stop. Unless he thinks you were eaten by those things out there and that you're really dead and gone, he won't stop hunting you. The Reverend gets what he wants. Always."

"I've had plenty of experience disappointing narcissistic, ambitious old men." She nodded at the Bishop. "What makes your Reverend any different than this Bishop? He wanted me, too."

"I'm not insane," the Bishop answered.

But Jack was shaking his head. "The Reverend's not crazy either. He's ruthless, but he's also careful, calculated. He knows how to play the game well. He says the right things to the right people to get what he wants—fundamentalist religion, forced morality, white nationalism—but I don't think he believes any of it. He believes in his own superiority, plain and simple. That's what makes him different.

"The Bishop and the Rabbi, they were fighting for something—a cause, for God, for good against evil. But the Reverend? He's just fighting for himself." Jack picked at a crumb on the table. "It's his wife, Kitty, who's the fervent one. She believes she has a mandate from God to wipe out evil on the Earth. Her fanaticism feeds into the Reverend's thirst for absolute power. They both want to tear it all down, destroy the world as we know it, because Kitty believes God will rebuild it in the way she imagines, prim and proper, and the Reverend believes he will be the last man standing to rule over it all."

"Why didn't you tell me any of this, Jack?" Mouse asked.

"You said to give you answers only when you asked for them. You didn't ask." He was more than a little smug.

Mouse stared at him until the smirk slipped from his face, and then she turned to the Bishop. "Why aren't you dead like all your council buddies?"

"I knew what was coming." The Bishop shifted in his seat. "Jack came to me after Australia, told me what the Reverend had done. I knew he'd move to take the Novus Rishi sooner or later."

"But you didn't warn the others? Your friends?" It was more accusation than question.

"I couldn't without risking exposure. I needed time to prepare."

"There's that Christian altruism I've come to count on," Mouse said bitterly.

The Bishop shrugged. "I confess I expected he'd try blackmail or subterfuge first, but he went for the quickest and quietest path—a little poison here, an explosion there. He wiped them all out within a day. Everyone except me."

"The shock and awe wouldn't be the Reverend," Jack countered. "That'd be Kitty. She really likes the stories about God using his almighty power to strike down the enemies of his people. Her personal favorite is the one about Elisha getting teased by a group of kids. You know, the one where God sends two bears to rip the children apart?" Jack blew out a soft whistle. "She loved to tell that one to kids' groups. Part of her anti-bullying campaign."

Mouse silently added another name to her list—the Bishop, the Reverend, and now Kitty Ayres. She still hadn't decided what to do about Jack. But she was tired of talking. The more time she spent with the Bishop, the louder his grief called to her own. It spread like a contagion, and she needed to stay ahead of it to keep her edge.

"None of this matters," she said. "Just tell me where to find the Reverend."

"I don't know where he is now—he's been in hiding since he killed the council," the Bishop said. "But I can figure out where he'll be next."

"How? Your toy army has been taken away from you."

"Not all of it. That's why I couldn't take the risk to warn the others. I needed to pull my most valuable resources off the field, hold them in reserve until—"

"Until the Reverend's arrogance and appetites inevitably lead him into a more vulnerable position," Jack said, and then answered the question in Mouse's eyes. "His empire's built on appearances—public piety, charm, conspicuous wealth, power. He has to be seen in order to maintain that image. He can only hide for so long."

Mouse lowered her chin to her hand. "So we wait until he comes out of hiding."

"And then you kill him," the Bishop said.

"And then I kill you." She smiled. "Until then, you text Jack every day with updates."

"Wait, where am I going to be?" Jack asked.

"You have an apartment around here somewhere, right? I'll walk you home. Then I can pop in whenever to check on you, and see what the Bishop's had to say." She let her eyes give him the unspoken warning—if he ran, he died.

Jack looked down at his hands and then back up. "I want to go with you."

"What?" the Bishop and Mouse asked at the same time.

There was a new hardness to Jack's voice when he said, "I want to be there when you go for the Reverend."

"You can't come home with me."

"Then take me back to where you were keeping me. Only let me get some fresh clothes and a toothbrush and maybe a book or two—I'm going nuts shut up in there by myself."

"Suit yourself, Jack." The metal legs of Mouse's chair scraped the sidewalk as she pushed back and stood. She paused and looked down at the Bishop. "You betray me, old man, and I'll be on your doorstep." She glanced over his shoulder toward the Vatican. "And anyone and anything you ever cared about will be nothing but ashes when I'm done."

The Bishop stood slowly. "The only thing I care about now is seeing the Reverend dead." He turned and walked back toward his Holy City.

Jack and Mouse headed down the sidewalk in the opposite direction.

"Can we get some fruit somewhere?" Jack asked.

Mouse left Jack in her father's house, content with his fresh supplies and solitude. Snow was falling heavily when she got back to the chalet at Innsbruck.

Luc had just woken and was playing with Mine out in the snow, the puppy a fluff of black against the downy white. Mouse watched through the window. The kettle she'd put on for her tea began to whistle. She lifted it from the stove, but the squeal continued.

She turned toward the window. Luc was screaming, his high, childish voice pitched with something terrible. Mouse dropped the kettle and ran into the backyard to find him standing over Mine. She was too still, and as Mouse ran up to them, she saw the puppy's eyes open and fixed, snowflakes falling into them.

Luc threw himself, sobbing, against Mouse as she knelt to lay her hand on the little dog. She heard her father's steps on the patio behind them.

"What happened, Luc?" Mouse asked, though she already suspected.

"She was pulling on my coat," he said through his tears. "I told her to stop, but she didn't." Another sob shuddered through him. "I got mad. And I screamed at her to *stop*, and I was so mad at her, and I felt that hot thing inside—do you know?" He lifted his head from her shoulder, his eyes full of heartbreak and shame. For the first time in months, something loosened inside Mouse.

She pulled his head toward her and kissed him on the cheek and wrapped her arms gently around him. "I know, Luc. I know that feeling, too." She ran her hands through his snow-covered hair.

"And then she . . . stopped." It came out as a whimper.

"I am so sorry, sweetheart."

"But I didn't really mean for it to happen, Mouse. I love her so much. What's wrong with me?" Luc went limp in her arms, sobbing again.

Mouse held him tight. "There is *nothing* wrong with you." Her throat burned with the words that she had heard so many times from Father Lucas. Words she did not believe. Words she so desperately wanted her little brother to believe. "You just made a mistake. You and me, we have gifts, right?" He nodded his head against her chest. "That makes us special. But it also means we have to be extra careful." She swallowed against the wave of grief surging in her chest. "We have to control our tempers."

"How?"

"Look up. Do you see the snow?"

He nodded.

"When you feel yourself getting angry, right at the start, find something like the snow that you can count." She could almost feel the weight of Father Lucas's hand on her shoulder as she echoed his gentle teachings. "Once you start counting, it makes it harder for that hot feeling inside to get so big that it makes you do something you don't want to do. I'll teach you, okay?" The sting of her hypocrisy burned.

"You promise?" Luc asked.

"I promise."

"Mouse? Can I make her live again?"

"Do you think that's any more right than making her die?"

Luc put his little hand against the still puppy, his fingers sinking into the tufts of fur. After several silent moments, he finally shook his head and said, "I don't think so. I don't think I should make her do anything just because I want it. I think I should just love her. And I do, Mouse. I do love her. I just wish she wasn't dead." He buried his head in her shoulder again, sobbing.

While Luc was talking, their father made his way across the yard to them. He bent now toward the puppy and whispered, "Live." The ball of fur quivered and then stood. "There, Luc. Aren't you happy? She's yours again, just like you wanted."

Luc pulled away from Mouse and put his hand out. The puppy whimpered and cowered.

"She's afraid of me," he said, his voice shaking. His father took a step back, and Mine wagged her tail and jumped in Luc's lap, licking his face.

Luc looked over at Mouse, confused, not sure what to do.

"She's giving you a gift, Luc. She forgives you. It's okay to accept it and to forgive yourself. It's called mercy. She's doing it because she loves you."

"I love her, too. I love her so much!" He held the puppy gently to his chest, letting her nuzzle his neck. "I don't think I want to call her Mine anymore. Because she's not. She's her own."

"What do you want to call her, then?"

"What you said. Mercy. That's her name now. So I don't forget." He carried her into the house, snug against his chest. "I love you, Mercy. More than anything."

"You shouldn't have done that," Mouse said to her father once they were alone.

"I suppose I should've just let you go on and on about how wrong it is to use your power?" He laced his fingers behind his head, arching his back until it popped. "He's happy and he has me to thank for it."

"Part of growing up is learning that there are consequences for our choices. You say you want him to have a normal life, but you just taught him—"

"I never said I wanted him to have a normal life. I said I want him to understand what it means to be human."

Mouse studied him. He had that twinkle behind his eyes that she knew well. He was playing at some game. But she didn't have time to unravel his mysteries.

She shrugged. "Human or normal—doesn't make a difference. It was still a mistake." She went into the house.

"We'll see how long you feel that way," he said to himself, then stuck out his tongue and caught a falling flake.

CHAPTER FOURTEEN

The Bishop contacted Jack a few weeks later to let him know that the Reverend and his wife were going to be at the Bolshoi a couple of days before Christmas to see *The Nutcracker*. Mouse intended to go alone, but the Bishop and Jack insisted on being there, too. And in some ways, it made things simpler for her—the last four names on her list, all in the same place at the same time. A few minutes' work during intermission and it would all be over.

When she told her father she was going to *The Nutcracker*, he suggested that he and Luc go, too.

"I want us to do all the normal things a family does—after all, it's Christmas," he said, his voice full of mischief.

"We've gone shopping at the holiday markets in the village. We've baked cookies and wrapped presents and learned all the carols and decorated the house. I'll be back on Christmas Eve. We can do *The Nutcracker* next year," Mouse answered. But her words felt hollow. She had a dark Christmas wish she meant to ask of her father once everything was accomplished.

"There's no reason we can't go this year, is there?" he countered.

Mouse knew full well that her father already understood why she was going. The tease in his voice just confirmed her suspicions. "This isn't a game. The people I'm dealing with are dangerous. They don't know about Luc, and I'd like to keep it that way."

Her father waved away her concern. "He and I will be nowhere near your *dangerous* people. And even if they were to see him, they won't be around long enough to pose a threat, will they?"

Mouse didn't answer. She hadn't decided what to do about Jack yet. "I doubt you can get tickets this late," she said instead.

Her father smirked. "I assure you, we will have some of the best seats in the house."

Mouse had no choice but to acquiesce. "You'll keep Luc away from . . . what I'll be doing?"

"I promise I will keep him safe from your dangerous prey." He played with a bit of garland swirled around crimson candles on the kitchen table. "But won't your activities interrupt the show?"

Mouse looked out the window at Luc and Mercy playing in the snow. The puppy didn't seem any different than before her death and resurrection. If anything, the bond between the two had grown stronger, fed by Luc's newly discovered power of selfless love.

Mouse swallowed a little wave of sadness. "I won't do it there," she said quietly. "I'll go somewhere else."

"Ah, that's clever. Less distraction, and it eliminates the drama that's sure to stir if someone drops dead at the ballet. Where are you going to take—? Oh, I bet I know. The lake that's not a lake? The one that's full of salt and bitter with disappointment?"

She snapped her face toward him. "There's nothing funny about any of this. I know the lake. I know it'll be isolated. I know there's nowhere for them to run. It makes sense to take them—"

"Them? I thought we were picking them off one by one."

"They'll all be there that night—what's left of them."

"That's ambitious of you. Can you do it? Traveling with a companion is more difficult than traveling alone."

"I know that."

"Would you like some help?"

"No." She had been transporting Jack back and forth to different locations to touch base with the Bishop via cellphone. She didn't want anyone tracing the calls, and it was a good way to test her endurance. "I'll do one at a time."

"How will you—"

"None of this is any of your business!" she said sharply. "I have it all planned. You're the one screwing it up by insisting on bringing Luc. Just be sure to keep him away from it all. When it's done, I'll either join you back at the ballet or I'll meet you here."

"Okay, okay," he said, raising his hands in surrender. "Merry Christmas to you, too."

In the days leading up to the show, Mouse visited the theater several times, playing out various scenarios in her head, mapping out countless strategies. She found all the places to slip away from the crowd so she could come and go unnoticed. She anticipated what the Reverend and Mrs. Ayres might do during intermission, thought about how to snatch them one by one, considered who to save for last. Mouse planned for everything.

Finally, the night came when it would be finished. Mouse wore a tux like her father and brother. Her hair had been growing back and now covered her head like a thick, super-short pixie cut. Luc was thumbing through the glossy program, looking at the faces of the dancers he was about to watch. It would be his first *Nutcracker*.

Her father had been right about getting them good seats. They had a box on the *bel étage*—a perfect view of the stage and of much of the audience below and across from them; a strategic spot. Mouse had already picked out Jack and the Bishop, Jack's long, snow-white hair standing out like a beacon. They were on the floor toward the middle. The Reverend and Kitty Ayres were supposed to be in the seats to the right of the presidential box, but they apparently hadn't arrived yet.

"I like these," Luc said, nudging her with his elbow and pointing at the pictures of the Arabian dancers in his program. "Will we see them?"

"I think so, in the second part."

"When will the show start?" He pulled at the collar tight against his throat.

Mouse's leg was bouncing. "Any minute now."

And just as the words left her lips, the third bell rang, sending patrons scurrying for their seats. As the lights dimmed and the curtain started to rise and the first notes rang out from the symphony, she looked back at the seats beside the presidential box and saw a woman in a modest black evening gown take her seat. The opulent jewels at her neck glimmered in the last of the house lights.

Behind her was a face Mouse knew well. It traveled with her like a second shadow. She saw it in her mind when she woke and just before sleep claimed her. She dreamed it during that fitful hour or two of night, all the time her mind would give her body for rest. She called the face to her when she hunted. She toyed with it when her grief threatened to overwhelm her.

She knew the Reverend's face like it was her own. In her mind, she lingered over every gaping pore and blemish and deep wrinkle and scar in that bloated face until, finally, her eyes settled on the cracked lips, shaping the words that had framed her fate and Angelo's—words that would now seal the Reverend's own.

Mouse strained to filter out the music so she could hear his voice. The Reverend's high Southern drawl lay discordant against the sharp, bright trumpets announcing the march of the toy soldiers.

"Are you comfortable, dear?" he asked his wife.

A simple question; a gentleman's question. Jarringly different than those other words Mouse had watched him say at Lake Disappointment, words that ran over and over again in her mind—*Take the girl down. The priest doesn't matter. Kill him.*

Mouse's hand slid around her side, fingering the bone of the Seven Sisters where it rested against her back like a second spine, tucked into her waistband and held tight by her cummerbund. It vibrated with anticipation. The bone wanted this one—this man would make a worthy kill.

But not yet. Mouse forced her hand back onto her shaking thigh. Luc reached over and threaded his fingers between hers, their entwined hands resting on her leg, now stilled. He leaned his head against her arm, and they watched the opening scene of *The Nutcracker* together. Their father, who sat on the other side of Luc, smiled over at them and stifled a yawn.

As the Christmas party played out on stage, Luc lost interest. From the corner of her eye, Mouse could see him watching the people in the audience, studying their expressions as they watched the ballet. She found it unnerving that her father was doing the same thing. She leaned down, about to whisper something to Luc to draw his attention back to the dancing dolls on stage, when she felt someone watching *her*. She looked first at the Reverend and Mrs. Ayres, but they both seemed enraptured by the ballet. Mouse doubted that the Reverend would even recognize her with her short hair and tux.

Her eyes turned down toward the seats on the floor. The Bishop was staring at her, and then his eyes grew wide as they slid to Luc beside her and finally to her father. He leaned over and said something to Jack Gray, who also turned and looked up at them.

With a sudden heaviness, Mouse knew she no longer had any choice about what to do with Jack. She turned her head back toward the stage. She could feel her father's eyes on her. She heard his gentle whisper in her mind: *I'll take care of it for you.*

Onstage, Herr Drosselmeyer conjured his magic, and the Christmas tree against the back wall, center stage, grew taller and brighter as Marie watched, wonderstruck, and the violins reached a crescendo. Luc shifted in his seat, tucking his legs under him to get a better view. He gripped Mouse's hand a little tighter as the music soared higher and louder.

Mouse turned to her father and shook her head. Something passed over his face, but she couldn't tell if it was pride or pleasure. Neither boded well for her soul. She leaned down and kissed Luc on top of the head.

"Look! It's you!" he said quietly, pointing at the stage. The Mouse King had just emerged from the trapdoor amid colored smoke. Luc grinned as he looked up at her. "It's the Mouse *Queen*."

He let go of Mouse's hand and leaned forward as the battle between the Mouse King and the Nutcracker began. He bounced with excitement when it seemed the Mouse King had won, but when Marie rushed forward and hit the Mouse King over the head, Luc sank back in his seat. As the Mouse King fell gracefully back into his soldiers' arms and was carried off, lifeless, Luc pressed his face against Mouse's arm. He didn't move even as the lights brightened for intermission.

"Is the Mouse gone?" he asked. "Forever?"

Mouse had already scooted to the edge of her seat, ready to stand, ready to finish what had to be done. She looked over her shoulder and saw the Reverend and Mrs. Ayres disappearing past the curtain into the shadows behind their seats. The Bishop and Jack were already making their way out to the lower lobby.

"I don't like this show. I want to go," Luc said.

"It's alright. It's just pretend. If you stay, you'll see the Mouse King at the end with all the others. I promise." Mouse pulled free of his arm.

"Where are you going?"

"I need to go to the restroom. I'll be right back."

"You're lying. I hear it. Where are you really going?"

"I'll be here with you, Luc," his father said.

"I don't want you to go," Luc said to Mouse, a note of panic in his voice.

"Let's talk about what you liked and didn't like in the ballet," his father said.

Luc shook his head. "I want to go with Mouse."

"You can't," his father said firmly.

Mouse looked down at the boy. She knew his unnatural senses were telling him that something was wrong, but she had no more time to waste. "Luc, I've got to do something and I'm nervous about it—that's what you're sensing. Okay? You stay here, but I have to go. I'll come back when I can." She pushed past him.

"Tell me what you liked and didn't like about the ballet so far," she heard her father say again as she moved toward the door at the back of their box.

"Leave me alone," Luc muttered as Mouse closed the door behind her.

The coat check was just down the hall. While she waited for the attendant to get her cloak, Mouse worked feverishly to douse her nervous energy and shift her focus from worrying about Luc to the task at hand. She realized that she'd come to rely on the mask Ngara had given her—it was like she could be something else when she wore it.

Tonight, though, she could wear no mask. Tonight, she would just be Mouse—she would *kill* as Mouse. She took her cloak from the clerk and pulled it around her shoulders. She forced her face to settle into an implacable, stony visage of hatred.

She was supposed to meet the Bishop and Jack in the White Lobby behind the presidential box. As she walked beneath the too-bright chandeliers, she scanned the room quickly. Sifting through the patrons, she realized that Jack and the Bishop weren't there. Neither were the Reverend and his wife. Mouse shifted plans in her mind and wove easily between the milling crowd, her unnatural senses on heightened alert. When she reached the top of the main staircase, she saw the Bishop and Jack on the landing below. They were talking to the Reverend and Kitty Ayres.

Everyone was smiling politely, but their hearts were running like horses. Mouse salivated at the adrenaline-saturated air. And then the Reverend looked up.

Mouse had been wrong. He most certainly recognized her.

He pressed back against the balustrade, his eyes darting from her to the crowd to the landing below him, clearly assessing his options as Mouse descended the stairs slowly, not wanting to draw any attention. His eyes flickered back up to her and then to the bone shard gripped in her hand and partially visible beneath her flapping cloak. The Reverend spun away from the others and down the stairs to the lower lobby.

Mouse tensed, ready for pursuit. And then a high voice called out her name.

"Mouse?"

It echoed against the polished marble walls and rolled down the stairs like a tossed ball. She looked up toward the White Lobby. Luc and her father stood at the head of the stairs.

"What are you doing?" Luc asked.

Mouse knew he was reading all of it—her cloak and the bone shard in her hand, the Bishop's fear and Jack's, Kitty's terror, the Reverend's flight. She could imagine the echo of the music still thrumming in Luc's ears, pitched and chaotic. She could feel his panic as he tried to make sense of it all.

"Mouse?" he said again, his voice shivering with confusion and fear.

Mouse felt her stony visage begin to crack, her mind full of a cacophony of choices. She had only a moment to decide, but she didn't know what to do. Her hand squeezed the bone shard, which vibrated with power, eager for release.

She lifted her eyes to Luc's, thinking to ask forgiveness for what she was about to do, but what she saw in his small face undid her. Mouse saw herself as Luc saw her in that moment—a monster, her face full of naked hatred, a mirror of what her father had looked like when he was killing her atop Megiddo.

Luc, who had only ever loved her, was now afraid of her, too.

Her gaze slid over to meet her father's, his eyes twinkling in victory, a contemptuous smile spreading across his face. And Mouse realized that this had been his plan all along—to have Luc watch Mouse murder these people in cold blood.

Shame at her own foolishness washed over her. She had let herself believe that her father simply didn't have the patience to parent well and that was why he wanted her with them. It was convenient for him and easy for her. But he had used Mouse for a far darker purpose. She had taught Luc about being human, about compassion, about love. These were the gifts she had that her father did not—gifts that gave her the power to sway multitudes, where her father could only manipulate the weak-minded, the selfish, and the greedy, one individual at a time.

Now Luc also understood his humanity. He knew how to love. He had the same power Mouse had. And her father finally had what he'd always wanted—a son to match his adversary's, a son who was both human and divine, an ally who could compel armies. A weapon. Mouse had given him all of it.

Her father didn't need her anymore. In fact, Mouse's continued influence over Luc could prove dangerous to her father's goals. But if Luc watched her kill these people—Mouse imagined what it might have been like to watch Father Lucas do something so cruel and violent. She would never have listened to him again. She would have turned her back on everything he had ever taught her. It would be the same with Luc. She would lose him forever, and he would become his father's son.

Mouse would not let that happen.

She lifted her arm to tuck the bone shard back into her cummerbund and realized that it was already glowing a brilliant, icy blue. She didn't know what else to do, so she did what she'd always done. Mouse ran. Down the stairs, not after the Reverend—just away. The bells rang for last call. She edged back a little behind the stairs and started to pull her cloak around her, an easy escape from the turmoil and the crowd now bustling back toward the doors into the theater. But then she smelled something familiar. A scent not quite the same but still recognizable, still unique. Still his.

Linen, a hint of coffee, the sweetness of olive oil.

Mouse let her gaze follow her nose. He was across the room, leaning heavily on a set of forearm crutches that bunched against the sleeves of his tuxedo. His legs seemed thin and slightly twisted under the loose legs of his pants. He was gaunt, his face almost unrecognizable in its hardness. But he was alive.

Angelo was alive.

PART THREE

There is that might-have-been which is the single rock we cling to above the maelstrom of unbearable reality.

—William Faulkner, *Absalom, Absalom!*

CHAPTER FIFTEEN

Angelo hurt. Everywhere.

He punched the snooze button on the hotel clock. Jet lag clung to him like a weighted blanket, but he had something he needed to do. He took a deep breath and filled himself with purpose, driving away the pain and fatigue.

When he'd left the hospital almost seven months ago, he had refused to take the pain medication his doctors prescribed. He'd already spent months in a drug-induced haze, floating in and out of reality as his body healed. He wanted his mind clear now. The drugs had robbed Angelo of his chance to grieve.

Those first weeks in the hospital, waking only for a few minutes at a time, awash in the agony ransacking his body, he would call out for Mouse.

"She's gone, honey," a woman would answer. She was there every time he begged for Mouse, and every time she told him Mouse was dead. He learned the woman's name—Kitty Ayres.

He'd heard the account from Mrs. Ayres so many times now that it only ever came to him with her words, her cadence, her voice in his head. The images in his mind weren't his, either—he'd been unconscious when it happened at Lake Disappointment—but he could see it play out all the same, just as Mrs. Ayres told it, like still shots run through a projector, staccato and disjointed: Mouse dragging Angelo away from the demons and bullets. Her father appearing. His long cloak, black like a drop cloth against the flying salt and sand. Her father grabbing her by one arm, then the other, and pulling until she ripped. Her father flinging the shredded arms to the demons like he was chumming water. Her father lifting her up as she screamed for her life. Her father throwing her out among the ravenous baited beasts. Her father laughing as they devoured her. Her father disappearing once she was gone.

Her father.

By the time Angelo was finally awake long enough for the truth to take hold, Mouse had been gone for months. He tried to breathe a flicker of faith to life that she might have survived this as she had her death at Megiddo, but reviving pieces of dismembered and devoured flesh was beyond imagining, even for Mouse. His acceptance that she was gone offered no healing, just scars, twisted and thick as the ropes of slick flesh that now ran across his torso and back.

The doctors had called his recovery a miracle. There were more than a dozen entrance and exit wounds, but no shots to the head. Nicked arteries and damaged organs, but he hadn't bled out. A severed spinal cord, but he was still breathing and walking. It was impossible, they said. But Angelo knew it wasn't a miracle—it was Mouse. Somehow, she'd saved him but not herself. She'd broken her promise.

And Angelo would never forgive her for it.

The alarm clock cried out again. He didn't have time to wallow in bitterness—Angelo had something he needed to do.

Sighing, he reached down and tugged at one leg and then the other, dragging them off the hotel bed and rolling up to a sitting position. He dropped his head in his hands, letting the searing pains in his back ease to a duller throb before reaching over for his crutches. After a month in the hospital and another three in rehab, he was able to walk again. He was stronger, his arms and shoulders and upper back more muscled than they'd ever been, but his legs would forever be weak, the doctors said. He would always need the help of the crutches. He would always be in pain.

Angelo pulled himself upright and took a couple of stiff steps to the hotel window. He leaned heavily on one crutch, his bicep bulging as it took the weight; he lifted his other hand to yank back the curtains and let in the blinding sun. The uneven rooftops of Amman, Jordan, swept out before him like scattered stones.

Angelo didn't remember what had happened at Lake Disappointment. Those memories had been stolen by the drugs and replaced by Mrs. Ayres's version. But he did remember some of what had happened before. He remembered Jack Gray. He remembered the race across the outback. He remembered who was chasing them. So when the Reverend had come to his hospital room the first time after he was fully awake, Angelo had raged at him—impotently. His voice thin and shaky from weeks of intubation, his body too broken to even free himself from the hospital bed linens, all he could do was send the monitors blaring as his heart raced. The nurses had come running, and then the sedatives had stolen his anger as they had his memory and his grief.

It was Angelo's first lesson: he needed to marshal his anger. In his condition, he could not hope to reap justice on everyone who was responsible for Mouse's death. He needed to pick one.

Angelo had then remembered the dream he'd had at the outstation the day before Jack showed up. Most of it had been the usual nightmare—Mouse's father doing terrible things to people, Angelo feeling helpless. But it had been more real, more like a portent of what might be rather than a fuzzy hodgepodge of worries put together by his subconscious. With a sudden jolt, as if he'd been punched, Angelo had remembered a detail from the dream—his legs wouldn't work. It hadn't made sense at the time, but he realized now that it must have been a prophecy, a vision sent to prepare him.

With the clarity he'd been searching for all his life, Angelo had finally understood his purpose. He'd been saved in the car crash that took his family, saved from his own suicide in the Thames, saved in the burning church at Onstad, saved even as Mouse died in the outback. It was too much coincidence. It was providence. Angelo lived so that he could finish what she could not. He would rip the root of evil and suffering up from the dark depths of the world and watch it wither in the sun and die by his own hand.

On that day, Angelo became a soldier, and his life became solely about the thing he needed to do: take down Mouse's father. Her father, who had been the source of all her suffering, who had killed her at Megiddo, who had destroyed her with a terrible finality at Lake Disappointment. Angelo would take all that suffering and destruction and return it to her father tenfold.

And Kitty Ayres was eager to help. Angelo had thought about reaching out to his former mentor, but Bishop Sebastian belonged to a different Angelo, a different life, a life that had Mouse in it. Kitty Ayres belonged in this barren new landscape with the twisted, broken Angelo. She'd sent her husband away for Angelo's comfort. She let Angelo brood in silence for weeks at the hospital and rehab center. She patiently took the blows of his caustic hate for the Reverend. And she believed in his cause. She fed his faith that he was the result of a God-driven life, that he had been brought to this moment for this singular reason—Angelo was meant to be God's warrior. And she was meant to help him.

Like any good soldier, Angelo refused to get tangled in the ethics of his allies. He had something he needed to do and he couldn't do it alone. He would take Kitty and the Reverend's money. He would take their time, their resources, their help, their blood, their souls—whatever was necessary for him to accomplish his mission.

Angelo turned from the view of the city spilled out below him and headed to the shower. The water splashed against his back, firing all the damaged nerves along the scars. He stiffened with the pain. It drove him upright, straight.

When he'd been released from the private rehab facility in Sydney, Angelo had gone to live in the guesthouse at the Ayreses' expansive Australian estate. They owned homes all over the world. The Reverend was rarely there; Kitty almost always. She begged Angelo to teach her what he knew about the world of angels and demons. He knew nothing about the first but told her what he could about the second—what kinds of creatures he'd seen, what they could do, the spells he'd learned. But when Kitty slipped in questions about Mouse, asking about her age, her limitations, her weaknesses, her powers, Angelo shut down. Mouse was off limits. Mouse was his.

Instead, he had redirected Kitty's energies into looking for anything that might help him when he faced Mouse's father. Together, they'd scoured online library catalogs and searched through personal collections, hunted down bread crumbs dropped in blogs and forums about old books, mysterious books, dangerous books, lost books. When they found something they wanted, Kitty called the Reverend. Their only harvest had been an assortment of binding spells, protection spells Mouse had already taught Angelo, and a couple of summoning spells. But these spells were pointless for the battle Angelo meant to wage. Before he summoned her father, he needed something that could kill him, a weapon that could annihilate an immortal, a weapon which Mouse, in all her years, had never found.

Angelo had begun to think that such a weapon didn't exist—until a week ago, when the Reverend got a call from an antiquities dealer in Amman who'd heard that he was looking for unusual artifacts. He had something he wanted to sell. He said it was very old. He said it came from Israel. He said it was called the Book of the Just.

"We need tickets to Amman. Now," Angelo had said, his spine tingling as Kitty relayed the information.

"Why? Sounds like some dusty old Jewish law book," Kitty had answered.

"If the Book of the Just is what I think it might be, it's the answer we've been searching for."

She looked up at him, a new, fiery curiosity in her eyes.

"There's a book mentioned in Samuel and in Joshua that some call the Book of Jasher," Angelo explained. "But most scholars think that name is wrong, a mistranslation, and that the book is really called the Book of the Upright or the Book of the Just Man." His voice had been singing with hope. "The book has been lost since Old Testament times. There's a version out there, but most scholars believe it to be a forgery. The real book is just a matter of speculation. Some people think it was a book of military tactics or a catalog of battles. Some think it's full of victory songs. But the only actual reference we have to it suggests it could be something much more—a book of spells, ones full of unimaginable power." He'd looked at Kitty, excited. "When the writer in Joshua mentions the Book of the Just, he talks about learning to hold the daylight at bay, keeping it dark so the people could—"

"'And the sun stood still, and the moon stayed, until the people had avenged themselves upon their enemies,'" Kitty had read from her phone. "'Is not this written in the book of Jasher? So the sun stood still in the midst of heaven, and hasted not to go down about a whole day.'" She'd shivered. "A book with that kind of power? What couldn't we do with that?"

Angelo's voice had gone stony. "If this book is real, it's for one thing, Kitty, and one thing only. For me to do what I have to do."

Just a few hours later, Angelo and Kitty had been on the plane to Amman, though Angelo had made it clear he was going by himself to meet with the seller. Kitty understood; Angelo was God's chosen warrior and so went to battle alone, like David against Goliath.

Angelo stepped out of the shower now that the hot water had eroded much of his jet lag. He wiped the fog from the mirror as he leaned against the counter. He no longer looked at his body these days. But his face—his face was a mystery to him. He didn't think he looked like himself anymore. He'd suffered no damage there—Mouse had curled herself around his head, or so Kitty had told him. He just looked *wrong* somehow. Different. He wondered if it was because he never smiled. He tried now, but it made no difference. It was still a stranger looking back.

He shoved away from the counter and grabbed the top of the door-frame, digging his fingers over the edge of the wood and pulling himself up again and again, until his muscles welled with blood and heat. He could feel the strength in his arms and across his back and up his neck even as his thin legs dangled weakly below him.

He was at least half a soldier, and he had something he needed to do.

The antiques store sat next to an ice cream shop on a typical Amman street. But the inside wasn't what Angelo expected. The long, low tables held gold dishes and cups crammed up against old radios and tourist trinkets. None of it had the dusty solemnity of authentic antiquities. As he ducked under guitars and lamps hanging from the ceiling, Angelo felt certain he was either in the wrong place or the victim of a scam.

Navigating the cluttered store with his crutches took time, but finally he made it to the counter in the far back corner. A young boy sat on a stool and stared at him.

"I'm looking for a Mr. Khalid," Angelo said. "He's expecting me."

The boy slid off the stool and came to stand in front of Angelo. He looked him in the eye for several moments, saying nothing, and then walked to a large carpet hanging against the back wall. He motioned for Angelo to follow and pulled back the edge of the carpet to reveal another doorway that led to a shallow, dimly lit hall.

This was more what Angelo had expected—breaking dozens of national and international laws seemed to warrant some level of sub-terfuge. A thrill of anticipation ran through him.

The hall opened to another, smaller room crowded with crates and scattered packing materials. An older man stood near the far wall, speaking to a group of four young people. Angelo judged the oldest to be about twenty; the youngest was just a toddler. Based on their clothing, Angelo guessed they were Bedouins. One of the girls saw Angelo first. She pulled at the older boy's sleeve and lifted her shawl to cover her face. The other girl followed suit, and the toddler whimpered and held his hands out, asking to be picked up.

The older man approached Angelo. "You are Mr. Angelo D'Amato, yes?" His English was excellent. A thick wave of sweet-smelling incense washed over Angelo as the man came near.

Angelo nodded.

"I am Khalid." He reached his hand out to shake Angelo's, then saw the crutches and moved with both hands to Angelo's shoulders, half patting, half hugging. "Come, I have tea and chairs here at the back."

Khalid led the way to a small curtained area at the side of the room where there were several seats on a soft rug crowded around a low table set with tea and dates. Angelo sat down as directed. The other four came and took seats as well. Khalid stood.

"This is our friend who has the artifact your Reverend wishes to procure," he said to Angelo. "Our friend does not want to give his name, but please understand it is because of the danger this might bring to his family that he wishes to remain unknown."

"Please tell him that I have no intention of revealing where or how I obtained the artifact," Angelo said to Khalid. "He and his family are safe. You have my word."

"You may speak to me yourself. I understand English, sir," the young man said. "As do my sisters. My little brother is learning." He smiled at the toddler sitting on the lap of the older girl.

Khalid poured tea and insisted that everyone drink and take a date. "Mr. D'Amato, our friend wanted to meet you because he wishes to know what you plan to do with the artifact."

Angelo hadn't anticipated the question and had no way of answering.

"What Khalid means," the young man said, "is that I need to know that it will not go to museum or university for study. I know the law says—"

"I don't care about the law," Angelo interrupted. "And I have no intention of selling it to anyone else. It's for my use alone." His forehead creased as he studied the young man. "But may I ask why you don't want it to end up in a museum?"

"It was my family's land, you see. My great-grandfather knew about the pots left behind in the Qumran caves."

"You mean the pots that held the Dead Sea scrolls?"

"Yes. But this was before any others knew they were there. My great-grandfather's father had told him, like his father before—they all told the same tale and they all agreed. The pots should be left as they are." He leaned forward, his checkered *smagg* sliding farther down his shoulders. "They weren't for us, you see. But my great-uncles had other thoughts. They knew they could sell the pots for money. Times were hard for the Bedouin then." He looked over at his sisters. "Not as hard as now."

"Your family found the Dead Sea scrolls?" Angelo was surprised at the awe in his voice; he didn't think he cared about such things anymore.

The young man nodded. "Against my great-grandfather's wishes, my great-uncles sold them. All but one."

Angelo set his cup of tea back on the table. "Why the one?"

"It was not in the cave with the others to be sold. It had already been saved."

"What do you mean?"

"The story my family tells comes down the years, passed from old mouths to young ears. It is a story of warning, which is why I give it to you. You understand?"

The toddler babbled, playing with a loose lock of his sister's hair. Angelo felt like he was in a dream. He ran his hand down the back of his neck to stop the prickling nerves. "I understand."

"Many, many years ago, not long after the Essenes left Qumran—you know the Essenes?"

"They lived in the caves. They were like monks, but Jewish, then later some Christian," Angelo answered. "They lived by themselves in a kind of commune. They read and copied a lot of books—which is why we have the Dead Sea scrolls. They were also very interested in the apocalypse."

The young man nodded again. "The caves where they lived were part of my people's land. After they left—no one knows why—one of my ancestors, a girl, wandered into a cave to hide from a storm. She found clay pots. She was a curious girl and so looked inside them and pulled out the scrolls, but she could not read. She put them back and moved on to another pot and then another, looking for something of value. She came to a small stone box at the back of the cave behind the stack of clay pots. She started to open the box, but an angel appeared and told her to stop."

"An angel?" Angelo asked.

"Yes. You believe in angels?"

Angelo sat back in the chair and looked at the faces of the brothers and sisters. Mouse would've been able to tell if they were lying. Angelo had to guess.

"I believe," he said quietly.

"Me, too," Khalid offered as he patted the young man on the back.

"This girl, my ancestor, was afraid," the young man continued. "So she got up to run away, but the angel called her back. He handed her the stone box and told her to take it with her. She was not to open it. She was not to sell it or give it to anyone, not even her own father."

The older brother bent down to the leather bag hanging from his shoulder and untied the flap. "She kept this box as she was told. She never told anyone until she was an old woman and knew she was dying. She gave it to her son. And, later, he gave it to his son."

Angelo leaned forward, thinking the story done and ready to see the book he'd come to buy, but the young man wasn't finished.

"This son was tempted to open the box. On the night he tried, the angel came to him and warned him. He told him that inside was a book called the Book of the Just. He said it was as old as the earth and held much power and that to read the book meant death. The son did not open the box or read the book, and he told this warning to his son when he passed the box to him. Finally, it came to my great-grandfather."

The young man pulled a stone box from his bag and put it on the table. It was smaller than a sheet of paper and stood about three inches tall.

"It's never been opened?" Angelo asked.

Both the young man and Khalid shook their heads.

Angelo reached his hand out to touch the box, but then he sat back, his hand pressed against his lips. "Why are you selling it now?"

It was Khalid who answered. "These children must move. They have no family left. They were driven from their lands in the Negev in Israel. They came here and want to go to the West."

"I want a different life for my sisters and brother," the young man said. "This is why I take your money. But this is not why I have brought you the book."

"Why have you brought me the book?" This time, Angelo couldn't stop his skin prickling in warning.

Khalid looked at the young man and shook his head. "He will think you are crazy. He will not want to buy your book then."

"This man should know before he takes the box, Khalid," the young man argued.

"Know what?" Angelo asked.

"It was meant for you." It was the youngest girl who spoke, her voice high and light. It didn't belong in the back room of a shop in the midst of a black-market sale, or as part of a conversation about ancient books and the end of time.

"What do you mean?" Angelo asked.

"The angel told me." She scooted to the edge of her seat, closer to him.

"You saw an angel, too?" Angelo's heart was pounding in his ears.

"The angel came to her weeks ago, out in Wadi Rum," the girl's brother explained. "It told her to take the box to Amman. It told her to give the box to a man called the Angel loved by God."

The knot in Angelo's throat erupted out of nowhere and flooded his eyes with tears. He saw Mouse in his mind—his Mouse, not the one painted for him by Kitty Ayres's memories. He heard Mouse's voice as she lay nestled beside him, whispering the meaning of his name after she'd heard it for the first time. He'd forgotten what she sounded like, and the memory given back to him was a treasure.

"You are Angel loved by God, yes?" The little girl put her hand on his knee.

Angelo nodded. "I'm sorry," he said gruffly as he pressed his hand against his eyes, trying to stop the tears. Khalid handed him a handkerchief and put his hand gently on Angelo's back. It took several minutes before Angelo was able to speak again.

"What did the angel look like?" he asked, his heart full of an impossible hope.

"He had writing on his skin. He looked like a man, but his face . . ." The girl shuddered and hid her head behind her brother's arm.

Angelo sagged with disappointment, chiding himself for believing it might be possible for Mouse to still be alive, or for some version of her to be working to help him.

"I'm sorry," the young man said. "That's all she would say to us as well. She is young."

"How old?"

"Seven."

"She's special," Angelo said against the knot still stuck in his throat.

"Yes. It is because of her we are alive. She warned us about the raid that killed my parents. They would not leave, but they sent us into hiding." He put his hand on the scarf covering his sister's hair. "It is she who tells us we should leave Jordan. And so we go."

"Where?"

"Germany, first, and then . . ." He lifted his hands and shrugged.

"Well, you'll have plenty of money to help you get settled. It should be enough to care for you and your sisters for the rest of your lives." Angelo pulled his cellphone out of his pocket and dialed a number. He waited just a moment. "We're good to go," he said, then hung up and looked at Khalid. "The Reverend has it all set up. If you check the various accounts you've given us, you should see the transfer of funds."

Khalid got up and went to a computer on a counter covered with packing pellets. He returned after a moment, smiling and nodding. "It is all there, in all the right places."

The young man stood and took the toddler from his sister, swinging him up onto his shoulders. The little boy giggled. His sisters also stood. But as they were leaving, the youngest paused and laid her hand against Angelo's cheek and whispered words he did not understand. Then she followed her siblings out.

Khalid came back as Angelo was pushing himself up onto his crutches. "It was a Bedouin blessing she gave you," Khalid explained. "She says your heart will be restored to you."

Angelo shook his head but said nothing. He was reeling. The sudden undertow of grief pulled him down while the girl's revelation set him spinning.

Khalid put his hand on the stone box. "I will pack this so you can take it through the airport, yes?"

"Sure."

Angelo watched as Khalid carefully placed the box into a foam-lined cutout of a resin replica of the Ancient City of Petra, a typical tourist trinket. Once the stone box was settled inside, Khalid glued the back on the resin statue. The edges fit neatly as if it were one whole piece. No one would suspect from looking at it that inside was an antiquity worth more than five million dollars.

After letting the glue dry for a few more minutes, Khalid put the resin Petra in a small crate that looked like a miniature wooden pallet with open slats. "Most likely they will be happy just to see it without asking to open the crate and examine it," he said as he hammered tiny nails into the back casing, "but even if they do, the glue will hold and they will not find the real treasure inside."

"Thank you," Angelo said as he took the box and slid it into the canvas satchel hanging from his shoulder. He leaned heavily on one crutch and freed his other hand, stretching it out to Khalid. The man took Angelo's hand in both of his own, shaking and then kissing it.

"May your heart be restored to you," he said as Angelo slipped past the hanging carpet and back into the front of the store, then out onto the street.

Angelo walked a few steps toward the corner, where he could catch a cab back to the hotel, but the wave of emotions he'd been holding back surged over his makeshift dam. He turned into a narrow, empty lot and sank to his knees, surrounded by broken concrete and shattered glass. He held his head in his hands, rocking back and forth as he wept until the haunting call to noon prayers rang out over the rooftops of Amman and lifted Angelo from his grief.

CHAPTER SIXTEEN

Kitty was waiting for him in the lobby of the hotel. "Let's see it," she said, her eyes lit up with desire.

Angelo shook his head and kept moving toward the elevator. "It's packed to get through customs."

"Well, what does it look like? Is it a book? A scroll? On parchment or—"

"I haven't seen it yet."

"What?" The smile slid from her face. "You just authorized my husband spending—"

"I saw the outer box. It has an ancient Jewish inscription on it. I met the seller. I know what I bought is authentic." He wasn't about to tell her his faith came from a story about angels from the mouth of a child.

"What *you* bought? I don't think you bought a thing, Angelo," she snapped. "And it sounds like we bought an old box. Let's go check and see if you owe us five million dollars." She pushed the elevator button.

"We will check, and you'll owe me an apology when you see that I'm right about what's in the box, but not here," he said quietly as the elevator doors opened. "We need to get it out of the country first. And then we'll need to go somewhere secluded to open it."

"Why?"

"You never know what might happen when you open a book." It was a lesson he'd learned from Mouse.

Kitty followed him into his hotel room as he started gathering his things. "What do you mean? What might happen?" She sounded both accusing and excited.

"If it's truly a thing of power like I think it is, sometimes other . . . creatures can be drawn to it, or bits of the power can slough off, like dead skin. Things can get out of control. I don't want to take that risk in the middle of a city full of innocent people." Angelo grabbed a rolled-up pair of pajama bottoms and crammed them into his bag. "Do you?"

Her answer was another question. "What's that?"

Angelo turned his head to look where she was pointing. He turned back to his bag quickly, working fast to mask his face. "Nothing. Just an old trinket of mine."

It was a small stone angel, sitting on the table beside the hotel bed. It had once belonged to Mouse, a christening gift from Father Lucas a very long time ago and a token of his faith in her goodness. She had carried it with her for more than seven hundred years, leaving it with Angelo when she'd gone to Megiddo to confront her father.

"It looks very old," Kitty said.

"I've had it a long time," Angelo lied. Mouse had teased him about giving the angel back to her, but Angelo claimed it as a penitent offering for the hell she'd put him through. After Megiddo, the stone figure had been his anchor during the three days Mouse had lain dead in the convent in Haifa. Angelo had cradled it when he wept, and it had given him hope. He had caressed it like a rosary while he prayed over Mouse's pale, cold body. The angel had watched over them both when Mouse, against all odds, took her first resurrected breath.

"Is that blood?" Kitty's hand stretched out, about to touch the chipped wing covered in dark streaks. Angelo wrapped his fingers around the angel and laid it gently among the socks and T-shirts in his bag.

The angel had been with him in his backpack at Lake Disappointment, and, like him, it had miraculously survived. He ran his thumb softly over the delicate stone face. Angelo had pulled the statue out last night, like he did every night, trying to remember Mouse's face, her smell, her touch, her sound—anything that belonged to his own memory of her and not Kitty's implanted vision of Mouse broken and bloody and dead. He'd gone to sleep empty once more.

But today, the little girl had given Mouse's voice back to Angelo. He could hear her again in his mind, saying his name. *Angelo D'Amato. Angel loved by God.*

His back turned to Kitty, he lifted the angel to his lips.

"Well, hurry up," she said. "The pilot's got the plane ready. I know the Reverend will be anxious to see what he's bought."

"Do you always call him the Reverend? Does he call you Mrs. Ayres?"

Angelo swung his bag over his shoulder, leaned against his crutches, and moved to the door, the muscles in his back tight against his shirt.

"Someone needs a nap," Kitty said. "You should sleep on the way to Moscow."

"We're not going back to the house at Australia?" he asked as the elevator doors closed.

"You want secluded. I have just the place."

An hour later, Angelo dropped into one of the deep leather seats on the Reverend's private jet and pulled out his phone. He wanted to let Khalid know that he had made it through customs without a single agent asking to examine the Petra statue. He wanted to thank the man for his kindness and to ask him to call when the kids got settled in Germany.

Kitty stretched out on the couch on the other side of the cabin, watching him. Khalid did not answer the phone.

Angelo dialed again, trying to silence the whisper of foreboding as Amman fell away beneath the ascending plane.

The Reverend met them, in his bathrobe, at the door of what Kitty called the farmhouse. It was a renovated Russian castle.

A television blared from a room to the left of the foyer. The modern sounds clashed against the old stone walls and rich wood bannister that twisted up to the second and then third floors.

"Where is it?" the Reverend asked, greeting neither his wife nor Angelo.

Angelo patted the satchel hanging from his shoulder.

"Bring it in here—the game's on." He led them toward the television, an enormous flatscreen mounted over an even larger fireplace. The wavering glare filled the otherwise dark room. The walls were lined with empty bookshelves.

"Now just a minute, Rev—" Kitty stopped herself and took a step forward, laying a hand on the Reverend's arm. "Kevin, it's been a long trip. Why don't we get a drink and let Angelo tell you what he knows first? And then we'll see about opening it."

The Reverend kept his eyes on the television. "I don't care what he's got to say. I paid for the thing. It's mine."

Angelo lowered himself onto a large settee in the corner near the vacant fireplace. Hours on the plane and then the long car ride had the nerves in his back and legs screaming. His tolerance for pain was reaching a threshold, his vision blurring and his mind a fog of worry about Khalid, who still had not answered his calls.

The Reverend was suddenly yelling at the football game, and Kitty was directing a maid to bring in drinks and something to eat. Demons and angels and ancient books had all felt natural in Mouse's world, but here, against a backdrop of wealth and banality, Angelo felt unsteady; the landscape seemed unreal. He lowered his head into his hands, pressing against his eyes. He needed his head clear for the battle to come.

After a few minutes, he heard the slap of the Reverend's foot against the gap of stone floor between the carpets at the corner of the settee. "It's halftime. Give me what you got, boy."

Angelo looked up at the Reverend, trying to mask his hatred. He knew his best chance was to play a careful game of feigned aloofness. If the Reverend saw how much Angelo wanted to be alone when he opened the book, he'd do anything to make sure it didn't happen.

He pulled the crated Petra statue out of his bag and laid it beside him on the settee. "Here it is."

The Reverend picked up a poker from the fireplace and jammed it against the loose slats, prying.

"Oh, honey, be careful! That thing's priceless!" Kitty said.

"It's never been opened," Angelo said, trying to keep his voice steady. "If it's as old as I think it is, depending on what it's made of, it might disintegrate in the wrong air."

"What do you mean?" the Reverend asked as he popped another slat free and reached in to pull the Petra statue out of what was left of the splintered crate.

"Well, once it's unsealed, if it's made of some kind of parchment, the fresh air might be too hot or too humid or too dry, and the book could just . . . dissolve. All five million dollars' worth."

"It's hidden in the back here?" the Reverend asked, turning his head back to the television.

"Yes. Would you like me to—?"

"No." The Reverend strode across the room to a desk and pulled out a letter opener, digging the point into the seam at the back where Khalid had glued it.

"Oh, for heaven's sake, honey, you're going to tear it up. Let me do it." Kitty took the opener from him and sat down at the desk, more carefully dislodging the back of the statue.

"Khalid did a nice job of hiding it, don't you think? Customs officers barely even gave it a glance," Angelo said. "I tried to call him to thank him, but I couldn't get through. Have you spoken to him?"

"No."

Kitty almost had the back off. "You should tell him what you told me, Angelo, about what might happen when we open it."

The Reverend looked at him, waiting.

"Objects of power, like I think this is, often release a bit of that power when they're opened or disturbed. It can sometimes draw—"

"He thinks something might come, Kevin. Something bad." Her voice was laced with awe.

But the Reverend's face twisted into a disdainful sneer. "That's bullshit, Kitty. He just wants to open it by himself, be the first one to see what there is to see. He's trying to scare you off."

Angelo shrugged, but his heart was jackhammering against his chest as he watched the Reverend snatch the statue, tilting it until the stone box tumbled free into his fat hand.

"That's a little thing for how much I paid. There better be something worth a whole lot inside," he said. He shook the box. A sharp, bright clink sounded and then was eaten by the commentators on the television discussing rushing yardage.

Kitty gasped. Angelo held himself still.

"That sounds like something solid in there. Not paper," the Reverend said, a new gleam in his eye.

"It would likely be a scroll rolled on a wooden dowel. If you open it, it might—"

"I didn't build an empire on being scared of what might be. I can't be so afraid of losing something that I won't take a risk." He wrapped his thick fingers around the top of the stone box.

"But what about the creatures that might come, honey?" Kitty whispered, poised as if she was just as eager for him to open it as she was afraid.

"This thing belongs to me now. I don't care who shows up to take it."

Angelo sat up. He could feel the change in the air before the Reverend even started to pry the top. He'd felt this kind of energy before—with Mouse at the ruins of Podlažice and in the Onstad church with the Devil's Bible.

He started to reach his hand toward the box, but the Reverend tugged and a tiny wisp of air escaped through the broken seal.

The Reverend screamed.

He either would not or could not let go of the box. The lamps around the room crackled and popped with raw energy, and the flatscreen flashed a blinding light. The voices of the commentators exploded into the room as the volume surged.

Angelo snatched the box from the Reverend's frozen grip and the surface of the flatscreen shattered and went dark, the room quiet and still.

Kitty was crying. The maid brought in a candle. The Reverend had fallen back against the couch, his great round belly erupting from his bathrobe, which lay limp on either side of him.

"You okay?" Angelo asked as he touched Kitty's hand.

She jerked it back like she'd been bitten and looked up at him with wide, tear-filled eyes.

"I'm so blessed," she said softly and then started sobbing again.

An hour later, Angelo found the Reverend sitting out on the balcony smoking a cigar. They had put Kitty to bed.

"So, what do you need?" the Reverend asked gruffly, not looking at Angelo.

"A place where I can control the conditions, someplace fairly isolated. I need to work alone. And, assuming I get to open the box and read the book, access to a theological library would be helpful. I'll need to be able to translate and contextualize what I read."

"I know a place."

"Okay." Angelo looked out over the dark expanse, dotted with a few lights from the nearby village. The last of the summer insects were singing. They sounded sad. Maybe it was the touch of fall in the cool air.

"Anything else?" the Reverend asked.

"What happened to Khalid?"

"Heard he had an accident. He's dead."

Angelo could hear the monks still singing as he stepped off the boat on the shore near the Ascension Chapel of Valaam Monastery. Thin clouds drifted over the moon. He tasted rain in the air.

He followed his lamp-holding guide up a pebble path to the main buildings of the Gethsemane *skete*—a tiny complex for monks seeking a deeper isolation than the main monastery offered. Angelo could make out the spiked towers of the small church in the sketchy moonlight, but the low building where Angelo would be staying erupted from the darkness without warning. He stumbled against his guide, his crutches clanking, but he recovered his footing as the man stepped down into a narrow doorway and light tumbled out from the hall inside.

The Reverend's helicopter had dropped Angelo off at the main complex of the Valaam Monastery just hours earlier. He had joined the Vespers service, staying at the back as dozens of black-clad Orthodox monks had led a small procession of locals and pilgrims into the ornate Saviour Transfiguration Chapel. The monks' voices ran in two threads—a rich melody dancing along the *ison*, which droned underneath and anchored the music to its ancient predecessors. Angelo wondered if this had been the soundtrack of Mouse's childhood growing up at Teplá Abbey centuries ago. Though the music drew him in, he held himself apart from the worshippers. The gilded dome decked out with brilliant mosaics of hundreds of saints bore down on him. He sensed judgment in their porcelain eyes.

Khalid's death weighed heavily on Angelo. He wondered what his soul would look like to Mouse now—surely not nearly as bright or as full. He'd forfeited too much of it for this alliance with the Reverend and Kitty. But to stop would mean no vindication for Mouse. Khalid would have died in vain. At least that's what Angelo had told himself when he'd climbed into the helicopter and let Kitty kiss him good-bye on the cheek. He had something he needed to do, he kept reminding himself. He was a soldier on a mission. The words now tasted like empty excuses in his mouth.

Angelo's guide gave him the oil lamp and wordlessly directed him down a hall lined with monastic cells. Angelo's was the last door on the left.

Valaam Monastery provided exactly what he needed to begin his exploration of whatever was waiting for him inside the stone box. Isolated on an island in the middle of Lake Ladoga on the border between Russia and Finland, the monastery saw only a few monks and a handful of locals who worked at the monastery farm. Valaam had also been the recent beneficiary of a wealthy patron and so had undergone sweeping renovations and updates. There was an extensive library and, in addition to the main complex, a dozen smaller churches with tiny communities of monks scattered among the little islands and inlets. Angelo had chosen to stay at the one they called Gethsemane.

He startled as the guide-monk closed the door behind him, shutting out the night and leaving Angelo alone. He had the *skete* to himself. The oil in the lamp swished as he swung his crutch forward. A sense of déjà vu pressed against Angelo as he made his way down the hall to his room. After a few steps, he realized why the place felt familiar—it was like the hall of doors he'd seen in the ruins of Podlažice with Mouse.

A sense of calm chased away his foreboding. This was as it should be. Mouse had come to a place like this to pay penance for causing the deaths of thousands of soldiers—an accident, but dead by her command all the same. She had crafted the Devil's Bible to carry her guilt. Now Angelo would unlock the secrets of the Book of the Just as penance for his part in Khalid's death. Mouse had put a book together; he would take one apart.

With a new assurance, Angelo turned the knob on the door to his cell. The room fit a single cot against the side wall and a desk at the window. There was a picture of Jesus over the bed. On the bed was the rest of Angelo's luggage, including a new satchel, which he unzipped and flipped open to reveal an assortment of tools he would need to examine the book. Everything was at the ready. Almost.

Angelo grabbed a scalpel from the satchel and reached into his carry-on to pull out a bag of salts. He scattered them in a circle around the perimeter of the room and then quartered it with a cross. He pulled the blade across his forearm, let the blood drip at each end of the cross, and said the words of the spell. Just like Mouse taught him. He imagined her voice saying them, and for a precious moment, he felt her near. Then the moment was gone.

He wrapped his arm with the gauze he'd brought and pulled the stone box out of the bag that hung at his hip. He set it on the table in the glow of the lamp, put on a pair of archive gloves, and pried at the corner the Reverend had already loosened. And then he worked on another corner and another. There was no pop or buzz of overrun electricity like before, just the soft sound of rain falling against the window. He wiggled the stone lid gently until it finally slipped free of the lower box with a last hiss of air.

Angelo held the top carefully still against the bottom and waited. He looked out the window. Turned to look behind him. He listened.

But there was nothing. Where was the angel to tell him to stop as it had the girl in the cave and the tempted son, Angelo wondered, a little disappointed. He sat back as a thought came to him for the first time. The spell of protection he cast would keep out creatures of evil intent. What if the angels in the young man's story were really demons, emissaries from Mouse's father and not heavenly ones? It would explain how the supposed angel had known his name. It would also mean that whatever was in the box was most likely a trap.

Angelo stared at the loose lid on the stone box in the glow of the lantern. The rain fell harder. What choice did he have? He held the base of the box in one hand and slowly lifted the lid. His heart beat like a drum in his head.

His eyes narrowed and eyebrows pinched together as he worked to make sense of what he was seeing. The box was filled with ebony ash, but it wasn't like any ash Angelo had seen—blacker than normal, powdery but with a shimmer, and with strange threads of silvery white ash snaking through the dark.

His heart sank as his worst fears lay splayed out in the lamplight. The book—or whatever it was—had been in the box, jostled on horseback or camelback across thousands of miles in the worst heat, stored

God-only-knows-where in a Bedouin tent over hundreds of years. It would be a miracle for such a thing to survive. Angelo had been foolish to hope.

He didn't realize he'd been holding his breath until he let out a little sigh. The tiny burst of air sent the ash nearest him dancing, and underneath he caught the glint of gold. His eyes widened, and he turned to grab a feathered brush from the satchel on his bed. Angelo leaned close and gently pushed the ash to either side of the box as if he were a painstakingly precise street sweeper clearing a road of brilliant gold. Not a particle of ash left the box.

It took hours. His back screaming at him, he finally pulled up, stretching, his eyes blurred and his mind so languid with a need for sleep that he barely registered the soft light of dawn tapping at the window.

Angelo stood, holding the back of the chair for balance, and looked down on the exposed treasure. A rectangle of gold, embossed with symbols and script, some of which seemed familiar, lay framed in the shimmery ash. Two gold rings pierced the short end of the gold leaf and circled back to disappear in the ash. Angelo was sure they promised more gold leaves under the first.

The box didn't hold a lost scroll after all. It was a book of gold plates. A book with writing. A book for him.

He knew he needed sleep or he was likely to make mistakes. He bent forward and picked up the lid and carefully placed it back on top of its base, enclosing the ash and gold. Was this the lost Book of the Just?

CHAPTER SEVENTEEN

In the dark hours of the morning, a day later and after hours of meticulous work clearing the rest of the plates, Angelo laid the gold book down on the desk, free from the ash and stone box for the first time in centuries. He waited once more for an angel to come with a warning. Or a blessing. But there was nothing.

The book shimmered like a Roman breastplate of ages gone. There were six plates altogether. Cautiously, he lifted one and then another, easing them down the golden rings that bound them. Each was covered with raised writing. He thought it was a variation of Hebrew, perhaps an earlier form than what he'd learned at seminary. He could guess at some of the words, but any real work would have to wait until daylight, when he could go to the library at the main complex.

His eyes turned instinctively to the low cot covered in disheveled linens. He hadn't slept well, and his body was begging for another chance, but as soon as his focus shifted from the book, his mind filled again with the dream that had woken him, that had tormented him in the few hours he'd tried to sleep. It had come again and again when he'd let himself drift off, until he'd finally given up and gone back to work on the book.

The dream was like the ones he'd had at the outstation, too vivid, leaving his senses splayed and overrun. He woke wanting Mouse—to sing to him, to calm him, to pull him out of his fear. She had been there, in a way, but not as comfort. Mouse was the thing haunting him in his dream.

He'd seen her—not Kitty's image of Mouse but not a memory of his own, either. She was wearing her father's cloak. Her head was shaved. She was standing over a sleeping man, in the midst of men, and she had the bone from the Seven Sisters. She was wearing the mask Angelo had seen her wear in his dream at the outstation, its wild feathers and crazy patterns making her look like a monster. The bone shard was lit up, eerie blue, like when they'd found it in the cave, only brighter. Angelo even thought he could smell something—cedar, maybe.

The sleeping man woke, grabbing at his chest, panicking as he stared at Mouse, his pupils huge as they drank in the light. Then they turned to icy terror—but only for a moment. Angelo and the dream-Mouse watched the life slide slowly out of the man's eyes. Angelo had never seen a man die before. Mouse was crying. Angelo had woken reaching out for her, the faint scent of cedar still in his nose, his hair damp with tears.

That had been hours ago. His work on the book had driven back his grief, but he could feel it stalking him like a cat. He grabbed his coat, hanging on a hook in the wall, and wandered out into the wee hours of the morning. Angelo left the door open as he walked down the path toward the lake, the bit of scattered light all he needed with the bright, full moon not yet set. He watched the chill breeze play with the water, listened to the gentle slap of it against the shore. The air had turned cold; winter was coming.

Angelo shoved one of his crutches under his arm and bent to pick up a stone. He threw it across the surface of the water. It bounced along a clear path until it sank. He looked out to the far shore where the lights of another *skete* twinkled in the gentle sway of the pine boughs.

Angelo thought he remembered someone telling him it was called Resurrection. Here he was in the dark hours of loneliness in the Garden of Gethsemane facing the light of the risen in Resurrection—did that make the lake Calvary?

He took a step closer to the edge of the shore, the water easing up under his sole. A louder clap against the surface of the lake startled him from his reverie, and he looked up to see a boat emerging from one of the hidden inlets. At first Angelo thought a monk stood at the bow of the boat. But it floated into a wash of moonlight, revealing a white tunic—not Orthodox black—tousled by the wind, and a man with no beard.

Angelo squinted, trying to make out the man's face. He had tattoos inked along his neck. Just like the man in Angelo's dream. Just like the "angel" in the little girl's story.

The boat floated out over the lake, eerily silent, and then stopped dead in the water.

"Who are you?" Angelo called out. The man made the sign of the cross and the benediction.

"I have the Book of the Just." Angelo's voice was thick with the cold and fear. "Why did you want me to have it? I am not a just man."

"Peace be unto you," the man said. His voice was mesmerizing, soft like water easing over river stones but vibrant and haunting, too, like wind whipping through a forest. Angelo stood hypnotized, trembling, until the little boat disappeared behind a copse of trees into another masked inlet.

"Wait!" Angelo cried. "Will you help me?" But there was no answer.

In the wake of silence, Angelo felt very alone. He needed to unburden his guilt about Khalid and his worry that he wouldn't be able to translate the text on the gold book, but most of all, he needed Mouse.

Angelo swallowed at the thick longing in his throat. He turned and made his way slowly back up the path, but he didn't turn in toward the low building where he was staying. Instead he followed the trail, which grew narrower and darker as the old-growth evergreens crowded near, until they opened like a hand to reveal a clearing and a tiny church—the one whose steeple he'd seen on the first night. Angelo climbed the few steps and opened the door to the chapel. The rich smell of polished wood washed over him as the trapped air ran out into the night. He made his way toward the iconostasis at the back of the room. Faint moonlight shone through the windows and slid over the carved wood, lighting up the raised places, the arches and crosses, but deepening the dark in the dips and valleys.

"I'm in the valley," Angelo whispered to the painted saints before the altar. "Help me." He gripped his crutches and eased himself onto his knees, and he prayed. It was the first time since Lake Disappointment.

The clang of bells ringing over his head announced the dawn as Angelo stiffly pushed himself upright. The monk who'd been set to guide and watch over Angelo met him at the stairs of the church, coming down from the bell tower.

"I need to go to the library," Angelo said, his voice still raspy from the cold air. "Can you help me?"

The monk nodded.

"Let me grab some things from my room first, okay?"

The monk nodded again and pointed down the path toward the lake. Angelo understood—he'd be waiting at the boat. Back in his room, Angelo wrapped the gold book in what was left of the gauze and slid it into his bag. The ash-filled box was closed and nestled in the corner of the desk against the wall of his cell.

He started back down the path toward the lake when his phone buzzed—a text from Kitty: ANY CREATURES? ANY NEWS?

He wasn't sure what had visited him on the lake—angel or demon or his own mind giving him something he thought he needed—but a sense of urgency ran through him now. He felt like a clock was ticking somewhere, but counting down to what, he didn't know. His hour of prayer in the church had not quieted that urgency, but it had driven back some of his despair. He felt sure he was on the right track.

Angelo wasn't about to share any of that with Kitty. ON THE WAY TO THE LIBRARY NOW. MORE TOMORROW MAYBE, he texted instead.

The boat rocked violently as Angelo stepped in and took a seat. The monk used a pole to push them away from the shore and toward the tall spires of the Saviour Transfiguration Chapel. The brilliant blue domes seemed to dangle above the trees like pieces of fallen sky.

A handful of monks were in the library. They looked up as Angelo entered. He wondered again at the strings the Reverend must have pulled to get the Orthodox Russians to admit a onetime Roman Catholic priest among them.

Angelo found a Hebrew primer to refresh his sketchy study of the language. He kept the gold book hidden in his bag. He read all day, through Vespers, until his co-habitant at Gethsemane came to tap him on the shoulder. Angelo took some of the books with him. When he got back to his cell, he pulled out the gold plates and the books of Hebrew and worked until his body betrayed him and demanded sleep.

The first snow fell a couple of days later. Kitty texted again. Angelo was no closer to uncovering the secrets of the book. He could read most of the words now, after deciphering ancient forms of the Hebrew letters and recognizing some of their antecedents. It was like undoing a puzzle only to reconfigure the pieces into something different. It took time.

The text of the gold book read like the Psalms—lyrical, so that without context it made no sense. Angelo felt like he understood the emotions conveyed in the beautiful words: the gnawing hunger for something that the writer also feared, a bone-deep weariness of journeying, and the elation of the promise that it would all be over soon. But Angelo didn't know what was being hungered for, or what would be over and why. He felt sure Mouse would have known. He slammed his hands down against the desk, his frustration and disappointment biting at him like ants and a nasty worry beginning to burrow deep into his chest. He was pretty sure that this wasn't the Book of the Just. Or, if it was, it offered no answers about how to defeat Mouse's father. It offered no hope.

This book was clearly old—the language itself marked it as being from long before the time of Christ, and the nature of the book, with the writing embossed on hammered gold plates and bound by rings, surely signaled its authenticity as an ancient artifact. But Angelo could find no evidence that it was the Book of the Just—no catalog of battles or songs of victories that might be spells, nothing about how to still the sun and moon as mentioned in Joshua. The text of the gold book seemed personal, more like a poem of lament—how terrible life was, the wish for an end to it all, the hope of victory of the good over the evil.

It fit with what Angelo knew of other apocalyptic texts, like a lyrical version of Revelations. But it wasn't nearly as specific or detailed. It did mention Sons of Light and Sons of Darkness, which made Angelo wonder if the gold book was really just the origin of another Dead Sea text—the War Scroll, which relayed in great detail a prolonged battle between the Sons of Darkness and the Sons of Light. Maybe one of the apocalypse-obsessed Essenes got frustrated with the vague, metaphoric language in the gold book and decided to fix it—make it concrete, make battle plans.

But none of this speculation helped Angelo understand why the book had been sent to him or what he was supposed to do with it. Where was the secret that would give him the power to make Mouse's father pay for what he'd done?

Without warning, grief ripped through him like shrapnel, stealing his breath and sending him staggering from where he stood at the desk, back onto his cot. He didn't have time to give over to it—he balled his fists in the sheets and lifted his head, trying to breathe, trying to push down the hotness welling in his chest. Frantically, he pulled at his backpack, yanking it open, searching. He tossed out clothes and drove his hand deep into the bag, feeling for it, his anchor—Mouse's stone angel.

It wasn't there.

He scanned the room quickly, though he knew he had not seen the angel since he'd come to Valaam. He lowered himself to the floor, searching under the cot, crawling along the floor of the tiny cell.

The angel was gone.

He buried his head in hands and slid out prostrate on the floor. He'd lost his last piece of Mouse. She was fully and completely gone.

He lay there, for minutes or for hours he couldn't say and didn't care. It was the singing that brought him out of his mourning. His mind, wanting something to make her real again, tricked him into thinking it was Mouse at first, but then the low, uniform bass shattered his dream. It was the monks. They were singing a song she'd sung, an old Bohemian hymn, "Lord Have Mercy on Us."

Angelo opened his eyes. He was looking up at the snow falling outside the window. An eagle owl roosted in a spruce near the rock cliff behind the building, his speckled feathers standing out against the snow, his orange eyes huge and watching Angelo. Angelo reached up to grab the corner of the desk to pull himself up, and his fingers brushed the rings of the gold book precariously perched at the edge. He squinted at the stacked ends of the plates where they fastened to the rings that bound them. There was something odd about them.

He shoved himself up to his knees, his eyes on the same level as the plates, his breath held tight with excitement. Along the top edges of each plate were little gold hills and valleys, too precise to be happenstance. They looked like the tongues and grooves of something that fit together.

A thrill of discovery ran through Angelo as he clutched at the nearby chair, dragging himself onto it. He didn't bother with the archive gloves or the tweezers. He just carefully pulled at the joint where the ends of the gold rings met until they slowly opened, just enough for a plate to slide through.

He freed the plates, one by one, and examined the top edges, which he had initially dismissed as margins, areas left empty where the book was bound. But they weren't empty at all, as he now saw. They were carefully laid out with a neatly fitted system of teeth that paired with another plate. He fitted the tongues and grooves together for each of three pairs. Once all six plates were correctly matched, what he saw astonished him.

The top plates rested with their text side down. He'd never thought to study the undersides of the plates. He'd assumed they were blank. But each of the three plates had a shallow etching visible only from one direction, like a perspective picture. When Angelo looked from either side or from what would be the bottom of the plate, he saw nothing, but from the top, the side where the rings attached, he could see a ragged line that ran across each plate. The end of the line on one plate perfectly matched the beginning on the next. The twists and turns looked like a road or a river. On the third plate, the line twisted back, spilling onto the middle plate once more and then turning back to sink down to the lower corner of the third plate—like something jutting out, perhaps an inlet or a peninsula. Maybe he was looking at a coastline.

The bottom plates were still right side up, filled with the text that Angelo now knew well. But if the top part was hiding something, he needed to look at the bottom plates differently, too. He bent his head down to the table, laying his face flat on the surface so he could see across the plates. The script rose up like tiny gold mountain ranges and sank into gentle valleys. With his naked eye, he couldn't discern any significant difference in the heights of the lettering, but he felt sure it was there. He sat back, thinking.

As an idea came to him, he tugged at the center drawer of the old desk. Equipped for a monk's study and meditation, it held a pad of paper and several pencils. Angelo ripped a piece of paper free and laid it across the bottom three plates. He rubbed the side of the pencil gently against the raised script. But he pressed too hard on his first try and ended up with a smudged copy of the words he already knew well. The second time, he kept his hand light, barely letting the pencil rest against the paper as he brushed it back and forth across the plate. A design emerged from the shades of graphite left behind.

For the first time since Lake Disappointment, Angelo smiled.

It was a map. Some of the letters had been shaped to be a little higher than their neighbors and left a trail of dashes and dots that led to a peak.

Not quite an X to mark the spot, but little stars that erupted from the text, one on each of the three plates. Angelo had discovered a map, a map that led to three somethings. But where—and what?

He took another piece of paper and made a rubbing of the winding road or coast etched into the upper plates. He would see if he could match it against anything. The library at the main monastery complex had Wi-Fi; maybe the internet would help him track down *where* he needed to start looking.

But he still had no clue *what* he was looking for. He scanned the text of the three upturned plates, skimming over the now familiar words. About halfway down the second, he realized that the letters that now butted up against each other made new words—some letters at the far right edge of the first plate joining letters on the far left edge of the second. His eyes jumped to where the second and third plates met, and they, too, had a new set of words.

Angelo wrote them down.

> *I am*
> *Beyond the waters raised by God*
> *In the land of the lost ones,*
> *And deep in the mountain,*
> *Bitter with loss.*
> *The journey is long*
> *But the end is sweet,*
> *And the lion watches over me.*
> *May the breath of God guide you,*
> *And the Book of the Just redeem you.*
> *Peace.*

So it *was* a map. And there were three places to visit—beyond the waters, a mountain or cave, and a third place, some kind of an end. End of the road? End of the search? But what did it mean that "the end is sweet"?

Angelo's phone buzzed with another text from Kitty: IT'S BEEN DAYS. YOU SEEM STUCK. I'M COMING TO HELP. SEE YOU TOMORROW.

The euphoria of his discovery fell away like shed skin. But it was more than panic at knowing he was out of time. When he saw her name lit up on his phone, his mind made another connection. Mouse's angel—Kitty must have taken it.

His face flushed with heat, angry at the arrogance that made her think she was entitled to whatever she wanted, whether it belonged to her or not. But quick on the heels of his anger came confusion and worry.

Why had she taken it? She had wanted to know how old the angel was, but that didn't justify stealing it. What else had she said about it? Angelo's body went slack with realization. "Is that blood?" Kitty had asked. She had zeroed in on the smears of blood on the wing.

The only reason Kitty would want someone's blood was for a spell. Protective spells used the caster's blood, but summoning and binding spells required the blood of the person or thing being summoned and trapped. Kitty already had Angelo on a leash; she didn't need his blood. Obviously, she thought the blood belonged to Mouse. She was right, but Mouse was dead. Who or what did Kitty think she could summon with the blood from the angel?

And again the answer came to him like a punch in the gut. Siblings share the closest biological relationship. His stomach twisted with the truth that seemed more clear as his mind moved through the possibilities. Angelo had assumed no one else knew about Mouse's brother. And yet, they had known about her. Why wouldn't they know about the boy, too? And if Kitty and the Reverend knew there was a brother, Angelo was sure they would do everything in their power to procure him. They had hunted long and hard for Mouse.

Angelo let out a hiss. He'd been so focused on Mouse's father, he'd never given her brother a thought. If Angelo was right about all this, the boy was in danger. But that worry was based on a lot of ifs.

Angelo grabbed the back of the chair and pressed himself upright. He didn't have time to figure everything out now. He needed to be gone before Kitty got here. He turned, hobbling across the small space without his crutches to snatch clothes and cram them into his bag. He packed everything quickly except the book and the box of ash, which he carefully hid in the back of the Petra statue.

The night the Reverend had told him that Khalid was dead, Angelo had started planning. He would not have someone else's blood on his hands. He knew then that he had to find a way to get lost, like he and Mouse had been lost. At her urging, Angelo had kept a fake ID and a credit card hidden in the lining of his bag. Once he was away from Valaam, he would use them to go wherever the map sent him. He would travel like a shadow, untraceable. Just like Mouse had taught him.

He paused at the threshold of his cell, leaning on his crutches, his bag hanging on his back as he looked down the monastery hall. A bittersweet smile played at his lips. Mouse had been on the run, too, when she'd fled Podlažice. He was just following her lead—like always.

CHAPTER EIGHTEEN

The jeep churned and bumped its way up into the highlands from Asmara, Eritrea. Angelo looked out over the coastal plains spilling down to the Red Sea. The Buri Peninsula jutted from the coastline at a sharp angle, the beacon landmark that had brought Angelo here. It looked almost exactly like the etched line from the backs of the gold plates.

He'd been surprised at how quickly he'd found the map's origin of location—just hours after fleeing the Valaam Monastery ahead of Kitty's arrival. Obviously, his search had centered on the Middle East, but that still left an enormous expanse of land with tens of thousands of roads, hundreds of rivers, and dozens of coasts that might match the twisty line on the map. As old as the text was, Angelo had reasoned that if it had been a road laid out on those gold plates, he'd likely never find it—roads changed as easily as people did. His only hope had been that the line represented something more timeless, like a river or a coastline, something that had a hope of still resembling the mapmaker's source.

Limited to what he could search on his phone while being jostled about in the back of a Russian cargo truck on its way from Valaam to St. Petersburg, Angelo had known he needed to narrow the search further. The poem he'd found hiding in the margins of the plates was clearly meant as a guide. He had read over the lines, again and again, until he could see them emblazoned in his mind when he closed his eyes. *I am beyond the waters raised by God in the land of the lost ones.* He had no idea what the first meant—*waters raised by God*—but the last part of the line, a land of lost ones, had pricked at him. A text written in ancient Hebrew and a writer talking about lost ones—maybe it simply meant the lost dead or damned souls, but it could also be a reference to the lost tribes of Israel.

As a seminary student, Angelo had been drawn to anything mysterious or unknown, so he had spent his fair share of hours hunting for the legendary lost tribes of Israel. Most scholars agreed that the ten lost tribes had likely scattered into what was now Syria and Mesopotamia, though some argued that a few had filtered into Africa. In fact, the only modern-day group claiming to be descendants of a lost tribe who had actually been accepted by the Israeli government as constituents under the Law of Return were the Ethiopian Jews. Thousands of them had been allowed to immigrate to Israel. There was even a tiny church in the Ethiopian city of Axum that claimed to have the lost Ark of the Covenant.

Angelo had shifted his search to Ethiopia and branched out from there, which had led him almost instantly to what he was looking for. It was on the southern end of the Red Sea, not quite Ethiopia, but close. A small section of the coastline of Eritrea followed the map line almost perfectly.

Angelo had tossed his phone in the trash at the bus station at St. Petersburg so Kitty and the Reverend couldn't trace it. At Moscow, he'd bought a one-way ticket to Eritrea with his fake ID. He had landed at Asmara four sleepless days after he'd first fled the monastery and had meant to take a day to rest before beginning the hunt for the first mark on the map, but Fate and his body had had other plans.

He had woken the morning after his arrival at Asmara violently sick and so weak he had to crawl from the hotel bed to the bathroom. He had assumed it was a consequence of his hectic travel, but then his fever spiked. The woman who cleaned his room, Abrihet, had brought a doctor, who worried about meningitis. The doctor had drawn blood for a test and left antibiotics. Abrihet had cared for Angelo day and night while they waited for the results. When the word came that it was influenza and a few days in bed should make the mends, Abrihet had gone back to work and sent her teenage son, Birhan, to sit with Angelo.

Once the worst of the illness had passed, Angelo had grown impatient, the clock ticking in his head again. He'd covered his tracks, just like Mouse had taught him, but she had also taught him that eventually the hunter always caught up with the prey. The Reverend had access not only to his own extensive resources but also to the unlimited reach of the Novus Rishi. Questioning the people coming and going from Valaam or utilizing face recognition software to search the footage at the Moscow airport—whatever the means, Angelo knew it was probably only a matter of time before they found him. And, if Kitty was using the blood on Mouse's angel to craft a spell to summon Mouse's little brother, Angelo was also running out of time to decide what to do about it—if anything.

"Mister?" the young driver said to Angelo, pulling him from his thoughts as he watched the coastline disappearing behind trees and clouds. "My mother say something to you before we leave. What did she say?"

"She told me to make you mind your manners," Angelo answered. "And I wish you'd call me Angelo."

"Mister is Mister—*these* are my mother's manners," Birhan said as he tugged on the steering wheel. "And what else did my mother say?"

"Your mother said she wanted you to leave Eritrea," Angelo answered, squinting at the suddenness of the sun climbing over the far mountains.

"As I thought," Birhan sighed. "I must join the army like all boys my age. She tells you this?"

Angelo nodded but looked away. His face, he knew, was full of shame.

It had been Birhan who had returned Angelo's hope that he might yet uncover the map's secrets before Kitty and the Reverend caught up with him. While still bedridden, Angelo had pumped the boy for information, asking about archaeological sites or place names that might have something to do with God and water.

"We are looking for something?" Birhan had asked. And with that first question, despite Angelo's misgivings, the boy had inserted himself into the hunt.

"I am looking for something."

"What is this thing we look for?"

Angelo had opened his mouth to answer and realized he couldn't. He didn't have a clue. "I think I'll know it when I see it," was all he could say.

Birhan had laughed. "We do not know what it looks like? Do we know maybe where it could be? Where to start looking for this thing we do not know?"

Angelo had shown Birhan the rubbing of the map, the book itself still sealed safely in Khalid's Petra statue. Birhan knelt on the floor beside the hotel bed so he could get closer to the pages. "This thing we look for is old or new?"

"Very old. And someplace where maybe there was an old kingdom. Or maybe a community of ancient Jews?" He tried to give pieces of the puzzle without really revealing anything.

Birhan had sat back on his heels, his face puckered in disapproval. "Is Mister looking for the Ark of the Covenant, like Indiana Jones?" he'd asked, his voice dripping with disdain.

Angelo had smiled again. "No, but something like it maybe. Certainly something old like it."

"Well, this place," Birhan pointed to the star on the first plate, "this could be Adi Keyh, a market city, but if Mister is looking for something very old, this is more like to be Qohaito or Toconda."

"What are they?"

"Places where there used to be cities. Very old. There is a dam and ruins and tombs."

"What do you know about the people who lived in those old cities?"

"Not much. I mostly learned modern history in school. Why look back, eh?" Birhan had laughed. "But when doctor says Mister may go, I take you. Yes?"

"No. I'll go alone." Angelo had stopped talking then, unwilling to let anyone else get wrapped up in his trouble. He liked the boy. He had liked Khalid, too.

But when Abrihet had come to clean his room later in the day, she had also come to beg. Birhan was about to come of age and would be conscripted into the army—decades of difficult service and too often a death sentence. Hundreds of boys were fleeing Eritrea illegally, but they, too, faced the dangers of border crossings and human trafficking, only to find themselves, if they were lucky, in a refugee camp. Abrihet wanted Angelo to take Birhan with him, to help him get out of the country.

Angelo had refused, for the same reason he couldn't commit to trying to rescue Mouse's brother. In the deep parts of himself, the truth was coming to light. He didn't mean to live past a confrontation with Mouse's father. It wasn't that he meant to fail; he just meant to die in the killing. He didn't want to live in a world without Mouse.

But after their kindness to him, Angelo wanted to do something to help Abrihet and Birhan. He had asked the boy to be his guide; Angelo would pay well for his service. Then maybe Birhan could use the money to get out of the country, one way or another.

Angelo had told Abrihet this, but he'd said nothing to Birhan. He didn't know what hopes the boy had hung on him. "Your mother said you don't want to join the army?"

"No boys I know want to die at seventeen," Birhan answered as the jeep twisted around a corner and the road opened up to the highlands of Eritrea.

Looking out at the jumbled peaks of the mountains, Angelo felt their great age sink into his soul as if he was being transported back in time. And then Birhan turned on the radio and a tinny blast of music broke the spell.

"Now what do we do?" Birhan asked. The sun was sinking lower against the mountains. They'd arrived at Adi Keyh in the middle of the morning and then trekked out to the ruins at Qohaito.

Angelo hadn't expected them to be so spread out—it really had been an ancient city. And he didn't know what he was looking for. *The breath of God to guide him?* What the hell did that mean?

He felt lost, stumbling over the expansive, stony ground from monument to monument, the heat of the day baking his back. He touched the stone walls, the pillars and their etchings, the flowered cross in the tomb, the paintings in the cave—but he felt and found nothing. No trace of power, no hidden compartments. Just nothing.

They'd finally walked to the north end of the plateau. Angelo's legs were trembling and weak.

"Mister should rest."

Angelo shook his head. "I see some pillars up ahead. Let's try there, and then we'll head back. Looks like there's a storm coming in, anyway."

Birhan looked out beyond the mountains. "No rain. Just clouds."

They walked in silence, wind tearing over the plateau and carrying the intermittent sounds of the goats and cows that belonged to the small, scattered communities of Saho, who called Qohaito home. The last of the sun beamed down as Angelo and Birhan reached the four pillars built on a mound surrounded by a stone wall. Steel rods had been run into the ground around the site, but the wire between them, meant to keep people at a distance, had either broken away or been cut. Angelo made his way slowly toward the ruins.

"What is this place?" he asked.

"A temple I think," Birhan answered.

"But how old?" Angelo meant the question for himself, though Birhan answered this one, too.

"I do not know, but he might." He pointed at an old man herding goats. Birhan called out to him. The old man made his way to the would-be fence and stopped and yelled at them. Angelo didn't need to know Saho to understand the old man was telling them they weren't supposed to be there.

Birhan jogged over to him and put him at ease somehow. Angelo saw the man's face light up. He caught snippets of animated words and watched the old man's withered hands point and flail as they helped tell whatever story he spun.

"It's as I say, a temple," Birhan said when he came back. "Old."

Angelo waited for the rest, but when it was clear it wasn't coming, he looked at Birhan's face. He was waiting to be asked.

"What else did the old man say?"

Birhan smiled and nodded. "He says is very old. Not as old as the cave paintings or the houses underneath." He stomped his foot on the ground and a hollow echo reverberated. "But older than most of the other places."

"What kind of temple?"

"He does not say."

The thick band of clouds had descended on the plateau, crawling like fog from the east and swallowing the sun.

"But he says we should not be here."

Angelo was looking at the pillars—the ones still standing and the broken and fallen ones, too. His hands hovered over the faded etchings. "Did he say if the temple has a name?"

"He says his people have always called it Mariam Wakino."

The mist rolled over them, bringing a touch of coolness in the air, and Angelo shivered. He walked between the remains of the pillars marking the entrance, and the hairs along his arms tickled and rose. The temple itself was gone, but there was no telling what artifacts might be hiding under the rubble. If the object marked on the map was here, it would be years before Angelo uncovered it.

He closed his eyes, his hand resting against one of the pillars. Some of the lettering seemed familiar; the script resembled the primitive Hebrew in the gold book. But it was blended with Ge'ez, the language scholars believed was common during the heyday of Qohaito.

Mariam Wakino. Angelo played with the name of the temple, some-thing worming its way forward from the back of his mind. Mariam was a common name for Christians and Muslims alike in Eritrea. Some thought it meant "beloved." A modern Hebrew interpretation was "rebellious." But Mariam was a modernization of Miriam, an Old Testament Hebrew name, most notably the sister of Moses and Aaron. Among the earliest transla-tions, *miriam* was often associated with water—*strong waters, bitter sea.*

"I may be wrong, Mister. There may be rain," Birhan said.

Angelo looked over the boy's shoulder to flashes of lightning in the steel-gray clouds moving swiftly over the mountains, but his mind was turned inward, putting pieces of a puzzle together.

One of the reasons the Israeli government had accepted the authen-ticity of the Ethiopian Jews was that they traced their lineage from the tribe of Dan, one of the lost tribes. The Danites were the only known Israelite seafarers. Biblical and apocryphal texts spoke of them making their homes in their ships, tethered to shore or out at sea. They loved the water. Once they were displaced with the other ten tribes and lost to history, the best oral traditions traced the tribe of Dan from Egypt down into the kingdom of Kush, in modern-day Sudan, and then farther still into Ethiopia. Pockets of the tribe had seemed to settle as others had moved on. Both modern-day archaeology and DNA testing sup-ported these theories.

What if a splinter group had migrated into Eritrea? Settling in the landlocked mountains, they would surely have longed for the sea once more. If the ruins here at Qohaito were from a Jewish temple built by the fragments of the lost tribe of Dan, might they have named their temple after their hope to return to "strong waters" someday?

If this was an ancient Jewish temple belonging to the Danites, maybe the writer of the gold book had once crouched in the shade of this very spot and etched the star on the map.

Angelo looked up at the highest pillar. "What does *Wakino* mean, Birhan?"

"Is the name of the temple, like Mister."

"*Wakino* doesn't have any other meaning in Tigrinya or Saho?"

Birhan shrugged. "Maybe is old?"

Wakino, Wakin. What if it was a name like Miriam—Joaquin? But old Hebrew, Joachim. *Raised by God.*

His mouth went suddenly dry. *I am beyond the waters raised by God in the land of the lost ones.* Twisted through tongues and the ages, the name meant 'Waters Raised by God.'

But the passage in the poem said "*beyond* the waters." Angelo looked up and out across what was left of the mist-covered plateau. Of course they wouldn't keep treasure in the temple. Temples got raided, especially in a stranger's lands. The Danites would have hidden their valuables somewhere else. Somewhere *beyond.*

He began walking to the plateau's edge.

"Wait, Mister," Birhan said as he followed. "There is no more to see."

"What about down there?" Angelo asked, pointing at a faint footpath descending steeply down the escarpment.

"The shepherds come and go to take their goats down to the river for water in the dry season. Mister cannot climb down there."

"We have to." Angelo's blood was jumping with discovery. "It's down there." He stiffly lowered himself to the ground.

"Stop, Mister, please." Birhan sounded scared.

Angelo eased himself over the edge, his feet dangling just a few inches above the top of the footpath, his thick arms bulging with his weight.

"Angelo, please." It was the first time Birhan had used his name, and it made Angelo stop. "Let me go first. I catch you if you fall." He jumped down to the footpath and turned with his hand outstretched. "Give me your bag. I carry."

Angelo hesitated a moment, but he knew Birhan was right. It would be a miracle if Angelo's legs didn't buckle and send him tumbling down to the river below. Carrying the extra weight of the satchel would make it almost certain to happen. "There are very valuable things in that bag," he said as he handed it over.

"Maybe I should carry Mister, too?"

Angelo shook his head. He didn't think his pride could handle feeling any more helpless than he already did. But he did take Birhan's hand to steady himself as he dropped the rest of the way onto the footpath. As they inched their way down the escarpment, he kept envisioning the goatherd creeping his way along the path—if the old man could do it, so could Angelo.

The heavy clouds seemed to sink down the mountain with them. Angelo's legs were trembling violently, and his arms were burning with the work of moving his crutches and balancing. The path started to level out and then twisted to the right of an outcropping and dropped sharply down again, but there was another, narrower path that led to the left, as if the rock had erupted from the mountain and split the path in two.

"Let's try left," Angelo panted, not sure he could keep going down and certain he would never be able to go back up. As he took a first step onto the path, which was covered with some kind of wiry grass, he knew. "Yes," he whispered. "This is the way."

He had to remind himself to take deep breaths as they moved through the narrow passageway onto a leveled terrace hidden under a shelf of rock that jutted out from the side of the escarpment like an awning. Excitement fluttered in his chest—an obelisk stood at the far end of the terrace. It was not as large as many up on the plateau, but it was carved more elaborately. It looked like a model tower—foundation blocks and then windows chiseled into the stone all the way up to the top, where it rounded into a half-circle, like the sun or moon rising. At the base was a set of carved stone doors, marked with the perfect details of a frame, doorjamb, handle, and even a lock, as if they were meant to allow tiny people to come and go out of the tower. But the doors appeared to be solid rock.

Angelo stepped closer and then circled the obelisk.

"This stone is not like the others, right, Mister?"

Angelo looked up as he heard the awe in the boy's voice. Birhan felt the power of the place, too. "This is different."

After running his hands along the sides of the obelisk, pushing on the doors and pressing against the indentations of the carved windows, Angelo was at a loss as to what to do next. He could see no words on the stone.

A fine mist had started to fall. "We must go soon, Mister," Birhan said. "We cannot go up if the path is very wet."

Angelo glanced up at the sky and nodded. "Can I have my bag?"

He lowered the satchel to the ground, little plumes of dust rising up around it, and reached in to pull out first the Petra statue and then, from its back, the stone box. Angelo hesitated before opening it. He remembered when Mouse had lifted words of a spell from an old text, how those words had to be said as they had been originally scripted in order for the magic to happen. The words themselves didn't really matter. It was the intention, the energy put into them by the writer, that made the spell work.

He wiggled the top off the box, but before he could even lift the gold plates from the ashes, a wisp of wind whipped around the obelisk and lifted a finger of the fine ash up and out of the box. It twisted as it snaked toward the door carved into the obelisk.

Birhan muttered something Angelo didn't understand. Angelo was trying to stay as still as possible, to hold the box steady, to do nothing that might break the flow of air that drove the tendril of ash into the sculpted lock on the door. He thought he heard a click. The ash shot back into the box, the air now completely still. And the doors opened.

His hands shaking, Angelo put the lid back on the stone box and then inched toward the obelisk on his knees, like a penitent come to pray at the altar. Fat raindrops now fell intermittently around him. He could see nothing in the interior of the stone tower, and so he blindly slid his hand through the open doors, groping in the darkness. All was smooth, dusty stone. His mind kept playing images of lurking scorpions or spiders as he pushed his neck and shoulder hard against the monument, stretching his arm inside as far as he could.

Leaning his face against the stone, his lips muttering a silent prayer remembered from seminary, Angelo's fingers brushed against something hard and long and round. He closed his fingers around the thing and dragged it into the light.

Birhan took a step closer and bent down over Angelo's shoulder. "We came all this way for a stick?"

CHAPTER NINETEEN

It certainly looked like a stick, Angelo thought bitterly as he rolled it between his hands back at the hotel in Adi Keyh a couple of hours later.

Birhan had gone to get them supper—Angelo was too tired to move. His arms were weak from carrying most of his weight all day, marks from the crutches deep and red on his forearms. His legs and back spasmed with sharp, hot pain. Even a warm shower had offered little relief. But it was really his spirit that was pulling Angelo down. He'd had to let Birhan carry him most of the way back up the path to the plateau. He'd had to stop several times to rest. He had pushed his body far beyond its limits, and for what?

It was about as long as his forearm and as wide around as a child's wrist, though it tapered slightly from one end to the other. It was knotty but smooth, with gentle hills and valleys running along its length. It was made of wood, but Angelo couldn't tell what kind. It seemed to have been sheared of its bark, but the grain itself was dark with tints of red and gold playing in the light.

With a sigh, he shoved it back in the bag. He could only hope that when they found the next X on the map it gave them some answers. *If they found the next place.* He threw himself back on the bed and picked up his journal, pulling out his rubbing of the map. The next marked star came from the middle panel and rested close to the left-hand edge, just a little higher and a finger's width away from the first. They needed to be looking south, but not far, and a little east, closer to the coast.

And deep in the mountain, bitter with loss, the writer had said. Assuming that the poem was meant as a guide and the lines drafted to move the searcher from one point to the next, Angelo believed he was looking for a cave. He rolled over and pulled a crinkled map of Eritrea out of his bag. He was hunched over it when Birhan came back, carrying a large plate of food.

"The woman in the kitchen, she knows my mother," he said, smiling. "She cooked for us. Smells good." He set the platter down on the bed and knelt beside it.

"Yes, it does," Angelo said as he sat up. He tore at the flatbread and dipped it in one of the stews piled on the plate. In between bites, he asked, "Do you know the mountains southeast of here?"

"Some. Is that where we go to look next?"

Angelo nodded, chewing. "Are there caves?"

Birhan shrugged. "Caves have bad bugs in them. What would I be wanting with them?"

Angelo swallowed at the sudden tightness in his chest and the memory of Mouse saying nearly the same thing, of him teasing her as they explored the cave that took them to the bone shard of the Seven Sisters. He wasn't hungry anymore. He laid his head back against the wall.

"Mister?"

"I'm just tired. But I need to know if there are any caves around here—particularly south and east, like this." He pointed to the rubbing of the map. "The book says we should look deep in the mountains bitter with loss. I don't understand the last part, but I'm pretty sure the first means a cave."

Birhan took another chunk of flatbread to scoop up a heap of stew and shoved it in his mouth as he stood again. "Cave in the bitter mountains. I find someone. Be back like the Flash." He smiled over his shoulder—he'd been trying out English slang and idiom. "Yes?"

"Almost. 'Back in a flash,'" Angelo answered.

"Not superhero?"

"No." Angelo cocked his head. "But now that I think about it, I like yours better."

Birhan shrugged and closed the door.

Angelo took out the piece of wood again. His memory of Mouse and the bone shard had him wondering. The shard had been lost with Mouse. According to Kitty, there'd been nothing left of her, not even her clothes or backpack. Was this piece of wood supposed to be a replacement, sent by whatever had sent the bone? So that he could finish what he and Mouse had started?

He was asleep when Birhan came back, excited. "I know the bitter mountain!"

"The cave?" Angelo asked sleepily.

"Just a mountain. Not a big one. Its name is Maror. Means 'bitter' in my tongue."

Angelo was suddenly very awake. "Maror? Is that what you said?"

Birhan nodded.

"That's also a Hebrew word. It means bitter, too, specifically the bitter herbs Jews eat at Seder. It is a reminder of their suffering as slaves in Egypt."

"I know this," Birhan said disdainfully.

"You know where the mountain is?"

"Yes. Not far."

"But there's no cave?"

"The old men say no caves anywhere around here." Birhan started picking at the cold food left on the plate. "But old men do not know everything. Right, Mister? Would they have known there was a stick hiding in the tower at Qohaito?" He shook his head. "We know better.

We find cave at the bitter mountain." He put the plate on the floor beside the bed and stretched out beside Angelo. "But now we sleep." And he did just that.

Angelo, however, lay awake, excited again, though it was the pain that kept sleep at bay—the searing shots of flame up his legs and the ache of missing Mouse, which seemed to grow at every step he took toward avenging her.

○—✦—○

Angelo sank onto the rock wall outside one of a handful of low, flat houses on the far side of the plateau of Mount Maror. He bent over, stretching his back and rubbing his legs. A camel was slopping water from a trough behind him. Birhan had thought ahead—when one of the old men he'd asked about caves and mountains had offered the use of his camels, he'd accepted.

Angelo's first notice of this new plan had come the next morning when they'd gotten out of the jeep at the foot of the mountain, ten minutes down a well-paved but winding road from Adi Keyh. An old man and three camels were waiting beside a jagged footpath that led up the stony face. Resentful at what he saw as pity, Angelo had let Birhan lift him up to his mount, trying to swallow his bitterness and acknowledge the boy's thoughtfulness. He'd only managed a muffled "Thank you."

But now, a few hours later, he was beyond grateful. He put his arm around Birhan, who sat next to him on the wall. "I couldn't have made it without the camels. I owe you."

Birhan lowered his head and shook it. "No, you owe the old man when we go back down the mountain."

"No, I meant I—"

Birhan laughed. "I got you! I know your saying." He punched Angelo in the shoulder but then said quietly, "You owe nothing. We have seen the wonders of Allah together. We are brothers now. Yes?"

Angelo nodded.

"Now we find more wonders." Birhan turned to speak with a young boy who lived in the tiny village—he'd been the one to see them coming, had run out to meet them and invite them to come drink and water the camels. Angelo felt his hopes sink when the boy began to shake his head at whatever Birhan was asking.

"No caves?" Angelo asked Birhan.

"He says no."

"So that's old men and young telling us there aren't any caves in these mountains. Can you ask him where the mountain got its name? Why is it called 'Bitter'?"

"I bet it was love," Birhan said, chuckling as he turned back to the other boy. "Love makes everyone bitter, yes?" He looked back over his shoulder at Angelo, then asked the boy how the mountain got its name.

The other boy did not laugh. He made the sign of the cross.

"Wait. Is he Catholic?"

"Yes. These are some of the Irob who live among the Saho. Some Christian—Catholic, like you, and others Orthodox—some Muslim, like me."

"Why did he react that way to your question?"

"I do not know. I can—"

The boy started speaking again, holding his hand up, and then he ran into one of the low houses. He came out with an old woman and said something to Birhan.

"She is the grandmother, he says. She tells us about the mountain."

Apparently, her grandson had already told her what they wanted because she started to speak without being asked. Birhan bent close, listening. Angelo watched the old woman tell her story. At times, her eyes grew wide with wonder or fright and other times narrowed in warning or anger. Her hands, knotted with arthritis, held a dark wooden rosary and stayed mostly still except to make the sign of the cross or, at the last, to point toward the northern face of the mountain, shaking her head. When she was done, she kissed her rosary and came first to Birhan and then to Angelo and ran her thumb over their foreheads in blessing, though the look on her face made Angelo wonder if it was meant as a last rite.

"What did—"

"First, Mister, I know where we must go."

Angelo pointed the way the old woman had pointed.

"Yes," Birhan agreed. "And down."

"Great." Angelo was already grimacing, his muscles still tired from yesterday's climb at Qohaito.

"She says she knows we will go anyway, but tells us to stay. She says the mountain is bitter because of the dead people who live in it."

"Dead people?" Angelo asked skeptically.

"Is why this big plateau has only this tiny village. No one else will live here but the Irob. They take turns praying."

"For?"

"The dead that live in the mountain. Otherwise, she says, the dead might go wandering and bother other mountains and other people. The Irob Catholics and the Irob Muslims take turns praying for the dead to have peace."

"Who killed these people?"

Birhan shrugged. "She say the story is lost now, but her grandmother say it was long, long ago. People from there"—he pointed toward the Qohaito plateau—"came here to hide. No one knows now what they hid from or why."

"What about where? Did she say there was a cave?"

"She say no one can answer for the north mountain if there is a cave or not. The Irob forbid their own to go to the north mountain. Bad things happen, she say. When she was a girl, her brother knew not to go but he and his friend went anyway, and God sighed, and the boys fell. She says not to go, but—"

"She knows we will anyway," Angelo finished, staring out across the plateau toward the north.

They sat for a few minutes in silence, then Birhan put his hand on Angelo's back. "Allah calls. Ready, brother?"

They took the camels with them. When they neared the edge, Birhan took a long iron spike and small hammer from a leather pack slung over his camel. He tethered the camels and then came to stand beside Angelo, looking down over the side of the mountain.

"There's no way down," Angelo said. In his mind, he was cursing God—*You broke me and then ask me to do this. What kind of Father are you?* They were his words, but it was Mouse's voice he heard in his head.

Birhan held out a coil of rope. "Our way down." He tied one end to the tether stake and tugged on it to check that it held, and in the next breath, he was over the side of the mountain.

"Wait! We don't even know if we're in the right place!" Angelo called down. The northern face was oddly jointed, as if a cat had been at play with the mountain, its claws shearing away bits and leaving behind jagged shards. Angelo moved closer to the edge, sat down, and rolled over onto his belly so he could peer over, trying to get a glimpse of Birhan. He could see nothing except the rope dancing as the teenager scurried along it. Then there were hands and arms. Angelo reached down and grabbed them, his upper-body strength powering him as he pulled Birhan back up.

"Nowhere there but down, Mister."

Angelo was angry. "Don't do that again. Think about your mother. What if I had to go back and tell her that you—"

"I just go a little bit to see if there is some place to stand or walk, a path not seeable from up here. Is okay."

"It is not okay. If you're going to take risks like that, we're going back to Asmara. I won't have your blood on my hands, too."

"Too? What else blood is on Mister's hands?"

But Angelo wouldn't answer. He wouldn't even look at him.

Birhan scowled. "I know where to go now, anyway." He whipped the rope to the left several feet. "There is a ledge maybe two meters down. You can climb rope?"

"Yes, but I don't want—"

Birhan had already gone over the edge again. Angelo gripped the rope and eased over the edge, too.

Surprisingly, he found climbing down the rope immensely easier than navigating yesterday's steep footpath. He only needed his legs for steadiness against the rock; his arms and shoulders did all the work. He found himself standing beside Birhan on a narrow outcropping that wrapped around one of the shards of mountain jutting out from the base.

Blowing out a sigh, Angelo looked up. He'd left his crutches on the plateau. He couldn't carry them and climb the rope. But his legs could hold his weight for short periods. The crutches offered support when his legs tired—support and balance. Who'd need that on the side of a mountain?

He looked down. A sharp angle and long descent ended at a thin line of river. He looked forward. The outcropping was less than a meter across.

"What can I do?" Birhan was watching Angelo's face.

Angelo shook his head. "Let's just move slowly and see how it goes. I may have to stop and rest a lot."

Birhan turned around and took a few wobbly steps along the rock shelf, Angelo following in his wake. He felt fine until they got to the rocky shard and the path turned sharply to the left. It got narrower as it twisted around the jagged front. Birhan went around the corner and Angelo got a glimpse of his face—sweat shining and his eyes full of fear.

Angelo felt the world tilt as his balance shifted. His body started to sway to the right into open air, but he caught himself and willed his weight toward the rock face, landing heavily against it, panting, and trying to find some handhold in the crevices.

He inched his way around the corner, trying not to think about his quivering legs or his pounding heart. He would not look up or down or out—just a few inches ahead and then a few inches more. He tried not to think about having to come back the same way, with or without a new treasure.

Birhan took him by the arm as he came around to the other side.

"It gets wider here. Better." Birhan's voice was still shaky, but Angelo looked up and saw that he was right—the path stretched out wide enough for two to walk side by side. Birhan offered his arm to Angelo, who took it, leaning on him lightly for balance. His legs were growing tired. He would have to rest soon.

They had gone just a few steps down the path when the wind struck. It whipped at their clothes and tugged at the satchel hanging across Angelo's chest. The gusty wind of the plateau dropped down into the channel between the two narrow slivers of mountain and hammered against them like a torrent, stealing their breath, blinding them with blown grit, and pushing them back little by little to the shard's edge.

Birhan dropped to his knees and pulled Angelo down with him. Though still fierce, the wind softened just a little, lower to the ground. Birhan motioned for Angelo to stretch out on his stomach. They pulled their shirts up over their mouths to filter out the dirt and sand, and they inched their way forward through the tempest.

Finally, Angelo saw it. He clapped Birhan on the shoulder and pointed to a large round stone pressed flat against the mountain face. It looked like it had broken off from the cliff above and landed on the outcropping. To anyone not searching for a cave or a secret, it would look like any other slightly odd rock formation in a land of mountains. To Angelo, it looked like a door.

He tried to stand as he neared the stone, but the wind here was especially fierce. He felt it fill his shirt and threaten to lift him up and away. He remembered the old woman's story—*God sighed and the boys fell.* Angelo lay back down and pushed against the stone, but it wouldn't move. It seemed fitted into place, as if it had always been there, as if it would always be there. He and Birhan could not fight the gusting wind and force the stone away from the mountain. They'd be blown off the ledge.

Angelo had one choice left and it terrified him. In this wind, at this height, if he was wrong, he would lose it all.

He pulled the stone box carefully from his satchel. He found Birhan's eyes for a moment, looking for courage. And then he opened the front edge of the box. Just a little. The wind snatched the ash like a vacuum, all of it lifted into the air and spread on the wind. Angelo felt his stomach flip, sure it was all gone.

The wind gathered the fine ash in a cloud, then rained it down on the stone, where it slithered along the edge like fingers of a hand feeling for purchase. Angelo heard a hiss of air, and then a last, mighty push of wind shot back at him, black and silver with ash, and thrust through the opening of the stone box once more. Everything went still.

Angelo bent to close the stone box, filled again with ash, when Birhan reached forward and squeezed his calf. "Mister," he whispered. "Look."

The stone had rolled to the right. It left a small gap of darkness in its wake—an opening wide enough for a person to crawl through.

Angelo looked back at Birhan, who was grinning.

"Old men do not know everything," the young man said.

Angelo laughed and crawled through the opening. The cave ate his laughter and sent it back to him in a hollow echo, but it was what he could see in the faint light filtering through millennia-old dust in the newly disturbed air that silenced him.

Most of the cave was swallowed in darkness, but along the walls near the door, Angelo could see a cairn, rectangular, about three or four feet long and a couple of feet high. Some of the stacked stone had shifted and fallen, and a skeletal foot lay exposed to the air. Beside the first was another burial cairn.

Then a beam of light blinded him. Birhan had crawled into the cave after him and turned on his flashlight. Angelo reached into his satchel and pulled out his own.

"Peace be upon you, people of this abode." Birhan muttered the Muslim prayer when he saw the cairn. "These are the dead people in the mountain old grandmother tell us about."

Angelo nodded. He ran his beam of light along the wall of the cave, exposing cairn after cairn in a ramshackle line, farther back into the dark. Birhan helped Angelo to his feet, and they made a solemn, slow progression through the dead. Bowls and clay pots and even desiccated woven baskets lay scattered in the open spaces between graves.

"Who are they?"

"Based on what the grandmother said, if the oral history bears any truth, they are the people who once lived at Qohaito," Angelo replied.

"Why come here when *there* is better?"

"There must not have been better for some reason." Angelo shrugged. "Maybe they were invaded? Driven out? And they came to hide here until it was safe to go somewhere else."

"Why die?"

"Maybe they fought a battle before they came and these were the wounded who didn't make it?" Angelo sighed. "I don't know."

But as they moved farther back into the cave, he was noticing something unusual about the cairns.

"They were small people," Birhan said before Angelo could give voice to his own thought.

Angelo let go of Birhan's bracing arm and knelt at a particularly tiny stack of stones. "A child, a baby." He looked around at the cluster of graves. "I think many of these were children."

"Who would kill children?"

"It was probably starvation or disease. The group came here to hide but didn't have enough to eat or drink. Dehydration affects children first. They got sick." His vision blurred as he imagined the horror of being a parent trapped in the cave, hiding from death outside only to find it had crept into the dark with them and was stealing the children. The agony of trying to decide what to do must have torn them apart. The words of the gold-book poet came to him—*Deep in the mountain, bitter with loss.* The author must have been here. He must have watched these children die. Had one of them been his own?

Angelo reached out and picked up a loose stone that had fallen from the infant's cairn. Tenderly, he stacked it again, a prayer on his lips. As his light flickered downward, he saw the words scratched into the cave floor at the base of the grave—a name, this one Anaiah.

Angelo crawled to the next. Lemuel. He reached out for Birhan to help him stand.

"Look at the names. Look for anything that stands out."

"Like what?" Birhan asked.

"I honestly don't know. I just hope we know it when we see it."

"Maybe you should open box again."

Angelo considered the idea and then said, "I don't think so. At the obelisk, it unlocked the door. Here it rolled away the stone. I think it's done what it's supposed to do. The rest is up to us."

It was Birhan who eventually found it, and it wasn't with one of the cairns. A small table of stone jutted out from the wall at the far back of the cave. "I found sticks, Mister," he called out to Angelo, who was replacing more fallen stones at another grave.

The sticks were slightly thicker than the one he'd taken from the obelisk. There were four of them protruding from holes that had been carved in the stone. They looked like the legs of a small table or stool, all of them even so whatever rested on them lay flat. They all looked the same.

Angelo reached into his bag and pulled out the stick from the obelisk.

"Hand me one, please," he said to Birhan, who tugged at one of the four sticks and passed it back to him.

Angelo measured each one against the original. They were all the same length. In the dim light, he couldn't make out whether the grains of wood matched, but they all felt the same. The four were all a little thicker than the first.

"See if they fit together, like puzzle," Birhan suggested.

Angelo tried one end and then the other against the ends of the obelisk rod. He found a match on the third try. The end of the wider stick fit perfectly against the thicker end of the one he'd recovered yesterday—they belonged together. He cocked his head, waiting, half expecting them to magically knit themselves together, craving some clue to their purpose, some sign that he was doing this right. He got nothing.

"We go now. Still have to fight the wind and climb the mountain," Birhan said as he laid a hand on Angelo's shoulder.

"I want to do something first."

Angelo went from cairn to cairn, praying. It was the mourner's kaddish from the Jewish prayer service for the dead—as much of it as Angelo could remember from his studies, anyway. He said it in broken Hebrew twenty-seven times.

"Now they have Jewish prayers and not just Muslim and Christian, they be at peace," Birhan said quietly as they crawled out of the cave.

"Maybe," Angelo said. And the stone rolled closed behind him.

CHAPTER TWENTY

E thiopia?" Angelo asked. "You think it's that far?"

Birhan was on one side of the map spread out on the hotel bed and Angelo on the other.

They'd made it down the mountain just after nightfall. Angelo had paid the old man extra for the use of the camels, grateful for their sure-footedness. Now he and Birhan were trying to figure out where to go next. The last mark on the map was in the far low corner of the third plate—much farther away than the second had been from the first.

Birhan shook his head and took a bite of food. "Not really far. No farther than Asmara from here, but is trouble."

"Because we can't get across the border?"

"There's still fighting—not as much now the war is over, but the law says no one goes from Eritrea to Ethiopia."

"I don't care so much about the law if there's a way to get across."

"There are ways, Mister, but there are rebels on both sides. They like to kidnap people like you for ransom, and they like to make people like me carry guns. There is also army to keep people from going or coming and they are sometimes shooting. I know boys who have died trying to cross."

"Is there a way to get there legally?"

"For you, yes. Go back to Asmara and get visa to go to Sudan and then get visa in Sudan to go to Ethiopia."

"How long will that take?" The clock in his head started ticking louder—Angelo didn't have time to waste on red tape.

"Not so long. A day, maybe two. Eritrea like Sudan, and Ethiopia like Sudan. I know a man in Asmara who can get the paperwork through quickly." Birhan wasn't looking at him. Angelo knew why.

"But you couldn't come."

"They will not give me a visa to leave Eritrea. They want me to fight. They know if I leave, I will not come back."

"Your mother wants you to leave," Angelo said.

"Yes. But the only way out for me is with the smugglers. She cannot make the journey. Is very dangerous. Is only for the young. And many of them die anyway."

"Would you go if she had to stay behind?"

Birhan pressed his lips together, thinking. "She is safe in Asmara. She has good job. She has friends and my uncles and aunts. The military does not want her. I would miss her and hope to bring her with me some day. It will make her sad to have me gone, but I think it will break her heart if I let them teach me to kill. She wants me to go to school."

"What do you want, Birhan?"

"I want to live. I want to not take a life. I want to find this last piece of Allah's puzzle with you."

Angelo's chest burned with unease; it was such a terrible risk, trying to cross the border illegally with Birhan at his side. He thought about the impossible choice the parents in the cave must have had to make, running from the danger they knew, only to be caught by another, unseen. Birhan's mother's choice was also impossible, to send her son away, perhaps to his death, or to lose him forever when the army taught him to kill—or to die. How was Angelo supposed to pick which gamble to make?

"I don't know what to do," he said.

"But I know," Birhan said softly. "If you go here," he pointed to the mark on the map, "I go, too."

"I don't have a choice, Birhan. I have to go."

"Then I choose to go." He took another bite of food. "We are looking for more mountains? Maybe happy one this time?" he asked, his own decision made.

Angelo's decisions were anything but made, though there was no point talking about them anymore. With a sigh, he opened his journal to the guide poem. "The writer says, '*The journey is long, But the end is sweet, And the lion watches over me.*'"

"Long? But this is not long." Birhan pointed at the distance on the map.

"Well, it would've been on foot. And I'm not sure if he means the actual journey or if we're supposed to read it as a metaphor—'journey' as life."

"Ah, so makes 'end' a death, yes?"

"Maybe."

"So much for happy." Birhan clapped his hands to clear away the crumbs.

"He says it's sweet," Angelo offered.

"He must be old, then."

Angelo chuckled. "Any ideas on the lion?"

"We have lions, but they eat you, not watch you."

"He could mean the lion of Judah or a statue or something." Trying to untangle the clue quieted Angelo's other worries.

"We understand it when we need to," Birhan said as he stretched out on the bed. "Like bitter mountain. Now we know why is bitter. Soon we know why end is sweet and why lion only watches."

He was asleep minutes later, though Angelo lay awake long into the night trying to justify the risk he was taking with Birhan's life. He ran from that thought into another. Birhan's life hung in the balance of the decisions Angelo made, and so, too, did Mouse's little brother's. If Angelo did nothing, Kitty and the Reverend might find a way to capture him.

Mouse whispered in his mind: *He's just a boy.*

❋

The sunrise prayers played out from the mosque speakers. Birhan rolled out of bed and went sleepily into the hall to pray.

Angelo, already awake, was sitting on the side of the bed, back hunched, his head bent as he stared at his hands in the murky light. He'd slept very little, just long enough to have a dream, another like those he'd had at the Martu outstation and at Valaam. He could see the Mereb River at the border of Eritrea and Ethiopia. Moonlight lay across the coffee-colored water like icing. Then flashes of light and the rattled pop of gunfire ran like a line of fireflies behind him and in front of him. Birhan scurried out of the shadows, shouting at Angelo to get down, until blood splattered out of his mouth and he arched backward, grabbing at his chest and looking down at the holes in his shirt, blood leaking out. He fell to his knees. Angelo caught him, but he was dead already. On a hill rising up the near bank of the river, Angelo saw the tattooed man, the man who was not a man and whose face, like Angelo's, was haunted with remorse.

Angelo had enough faith left to believe this dream was a warning. He sat for hours listening to Birhan breathe, feeling the weight of the boy's life in his hands. Take him across the border and he died. Leave him behind and the army got him and he died—in body or in spirit.

Angelo needed someone who could help him get Birhan out safely. Mouse had left him a contact who could forge passports and visas, but working that thread would take access to technology he didn't have in Eritrea. His only other option meant taking a terrible risk. But what choice did he have? His hands shook as he punched the numbers on the phone.

"Hello?"

"I need help."

"Well, bless your heart." Kitty sounded like she'd been expecting his call.

He pulled at the tendons on the back of his neck. "Please."

"Where are you?"

"Eritrea."

"Where?"

"Africa."

"Why on earth there?"

"Following a lead from the gold book."

"Have you found anything?" There was a breathless anticipation in Kitty's voice.

"My last hope of finding anything useful is in Ethiopia." The answer was technically accurate, but it hid the rest of the truth from her—another skill Mouse had taught him. "I know I shouldn't have left without telling you. But . . . I don't like your husband. I don't like being bullied. I want to do this on my own."

"Clearly you can't."

Angelo's jaw locked tight. "You're right," he finally said. "I need your help."

"What can I do for you?"

"I need visas to get from Eritrea to Ethiopia, probably by way of Sudan. One for me and one for someone else."

There was a moment of silence, and then, "Someone else?"

"A guide. Someone who knows the area. But it will be tricky getting him out of Eritrea."

Kitty laughed lightly. "Just give me his information. I'm good with tricky."

Angelo had just hung up when Birhan came back into the room, yawning.

"Grab your things," Angelo said. "We need to get to Asmara by noon."

"Asmara? I thought we were headed to the border. Tonight."

"Change of plans."

"What has happened?" the boy asked.

"Nothing. I just decided we're going to fly instead."

Birhan sank onto the bed. "You are leaving me behind."

"No, Birhan. It's just too dangerous to try the border. If you were to—"

"But I cannot get visa." A note of panic threaded through his words.

"There'll be visas waiting on us at the airport, one for me and one for you. I promise. We are brothers, yes?"

Birhan jumped onto the bed and wrapped Angelo in his arms. "How have you done this thing?"

"I called . . . a friend." Angelo pulled away from the boy's embrace and nervously ran his fingers through his hair. He was already counting down the time he had to get ahead of the traps Kitty and the Reverend would inevitably set.

"I am going with you. I am leaving Eritrea. Truly?" Birhan's face was lit with joy. "Thank you for this miracle, brother. Thank you, Angelo."

⚬━━⚬

Birhan blasted his music in the jeep, half dancing and half driving back to Asmara, leaving Angelo to wrestle with doubt. The call to Kitty hadn't just been for Birhan's sake.

The bones of the dead children in the cave had been rattling in his conscience. Images of the suffering they must have endured played on a loop in his head whenever he closed his eyes. His imagination painted faces on their small bodies. They all had delicate features and brown hair. They all had green eyes. In his mind, they were all versions of Mouse—but not her. They were all her little brother.

The truth had been stalking Angelo since his night of prayer in the tiny church at Gethsemane. It had finally sunk its teeth into him last night after his dream and would not let him go. His conviction that he was God's chosen warrior was a lie fed by his bitterness and grief. He hadn't really wanted to be a warrior; he just wanted to die so he could be with Mouse again.

In the dark hours of the morning, Angelo had decided to do something much more difficult. He would live in a world without Mouse. He would live to honor her. She would not have wanted Angelo to kill her father—she'd had that chance at Megiddo, and she had chosen not to fight. Mouse wouldn't want him to fight either. Mouse would want Angelo to save her little brother—it had been her last wish. And so he would. He would be Father Lucas to the boy and raise him to be like Mouse. Armageddon would just have to wait.

Angelo had called Kitty to help him get Birhan out of Eritrea, but he also needed to know if his suspicions were right. Was she planning to use the blood on the stone angel to track Mouse's little brother? Had she done it already? Angelo's best chance of finding answers was through her.

He still needed something to protect him from Mouse's father, something that would get him past the demon minions and back out again with the boy, alive. Angelo had no idea how sticks and gold plates and a box of magic ash were supposed to help. Where was the Book of the Just? Would he be able to find it and hide Birhan before Kitty and the Reverend caught up to him?

When he and Birhan got to the airport at Asmara, a courier was waiting for them with everything they needed—visas, tickets, and a new cellphone for Angelo. It had a text from Kitty. I'VE MISSED YOU. WELCOME BACK.

Before their flight to Khartoum, they had just enough time for Birhan to call his mother and say good-bye, and for Angelo to pick up a map and guidebook to Ethiopia. Birhan was quiet on the plane, watching out the window as his homeland fell away behind him. Angelo thumbed through the travel guide, looking for anything about ancient cities and tombs and lions in the north part of the country. He found two likely candidates—Axum and Yeha. Both had been ancient cities: Yeha was thought to belong to the earlier kingdom of D'mt, and Axum, the eventual capital city of the Axumites. Both cultures were thought to have direct ties to the ruins at Qohaito. Both places also had excavated tombs, and Axum boasted several unusual obelisks, including one inscribed with what some scholars thought might be an early rendering of the Ark of the Covenant.

There was also an Ethiopian church at Axum claiming to have the actual Ark itself cloistered away, where they had watched over it for centuries after the son of Solomon and the Queen of Sheba brought the holy relic out of Jerusalem for safekeeping. With a little less dramatic flair, Yeha offered an ancient temple, thought to belong to a group worshipping a fertility goddess. There was not much known about the site and the people who had lived there. Neither entry mentioned anything about a lion.

Angelo picked up his phone to search the internet. There was another text from Kitty. SEE YOU SOON.

Worrying about her wouldn't help him, so Angelo shook her off and found what he needed with one hit. A travel blog mentioned an odd formation in the hills above the ruins of Yeha, a mountain outcropping that looked just like the head of a lion. There were even pictures. Today people called it the lion of Judah and claimed it guarded the ancient city. No one had excavated the area yet. No one knew if the formation was natural or man-made, but, to Angelo's eyes, the picture looked like a worn-down version of the sphinx, legs stretched out in front of a majestic lion's head elevated high over the surrounding valleys and rolling hills. It looked like a good place to be set to rest—a sweet end.

◦—⟊—◦

Angelo and Birhan ate breakfast in the rental car on the way to Yeha, the sun just easing up from the horizon as they parked at the lot below the path that led up to the temple ruins. They saw no one as they walked past the tombs and the temple and headed for the mountains on the west side of the village. The monument stood out, dark against the violets and pinks of the lightening sky, a clear silhouette of a lion's head, as if a child had drawn it, simple and stark.

"We think to look in the mountain and not the tombs?" Birhan asked.

"We found the other two objects—"

"Sticks."

"Sticks," Angelo conceded. "We found them in the mountains. Makes sense this one would be, too. And if it were in the tombs, at least the ones that have been excavated, someone would've already found it, right? Even if they didn't know what it was."

"Do we know what it is?"

Angelo grunted, "No."

"We think is inside the lion?"

"Or beneath it. Or below it. Or at its base."

"That's a lot of 'or' to be looking at."

"I know. We're going to split up to cover more ground."

As they neared the mountain, Angelo sent Birhan up what was a terribly easy slope compared to their climbs at Qohaito. He wanted him to search all around the lion's head. Angelo searched in the dip at the chest and along the rock jutting out like legs. The terrain was difficult—not as steep as Qohaito, but layered with loose stone that broke away under the weight of his crutches.

Hours into searching, the heat and lack of sleep beginning to sap his energy, Angelo rested against a rounded stone and pulled out his canteen. He could hear Birhan above him sending little avalanches down the lion's face, as if the beast was slavering shards of rock. Angelo could see people wandering around the temple below, tourists who would likely make their way up to see the lion's head soon enough.

The lion watches over me, he said to himself again and again. He looked over his shoulder at the lion's head. "You're not looking at the temple or the tombs, are you? You're not looking at me. What are you watching?"

Angelo turned slowly, following the lion's line of sight. That's when he saw it.

"Birhan!" he called up. "Come down! I think I know where it is."

The lion was staring directly at the rugged mountaintop beside it. It was really part of the same mountain with a section in the middle gone. Eroded or carved away—Angelo didn't know or care. With urgency, he pulled the straps of his crutches up his arms so they dangled loosely from his elbows. He scrambled over the rock in front of him and then slid down the other side, bits of jagged stone ripping his khakis and cutting his hands, his crutches bouncing and clanging as he dragged them with him. But he was sliding too fast toward the deep gap on the other side. At the last moment, he shot his leg out, wedging himself against the next outcropping to keep from falling. Angelo cried out as his hip twisted up against his spine, sending a flare of pain up his leg and back. The gap opened up below Angelo like a waiting mouth.

Birhan was on the lion's leg but made it to Angelo in a couple of running leaps. "I'm here, brother. I've got you." He grabbed him under the arms and pulled him free.

Panting, Angelo laid his head back against the rock, tossing his arm over his eyes to shield them from the sun, which was now high in the sky.

"You wait next time, yes?" Birhan clapped him on the shoulder and tugged him upright. "Where we going?"

"There." Angelo pointed at the rough, rectangular mountaintop in front of them, resting just a little lower than the lion. "That's what he's looking at."

"Ah! Yes, I see. Well, come then. Let us find another stick." He stood and pulled Angelo up with him. Birhan jumped to the bridge rock and reached back to help Angelo over the gap. There was level ground on the other side. And another stone to be rolled away. It, too, seemed to just be part of the mountain, but Angelo knew what to look for now. So did Birhan.

"Time to open the box, yes?"

Angelo nodded, reached into his satchel, and pulled out the stone box. The black and pearly ash rose up on a gentle breeze that had not been there moments before, and just as it had at Maror, it slid fingers around the stone and rolled it back. But this was not a cave; it was a tomb. The opening was cut into the mountain, straight and sure.

Angelo hesitated. A somberness settled on him, a sense of knowing this was a last step, that he was finishing something, and he wasn't sure he wanted it to be over.

"Let us see what Allah has for us this time," Birhan said softly at his side, a tender hand on his back.

Angelo nodded and stepped into the tomb.

The body was at the back of the carved-out space, which ran about twenty feet deep into the mountain. A table had been cut into the wall and the body laid to rest there. The stone at the man's feet was engraved with a name. *Joachim.* Like the opening lines of the poem that had guided them here—*I am beyond the waters raised by God.* It was an introduction. I am Joachim: Raised by God. They had followed him full circle.

"I am sorry to disturb your rest, Joachim," Angelo said quietly. "But I think you called me here." He was certain this was the man who had written the gold book, who had hidden the map and beckoned someone to find the treasure he had left behind. Angelo looked down at the empty eye sockets and the shockingly white teeth and tried to imagine a face. He felt like he knew this man, like he had shared a similar struggle, a life determined not by his own choices but by some unseen hand pointing him toward a destiny whether he wanted to go or not. Joachim had written about loss and anger. Had he also had a mission like Angelo's? Had he failed?

"Angelo," Birhan whispered, pointing to the skeletal hand resting on the side nearest them. "Another stick."

This one was thinner and tapered to a point, finger-wide. Angelo carefully lifted the bony hand and eased the stick free. He passed it to Birhan and then leaned over the body. Something shiny had caught Angelo's eye.

Under the other hand was another gold plate.

Angelo flipped it over, but the back was smooth and empty.

Birhan sighed, his shoulders slumped. "No more map? No new place to look? Just sticks."

"I've got a feeling these aren't just sticks."

After seeing this last piece, Angelo thought he knew what the three sections of wood made once they were all put together, and it was anything but useless or benign. Excitement welled up in him, a boyish anticipation brightening his voice. "Well, they are sticks, but together, I think they make—" His phone buzzed.

It was Kitty. AXUM? HOW INTERESTING! BE THERE BY 4. MEET ME AT THE AIRPORT?

"Shit." He looked at the time on his phone. He texted back—THERE'S A COFFEE SHOP NEAR THE MAIN EXIT.—then grabbed Birhan and steered him out of the tomb as he shoved the gold plate in his bag.

"Wait! Aren't you going to read the plate? Maybe there is new secret poem." Birhan sounded eager for more adventure.

But Angelo was driven by another emotion that silenced all the others—panic.

"We need to get back to the airport," he said, leading the way down the hillside, straining in his hurry and giving no time or breath for Birhan's questions until they got in the car.

"Where we going now?" Birhan asked, panting.

"Cairo." Angelo was already searching for flights on his phone.

Birhan looked over at him, an eyebrow raised. "Indiana Jones also goes to Cairo."

Angelo half-smiled, his tension easing a little as he found a flight that would have them on their way before Kitty landed. "Cairo is just the closest place that gives us what we need."

"What is it we need?"

"Modern resources and someplace big enough to hide while we wait."

"Wait for what?"

But Angelo just shook his head.

Birhan chewed at his lip. "Is someone chasing us?"

Angelo had not said anything about the Reverend or Kitty to Birhan—he wanted to keep the boy as far away from them as possible—so he hesitated now, but Birhan gave himself an answer first.

"Someone else want these sticks and that gold book—yes?"

"That's right."

"Like Indiana Jones." His eyes were wide and excited.

"We need to watch some new movies, Birhan." Angelo had pulled out the stone box and put the new gold plate on top of the others, nestling them all back in the resin Petra statue, but the three sticks were still stacked between his legs. He hadn't figured out what to do with them yet.

Birhan had been watching from the corner of his eye. He reached his hand over and tapped Angelo's forearm crutches. "Tube is hollow, yes?"

Angelo looked up, grinning, and began to dismantle the padded armrests from the metal legs. He worked the largest section of stick in first—it was so thick it barely fit into the tube. He had to twist it down into the opening and tried not to think about any damage he was doing to a potentially millennia-old artifact. The thinner two pieces went in the other crutch easily. "That was brilliant, Birhan!"

The boy smiled smugly. "I also watch James Bond."

CHAPTER TWENTY-ONE

Birhan slept on the plane to Cairo. Angelo did not. He had more decisions to make. They needed to hit the ground running.

Kitty had landed in Ethiopia, and she didn't sound happy to find them gone: NOW EGYPT? I'M TIRED OF PLAYING CAT AND MOUSE. STAY PUT UNTIL I GET THERE.

Angelo had not responded—he had no intention of staying put. He'd been trained to play cat and Mouse by the best, and the first rule was to keep on the move. The second was to plan ahead, but only by a little and with several contingencies. The underlying principle was to avoid predictability.

When they cleared the airport, Angelo steered them through the throng of taxis to a shuttle bus headed for downtown Cairo. He waited through several stops until they were in a commercial area. Several people were getting off.

He nudged Birhan toward the door. "Let's go."

"Hotel near here?" Birhan asked as the bus drove away.

"No hotel yet. We need an electronics store."

Birhan looked around and then pointed. "They tell us where to go."

He headed across the street to a group of teenage boys who were skateboarding on pink granite surrounding a statue. He spoke with them for just a few minutes and then jogged back to Angelo.

"City Star Mall they say. Take taxi they say. Quicker than bus. We want quick, yes?"

"The quicker the better."

Angelo paid cash for the taxi and then for the burner phones at the mall.

"You already have phone. Why you need two more?" Birhan asked as they left the store.

"One is for you actually." Angelo handed it over. It was an older model—another of Mouse's rules: simple things left fewer bread crumbs. "I'm going to text you so you have my number. Don't use the phone to call or text anyone else but me. Okay?"

Birhan nodded, his brow creased but a smile spread across his face. "So people chasing us cannot find us?"

"More James Bond?" Angelo asked as he stepped into a hallway leading back to restrooms and offices and out of the loud squall of shoppers. He pulled out some cash and handed it to the boy. "Will you go grab us some food while I make a call?"

As soon as Birhan left, Angelo punched in the number Mouse had made him memorize. She had made him practice what to say, too. His heart was pounding. He'd never dealt with criminals before. It was surprisingly easy and professional. He gave the code word, then someone asked for the necessary information. He gave them what they needed. They told him where to go and when to be there. It was over in less than five minutes.

Birhan returned with the food. They ate as they walked. Another taxi, lousy traffic, and an hour and a half later, they were sitting in an internet café filled with neon blues and pinks, flashing screens, and a clash of video game soundtracks interrupted by the groans of defeat and yells of triumph from dozens of gamers plugged into their alternate realities. It was a perfect place to commit a crime—surrounded by the protection of a public place in the midst of preoccupied alibis.

Birhan was playing a racing game. Angelo drank coffee and used one of the café's computers to upload a picture of the boy as he'd been instructed. The shot was of Birhan in the airport at Asmara; he'd wanted a last photo of himself in Eritrea. Now there was nothing left to do but wait.

Angelo stared out over the glaring screens, not really seeing them, playing instead with his suspicion about the pieces of wood hiding in the hollow aluminum tubes of his crutches. Smooth and simple, the three pieces were clearly part of a whole. Together they would make a staff or a rod, something about the size of a hiker's walking stick. But why would anyone go to the trouble to separate and hide a simple staff?

An idea had come to Angelo in Joachim's tomb as he'd held the third piece and looked down on the skeleton, which had been wrapped in woven cloth. Faint shades of color, not yet bleached by time, had revealed a striped pattern, broad lines running parallel to a darker central stripe, that draped over Joachim's bony shoulder. An image had flashed through Angelo's mind, a scene from a movie he'd watched with his fellow seminary students years ago—*The Ten Commandments*. They'd laughed and made fun of the movie, mostly for the outdated special effects, but some of the visuals had stayed with Angelo, especially Charlton Heston parting the Red Sea. It was the image of the patterned Hebrew cloth draped over Heston's Moses that made the connection in Angelo's head—the stripes ran over his shoulders and down to outstretched arms and a hand gripping the rod that commanded the water to part so the Israelites could escape the pharaoh's vengeance. The staff of Moses.

Angelo remembered reading something in seminary about the staff, but he couldn't recall the details. He typed a couple of keywords in the search engine and found a digital copy of the book he was looking for.

The staff wasn't Moses's—well, not his alone. It had also belonged to his brother, Aaron, who was a shepherd and had most likely used the staff to nudge wayward sheep. But the staff proved to be much more than a simple tool. By God's command, Aaron used it to threaten Pharaoh during the plagues and turned it into a snake that swallowed up all the other staff-snakes cast by Pharaoh's sorcerers. Moses used it to part the sea and draw water from a rock. Later, the rod miraculously bloomed to settle a dispute among the Israelites—another show of power.

Those were just the conventional biblical stories, but Angelo had never settled for conventional. He'd never admit it to Birhan, but he *had* once daydreamed about being Indiana Jones. As a student, he'd been hooked by the mystery of a magic staff, just like he'd been caught up in trying to find the lost tribes of Israel. Angelo's research had taken him to rabbinical teachings arguing that Moses's staff and Aaron's rod were one and the same. The rabbis believed that the rod was actually made by God in the earliest days of creation and given to Adam as protection against evil when he was exiled from the Garden. The rod had passed from hand to hand by God's blessing—used by Abraham, by Isaac, by Moses and Aaron, by David as he killed Goliath, and by the kings who followed him, until it was placed in the Ark of the Covenant to wait for a Messiah who would use it to annihilate the heathen at the end of days.

It might not be the Book of the Just, but if his hunch was right, Angelo had found the weapon he'd been looking for—a weapon he had no idea how to use. And it was crammed in an aluminum crutch in the middle of one of the largest cities in the world.

"Your coffee, sir."

Angelo looked up, confused. But the waiter set a cappuccino down on the table with one hand and slid a brown envelope into Angelo's lap with the other.

Angelo tipped him and then tapped Birhan on the shoulder.

"Time to find a place to sleep, my friend."

He picked a place at random—not a nice hotel—and paid cash. Birhan got the shower first. Angelo sank onto the bed. He was both terrified and tempted by what he now felt sure rested inside his crutches. He had thought he was beyond awe. Awe and excitement belonged in a world with Mouse in it. But the magnitude of history, the symbolic gravitas of those simple pieces of wood and what they meant to Jews and to Christians and to Muslims, pulled at him. He smiled as he imagined sharing this moment with Mouse.

And, again, Kitty interrupted. MY PLANE LANDS IN FIVE HOURS. GATE 2 IN THE INTERNATIONAL TERMINAL. BE THERE. NO MORE GAMES. I'VE FLAGGED YOUR PASSPORT SO DON'T TRY RUNNING AGAIN.

He texted back, I'LL BE THERE. NOT RUNNING. JUST CHASING DOWN LEADS. I HAVE SOMETHING.

Angelo bent down and pulled the Petra statue from his bag.

"No more hot water. Sorry. You wait, yes?" Birhan's hair was dripping on the soiled carpet. When he saw the gold plates laid out on the bed, he clapped Angelo on the back. "More adventure?"

"Not for you." Angelo put down the pencil he'd used to make a rubbing of the last plate and stacked the gold book back in the box with the ash.

"Why not?" Birhan's voice was already tight with suspicion.

Angelo shoved the brown envelope toward him and waited as Birhan scanned through the documents inside.

"This says I am Brian Lucas. Why am I Brian Lucas?"

"It's a fake passport. It comes with all the other necessary papers to prove that you are indeed Brian Lucas, an Italian citizen."

"So we can hide from the people who are chasing us?"

"Yes."

"Who are you now?" Birhan asked.

Angelo smiled sadly. The prepaid account with Mouse's secret contact only covered one new identity. "These are bad people chasing us, Birhan. They do whatever they want when they want. They have no guilt and no compassion. They take and they kill. They murdered the last person who helped me."

"This is the blood on your hands you talk about at Mount Maror?" Birhan asked.

"Yes. And I don't want the same thing to happen to you. I need you to go somewhere safe."

"That is not your choice to make." Birhan shook his head. "I stay with you."

"I've got you a flight to Rome and then a friend is going to pick you up at the airport and take you a few hours outside of the city to a monastery at Fossanova, where I grew up."

"I stay. My choice."

"I'm going to come to you just as soon as I can," Angelo said, but he could feel the lie in his voice. He didn't know if he'd live long enough to see Birhan again.

Birhan heard it, too. He put his hands on Angelo's shoulders and made him look him in the face. "We run together from these bad people."

"I can't run fast enough," Angelo said.

"I carry you."

Angelo swallowed against the knot in his throat. "Not this time. I need for you to carry something else."

Birhan backed away, his head hanging down as he leaned against the wall behind him. "What?"

"I need you to take the stone box with the ash so when I get away from these people, I can come to you and we can figure out how the sticks and the ash work together."

"What about the gold book?"

"I think we've gotten everything we can from it. It has no more secrets to tell. I'll give it to these people. That should satisfy them, and they'll let me go." It was more hope than expectation.

"What if they don't?"

Angelo didn't answer.

"Is there more poem, more clue?" Birhan pointed at the rubbing.

"There's something, but I haven't read it yet."

"Read it now."

"If I do, will you promise to go to Rome with the box of ashes like I ask? Regardless of what this may say?" There wasn't time to go anywhere else anyway, even if the poem gave them a new clue.

253

Birhan stared at the floor for a minute and then answered. "I will, but you must promise to call me if you find trouble."

"I promise." Angelo put his hand out, but rather than shake, Birhan pulled him into a hug.

Angelo cleared his throat and then turned to the rubbing of the last plate he'd just made. "'Be unto you,'" he read, his voice still heavy with emotion. "Ah, that goes with the 'Peace' at the end of the earlier poem. 'Peace be unto you,'" he said. "'Soldier of sorrow, Soul of my soul, Behold your treasure.'"

Birhan leaned forward.

"'A hardened heart hungry for justice, dead to the world, mighty in righteousness. Be it so with you as it was with me.'" Angelo paused, the weight of the bitter words sinking into him. "'May the Book of the Just protect you. May your heart be restored to you. From ashes have we come, to ashes we must go. Amen.'" Angelo bent to lay the paper back on the bed, but stopped short and snatched his hand back.

The stone box, sitting on the bed near the pillows, was shaking.

"Go, Birhan. Get out!" Angelo said, but Birhan didn't move.

The tremors grew stronger, shaking the whole bed. The gold plates were now sliding out between the lip of the stone top and the edge of the box's bottom. Something was lifting them up—something growing inside the box.

Angelo looked at his crutches, also lying on the bed; they, too, appeared to be shaking. In a flash, he imagined the ash, called to life by the poem, resurrecting Aaron's rod, and unleashing its power or a swarm of demons, like the ones from the church at Onstad. He lurched toward the bed, grabbing the box and clamping his fingers around the sides, trying desperately to close the lid, to contain the ash, but the box shook so violently that the lid pressed against his fingers, grating stone against stone, and then, a heartbeat later, it went still.

Everything was quiet in the room for a moment, and then Birhan let out a gasp of air. "What—"

"I don't know." Angelo kept his hands gripped around the box. All but two of the plates had fallen out onto the bed. "It feels heavier than it should."

"Something is in there?" Birhan's eyes grew wide.

Angelo nodded. "Why don't you go out—"

"No."

"It might be—"

"Open it." Birhan stepped close to the bed.

Angelo knew he had no choice. He held the bottom in one hand and lifted the top. The two remaining plates clinked out against the others on the bed. Their heads almost touching, Birhan and Angelo bent over the box.

"Is another book," the boy said as he sat down beside Angelo.

Angelo tried to swallow, but his mouth was dry. The black ash with silvery swirls was gone. In its place was a small, tattered book about the size of Angelo's hand. He had the sense that the book was very old, older than any book he had ever seen, including the Devil's Bible. There was faint, silvery writing across the front, but it did not look like any language Angelo knew. He could not read it.

"What is it?"

"I think it's . . . the Book of the Just," Angelo answered. He was shaking. He reached out with his finger and touched the book's cover, half expecting it to disintegrate into ash again. It felt almost like leather, but softer. Several times he started to slide his fingers around the spine and pull the book out of the box, but he couldn't make himself do it. He remembered Mouse talking about a book with impossible-to-read writing that she'd discovered when she was at the abbey. An ancient book, one she'd called the Book of the Angels, a book that had released a swarm of malevolent spiders to attack her.

Angelo snatched his hand back. The power rolling off the book felt much like the Devil's Bible had when Mouse opened it in the church in Norway. He was scared. This book. Aaron's rod. These things belonged to Mouse's world, not his. A world of gods and angels and demons and immortals.

"Are you going to read it?" Birhan was whispering.

Angelo whispered back, "No." If the poem made the Book of the Just whole, the book might make Aaron's rod whole, and even if he couldn't

255

read a word of it, he knew well enough that an object with that kind of power could make itself understood. All Angelo might need to do is lay his eyes on the words to set in motion . . . what?

Until he knew the answer, he had no intention of even opening the book. But time had run out for asking questions.

"We need to go. Your flight to Rome leaves in a couple of hours." And Kitty's was arriving not long after.

"What are you going to do with that?" Birhan pointed to the black book in the box.

The Book of the Just changed everything. Angelo had meant to send the ashes with Birhan to Rome, keep the pieces of the rod hidden in his crutches, and hand the gold book over to Kitty in the hopes it would satisfy her questions about what he'd been doing and regain her trust so he could find out if she was indeed hunting Mouse's little brother. Angelo's stomach churned at the thought of sending the power-laced book with Birhan, but his fear of what might happen if Kitty and the Reverend discovered the book and rod together overran everything else.

"You have to take it," he said as he finally closed his hand around the spine and pulled the book out of the box. He looked up at Birhan. "Are you okay with that?"

"I will keep it safe."

"You understand how dangerous it is?"

"Yes. I can feel it." He was whispering again.

"You must not open it. No one can open it."

"We must hide it."

Angelo nodded, then shoved his hand in his backpack and pulled out his journal. He tore out a thick stack of pages from the center and inserted the ancient black book. The elastic strap that held the journal closed snapped back in place. From the outside, it looked like a plain journal. He held it out to Birhan, who took it with trembling hands and slid it into his own bag among rolled socks and snack wrappers.

"You look terrible," Kitty said as her high heels clicked to a stop in front of Angelo's table at the coffee shop near the airport exit. He'd just sat down, his coffee still hot, after seeing Birhan off on his first leg to Rome.

"I was very ill in Eritrea," Angelo answered as he half stood and pulled out a chair for her. "It's partially why I was out of contact for so long."

"Partially?"

Angelo took a sip of coffee. "Can I get you something?"

"I need sleep. You've had me on quite the chase these last few days. But you were saying?"

"In deciphering the text of the gold book at Valaam, I realized we were missing a plate—at least one. I thought I had enough clues to know where to start looking."

"Africa?"

"Eritrea, yes."

"Why not tell us?"

"I wanted to find it on my own. This is my quest, my calling, not yours or the Reverend's." He was using reasoning he knew she would understand.

"We just want to help you. I think we all have the same goal."

"Do we? I'm not sure anymore. Not after what happened to Khalid." Mouse had taught him that a hard truth masked a million lies.

Kitty sat back in her chair. "I thought that might be the problem. I told the Reverend he shouldn't have—"

"I'm not comfortable with killing."

Kitty barked out a laugh. "What do you think you're going to do when you come face-to-face with your sworn enemy?"

"Khalid wasn't my enemy. Or yours."

"How do you know? He was a man interested in money, and he had information on the Reverend that would be worth a great deal to many of the Reverend's enemies. How do you think it would look if the Reverend were caught buying illegal artifacts on the black market?"

"You don't kill someone because they *might* be a threat."

"Yes, you do. If you want to win. And it's all for the greater good—to make the world a safe and wholesome place again." She smiled at him. "But no matter. What's done is done, right?"

Angelo just looked at her.

"You ran off because you were mad and you wanted to find the thing on your own," she said. "And then you got sick and then you got stuck, which is when you called me. Have I got it?"

"Yes."

"So you couldn't find it on your own, after all."

"No."

"Speaking of which, where is your friend—the one I had to help?"

"Thank you for that. You probably saved his life." Angelo swallowed the bite of irony to keep his voice sincere. "He's gone on somewhere to join family, I think."

"I had hoped to meet him. Oh, well." She yawned. "So where is this thing you found, and why didn't you wait for me in Ethiopia?"

"I needed a good library to translate the new text," Angelo lied. "And the closest one was here in Cairo. I knew if I took the next flight out, I could get here and do the research I needed before you even landed so we could get back to the Reverend more quickly. I thought you'd want that."

"I do. We actually have tickets to the Bolshoi *Nutcracker* day after tomorrow. For you, too, if you'll come."

"Sure," Angelo stammered, trying to understand the sudden shift in conversation. He'd forgotten it was almost Christmas.

"The Reverend will be pleased." She pulled her phone out, texting. "Now tell me what you found."

"It's the last plate of the book."

"The Book of the Just?"

"If it is, it doesn't have what we were hoping for."

"No spells of victory?"

"Not that I've found. But I've only just translated it. I need to be able to read it in context with the others. My first impression is that this last plate just completes the story—one we're familiar with in Revelation and the War Scroll—but I am convinced that this is the prototype, the earliest draft of those others."

"Why?"

"Two reasons—it's lyrical, like poetry, whereas other apocalyptic texts are more like battle plans or play-by-plays."

"If I'm going to war, I'd rather have the battle plan than a poem."

"Sure, but it's like reading the details of the Battle of the Bulge without understanding the context of World War Two. We need story to do that, to really capture what's at stake, what sacrifices are required and why. To understand what we're fighting for."

"We're fighting to win."

"It's not that easy, Kitty. What if the battle is over a single child—your side wants to save it and the other wants to kill it. Say you win the battle because you know how to wage war, you're good at it, but then you find out after it's all over that the child is dead at the epicenter of your victory. Did you win?"

Kitty narrowed her eyes at him. "I don't understand your gibberish. If my side takes the field, we win. It's that simple." She put her phone down on the table. "You said there were two reasons you thought this one came first?"

"You won't like the other reason."

"I probably won't care. What I want to know is if there's something in that book to help us do what we want to do."

"Bring about the end of the world?"

"Wipe it all away and start with a clean slate. Like Noah's flood. Then we can rebuild it as it was meant to be."

"That's why you won't like what the end of the book says. It's about forgiveness, especially about the writer forgiving himself for wanting vengeance. It's about not looking at each other to judge, but working to love regardless of what we've done or what's been done to us. It's—"

"It sounds like someone who lost his nerve and is trying to justify his weakness." Her phone lit up with a text. "Is that what's happening to you, Angelo? Have you lost your nerve?"

"No."

"Can this book help us or not?"

"I'll need to double check my translation," Angelo replied, "but there's a passage that suggests that the bearer of the book is protected from evil." It was true, though of course the book in reference was the one Angelo had sent with Birhan—the real Book of the Just. The gold book was just a man's story and a now useless map.

Kitty's eyes lit up for real, and the smile spreading across her face was genuine and joyful. "Well done, Angelo." She reached her hand across the table and stroked his cheek. "Now let's get you back home, where we can get you healthy and strong again. The pilot just texted that the plane is refueled and waiting on us."

Once they'd taken off, Kitty curled up on the couch and slept. Angelo stared out at the stars. He could see the Pleiades in the sky just beyond the wing's tip. He thought of them now as Mouse's Pleiades and imagined another bright spot in their midst, another sister gained.

The tears came without warning. They weren't sad or angry. They were a quiet good-bye, a final acceptance that nothing he did would bring Mouse back. He could not avenge her. He could only live to honor her—saving brothers and raising brothers. Mouse had all her long life refused to be a warrior. She lived to love. He would, too.

Angelo pulled at the collar of his tux. The tie was cutting into his throat. The discordant sounds of the symphony warming up rolled out from the auditorium into the lobby of the Bolshoi Theatre. He didn't want to be here. Kitty had insisted. Which put him on edge. Why did it matter to her if he came to the ballet with them or not?

Everything had felt wrong since they'd landed at Moscow the day before yesterday. The Reverend had been waiting for them when they drove up the chalky lane to the farm house out in the empty Russian countryside. A deep blanket of snow had stretched out between soft hills and glittered in the moonlight.

"Good flight?" he'd asked.

"Slept like a baby," Kitty had answered as she leaned into his massive belly, reaching up to kiss his cheek.

"Nice to have you home, Angelo."

"Reverend."

Angelo had spent the night feeding lies to the Reverend's questions about where he'd been, what he'd been doing, who had helped him, what they knew. Like Kitty, the Reverend's enthusiasm had peaked when Angelo mentioned that the bearer of the book was protected from evil. He'd demanded that Angelo hand over the gold plates.

"I still need to read the last against the others so I can see if there's a spell like Kitty wants." Angelo had counted on buying some time with pretending to do more research—time he needed to figure out what Kitty was up to with the stone angel, what she knew about Mouse's brother, and what his own next move should be.

"You've had your chance. Maybe it'll reveal its secrets to someone else," the Reverend had said as he stretched his hand out, waiting.

Angelo had no options. He had pulled the Petra statue out of his bag and laid it on the chair beside him. The Reverend had walked across the room to take it.

"Wait," Angelo had said as he peeled the backing away and tipped out the stone box, empty now of ash but still holding the gold plates. "I want to keep the Petra statue, if that's okay?" He knew it was sentimental, but for him, the cheap tourist trinket was as meaningful as the ancient text. He might work to forgive himself for his part in Khalid's death, but he would not let himself forget.

"You didn't get much for your trouble or travel, did you, son?"

Angelo had lowered his head. He didn't think he could hide the slight grin at knowing that the Reverend was the one walking away empty-handed. Angelo was the one who had cleared the table. He had Aaron's rod and the Book of the Just. And, perhaps more importantly, he had his soul back, too.

But he didn't know how long he'd have his life. Kitty and the Reverend had left him alone the next day; their absence rang like a siren in Angelo's chest. They had everything they needed from him—or at least they thought they did—which made him, like Khalid, a dangerous loose thread. The real question was why they were still leaving him hanging.

And why they wanted him at the ballet. The second bell rang, signaling the end of intermission, and many of the people in the corridor headed back to their seats. Angelo hung back, meaning to wait until the show started again and then slip out to catch a taxi and go back out to the farm—alone. He'd search the house for the angel and any sign of what Kitty had been up to, and then he'd leave before they got home. He'd disappear. He had some cash left, but he'd need real money to pay Mouse's friend to put together a new identity. He knew of only one other source for getting that kind of money.

With a sigh, he pulled out the burner phone and punched in a number he hadn't called in over two years. He had no idea what he would say to Bishop Sebastian. According to Kitty, his old mentor thought him dead, and Angelo had consented to leave it that way. How would he explain that to a man who had likely grieved for him?

But now Angelo could see no other way. He pushed the call button.

Leaning his weight onto his crutches, he brought the phone to his ear and cleared his throat. The bright, brassy bark of Frank Sinatra's "Come Fly with Me" rang out somewhere in the lobby, grating against the sounds of the orchestra and the shuffling feet of the patrons. Angelo lifted his head, searching the crowd, his phone dangling from his hand. The dusty brush drums and muted slide of trumpets filtered through the emptying foyer. It seemed to be coming from above.

His chest tightened as if all the air had been squeezed out. It couldn't be coincidence—that song had always been the ringtone for Bishop Sebastian's phone. Angelo took a step toward the stairs leading to the upper lobby. "Let's fly away," it beckoned and then was gone.

PART FOUR

The mystery in how little we know of other people is no greater than the mystery of how much.

—Eudora Welty, *The Optimist's Daughter*

CHAPTER TWENTY-TWO

Angelo was alive. It was all Mouse could think in the moment. He was impossibly, incredibly, miraculously alive.

The Bishop's phone was blaring from the landing above, and Mouse watched as Angelo took a step toward the stairs, but suddenly the Reverend was there, clapping his arm around Angelo and steering him away, back down a hall. Instinctively, Mouse took a couple of hurried steps out from behind the stairs to follow, but she was shaking and had to lay her hand against the balustrade to steady herself. Shock ran through her like a live current—*Angelo is alive.* She closed her eyes, trying to calm herself so she could run to him, so she could touch him and make herself believe it was real.

But she couldn't stop shaking, and the bone shard still radiated an electric blue glow.

An odd, delicate pinging filled the air. Mouse looked up and saw the chandelier trembling, all the crystal teardrops tinkling against each other. The flowers in the vase against the wall quivered and bounced. She felt the floor under her boots start to shiver.

"What is this?" she heard someone in the crowd say, a note of panic rising in his voice. "Is it an earthquake?"

Mouse knew better. It was her—her power building off the sudden, euphoric joy and leaking out around her. She couldn't stop it. She could feel it surging. She had to get out of here. The walls or the ceiling would start to shake and crumble next. Or, fueled by her power, the shard would start claiming victims. Casting a last, frantic look down the hall where Angelo had disappeared, she wrapped her cloak around her and was gone.

It was no surprise when she sucked in the arid heat of the Australian desert once more and stared out over the dark expanse of Lake Disappointment. She hadn't been thinking about where to go, but Mouse supposed this place would always be an event horizon for her, the place where everything had changed, where the black hole of despair had eaten all the goodness in her life. But it was joy that dropped her to her knees now and bent her down and pulled the tears from her eyes. Joy that set her power ricocheting out into a hundred shallow fissures along the surface of the dry lake.

She rolled over onto her back in the white salt-sand and stared up at the countless stars and laughed. She gave thanks. She played the image of him in his tux over and over again until the shock and wonder started to wane.

But even as she sat up and sheathed the now quiet bone shard, eager to return to the theater, the questions came. Angelo was with the Reverend. Why? Another question eroded the first with a terrible force: How? How was he alive?

And why had he not tried to find her? Maybe he thought she was dead—just as she had been sure he was. The joy came flooding back as she imagined his face when she showed up and surprised him. Her laugh ran like strings of light along the fissures and into the dark outback.

She pushed herself to her knees and took the edge of her cloak, ready to bring Angelo the joy he'd just given her. All the long days they would spend together spilled out in Mouse's mind. But as she glanced down on the place where she had watched Angelo's bright, beautiful soul start to leave his body, where she herself had died knowing she would live again, the question bloomed once more. *How* had Angelo survived?

And the word she spoke that day with the last of her breath echoed again out over the lake. "Father." But why would her father save Angelo? And why not tell her? Was he just using the two of them as pieces in some game? Her temper rising, Mouse snatched the cloak up around her.

The chalet at Innsbruck was dark—her father and Luc must have stayed for the second act of *The Nutcracker*. She sat in the den. The lights on the Christmas tree cast a magical glow over the room. They'd left the Christmas music playing. The "Bogoroditse Devo" from Rachmaninov's Vespers rolled like a river through the house.

Mouse waited.

Luc threw himself into her arms an hour later. "You broke your promise—you didn't come back for the rest of the show."

Mouse hugged him close. "I couldn't. Something happened and I needed to leave."

"Was it the people on the stairs I saw you with? You seemed really mad at them."

"They aren't nice people, and I was mad at them. Too mad. I needed to go somewhere."

"Where you could count things until you were better?" Luc looked up at her, his eyes full of understanding.

"That's right." She tucked a bit of hair behind his ear. "And I came home after because I thought you'd be here to help me. I didn't think our father would want you to be at the theater with those people you saw me with." She turned to look at her father.

"He was safe with me. And anyway, your friends all left after your little reunion." He tossed his cloak on the couch. "It was Luc who insisted on staying. He wanted to make sure the Mouse King was okay."

"And he was!" Luc exclaimed. "Just like you said. He came out and bowed. I clapped for him." His mouth stretched in a big yawn.

Mouse smiled. "Let's get you to bed. It's Christmas tomorrow." She pulled him up into her arms and carried him up the stairs. At the landing, she turned back to her father. "Don't go anywhere. I have questions for you."

"Ooh, what do you need to ask Father?" Luc said.

The high, clear sounds of a boys' choir rang out from the speakers. They were singing "Silent Night."

"Never you mind," Mouse said softly. "It might be about presents."

"We get to open them tomorrow, right?"

"First thing in the morning, if you want." Mouse hoped to give herself a present, too. She hoped to get the answers she needed from her father, and then go bring Angelo home.

All is calm, all is bright, the angelic voices sang up the stairs.

"Yes, please." Luc laid his head down on her shoulder. "I'm glad the Mouse King came back. I'm glad you came back."

"Me, too." She lowered him to his bed. *Sleep in heavenly peace.* A pair of pajamas covered in pictures of puppies with candy canes in their mouths lay folded at the end of the bed. "Get changed and I'll come back and read you a story. Okay?"

"Can Mercy sleep with me tonight? It's Christmas." He'd crawled over to kneel in front of the dog's crate. She was licking his hand through the bars.

"Sure. I'll be back in just a minute."

"I love you, Mouse."

She paused at the threshold. "I love you, too, Luc."

Her father was stretched out in the recliner when she got back downstairs. *Shepherds quake at the sight.*

"Why?" she asked. She'd had an hour to wrestle with the chaos of emotions slamming into each other—joy, rage, wonder, fear—and knowing that Luc was in the house, she worked to tamp them all down, safely under her control.

"Which why?" her father asked, tucking his arm under his head.

"Why did you save Angelo?" She stood by the Christmas tree, watching the lights blink and change colors—red, green, blue, white. Luc had picked them out.

"Wasn't it what you wanted when you called for me that day?"

Heavenly hosts sing Alleluia.

"Yes. But I asked *why* you did it. Surely you didn't do it just for me?"

He sighed. She looked at him. "I can't tell you because I don't know. I saw him lying there, your hands covering his mouth and trying so desperately to hold the life inside him." He shrugged. "I just did it."

Mouse had all her senses tuned for a lie, but he was telling the truth. "Then why not tell me when I woke?" Her heartbreak at the grief she'd suffered cracked her voice despite her efforts.

Silent night. Holy night.

"That's easier. I didn't want you to go after him. I wanted you to stay with me and Luc."

"You let me suffer. You let me—"

The music swelled, the children's voices singing *Love's pure light* and the descant hovering above the melody like a wavering star. Tears were running down Mouse's face.

"You let me lose myself, let everything I ever wanted to be get burned to ash in the fire of my vengeance. You let me kill. You let me—"

"I did none of those things, Mouse. You did them. They were your choices."

"But I wouldn't have done any of it if I knew that Angelo still lived."

"Does that matter?"

Mouse sank back against the wall. She despised him, but he wasn't wrong; it was her fault. She'd masked herself in sorrow and revenge and used it as an excuse to turn her back on everything she knew to be good and true. It was easier than mercy.

"Don't beat yourself up about it too much, kid. It's only human. You all have lofty ideals that you wrap in pretty words—love and forgiveness and compassion." The choir had come back to repeat the first verse, and he joined in, his voice as high and clear as theirs as they sang *All is calm, all is bright* for a last time. Mouse wondered at the beauty in his voice, truly the sound of angels.

He stopped abruptly, the choir moving on without him. "But you don't act on those pretty words, do you? You act out of anger or desire—everything comes back to what *you* want, what *you* deserve, what's *yours*. You know why? Because there's no such thing as love. It's a lie told by my old master to—wait for it—*get what he wants.*"

"Mouse?" Luc called down from his room.

"Be just a minute, Luc." She turned back to her father. "I don't think you believe any of that. I've seen your face when you watch him." She pointed upstairs. "You may not know it, but that warm burning that fills your chest and crawls up your throat and stings your eyes is love."

Her father slammed down the footrest on the recliner, then stood up. "You don't know what you're talking about. Creatures far older and with infinite knowledge tried to make me believe in love. They failed. Because I saw the truth—every day, in every person whose worthiness I judged, whose goodness I was sent to test. They failed—every one." He stood, stiff-legged, angry. "I wanted to love like you do. I wanted them to love me. But they didn't. And I couldn't." His shoulders sagged. "I can't."

"Yes, you can." She took a step toward him.

He backed away. "You'll learn, too. And here's your first lesson. The man you think loves you so much, your Angelo, whom you think to be full of compassion, has been working with the man who hunted you down and killed you. He's been living with the fat slob and his plastic wife ever since. He's been gathering up old books—ones that might have spells in them to come after me or you or Luc."

Mouse shook her head. "He thinks I'm dead."

"Does he? Why would he? He saw you after I had my way with you at Megiddo—you can't get much more dead than that. He watched your resurrection with his own eyes. And you think he really believes you were killed with bullets?"

"Maybe he—" But the worming doubt she'd been shoving back under the dirt all night erupted and slithered into her head.

"You know I'm right," her father said. "It's why you waited here for me instead of rushing off to find the beloved I returned to you. You don't trust him—and for good reason."

"Good King Wenceslas" droned out from the speakers now, still in the voices of a children's choir.

"Mouse." Luc sounded impatient. Mercy was whining.

Her father kept talking. "But there's more at stake than just your feelings." He sneered. "He's woken the Book of the Just."

"What?" Mouse asked, her body suddenly taut with alarm. She knew all about the Book of the Just. She and Father Lucas had spent hours talking about it—tempted by the power it would give her to protect herself from her father, to maybe even defeat him. A thousand times during her seven hundred years of running, Mouse had thought about looking for the book. But she remembered Father Lucas's warnings. The Book of the Just, woken and used, would mean the end of humanity.

"Why does Angelo have it?"

"Why else? To use it for its final purpose. To wipe out all the evil in the world—which means wiping out everything. And everyone."

"How do you know he has it?"

"I can feel it." He shrugged. "It used to be mine, you know."

"What?"

But her father didn't get a chance to answer. The shrill, panicked scream of a child rang out over the Christmas music.

Mouse took off running, her father following behind, but she fell in the hall outside Luc's room. Her legs wouldn't work, her body felt too heavy to move. She reached forward, digging her fingers against the hardwood floor, dragging herself through the doorway trying to get to Luc. Her father jumped over her, but he stopped short at the bed, looking down on his son.

Mouse could see Luc writhing on the bed, Mercy whimpering and turning in circles beside him. It was then she felt the pain. She saw the skin on her hands and wrists, boiling and bubbling, flakes of it peeling and lifting into the air. The breath in her lungs was hot, too, and just before her vision was blinded with heat, she saw her father wrap his cloak around himself and disappear.

The last thing Mouse knew before the darkness took her was Luc screaming and the lines of the carol echoing through the house—

Sire, the night is darker now
And the wind blows stronger
Fails my heart, I know not how,
I can go no longer.

○━✦━○

They rode in silence from Moscow to the farm. Angelo watched the Reverend and Kitty, trying to see them as Mouse would, searching for some sign of their intentions, looking for a weakness. His general impression was that they were both inordinately pleased about something.

The Reverend maintained a smug smile as he scrolled through his phone, though there were moments when Angelo caught a cloud pass over the rotund face. At one point, the Reverend slid his massive body forward to look out the windshield at the stretch of empty road ahead, but then he settled back with his phone once more. Kitty was literally trembling with what her eyes suggested was pure joy, like a child anticipating a much-longed-for present. Angelo didn't take their happiness as a good sign.

And he didn't understand what had happened at the ballet—why Bishop Sebastian and Jack Gray had been there, why the Reverend and Kitty were bringing them all back to the house. None of it made sense.

He could feel the Bishop's eyes on him the whole ride, but Angelo would not look at him. When Kitty had brought the Bishop and Jack to the car where the Reverend and Angelo were waiting, he'd caught his mentor's eye for just a moment. The look had been full of accusation and betrayal. Angelo didn't have time to deal with that now.

Jack Gray just looked out the window at the passing countryside.

When the car crunched and spat the gravel of the drive as they pulled up in front of the castle, Kitty finally spoke. "Sorry we had to miss the second act." One of the bodyguards came around to open the door of the car. "But I have plenty of sweets for everyone here. You won't miss any of that sugary decadence that rewards dear Clara for killing the Mouse King."

Angelo caught the Bishop's quick turn of the head at Kitty's words. His face, lit by the gas lamps in the courtyard, creased with some dark expression Angelo couldn't understand. He assumed that the Bishop and Jack were involved in the Reverend's plan, that it was somehow part of the Novus Rishi's mandate to prepare for a battle of Armageddon—a battle they meant to win at any cost. But the Bishop's demeanor suggested that maybe something had changed.

Kitty led the men into the spacious den. The curtains were pulled back, framing a wonderland of evergreens and falling snow. She turned on a lamp near the bar against the far wall. "I'll have one of the girls bring in some goodies for you. Make yourselves at home."

The Reverend lingered in the foyer, speaking to one of his bodyguards, then came and dropped into a deep leather chair near the fire. He kept his eyes on the window. Kitty sat down on the arm of the chair, leaning close to the Reverend, her breast brushing his cheek. She whispered to him, but not so low that Angelo couldn't hear: "Stop worrying. It won't take long now." She bounced back up. "I'll leave you men to talk business. Merry Christmas!" And she disappeared through the foyer down the hall to the kitchen.

Angelo heard muffled speaking, and then a door closed. Moments later, a woman came in carrying a tray of cakes and cookies.

"Would anyone like coffee?" she asked, her English thick with a Russian accent.

"What I want is over here." Jack walked to the bar. Angelo wandered over to the window.

The Reverend had pulled out his phone again.

The Bishop slipped up behind Angelo near the window. "I thought you were dead."

Angelo had been distracted watching Kitty Ayres shuffle down a path freshly covered with snow toward a low outbuilding just visible at the edge of light cast from the house.

"I'm sorry." He didn't know what else to say.

"Why?" the Bishop asked, his voice heavy with hurt.

"I didn't know who to trust."

"You truly believe I could have had anything to do with what happened in Australia?"

Angelo shrugged. "It doesn't matter now."

"It does, very much. You need to—"

"What I need is a cup of that coffee. Excuse me." Angelo turned on his heel and headed toward the kitchen. He'd seen a light come on in the outbuilding. What was Kitty doing out there? And what did it have to do with the Reverend's nervousness?

Angelo gave the maids in the kitchen a small nod and stepped out the door onto the side patio. It was full of bodyguards.

"Where are you going?" one of them barked at Angelo.

"Mrs. Ayres asked me to come down and help her." He pointed in the direction of the outbuilding, though it wasn't visible at this angle.

The bodyguard looked down at Angelo's crutches, then nodded and turned back to the other men.

Angelo pivoted around the corner of the house and took a diagonal path across the huge back lawn toward the tree line. He was careful to stay in the shadows outside the house lights. He didn't want to be seen by anyone who might be watching at the den window. He stepped through the high drifts piled against the tree trunks into the cover of the woods and made his way toward the outbuilding.

There were no windows, only one door. The building looked as old as the renovated manor. Thick stone walls ran up to meet a slate roof. Angelo circled the building slowly, but he couldn't hear anything inside. He pushed his crutches onto the path where Kitty's footprints were filling up with new snow, and he nudged open the door.

A single, large room spilled out in front of him, twenty feet wide and at least twice as long. Most of it looked old—short walls made of weathered stone divided one side into what must have once been stalls. Huge, dark beams of wood, hand-hewn and uneven, crisscrossed the roof. But the floor was smooth concrete, and modern lighting illumi-nated the space.

Kitty glanced up from a long metal table at the back of the room. She had a vial of something in one hand and held a spoon against the side of a ceramic bowl with the other. The table was scattered with bottles and herbs. In the center, a sack of salt lay on its side, a handful of crys-tals trailing in a line from its open mouth and glistening in the light.

"Working on a spell?" Angelo asked.

Kitty's face had gone from the shock of unexpected discovery to a feverish thrill. "Yes."

"Need any help?"

"I think I can do this one myself. I've been practicing."

She gestured at something hidden from Angelo's view by the table. He shuffled over to the side where he saw a trapdoor propped open by an iron bar. Angelo caught a glimpse of some paintings on the wall of the room below, but his eyes were drawn to something on the floor beside the door. A four-foot-wide dark circle, quartered by a cross, marked the smooth concrete and glistened in the light. Freshly crafted, still wet—Kitty's spell.

"A binding spell?" he asked.

"Yes." She squeezed tiny drops out of the vial. They fell silently against the ceramic sides of the bowl.

"You did well. It looks finished," he said, nodding at the mark on the floor and stepping back around the table. "What are you hoping to bind?"

Kitty just smiled and started stirring what she'd put in the bowl.

He tried again. "What are you making there?"

"Another spell."

"For protection?" he asked.

"Nope. You already gave us that." She thumped the gold plates stacked on a stool beside her.

"What kind of spell, then?"

"Summoning."

Mouse had taught Angelo that protection spells and binding spells were static, stable—crafted by words and symbols, powered with blood, and sometimes enhanced with salt as a conduit. But there were also active spells, ones that required kinetic energy—like Jack Gray's locator spell that had hunted down Mouse in the outback. Those spells still needed blood, but they also needed a power source to serve as a catalyst to set the spell in motion.

"A summoning spell needs power to fuel it," Angelo said, sounding like a teacher coaching a student. That kind of power was hard to come by, and he had been counting on Kitty not yet having it.

"I know what I need," Kitty snapped as her arm shot out to grab the stool, turning it so Angelo could see what was hiding on the other side of the stacked gold plates.

A hiss of breath slipped through his lips. "You don't want that," he said.

She looked over at the stool. "Your little Mouse had lovely eyes, didn't she?"

Angelo kept his gaze on the stone shard covered with a painted green eye. Mouse had had it last—at Lake Disappointment. She'd taken it away from Jack. "You got it from the desert?"

She hesitated just a moment. "The Reverend brought it back for me. Brought you, too."

She didn't sound right. "That thing will mess with your head," he said in warning.

"You mean the tickle of power that comes from it? I can handle that just fine."

"It's dark power, Kitty. It belongs to Mouse's father."

"We use what we have."

"Who are you summoning?" He needed her to say it, to confirm his fear that she was using the blood from Mouse's stone angel to capture her brother.

"Someone I met this evening."

"At the ballet?" Angelo was genuinely confused.

She smiled again but didn't look up. "Did you know Mouse had a little brother?"

And there it was. "What?" Angelo's crutches slammed against the side of the table as he lurched forward in feigned shock, giving her what she wanted.

Kitty laughed. "I love surprising people! Especially at Christmas." She reached for something rolled in what looked like gauze. "I have to tell you, the boy was really cute."

"How do you know he was Mouse's brother?" Angelo felt sick knowing that he had set all this in motion. He clenched his jaw, working to find an angle that would get her to stop.

"You don't look happy. Is it because your little Mouse was more common than you realized?" Kitty slowly unwound the ball of gauze.

"Brother or no, Mouse was anything but common," Angelo said. "The reason I don't look happy is because you seem to be planning to summon the son of Satan to an old barn by yourself while you're still in your evening gown." He slammed his fist against the table.

His mind was racing. Maybe he was looking at this wrong. Maybe this was an opportunity—given the choice, he'd much rather try to take the boy from Kitty than from his father. "Let me help. Please," he said more softly.

"I want to do it myself," Kitty argued.

"Is that blood?" Angelo was watching as she used a pair of tweezers to pull fine strands of discolored cotton from a bandage. "Is that the boy's blood?"

Kitty pressed her lips together. "I know what I'm doing."

"Do you even know whose blood that is?"

Kitty looked up at him disdainfully. "I know it came from a special place." Her eyes shifted, looking over his shoulder.

"How did you get it?" Angelo asked as he turned to see what she was looking at.

Jack Gray stood in the doorway, lit by the scattered light drifting down from the house. A heavy curtain of snow fell behind him. "I gave it to her."

CHAPTER TWENTY-THREE

W hy?" Angelo asked.

"I had no choice," Jack answered.

"I wasn't talking to you, *stronzo*." Angelo took a step toward him, his hands gripping his crutches as he fought the urge to smash the metal against the soft, pasty face and watch all that long white hair run red, but Angelo didn't have time to indulge his anger. He spun back around to Kitty.

"I'm asking you—why? Assuming that it's actually the boy's blood, why bring him here now?"

Angelo needed to slow everything down, to give himself time to come up with a plan for rescuing the boy if Kitty managed to summon him. A plan for what to do if Mouse's father followed in the wake.

"Why risk waking his father's rage against us when we aren't ready yet?" he added. "I don't care what kind of protection spells or how many hundreds of bodyguards you have crawling all over the place—none of it will stop him. It won't even stop the first line of demons he sends to clear out your men. This place will be a pile of ashes before you can even finish calling out to God for deliverance."

"Your stories don't scare me anymore, Angelo. I have my faith instead. God's in the control booth and he says we're good to go!" Her voice over-bright, her smile too tight, Kitty kept working on the contents of the bowl. "Besides, the Reverend's tired of waiting. He has his armies ready and all his pieces in place—a few small but key countries pushed to the edge of chaos, waiting for our nudge; access to important political figures; strings in hand to manipulate the markets." She glanced up. "We just have to set it in motion. Then we sit back and watch it all fall down." A faraway look glazed her eyes for a moment before her forehead creased with a touch of worry.

"What do you need the boy for, then?"

Her lips pulled in a tight line of disapproval. "Don't try to play me, Angelo. You already know full well what we need him for—the spark to light the fuse, the voice to whisper the Reverend's orders into the ears of those key figures. He's a contingency plan if something goes awry—a force to make it all happen just the way we want."

Her smile had come back, though it didn't drive out the remaining worry in her eyes. "We thought to use Mouse, but that didn't work out, so her brother will have to do. We thought you would deliver us a weapon, the anointed warrior blessed by God to live again and again. But you failed us, too—at least in part. Though you did give us armor to protect us in our holy work." She grabbed the book of gold plates and held it to her chest. Angelo noticed for the first time that only three of the plates were held together by the rings. Kitty saw the look slide across his face. "Yes, Kevin has the others. So even if the boy's father comes running to the rescue, at least we're safe."

"What about your men?"

"They are prepared to die for their faith, and God will welcome them at St. Peter's gates."

"Jack and the Bishop?"

"I'm leaving before the fireworks start. Which is why I came out here, Kitty," Jack said. "The Reverend wants to know how soon and do you want him out here or can he stay in the house?"

Ignoring him, Angelo pressed Kitty for another answer. "The Bishop?"

"I leave the business part to the Reverend." Kitty looked down at the bowl, stirring slowly still. "You haven't asked about yourself."

"It doesn't matter."

"It does to me. The Reverend wanted to kill you. I wouldn't let him. I told him you'd tried your best. And I told him that I didn't want to be any part of killing you."

"Why not?"

"I meant what I said all those months ago, Angelo. God has called you to do great and wonderful things. He has lifted you from the clutches of death. Even if evil descends tonight, God will not let you perish. I believe it! Stay with us and watch as we set the foundation stone of our new moral empire." She shrugged. "Or you can leave with Jack."

"No. I'm with you." Angelo was still banking on a chance to get the boy and run—hopefully before Mouse's father showed up.

"Wonderful," Kitty said and then looked up after a moment of silence. "Oh, bless your heart—I didn't mean *out here* with me now. I told you, I want to do this part alone. Go tell the Reverend it'll be about five minutes, give or take. And then he can come down if he wants."

Angelo had no choice but to turn and follow Jack out the door and into the snow.

"I did what I had to do," Jack said as they walked back up the path to the house. "That piece of portrait and a bloody bandage bought me my life."

"You're not worth it. Now, shut up." Angelo was straining to listen for any sounds from the outbuilding, but all was quiet.

"Anybody else would have done the same thing," Jack said as they turned the corner onto the patio still full of armed guards.

The maids in the kitchen kept their heads down over another tray of food when Angelo and Jack walked through. The den was much as they'd left it—the Reverend was still looking at his phone, and the Bishop still stood looking out the window, though he turned when Angelo came back in the room.

"She said wait about five minutes," Jack announced to the Reverend.

"Thank you, son." With surprising grace for a man so large, the Reverend rose from the chair, pocketed his phone, and crossed the room to his desk. "And does she get to keep her little pet angel?" he asked as he opened the center drawer, looking over his shoulder at Angelo. "Are you staying with us?"

"If that's alright with you."

Angelo moved closer to the window, trying to get a view of the outbuilding. He saw the Bishop's reflection in the glass, his face hard and disapproving.

"Why are you here?" he said softly to Angelo, his words making puffs of cloud against the window.

"Why are you?"

"To die, I think."

"What do you mean?"

As the words left his lips, Angelo saw the flash of a gun in the reflection of the window. Then he heard a loud pop and turned just in time to see the side of Jack Gray's face explode as a bullet tore through and sprayed blood and cartilage across the hearth. Bits of something sizzled and sparked as they fell into the fireplace.

The Reverend pivoted the gun toward the men at the window. Angelo threw himself at the Bishop as a second shot rang out. The window shattered and a gust of cold air rushed in. Angelo was on top of the Bishop, shards of glass and snow raining down on them. His body tensed, waiting for the next bullet, his mouth flooding with adrenaline and bile.

But it was a scream, not a last gunshot, that broke the silence, and it came from the outbuilding. Angelo couldn't tell if it was a cry of pain or fear—or a yelp of gleeful surprise.

There was a sound of footsteps, dozens of them, and at the same time, Angelo thought he heard the Reverend call out for Kitty. Footsteps again, then silence.

Angelo slowly lifted his head to look out over the room. It was empty of everyone except himself and the Bishop and a dead Jack.

"Are you okay, Father?" Angelo asked as he rolled off the Bishop. He felt the wetness on his own shirt before he registered the Bishop's stillness and then the spreading ooze of blood coming from his mentor's stomach. "Oh, God."

Angelo pressed his fingers to the Bishop's neck. He was still alive. Angelo heard the shouts of the guards outside. He needed to get Bishop Sebastian out of here quickly.

He slipped and slid in the melted snow on the floor as he scrambled to the other side of the Bishop and grabbed him under the arms, dragging him toward the foyer. Angelo's crutches dangled from the leather straps at his elbows, his muscled arms bulging as they pulled the Bishop's weight. But his legs kept giving out under him until he finally stayed on the floor, his legs framing the Bishop's body as he used one arm to pull himself forward and the other to drag the Bishop with him. At the foyer, he dug his fingers into the grout lines around the centuries-old stone floor. He knew he'd never be able to get the Bishop into a car on his own.

He could hear the two maids crying in the kitchen. He swung his head in their direction and called out, just loud enough for them to hear. "Help! Please, this man is still alive. We need to get him to a hospital."

His answer was more crying.

"I know you're afraid. I am, too. But I really don't want to be here when the Reverend comes back. Do you?"

He waited a moment and, hearing nothing, reached up to the knob and pulled the Bishop to the side so the door could swing open. The Bishop groaned and lifted his hand toward his abdomen.

"Hold on, Father. I'll get us out somehow." Angelo's voice cracked with despair as he looked out at the entrance steps and the yards of snowy gravel between him and the nearest car.

Angelo snapped his head around as he felt a hand press against his shoulder. The maids stepped past him and slipped their arms under the Bishop's back, pulling him upright. Groggily, he seemed to try to help drag his feet under him.

Angelo pushed himself up on his crutches. "Thank you," he said as they all stumbled out into the cold night toward the car.

Angelo got in the back with the Bishop. He pulled his coat off and pressed it against the bloody wound to slow the bleeding. "Where's the nearest hospital?"

"Near Moscow." One of the women slid in behind the wheel, the other on the passenger side.

"No lights until we're well on the main road," Angelo instructed the woman driving. "And then go very fast. You understand?" She nodded. He looked out the back window at the disappearing house. No one was chasing them. He wondered what was happening at the outbuilding.

"Father, can you hear me? We're going to get you to the hospital. You have to hold on just a little longer. Okay?"

The Bishop grunted and nodded. He opened his eyes a little. "I missed you. God . . . sent you back . . . to me." He smiled and then closed his eyes again.

"That's right, Father. I'm here now. It's going to be okay."

Angelo couldn't stop shaking, but he couldn't afford to break now. He needed a plan. He pulled a wallet and cellphone out of the Bishop's tux, took a credit card and the cash, and then tucked the wallet back inside the coat pocket.

"When we get near the hospital, I need you to let me out," Angelo told the woman driving. His guilt at leaving the Bishop, knowing there was every chance his mentor would die, twisted his gut, but he couldn't afford to get caught up answering police questions about a gunshot wound.

"You are leaving us?" The woman's voice was shrill with fear and accusation.

"Someone else is in danger, a boy, and I need to help him."

The woman pulled over in a shopping mall parking lot a few minutes later. Angelo could see the signs for the hospital. He opened the door, then leaned down and kissed the Bishop's forehead.

"I'm sorry if I disappointed you, Father. I'm trying to make amends. Be well."

"Wait," the Bishop mumbled. "You need . . . she's . . . do you know?" But his words were lost in a low groan of pain. Angelo closed the door and watched the car speed out into the traffic. As he walked toward the mall, he scrolled the Bishop's cell for a taxi service. While he waited, he prayed—not for his mentor, not for himself. He prayed for a little boy he'd never met.

⚮

Mouse woke shivering in the dark. She took a raspy breath of air and opened her eyes but could see nothing. The floor felt like stone or concrete. It was smooth, and wet with her own urine. She inched forward on her knees, feeling for Luc, not sure she could speak yet, her throat ravaged by the heat and her screams. When she moved, lights clicked on overhead. Too bright, they stung her eyes and took away her hope.

Luc wasn't here.

Her clothes and the cloak lay in tatters around her, the edges of the pieces charred and whole sections burned to a fine ash. The walls and floor were covered in writing and symbols, many Mouse recognized. They were spells of summoning and containment, spells to drain power, spells to bind.

She stood and lifted her nose like a dog, sniffing—sickly sweet perfume and the brassy twang of hairspray hovered in the air. She'd smelled them earlier that evening on the landing at the Bolshoi. Kitty Ayres.

Mouse's lips pulled into an angry sneer as she lifted her hand to the wall. "These work on demons, you fool," she said. "I'm part human. You can't hold me." She pressed her hand against the wall and commanded the surface to break. Her power swelled between her palm and the concrete, surging until it lifted her and threw her back against the opposite wall.

She shook it off and fed her power with the rage she meant to unleash on Kitty Ayres. This time, Mouse hurled the force against the corner across from her. It shot back like a boomerang of heat and ill will, crushing her against the concrete. She heard her ribs snap, the pain rushing into her chest and stealing her breath. She slid to the floor, moaning and grabbing at her side.

Furious, she rolled over onto her knees, her hands spread wide on the floor. "Shake," she commanded through gritted teeth, tears of pain and wrath mixing with her spit as she sent the full force of her power down against the floor. The air inside the concrete cell began to vibrate like the concussion from a dropped bomb. It rose up against the ceiling, hit the spells painted there, and fell back down on her, pressing her into the floor until she couldn't breathe. Her consciousness slid away from her like smoke in the wind.

It was dark again when she came to and opened her eyes. She lay still, trying to understand—why were these spells working against her when all the spells Bishop Sebastian had laid in the Vatican had failed? There was nothing unique about the spells themselves. They were all familiar to her. So how were they taking the force of her power and turning it against her? And where was her little brother?

She sat up, frantic, a fresh wave of panic about Luc flooding her mouth with bitter adrenaline. The lights flared again, and Mouse, blinking and half blind, looked up to the ceiling. It was also covered in spells. She saw a small rectangular door to the side of the light. If she could find a way up, maybe she could force the door open, but it was too high to jump. Her eyes moved from the door toward the wall.

And in that moment, she found her answer to why the spells were working against her. Her stone angel, a christening gift from Father Lucas, dangled on a rope from the high ceiling. Swaying gently like a hovering emissary from God, it taunted Mouse. Sections of the wings had been scraped or chiseled, exposing new stone beneath and leaving wide, white, gaping streaks where Mouse knew there had once been blood.

She dragged herself over to the wall and licked the nearest letter of a spell. Clary sage and clove oils—and a trace of blood. Her own.

Mouse looked back up at the angel. It wasn't hers anymore. She had given it to Angelo when she'd left to face her father at Megiddo. Now she wished she hadn't. Better yet, she wished she'd left the thing to burn in her house in Nashville.

The angel proved her father right. This cell had been meticulously prepared for Mouse by someone who knew her well, and only one person alive could make such a claim. Angelo. He had the knowledge of the spell work. He had the angel. He knew about Luc. And he had been with the Reverend and Kitty.

Mouse felt fissures spread out inside her as if she were a pane of glass breaking. Her heart, so sure that such a betrayal was impossible, could not silence what her mind knew to be the truth. In the past, such a wound would've sent her seeking some dark escape, like a river to carry her away. But not this time. She had Luc to think about.

"So be it," Mouse said, her mind already adapting to the new rules and crafting a plan on how to get out—and what she would do when she did.

CHAPTER TWENTY-FOUR

Mouse held herself perfectly still in the dark so the motion-detector light wouldn't turn on. She breathed against two charred pieces of what was left of her cloak, the smell of burned fabric stinging her nose.

"Be one," she said on her breath, so softly her own acute hearing barely captured the sound. She felt the silky cloth slide over her palm, tickling the delicate skin, knitting itself together. When it stilled, she moved quickly, the light glaring as she snatched up a dozen more pieces and then settled again at the end of the room, her back to the ceiling door. She slowed her breathing and waited.

The light shut off. As soon as the blanket of darkness descended, Mouse went to work again, not wanting anyone who might be watching from above to see what she was doing. It was tedious—she could only use a sliver of power, more like a mirage than anything real. At first, she had tried a single, forceful command to bind the ruins of her cloak. As with her attempts to escape, the power had ricocheted off the spells on the walls and scattered the pieces of black cloth into the air like a murder of displaced crows. Little by little, Mouse had gathered them together. Breath by breath, she had made them whole once more. They would not make a full cloak—too much had turned to ash—but she would have enough. Just a few more pieces, a few more exhaled commands.

Mouse kept a clock ticking in her head while she worked, literally counting seconds. It had been about two hours since she'd regained consciousness, but she had no idea how long she had been in the cell before that, how long it had been since she and Luc had been taken. Her mind wanted to fill her with all the things that might have been done to her little brother in that time, but she built a wall against them. The spells in the cell seemed to feed off her power when she fueled it with anger or fear, amplifying it and turning it against her, but when the power was soft and her mind at peace, she could use it in small portions. She had to silence her wrath and sorrow. Harder still, she had to leash her panic. She needed the focus and patience of a Norbertine monk.

As always, when Mouse was in need, Father Lucas came to her, even now after she had turned her back on him.

In her memory, she saw herself picking up grains of rice he had scattered in the Mary Garden—a practice in controlling her anger. The cell blurred into the trellised garden walls, covered with pink climbing roses and morning glories. Mouse breathed out the stench of her own sweat and urine and stale air and breathed in the sweet aroma of hollyhocks and rosemary. She shut out the droning hum of silence and frantic racing of her heart and let Father Lucas's voice fill her ears. His gentle voice had once given her the strength to pinch her fingers around the next grain and the next. Often, he had read from the Psalms, but they weren't the words she needed tonight.

Help me, Father, Mouse said silently.

And the words from another book came to her, a book he'd brought from one of his many trips abroad—*The Conference of the Birds*, a book of Muslim wisdom written by the sage Attar. Unlike the books that normally drew Father Lucas out on such quests, this one was not a treasure of spells or apocryphal knowledge. This one was about hope in the darkness. A primer to prepare Mouse for what Father Lucas, with terrible foresight, knew would be a long life of struggle.

She heard his voice now as clearly as she had back then.

As soon as you set your foot in the first valley, that of the search, thousands of difficulties will assail you unceasingly at every stage. Every moment, you will have to go through a hundred tests.

Father Lucas's reading filled Mouse's mind as she scrambled to collect the last scraps of cloth, her eyes shut tight against the blinding light.

You will have to remain for several years in the valley, and advance with great patience and perseverance.

"I will, Father."

In the falling darkness, she breathed into her palm once more, and the cloak was finished, mended enough to do its work. Mouse pulled it over her shoulders, the seared fabric shimmering under the sudden glare of harsh light as it dangled over the tatters of her tuxedo, down to her waist.

To use the cloak, she needed to summon more than a breath full of power, and though the magic would be funneled into the cloak and not directly against the spells that jailed her, she felt sure a broad release of her power would still be turned against her. This locked door needed finesse, not a battering ram.

She found what she was looking for in a corner of the cell—a containment spell that crossed from one wall to the other and stretched down onto the floor, about two feet long and wide. It was one of many containment spells around the room, but she didn't need to worry about those. She just needed one spell, one keyhole, and the patience to work the lock.

Mouse had seen spells undone before. In an ancient church in Onstad, Norway, she had watched her own spells unravel, dehydrated from heat billowing out of the Devil's Bible. Angelo had been there, too, but Mouse scrubbed her memory free of him, erased him before the pain of his betrayal could suck her under. She'd think about him later. Now was about Luc.

She needed to focus on how the heat of the Devil's Bible had undone her spells. The heat came from the power in the book—her father's power. But it was her power, too. If she could use it to peel up this containment spell, it would give her enough opening for a way out.

She folded her legs under her and bent her head toward the corner, using her body once again to shield what she was doing from anyone who might be watching overhead. She siphoned the power coursing through her body, pulling it all into her hands, her long fingers caressing the wall, tracing the symbol—a simple design of the Chi Rho, an ancient monogram for Christ, with the marks of Alpha and Omega on either side.

The layering of her power over the spell had to be delicate and gentle, and she had to hold her fear and anger in abeyance. If she tried to force it, to hurry it in her panic over what might be happening to Luc . . .

Mouse gasped as she yanked her hand back, her fingers blistered and red. She took in slow, deep breaths. She called up images of Luc again, but happy ones, real ones, not imagined horrors. She wove them with Father Lucas's voice and the poet Attar's story of a man journeying through the Valley of Love.

He must not for a moment think of consequences.

She lifted her trembling hand once more to the rust-colored Alpha to the right of the Chi Rho on the wall. She held her fingers, spread wide, hovering over the symbol, so close but not touching. She saw Luc and Mercy playing tug-of-war in the backyard.

He must be ready and willing to fling a hundred worlds into the fire, knowing neither faith nor infidelity, neither doubt nor belief.

Mouse moved her left hand over the Omega, her skin sizzling as the power leaked out, slowly burning her and the blood on the wall. She saw Luc's face lit up with a smile, whipped cream on his nose and his mouth framed with the leftovers of his first hot chocolate.

In this road, there is no difference between good and evil.

She opened her eyes to see the blood-spell under her hands curl away from the wall and float up on the heated air. Alpha and Omega were gone. She moved her hands to each side of the Chi, a great X crossing the stem of the Rho. She saw Luc cuddled beside her as she read to him before bed.

Here neither good nor evil exists.

Her fingers were so swollen with blisters she could not bend them. She laid her hands on the lower part of what was left of the spell, the stem of the Rho, which looked like a stretched-out P and curled down to the floor. She could not stop the tears of pain rolling down her face, but she filled her mind with Luc curled up on his side asleep, his hand still wrapped around hers.

Love transcends both.

She was fading, losing consciousness. She slid her hands to the last of the symbol. She could smell her burning flesh.

And heard Luc's voice, whispering, "I love you, Mouse."

She sank to the floor, pressing her forehead into the concrete, her lips clamped between her teeth to keep from screaming, her burned hands held up and away from her though even the touch of the air was agony. Mouse reached out with her senses and felt an openness where the spell had once been and was no more—like a fresh breeze coming through an open window.

"Thank you," she said to Father Lucas.

She let her hope drive out her pain and lay still to let the light die one final time. As the darkness painted the floor, Mouse curled under her cloak and dove into the spell-less section of the wall. She wasn't thinking of a place to be transported. She was where she wanted to be. She just wanted to be outside, not in.

She felt her body slip over into the between space her father had taught her to travel, but this time it was more like standing still with everything moving around her, rather than her launching out into the current and being whisked away. She was no longer in the cell, but she could feel something pressing against her on either side. She imagined herself going up, and suddenly she was—up and surrounded by open air. Slowly Mouse became aware of the sharpness of the cold seeping up though the melted holes in the soles of her boots. She also felt her power surge, finally free of the suffocating spells, dancing and ready.

The sky was clear, stars out. A low stone building stood before her. She walked around the corner and saw a door. She kicked it open and searched the single, long room in an instant with her unnatural senses, but there was no one here. A lamp at the back lit up a metal table covered with bottles and bowls. Mouse's nostrils flared: anise, frankincense, pine . . . clove and clary sage, just like the spells in her cell. She crossed to the table in long, bold strides. With a glance, she scanned the disheveled debris for anything of Luc's, any clue about where he might be. There was nothing, but as she started to pivot back toward the door, she saw the quartered circle on the floor. In the center was a seared piece of pajama decorated with a dog holding a candy cane in its mouth.

Lifting her charred hands out beside her, Mouse dropped to the floor next to the circle and licked the brownish residue—oils and blood, this time Luc's.

Her mind gave her the answer before she even asked how. Jack Gray was the only person who would've had access to anything belonging to Luc. It must have been something she'd left at her father's place where she'd imprisoned Jack. A white flame of hatred flared in her chest, along with the heaviness of guilt.

Love transcends both. Father Lucas's voice anchored her again. She didn't have time for hatred or guilt right now. She needed to find Luc.

"Burn," she said, wincing as she laid her hand on the threshold of the door. "Burn hot!"

She didn't look back as the instant wave of heat lifted her hair and the acrid odor of scorched wood stung her nose. She knew there would be nothing left, not of the building or of anything inside. No stone angel. No residue of blood. Nothing but useless ash.

Mouse kept her eyes on the next target—it looked more like a castle than a home. She saw fifteen armed guards standing sentry along the back and nearest corner of the house. And they saw her. But she didn't care. She'd seen castles and armies before. They hadn't stopped her then. They wouldn't stop her now.

They all deserved to die for what they'd done. But even as her tongue curled around the words of command, a little voice somewhere in the back of her mind whispered: *Love and discipline have brought you this far. Not hate. Not vengeance. Love transcends.* It didn't sound like Father Lucas this time—it sounded like her own voice, clean and bright, like when she'd been a girl and a young woman in love and a mother.

As she took off running up the path toward the guards, Mouse made a small, tight gesture with her hand, like she was unscrewing a bottle. "Blow," she said. All at once, driving winds whipped up the snow and ice like a white tornado with Mouse at the epicenter. The guards couldn't see; some lost their footing in the fierce winds and undulating snow. Others were pulling back toward the far corner of the house, trying to use the stone walls as cover while they shot at her. But Mouse had seen the shattered window at the back of the house and made for it.

"Down," she commanded the wind. The torrent of ice and snow collapsed on the men, half burying them. As Mouse stepped through the broken window, she reached back and laid her burned hands against the drifted snow. "Freeze."

The fluffy softness constricted into a compact, ice-hard surface and branched out from the window into the yard like a tidal wave. Many of the men were trapped in it. Some were screaming. Mouse turned away from them and closed her eyes, searching for Luc's bright, little glow, but she couldn't find it anywhere in the house. Maybe Kitty's spell masked it.

Mouse walked through the den, breathing deeply and filtering the smells. Blood—lots of it. She didn't have to look at the body on the floor by the side of the couch to know Jack Gray was dead. There was someone else's blood, too, but she didn't know whose. It wasn't Luc's, and that was all that mattered. She pushed away the sharp odor of blood and focused on the other smells—the Reverend and Kitty, just as they'd been at the ballet earlier, smothered with luxury perfume, high-end cigars, and dry-cleaning chemicals. She smelled the familiar scents of Bishop Sebastian . . . and Angelo. A wave of despair crashed against her, but she would not bend. And then she found what she was hoping for—the honey-vanilla of Luc's shampoo mixed with a touch of Mercy. He'd been here.

She paused at the threshold between the den and the foyer, where a grand staircase wound around to the upper floors. She cocked her head, listening. Her ears picked up the Reverend first because she knew him best. He was upstairs to her left. He was ranting about something on the television. Kitty called out from another room near the Reverend, telling him she was almost ready. A handful of other people Mouse didn't know—servants or guards—were scattered through the house, but several were clustered outside, just a few feet away from her on the other side of the door. She'd try there first, and then move up to Kitty's room.

The nails in the soles of Mouse's boots, exposed from the melted rubber, clanged against the stone floor of the foyer. She flung open the front door. A dozen faces looked back at her from the gravel courtyard in front of the house. They were standing around a line of three black SUVs. A couple of men were lifting what looked like an old wooden trunk into the back of the lead car.

Mouse could smell him, could smell the happiness of the bath he'd had before *The Nutcracker*, could smell the fear from where he'd wet himself and the saltiness of his tears. And blood—she could smell Luc's blood coming from that trunk.

She fought back a flash of rage and a powerful wish to command them all to drop dead.

"Love transcends both," she whispered to herself as she stepped out onto the landing and dropped to a crouch, her blistered, melted hand slamming against the stone as all the eyes of the people watched her. She funneled the full force of the power coursing through her down into the ground.

"Shake," she commanded.

The ground erupted. Gravel rained up as the driveway rolled like a wave. The centuries-old stone squealed as the mortar was ground to dust and poured out over the castle façade. The cars shook violently, the glass in their windows shattering. The people in the courtyard fell back, tumbling to the ground, and then took off, half running, half falling away from the castle, away from Mouse.

All but one. One of the guards who had been loading the trunk, which now rested on the ground, crouched beside it, his gun pointed at Mouse. She took a step forward. The man's finger hovered over the trigger. A huge piece of stone fell from somewhere high up on the castle, crashing down into the courtyard, spraying stone shrapnel against the cars.

Mouse could hear Luc crying. She looked at the man with the gun. "I can kill you with a word. But I don't want to." She took another step forward. She would not be stopped from saving Luc, no matter what she had to do.

"I want my brother," she said. "He's in that box. I can hear him crying. Can you?" She stood over the man now, looking down on him, watching his face soften with compassion, her own face wet with tears. "He's just a little boy."

The man nodded. Mouse knelt and tried to unfasten the locks on the front of the trunk, but her swollen, blistered fingers couldn't close around the latch. The man slid his black-gloved hand under hers, snapped the locks open, and tugged the lid of the trunk up.

Luc was naked and curled in a ball. The entire surface of the trunk inside was covered with spells, like Mouse's cell had been, but these were made only of blood. Luc's blood, fresh, sticky, and glistening in the lamplight.

"Gospodi," the man gasped.

"I don't think God gives mercy to someone who does this to a child. Do you?"

Mouse knelt and bent over Luc. He kept his head wrapped in his arms, his eyes closed. He was shaking.

"I'm here, sweetheart. I've got you." She eased her arms under him, wincing at the pain when her hands scraped against the bottom of the trunk. She pulled his body to her chest, kissing him gently on the cheek, her tears sliding down to mix with his.

She looked over to thank the man who had helped her, but he was gone.

When she turned back, she saw the Reverend and his wife being helped down from an upper landing at the far side of the still-quaking house. Kitty saw Mouse, too. She raised her hand, pointing and screaming something.

But Mouse couldn't hear because she was singing to Luc as she held him with one arm and tugged her tattered cloak around them both with the other. The song she sang was a lullaby—one her mother had sung to her in their seconds of a life together.

"You are loved, little one. You are loved."

And she folded them into the dark.

CHAPTER TWENTY-FIVE

The glare of fire flickered against the back window of the SUV.

"Will there be trouble?" Kitty asked. Her voice was hoarse from the smoke and from screaming in rage as she watched Mouse and the boy disappear. She bent over, wiping at bloody scrapes on her legs. They'd barely managed to get down from the landing before the whole wing collapsed and erupted in flame.

The Reverend was only a little dusty. The sweat slicking his face and neck was the only sign that he'd nearly died. He looked up from his phone. "This is Russia, Kitty. People like us don't have trouble here."

"What about when they find what's left of Jack?"

"We have the necessary connections. There'll be no questions asked."

"Were there others trapped inside?"

"I don't know—it won't make a difference. Why do you care?"

"I don't. I just wanted to be sure there wouldn't be any lingering consequences, something that might slow us down."

"I think your failed stunt managed that all on its own."

"My failure?" Kitty sat up sharply. "I did just what I said I would do—I captured both the girl and her brother. Your men let them go—one of them even helped her!"

"Yeah, and as soon as I find him, he'll be dealt with. All the cowards who ran will be dealt with." He looked back down as his phone pinged with a text. "But it doesn't change the fact that something you did to trap that girl didn't work. She got out."

Kitty laid her head back against the seat. "It was my first time with those kinds of spells. I can do them better next time."

"Next time?"

"Yes, of course. We have to get the boy back."

"Why?" He sounded far away, distracted.

"He's critical to our plan." She pulled a compact out of her purse and started patting at smears of dirt on her face.

"Not really. Now that I've got the Novus Rishi network fully integrated with my own, we've got people everywhere. There's no politician we can't own, no country we can't manipulate. It's all ours now, to play with as we wish. The girl—or her brother—would only make it easier. They offer a certain assurance of success. But I'm willing to take the risk without them."

"You're just talking about money and influence. We need the boy to start the Crusade. He can wipe out the vile, disgusting masses and turn the tide so the righteous can rule this world again. We'll lead the way."

She turned to him, but he was still staring at his phone, smirking.

"What makes you think the boy will do any of that?" he asked. "What makes you think he can? Some old book you read? Something your pet angel told you?"

"You saw with your own eyes what the girl can do."

His eyebrows lifted. "Yes, her I believe in."

"If she can do it, why wouldn't her brother be able to do the same? We get him while he's young and break him so he obeys without question. So he belongs to us."

The Reverend licked his lips, and they shone in the glare of his phone. "I could break the girl if I had the chance."

Kitty's hand lashed out and slapped the phone down onto the floor-board between his feet. "Stop your sick texting with whatever slut you have on the hook right now. You know, just because it's words—"

The Reverend grabbed the back of her neck and pressed her head between his legs toward the floorboard. "Pick it up."

"Get your hands off me."

"Pick it up, Kitty."

She wrapped her fingers around the phone, and he let go of her neck. She handed him the phone. "Look at that, I broke a nail."

The Reverend chuckled.

Kitty waited a beat. "I'll remind you that you need me as much as I need you."

"What do I need you for?"

"You need me not to expose you. What would happen to your horde of acolytes if they learned about your hobbies? You wouldn't be their 'Righteous Reverend' anymore, would you?"

The Reverend put the phone down and looked at her.

"And don't think about getting rid of me like you've done with so many others. I've planned for that. I'm part of the most powerful tech dynasty in the world, remember?"

They let the silence drag out, each of them cataloging their vulnerabilities.

"What do you want?" he finally asked.

"I want the boy back."

"And the girl?"

"You can have her if you want. She's too nasty for my tastes. The boy still has some innocence, some malleability. I want the boy."

"I think I know how to get them both."

⚬━━⚬

Angelo sank onto the bed in the small room at Fossanova Abbey outside Rome. Birhan leaned against the wall beside the door.

"You look bad, brother," he said, shaking his head. "You need sleep."

Birhan had been overcome with joy when he'd spotted Angelo coming through the courtyard beside the cloister earlier in the day. But worry and exhaustion had sheared away Angelo's happiness at the reunion—he couldn't help but think he was bringing more trouble into the boy's life.

"I tried on the plane," Angelo replied. During the four-hour flight from Moscow, all he'd been able to see were faces—Jack Gray's exploding into crimson confetti and the Bishop's drained of color. They kept repeating, like some morbid video loop, when he closed his eyes. When his eyes were open, his imagination rolled out scenarios of what might be happening to Mouse's brother at Kitty's hand. He'd taken a taxi back out to the castle to see if she'd been able to summon the boy, but the chaos of lights flashing from half a dozen emergency vehicles lining the drive had warned him off. Neither Kitty nor the Reverend would let themselves get caught in that kind of mess; they were surely gone, and, if Kitty had been successful, the boy with them. Despite a growing sense of urgency, Angelo had to wait. He needed to prepare something before he tried to rush to the rescue, and he needed the solace of the night to get it done. Afterward, he hoped the way forward would be clear.

"What I'd really like is a shower and some food," he said to Birhan. "And then we have something we need to do."

"The rod and the book?"

Angelo nodded.

Birhan straightened his back against the wall, his shoulders square. "The bath is down the walkway to your—"

"I grew up here, Birhan. I know where the bathroom is." Angelo smiled as he pushed himself up onto his crutches and followed the young man out onto the covered walk. The warm air on his face felt good after the iciness of Moscow, but it didn't seem like it had been Christmas yesterday. "Can you go get your bag and the book and meet me back here? We can go eat at the restaurant just down the lane."

"Back in a flash." Birhan smiled over his shoulder as he headed down the walk away from Angelo. "I say that right this time, yes?"

Angelo chuckled. "Yes. Perfect."

"I am getting good at this English slang."

―⟐―

The water wasn't hot enough. Angelo felt like he needed to scald away a layer of skin to feel clean again. He didn't hold Jack's death on his conscience—Jack Gray got what he deserved. And he didn't think he was to blame for the Bishop getting shot; his mentor's obsession with the Novus Rishi had led him into danger, not Angelo. But whatever Kitty meant to do to Mouse's brother was Angelo's fault, pure and simple. He'd been the one to help her find the books and the spells. He'd been the one to teach her how they worked. He'd been the one to align himself with her despite her desire to start a modern-day Crusade. He'd played along because it had served his own blind pursuit of justice.

The shower turned into a cold stream sliding down Angelo's back. No amount of water, hot, cold, or holy, would make him feel clean. He hoped that saving Mouse's brother might. *If* he saved Mouse's brother. *If* it wasn't already too late.

The sun was almost directly overhead when Angelo and Birhan walked through the ivy-covered archway at the restaurant. Just as they were seated, Angelo's phone buzzed.

"Not me," Birhan said, grinning.

"No. It's the Bishop's phone." Assuming the text was something meant for the Bishop, Angelo barely glanced at it as he started to swipe it off the screen, but his eye caught a word that electrified him. The text was from the Bishop. He was alive, but that wasn't the message he'd sent Angelo.

"Oh, God." He pushed back from the chair, tripping over his crutches.

Birhan shot his arm out to catch him as he fell and pulled him back to his feet. "What is wrong?" He put his hand on Angelo's back, steadying him. "Brother, what has happened?"

But Angelo shook his head and took off for the door. Birhan followed him across the cobbled lane and into a grove of trees.

Angelo stretched his head up, held his arms out. "I can't breathe. God, I feel like I can't—"

"Mama always say to lean your head down when you think you might pass out," Birhan said, shrugging.

Angelo leaned down against his crutches, letting his head drop low, and handed the phone to Birhan.

"'She is alive. She thinks you are dead. She seeks vengeance. She is with her father. Save her,'" Birhan read. "Angelo, who is this 'she'?"

"Mouse. Mouse is alive." He flung his head back and yelled to the heavens. "She's alive!"

He started to laugh, but something in the Bishop's message speared his joy. His mind was just registering Birhan's words—Angelo hadn't read the whole message, he hadn't gotten past the first sentence. "She's with her father," he repeated now. "Oh God, what have I done?" Angelo spun past Birhan and took off for the Chapter House.

"Where are we going?"

"Same place we were planning on—just several hours early. But we can't wait any longer."

"Why not?"

"I need the rod. And I need that book to tell me how to use it." His voice shook as he thought about the stone angel smeared with Mouse's blood. The angel Kitty now had because of him. "Mouse is in danger."

Birhan was having to jog to keep up with him. "And who is this Mouse?"

"She's . . ." Angelo didn't know how to answer. "She's everything, Birhan."

Birhan nodded, his jaw setting tightly. "Then we will save this Mouse."

They raced up stone stairs worn down by centuries of faithful feet traipsing up and down for prayers. The Chapter House had been a favorite spot of Angelo's when he'd lived at the abbey as a boy. Most of the tourists passed it over, so it was often a place of solitude, and there was a magic in the space that he was drawn to but could not explain. The room was simple and bare, with a trio of deep-set windows softening the light as it washed the chamber. The arched ceilings, with their runners and carved columns and capitals that looked like fountains of stone erupting, were the only ornate elements in the room. But they weren't what gave the space its magic—that came from the ripples in the plaster and chips in the stone blocks around the windows, and the shallow dips in the pavers on the floor, places where knees bent or hands gripped, places worn by human contact.

Thanks to Mouse, Angelo understood it now. It was magic of a sort, the power that comes from consecrated places, this one steeped in the centuries-old ceremony and worship of first Cistercian and then Franciscan monks. This place was layered with their confessions and their hopes, with moments of loneliness and of brotherhood. Mouse had taught him the power of such places. He hoped it helped him now.

He dropped to the floor where he always had as a boy, in the dead center of the room under the spot where the arches crossed on the ceiling. He pulled at the hand rest of one of his crutches, then shook out two of the pieces of wood he and Birhan had hunted. Birhan did the same with the other crutch, though it took much shaking to get the wider section of wood free of the hollow aluminum casing.

"The book?" Angelo's breathing was fast and shallow, his mouth dry.

Birhan pulled out the inconspicuous journal he'd carried with him since Cairo and handed it to Angelo with a sigh, as if freeing himself of a heavy burden.

Angelo said, "I don't suppose there's any point asking you to—"

"No." He folded himself down beside Angelo. "I'm staying right here."

The three pieces of wood lay on the floor in a line in front of them. Angelo held the Book of the Just in his lap. He made the sign of the cross as he readied himself to open it.

"In the name of Allah, the Gracious, the Merciful," Birhan whispered.

Angelo pulled the cover back. The internal pages were made of some black, thin, incredibly soft parchment. The face page was covered in writing—a tiny script and, like the words on the cover, written in a language Angelo could not identify. He flipped to the back cover and found letters crafted with the same silver ink as those on the front and the opening page, but they were written in the ancient Hebrew Joachim had used on the gold plates. And the lines were broken into three stanzas, like a poem, like the pieces of Aaron's rod on the floor in front of him.

"Here we go," Angelo said, blowing out a breath and lifting the book closer so he could read:

The Just are three:
Driven by compassion
Shaped by humility
Fueled by hope.
The Just are one.

"Angelo." Birhan touched his arm, and he looked up.

The smaller of the sticks was quivering and then began to undulate. The transformation from wood to something living happened so gradually that it was impossible to say when it became a snake. It lifted its head, tongue flickering, looking at Angelo as if it were waiting for something.

Angelo looked back at the book. He read the next stanza, his voice and hands shaking.

The Just are three:
Shaped by humility
Fueled by hope
Driven by compassion.
The Just are one.

He looked up as soon as he finished the line and watched the second stick slither to life. The smaller snake inched forward, mouth gaping, and sank its fangs into the tail of the other snake.

Angelo gasped.

"Will it eat the one?" Birhan asked, reaching out with his hand as if he meant to stop the violence. The second snake turned and hissed. Birhan snatched his hand back.

Angelo read.

> *The Just are three:*
> *Fueled by hope*
> *Shaped by humility*
> *Driven by compassion.*
> *The Just are one.*

The final piece twisted and shook, rattling against the stone floor until it, too, grew soft with flesh and skin, its scales glistening in the fading light. The second snake pulled itself forward, dragging the littlest snake with it, and bit into the thick tail of the third. All of them went still and straight, then a last tremor quaked along the length of them as they stiffened once more.

The rod of Aaron rocked with a quiet thunder on the floor in front of Angelo.

CHAPTER TWENTY-SIX

Mouse knocked against the dark wooden door with her foot, her arms wrapped tightly around Luc, holding the cloak against his naked body, trying to keep him warm. She had not known where to go. The chalet in Austria felt vulnerable, contaminated, as did her father's place. Besides, Mouse did not think seeing him right now would be good for Luc. The only words the boy had spoken so far had been whispered more than once, like he was trying to convince himself of something impossible. "He left me. He just left me."

Mouse could find no comfort for him.

Without thinking, she had come back home again to the abbey at Teplá. Somehow, it seemed right, a woman and a child in trouble going back to where Father Lucas had taken her in so long ago. There was good in the world, good in people. Father Lucas had taught her that. She hoped, for Luc's sake, that they would find that goodness here once more.

There was a light snow falling. Except for the occasional gentle slap of the river below, all was silent and dark—until a light shone out from under the door, and Mouse heard mumbling and the shuffling of feet. The door opened, not just a crack but wide, welcoming. It gave Mouse courage.

"We need help, please. Someplace to stay, just for a few hours." She heard the old accent commandeer her words as she spoke to the man in Czech. She was running on instinct.

The man pulled his robe more tightly around himself. He squinted in the dim light. "Am I dreaming?" he asked.

"No, Father. Please help us. We need sanctuary."

"Sanctuary?" the man said from the doorway, leaning out and looking up and down the lane. "From what? It's Christmas."

"Yes, Father. It's Christmas. Please, we have nowhere else to go."

The man's sight had cleared of sleep, and he looked at them sharply. He made the sign of the cross and then stretched his arms out, touching Mouse gently on the shoulders and drawing her in. "Come inside, child, where it is warm. You will be safe here."

An hour later and no questions asked, Brother Josef—no Fathers at Teplá, all were Brothers, he explained—had settled Mouse and Luc in the gardener's cottage at the edge of the monastery grounds. The abbey was between gardeners, so the house had been empty for weeks.

"It will be wanting people for Christmas to make it warm and happy," Brother Josef said as he stoked the fire he'd built in the wood stove. There was a pot of water warming on top. Luc lay curled under blankets on the small, low bed against the back of the room. Mouse sat beside him, her hand clenched in his. A stack of clothes and linens sat propped against the wall at the end of the bed.

Brother Josef had perused the cabinets and found an assortment of canned goods. "Enough if you are hungry now. Later, I will bring fresh food from town." He walked toward the door but paused. "We eat Christmas dinner after Mass. You are most welcome to come if you are feeling up to it." His eyes lingered softly on Luc and then met Mouse's gaze. His was sad. Hers was despondent.

"Thank you, Brother Josef."

As soon as he closed the door, Mouse was up and searching for a kitchen knife.

"I'm going to do some spells like I showed you—to protect us," she said, desperate to draw Luc out, to hear him speak, to know that he would be okay. "Do you remember, Luc?"

The swelling in her hands had gone down enough to grab a hilt—she was healing, but much more slowly than normal. She didn't understand why but thought it might be because the damage had been done by her own power.

"Do you remember the words? Do you want to say them with me?" She sliced into the flesh of her forearm. "No? That's okay. I can do it." She moved around the perimeter of the cottage, casting protection spells.

"Those will keep us safe," she said as she finally sank onto the bed beside Luc, faint from the loss of blood, fatigue taking over now that the adrenaline was gone.

"You don't believe that. I can hear it in your voice." He was quiet, monotone, but Mouse nearly broke with relief.

"You're right. I won't lie to you. I don't know for sure if the spells can stop . . . her. But I think they might." Mouse had used every spell she'd ever learned, fueled them with her own power-rich blood and the fierceness of her love. It would be enough to stop someone or something from coming in, but there was another worry that hung on Mouse. "Can you tell me what happened? Did she—"

"I don't want to talk about it." His voice went high with panic, and she could hear his little heart running.

"No. Of course not." She had wanted to ask if Kitty had taken more blood than she'd used on the spells in the trunk. If Kitty had more of Luc's blood, she could take him again. Mouse didn't know of any spell that could stop her. But Mouse wouldn't push Luc—not now. He'd suffered enough.

"Can you sit up so we can get you washed off? Brother Josef left a shirt you can use to sleep in."

"I want my own pajamas." He started crying softly.

Mouse worked hard to keep her voice steady and calm, just like he needed, but the effort burned her eyes and throat. "The ones you were wearing are gone, honey. The ones with the—"

Luc sat up suddenly. "Mercy! I forgot Mercy! Mouse, can you go get her? Please? She's all alone. She might have been hurt when . . . when the burning started. And she's with . . . she's with him. He might—oh, please, Mouse. Please go get her." He was sobbing so hard now that he was breathing in gulps.

Mouse didn't want to leave him here alone, even for the few minutes it would take, and she was so tired, she wasn't sure she could travel through the between space. "Honey, can we wait a few hours? I can get Brother Josef to sit with you and—"

"No! I want Mercy! Please." He curled in a ball again, the blankets tangled under him, exposing his blood-smeared little body.

The cuts had been bone deep, but they were only scratches now. Mouse wasn't worried about the physical harm—like her, Luc would always heal. But what must it do to a child just learning to love to have someone rip him from his bed on Christmas Eve, to have his father abandon him in the moment of his terror, to be tortured by a stranger and to not understand why?

Her mind filled with her own young self, ripped apart by despair and brought back to life by the unconditional love of a wolf who taught her to trust again. Mercy's love would heal Luc much faster than Mouse ever could.

"Okay, sweetheart. I'll go."

He nodded, still crying.

As she stood and lifted the tattered cloak from the bed, he said, "There's something under my pillow, too. Will you bring it?"

She bent and kissed him on the forehead. "Of course. You stay here, just where you are." She pulled the blankets back up around him and then took a step away, the edge of the cloak in her hand. "And, Luc. If anything happens . . ." She swallowed against a surge of fear. "If she, or anyone, if they . . . you use your power. Do you understand? It's okay to do anything you have to do to protect yourself."

He nodded again and she folded herself into the dark.

⚬━╼━⚬

The puppy was waiting, curled up in the middle of Luc's bed. Christmas music was still playing—"God Rest Ye Merry Gentlemen" sang out through the house. There was no sign of her father.

Mercy whimpered and cowered until Mouse spoke. "You have a little boy who needs you."

The puppy stood, stretched, and wagged her tail.

Mouse reached into a drawer beside the bed and pulled out a pair of pajamas and a set of clean clothes for Luc. She wouldn't take the time to bother with her own things—she was anxious to get back to him, and besides, she had lifetimes' worth of practice leaving everything behind. She started to pick up the puppy, but then remembered the something under Luc's pillow.

She assumed it was a book or a stuffed animal and so was surprised when her hand made contact with something hard. Her fingers painted the picture of what it was before she saw it. She tucked it in with the clothes as she bent and gathered Mercy in her arms and leaned into the black space of her cloak and stepped out onto the worn, wooden floor of the gardener's cottage at Teplá Abbey.

The dog was already squirming to get free before Mouse's second foot settled.

"Mercy!" Luc's arms opened and the puppy sprang into them, licking his face and whining with joy. Mouse saw a smile spread across Luc's face, all the way up to his eyes, driving out the dead, dark clouds that had hung there since she'd pulled him out of the trunk. As a healer, she knew it took time to recover from such wounds. She knew there would be nightmares. There'd be anger and fear. The clouds would surely come back again. But, hopefully, Mercy and Mouse would be there to drive them back once more.

310

While Luc soaked in Mercy's love, Mouse sank wearily into a chair between the wood stove and the bed. She put the clothes beside the linens Brother Josef had left. She held the thing from under Luc's pillow in her hands, rubbing her thumb over the smooth wood, following the grain that ran like locks of hair along the baby's head.

But for the first time since she'd carved it seven hundred years ago, it was the mother that held Mouse's focus. The mother nursing her son. The mother's soft face, smiling. The mother singing. The mother full of goodness, feeding her son on joy.

It had been Mouse's dream to be all those things—soft, a force for good, full of joy, a healer. But she'd turned her back on all of it after Lake Disappointment. The Mouse etched in the centuries-old wood in her hands was dead. She'd let vengeance suck out all the goodness, like a vampire draining its victim, and all that was left was a bitter, brittle shell.

"Are you mad?"

Mouse startled and looked up at Luc. She realized her face had gone hard and cold again. She tried to soften it. "Why would I be?"

"Because I stole it."

"I threw it on a pile of what I considered worthless trash." The tears stung her eyes without warning, rolling down her face and dropping on the statue. "The best parts of me—the joy, the love, the light—I tossed them away like they were nothing. I set fire to them and the memory of the people who'd given me those gifts." Her voice broke as she looked at the scorch marks along the bottom of the statue. "You didn't steal it, honey. You saved it—from me."

She handed it out to him.

"But it's yours," Luc said.

"Not anymore." She thought about all that she'd lost, all that she'd given away, all of it ash now—Mother Kazi's satchel of healing tools, Bodhan's lock of fur, Father Lucas's breviary, her own soul. She couldn't get any of it back. It was too late. She'd done too much, gone too far. "I don't deserve it."

Luc nudged through her arms and climbed into her lap, holding the statue. "Is this you?"

"It was."

"It is."

"Not anymore. I gave that girl away."

"It looks like you." He twisted in her lap and laid his hands on her face, gently pulling her cheeks back to make her smile, running his hand lightly over her forehead, easing out the furrows.

"Not really, not on the inside, and that's the part that matters."

He closed his eyes.

"Don't, Luc. Don't look, please."

She was an echo of her father atop Megiddo, when she'd used her gift to look inside him, searching for and finding the tiny flicker of a soul. She couldn't stand the idea that Luc, who also had this gift, would see the empty darkness inside. The soul she'd finally seen inside herself at Megiddo, a lightness and joy Angelo had seen in his pictures—it had surely drowned in her hatred and vengeance.

"I don't know what you looked like inside back then," he said in a faraway voice.

"Please, Luc."

"But I see a bright, golden glow that fills you up and spills out around you." He lifted his hand as if he were playing with something invisible. "It's dancing all around me. It's beautiful, Mouse."

She pulled him to her, kissing him on top of the head, holding him as she shed silent tears.

His finger traced over the words Mouse had carved into the statue so long ago. "This is French. You taught me French. I read the words, over and over again, but I didn't know it was a song until you sang it to me when . . . when you found me."

"Yes." She reached over and pulled a blanket from the bed and wrapped it around them. Luc had started shivering again. "My mother sang it to me, just once, before she died."

"Will you sing it again?"

"*You are loved, little one, you are loved. By God in heaven, you are loved. You are loved, little one, you are loved. By your mother, forever, you are loved.*"

"Mouse?" Luc interrupted as she started the verse again.

"Yes?"

"You don't have a little boy anymore, do you?" He was fingering the baby on the statue now.

"No. He lived and died a long time ago." The knot in her throat burned.

He was quiet a moment. The wood in the stove popped and snapped in the silence.

"What will happen to me now?" he finally asked. "I don't want to go back with Father. I don't want anyone to snatch me away again." He was crying.

"You don't have to. And I won't let them."

"Can I be your little boy and you be my mother?"

"If . . . if you want me."

"We can stay together?"

"Always."

He sighed and settled against her chest again. Soon his breathing grew slow and his body relaxed into sleep. She held him a little while longer, still singing, and then settled him into the bed, curling up beside him.

They spent Christmas Day eating canned soup and crackers. Brother Josef brought them leftovers from the abbey's Christmas dinner late in the day, along with some milk and bread and eggs. Mouse and Luc slept for hard, heavy hours at a time, until one or the other woke from dreams filled with horrors. Mercy was there to lick the nearest face. Later, Mouse found some rope to make a leash for the dog. She'd forgotten to get Luc any shoes, so she carried him on her back around the abbey grounds, telling him stories of her childhood and revisiting the ghosts of her past.

The next day, they started planning. Brother Josef had said they could stay at the cottage until spring, when the new gardener arrived. Luc liked the idea of being in the place where Mouse had been a child. He loved hearing her stories and seeing the place as it had been seven hundred years ago. But Mouse was already ready to run. And yet, underneath her instinct and drive to keep him safe, she also wanted Luc to have a normal childhood—as normal as he could, anyway. Soon enough, his immortality would make him a wanderer. Where could she go that would keep them off the Novus Rishi's radar? Lurking in that question was another problem Mouse had no answer for—if Kitty had Luc's blood, how could Mouse ever keep him safe?

The worry drove her outside for fresh air near sunset, when Luc had fallen asleep—his little body worked so hard to recover from the trauma that he ran out of energy often. It would get better, she told herself, but there was only one way she could think of making sure it didn't happen again. Here at the abbey, with Father Lucas so near and so far away, and now that Luc had restored her hope, Mouse didn't want to add any more names to the list of lives she had already taken. Not if there was any other way.

She was not surprised to find her father waiting at the threshold of the cottage door as she opened it.

"Seems I'm not welcome here," he said as he toed the bloody line of her spell.

"What do you want?"

"To check on my son."

"The one you abandoned?"

"I knew you'd save him."

"Go away." Mouse picked Mercy back up and turned toward the door again.

"Wait. There's something you need to know. Your little friend—"

"Angelo. And he's not my friend anymore."

Mouse couldn't deal with the bitterness of Angelo's betrayal and give Luc the love he needed right now. She pushed Angelo down and away, into the cage she'd once saved for the power that coursed through her. She'd considered it a curse. Now Angelo held that title.

"Well, at least we agree on that. He's awoken the Book of the Just."

Mouse remembered that her father had told her this just before the summoning spell tore her and Luc away.

"And now he's put the rod together."

Her uncanny intellect and seven hundred years of religious study made the connection quickly. "Aaron's rod? What does Angelo want with—"

"Technically, it's my rod. I had it first," her father said.

"What?"

"The Book and the rod, they were the tools of my trade. I was the Accuser." Her father said it dramatically, like a commentator announcing a competitor entering the arena. "I was supposed to test the worthiness of humanity. The boss believed that his clay puppets were good at heart, selfless, trusting, kind, and faithful. Not all of us agreed." He shrugged. "I was sent to challenge them. You know, like Job? I kept a catalog of my . . . clients. Who was tested and how. Who failed and why. Evidentiary notes to make my case against humanity."

"Why would that make the Book of the Just dangerous?"

"I scribbled down the spells I used to expose their—well, you might call it evil. The boss called it corruption and blamed it on those of us who'd come down to hang out with the humans even though he'd told us not to. But as I argued then, if they were infected with greed and lust and selfishness, he had only himself to blame—it wasn't my fault that I could see it in them, that I could pull it out of them. They were what they were. You can't expect a child to transcend its origins."

"Yes, you can." Mouse looked him in the eye. "It's called free will. It's called choice."

"Oh, you want to talk about the choices you've been making?"

"I have to deal with the consequences of my choices, and they're none of your business. But you might want to think about the consequences of some of your own." She nodded back to the cottage where Luc lay sleeping.

"How is he?"

"He doesn't want to see you."

"He'll get over it. You did."

"You're such a fool. You have a chance at redemption, at love, and you can't even see it."

"Love is a myth humans cling to in order to make themselves feel better about their pathetic existence. How's it gone for you so far?" he smirked.

Mouse wouldn't take the bait. Her wounds were her own to heal. "The Book has dangerous spells—I already knew that. But no one can use them without a power source, right?" Something clicked even as she said it and before her father could answer. "That's what the rod's for."

"Yup."

"How powerful is it?"

"Unfathomable—far beyond what even you can do. It fueled the spells I used to bring disasters on people."

Mouse shivered at the foreboding pricking at her skin, but something here didn't feel right. "Why do you care? Sounds like the spells are against people, not demons. I thought it was supposed to wipe out evil."

"That's the whole point, dearest. Evil is everywhere. And though you're right—me and mine won't be in the first wave of victims—my old adversary left the playing field on one condition: that the game was played fair. I gave up my Book and the rod, which meant I could influence only one person at a time. I could plant my seeds, one by one, but I had to let them grow as they would on their own." He smiled. "I think my garden's done well, and, as I told you, I have every confidence that Armageddon will be won in the beat of a single heart—the last one I claim as my own."

"The Book and the rod change the nature of the game? Whoever has them wins?"

"Bingo. You are clever—pretty sure you got that from me, kid."

"Why haven't you ever tried to get them back? They've been here all along, right?"

"I made a deal, remember? He leaves the field to me. I hand over the Book and rod and only work on one person at a time."

"But you had me, and then Luc, so we could do more than that. You want us to command armies, to coerce multitudes for you, to make them all love you."

"Yes. But *I* am only influencing one person—either Luc or you, though that hasn't worked out well so far. You're the ones giving me a leg up on the old competition. And technically, he cheated first. He had a kid, too, you know."

"Angelo has the Book and now the rod. Why don't *you* take him out?" A cold spear ran through her gut.

"The Book and the rod shield the bearer from all but the Just."

"Someone who's just is the only one who can—?" She felt a wash of relief run over her. "You need to find someone else, then. That's not me."

"No?"

"Not anymore." Her mind thumbed through all the things she'd done and said since Lake Disappointment. "I'm my father's daughter now."

He barked out a laugh. "Not quite. You're just being a coward. You're going to let the world burn because you're too afraid to confront your traitor lover." He nodded smugly. "See? I told you love was a myth and selfishness the ruler of the human heart."

Mouse eyed him, her temper flaring, but she knew he was right. "You still haven't answered my question—why do you care?"

"If someone starts using the Book of the Just and the rod of Aaron, my old adversary's going to get back in the game, and he'll bring a host of his friends, and it will be—"

"The end of the world."

The fractures that had feathered inside her when she'd seen the stone angel floating over her head in that blood-laced cell and realized that Angelo had betrayed her now grew deep and wide. She felt like her heart—and every truth she'd held there—were shards piercing her. She had to do whatever it took to stop Angelo.

"Can you take me to him?"

CHAPTER TWENTY-SEVEN

Angelo laid his hand on the rolling rod to still it. He could feel the charge of power dancing along the wood and reaching up to tickle his palm as he picked it up.

"What is it?" Birhan asked.

"The rod of Aaron. The rod of Moses."

"The one that split the sea?"

Angelo nodded.

"Can it still do that?"

"I don't know. I think it probably powers the spells in the Book. Can you hand it to me?"

Birhan grabbed the worn black book from the floor and passed it to Angelo, who rested the rod in the crook of his arm as he opened the Book of the Just. Many of the pages were covered with the same script as the first, in the language he did not know. But about halfway through, the writing changed—a different hand and a different script. Angelo could make sense of some of the symbols; they resembled the ancient Hebrew he'd translated from the gold plates. Toward the end, the script changed over almost completely to that same old form of Hebrew.

There were spells to make arrows fly true and hit their marks. Spells to shield armies. Spells to call a fog. He found the spell, referenced in Joshua, about holding the sun and the moon still. There was a spell to identify enemies with a bright aura. Angelo flipped back a few pages to the older script mixed with symbols he could identify and saw lines that talked about boils and calling out ferocious beasts from the wild. A last line with enough words he could understand talked about cleaving the heart of evil. He shuddered.

"What does it say?" Birhan asked. "Read it."

"No," Angelo answered briskly. "If I read these words out loud while I hold the rod, it would bring down . . . they're all curses, Birhan, ways to annihilate your enemy."

Birhan's face twisted with fear. "We should take it back, hide it again."

"Not yet. I have to use it first." Angelo had a faraway look in his eye, but his jaw was clenched, determined.

"Use it for what?"

"To save Mouse. And her brother." He used the rod to push himself up.

"How?"

"I'll figure it out when the time comes. I have to find them first—and fast."

"How?"

So much of Angelo's plan was guesswork and chance, but he knew where he had to start. He pulled out the Bishop's cellphone.

"Who are you texting?" Birhan's voice was loaded with apprehension.

"Kitty."

Birhan put his hand on Angelo's. "You can't put these weapons in the hands of these people, brother."

"I don't want to, but I don't have a choice. I can't find Mouse on my own. And I think Kitty has Mouse's little brother. She also has everything she needs to capture Mouse, too—if she hasn't already. If I have any hope of saving Mouse and her brother, I have to go to Kitty, and these are my ticket in."

Angelo punched in a simple text: HELLO KITTY. IT'S ANGELO.

The phone pinged with a response: WHERE HAVE YOU RUN OFF TO THIS TIME?

ITALY.

FUNNY. ME, TOO.

I HAVE SOMETHING YOU'RE GOING TO WANT TO SEE.

OH?

THE ROD OF AARON.

Angelo waited nervously for her reply. It was taking longer than he wanted.

WHY TELL ME?

I THOUGHT YOU WANTED A WEAPON AGAINST EVIL.

DOES IT WORK?

I CAN FEEL THE POWER POURING THROUGH IT. BUT I HAVEN'T TESTED IT.

WHY NOT?

I'M SCARED OF IT.

I'M NOT.

YOU WILL BE.

Another nervous wait.

CAN YOU COME TO ROMA MARINA YACHTING IN THE PORT OF CIVI-TAVECCHIA? WE'RE ON THE BOAT. I'LL LET YOU KNOW WHEN WE DOCK.

I'LL BE THERE IN A COUPLE OF HOURS.

NO SURPRISES, PET. THE REVEREND'S A LITTLE TOUCHY AT THE MOMENT.

I UNDERSTAND.

Angelo looked up at Birhan.

"You are going somewhere," Birhan said. "I am going, too."

"I need you to stay here as my backup. You still have your phone?"

Birhan pulled it out of the bag hanging on his shoulder. Angelo keyed in a number. "This is the number Bishop Sebastian texted me from. You can reach him here. If you don't hear from me in twenty-four hours, contact him and tell him what's happened. He'll know what to do."

"No, not this time."

"Birhan, if it all goes wrong, we need someone to get the Book and the rod back before Kitty and the Reverend figure out how to use them. That's on you."

Birhan sighed and lowered his head. "Then I will do this thing. I will stay behind. And I will pray to Allah that I may see you again."

o—▸—o

Mouse sent her father back to the chalet in Austria to fetch the bone shard the Seven Sisters had sent her. She couldn't imagine what had turned Angelo against her. Some part of her mind wanted to argue all the possibilities that would exonerate him—he didn't know she was alive, he was driven by grief and vengeance—but Mouse had seen him with her own eyes, friendly with the Reverend at *The Nutcracker*. And Angelo had been in the house in Russia with his old mentor, Bishop Sebastian, and Jack Gray, the traitor who'd sold out her brother.

Despite his betrayal, Mouse didn't think she could kill Angelo by her own command or with her own hand. Not even to save the whole world. If there was no other way to stop him, she could only hope that the shard would do the killing work for her as it had in the barracks with Citrus, Musk, Bay Rum, and Cedar. But she would have to draw her mind to the ready. She would have to be full of wanting Angelo dead.

Mouse stepped back into the gardener's cottage and heard the Brothers singing at Lauds as she closed the door.

"Mouse?" Luc called out, frightened.

"Right here," she answered. "I was just taking Mercy out." She sat down on the bed beside him. "You okay?"

He rubbed at his eyes. "Just hungry."

Mouse heard a rustling at the door. Their father was back.

"Who's that?" Luc asked anxiously.

"Let me fix you some toast and eggs." She moved to the stove.

"I don't want him here," Luc said. "I don't want to see him. You said I didn't have to—"

"You're not going with him. I am."

"No! Why?"

She kept her back to him as she talked, working hard to keep her heart and voice steady so he wouldn't be able to read her well. "The trouble's not over, Luc. We just ran from it. And I've spent a lifetime running—it's not what I want for you. I'm going to go deal with it so it's over, so no one can hurt you again."

She could almost feel his eyes boring into her as he searched for a lie. She wasn't lying, but she didn't want him to sense her fear. If Angelo and Kitty had the rod and the Book and knew how to use them, Mouse didn't think there was much she could do, but she had to try. She didn't want Luc sensing her worry that she might not come back.

"Okay," he finally whispered. "Do you want me to come help?"

Mouse shook her head, not able to talk.

"But *he's* going to help you?"

She cleared her throat. "Our father knows how to find them, and I don't. But once we're there, he's going to come back here and—"

"No. I don't want him. I'm fine here with Mercy."

"He can't come inside, Luc. The protection spells I did stop him. You just stay here and eat and play with Mercy. I'm going to go ask Brother Josef to come check on you in just a little bit, in case I'm gone longer than I mean to be." She brought him his plate of eggs and toast and a glass of milk, which she set on the bedside table.

He was staring at her face and then his crumpled. "Please don't go, Mouse. I want you to stay. We're safe here."

"We can't live our whole lives in this cottage, Luc. I want you to see the world. It's a beautiful place with beautiful people in it." She couldn't keep the heaviness from her voice.

"You don't think you'll come back." He said it in a breath and then launched into her arms, clinging to her. "Don't go. Please don't go!"

Mouse reached back and tugged his hands apart, then picked the dog up and put her in Luc's lap. Mouse didn't turn back when she got to the door. "I love you, Luc," she called back to him, but she wasn't sure he could hear her over his sobs.

She took the bone shard from her father, who stood just to the side of the door. He held out a new cloak as well. "Looks like your old one is a little worse for wear."

Mouse snatched it from him and let the tattered one fall to the ground. He pulled her *kurdaitcha* mask from behind his back and offered it to her as well.

She shook her head. "I'm done hiding. What I do now, I do as Mouse." She shoved past him. "I need to go speak to Brother Josef. Wait here. And don't talk to Luc. After you've shown me where I need to go, you come back here and you watch over him, but he's in charge. You understand? If he wants to talk to you, he will. Otherwise, leave him alone. Or I swear I'll get that damn rod and Book and hunt you down myself."

"You're charming this evening, dear," her father said to her back as she headed off to the church. When she'd turned the corner and was out of sight, he picked up the old cloak and mask, opened the cottage door, and stepped silently over the blood spatter of her spells and into the foyer. He laid the cloak and mask on the side table against the wall.

He was looking over the hedge down to Teplá River when she came back.

"Shall we?" He held his arm out to her, and just as he pulled his cloak around them both, he said, "You'd do well to remember that he's my son. He's hurt now, but our kind heal. And we're harder after the scars."

⊷

Angelo felt more out of place than he ever had in his life. He was walking down a pristine cobblestone path flanked by huge, sleek yachts, towers from the ancient port of Rome pressing up against the horizon.

He gripped the rod of Aaron against the hand rest of his crutch; it stretched out in front and behind him and looked every bit like an old-school fishing pole.

He turned his head at the sound of a helicopter coming or going, chauffeuring the wealthy from one luxury to another. Kitty had texted the quay number where their yacht was moored and the name of the boat: *The Redeemed*. Angelo was not prepared for the size, though he chided himself for the shock—he understood the Reverend's appetites were large. Why should it be any different for a boat?

A guard stood at the ramp leading up to the yacht. Another two were waiting at the top.

"I'm—"

Without a word, the guard nodded, stepped forward, and directed him up the ramp.

As Angelo stepped onto the boat, one of the guards, pointing at a spiral staircase to the right, asked, "Can you manage, Mr. D'Amato, or do you require assistance?"

"I can do it. Down or up?"

"Down, sir."

Angelo let his crutches swing loose from their straps and grabbed the rails on either side of the narrow stairwell. He held Aaron's rod in his right hand, upright against the rail, and let his upper body carry most of his weight. He felt like a mangled insect, legs dangling, as he clunked his way down one glossy, dark wood step at a time.

The room opened up at the bottom and ran half the length of the boat. On Angelo's end was a posh sitting area with couches and chairs covered in rich leathers and plush velour. Banks of windows offered vistas of other grand yachts and the promise of the open sea, turned amber by the late afternoon sun.

"They wanted to open the windows." The Reverend sat at the head of a dining table at the far end of the room. "But I told them seawater and fish smells and the caw of them damn seagulls belong to the Fourth of July, not Christmas. Christmas should be cold. Down home, we run

the air conditioner if we have to. I got them running it full blast now."
He smiled. "Come on and grab a seat. Get you a plate."

Angelo navigated the couches and chairs and took a seat at the table.
"That is a lot of food," he said.

"I missed my Christmas dinner yesterday with all the drama out at
the house, so they fixed it up for me here. All the Southern goodness.
Let me cut you a piece of prime rib."

The Reverend pushed back from the table. Serving spoons and glasses
clinked against each other in the wake. He stabbed a long-tined fork
into a chunk of meat and sawed at it with a large serrated knife. The
center of the cut was a deep purple-red and sent tiny rivers of blood and
juice rolling when the Reverend slid the meat down onto Angelo's plate.

"We got creamed potatoes and cornbread dressing with gravy, some
buttermilk biscuits—just make sure to save some room for the coconut
cake. That's a Southern delicacy, I tell you." The Reverend sat back
down with a quake and shoved a deviled egg in his mouth.

"Where's Kitty?" Angelo asked. Everything felt wrong.

"She's getting dressed. She'll be up in a bit. Get you some food now."

Angelo reached over to get a biscuit but jumped up at the sound of
a scuffle coming from the stairs. "What's that?" His hand had gone
instinctively to Aaron's rod, which leaned against his chair.

"Nothing. Sit down and eat." It was an order, devoid of his Southern
charm.

Angelo sat down but kept his eyes on the stairs and his left hand on
the rod. His right hand rested inside his bag against the spine of the
Book of the Just.

"What you got there?" the Reverend asked, nodding at the rod.

"A rod."

"That thing's only good for the catfish pond." He chuckled. "You
won't catch a thing out here."

"It's not for fishing. Is someone else joining us?" Angelo asked,
looking at the fourth place setting.

"Kitty! The food's getting cold," the Reverend bellowed. "Get up—"

"Stop yelling, Kevin." Kitty was slowly climbing up another spiral staircase in the doorway behind and to the left of Angelo's seat. "I'm sore. It took a little longer."

"What happened to you?" Angelo asked. She had scrapes down both legs and a few scratches and bruises on her face.

"We had a visitor after you left on Christmas Eve." She sat at the end of the table, plucked the napkin off her plate, and smoothed it onto her lap. She cut her eyes up to the rod. "Is that the thing you mentioned on the phone?"

"Yes."

"The rod of Aaron?"

"What?" the Reverend asked.

"You know your Bible, Kevin. This is the rod that Moses's brother used to best the pharaoh."

"The one that ate the other snakes? How's that supposed to help us?"

"It's more than that," Angelo said quietly. His eyes were still on the place set for a fourth person. "Who else is coming?"

"What else does it do?" the Reverend asked.

"It's the rod Moses used to part the Red Sea."

"Now that's more interesting."

"I can feel it," Kitty said, excitement playing in her voice.

Angelo turned to her. "What visitor did you have and how did they do this to you?"

"*She* didn't do anything to me. It was the house." Kitty leaned forward and touched his arm. "But I did it, Angelo! The spell. I caught them—both. And I would have kept them, if—"

Angelo shivered against the penetrating cold of the air-conditioned air as it seeped into his gut. "Caught both of whom? Mouse's brother and—"

"Mouse, of course." She studied him carefully. "I see you already know she's alive. Did your Bishop tell you?"

"Yes." Angelo was trying to master his fear. "Where is she?"

"Your nasty little girlfriend found a way through my spells."

326

"She took out my men," the Reverend added. "Destroyed the whole damn house. We barely got out." He sounded more awestruck than afraid or angry. "She's a force of nature, that girl."

"I had her trapped—no way out. I did it all like you taught me," Kitty whined. "I don't understand what went wrong. Unless—"

"Where's her brother?" Angelo's mouth had gone dry. He looked back at the fourth seat.

"She took him," the Reverend answered.

"It must have been the blood." Kitty was talking to herself, seemingly oblivious to the conversation. "The spells were working on the boy. I could hear him scream and cry. *He* didn't get out. So there must have been something wrong with the blood on that angel you gave me."

"I didn't give it to you," Angelo said, his words sharp, his body tensing. He realized he'd made a mistake coming here. But he'd thought that Kitty had the boy already, and maybe Mouse, too; he'd had no choice but to come. Angelo was prepared to use the rod and the Book to do whatever he had to do to save them. But they weren't here.

"Maybe the blood was too old. Maybe there just wasn't enough." Kitty shrugged and grabbed a biscuit. "But I got plenty from the boy. So, I know I can get him again."

"And the girl will come to rescue him again," the Reverend countered, meeting Kitty's eyes across the table.

"Which is where Angelo comes in to save the day," she said with a simper.

Kitty had all the cards—the spell, the boy's blood, and in Angelo, both a shield and a weapon against Mouse. Angelo was struggling to find a way out of the trap. "Why should I help you? You lied to me. You told me she was dead."

"What would you have done if I'd told you the truth? That her father whisked her away and left you for dead?"

Angelo seemed to have only one choice left. He'd take them out, the whole boat, himself included, before they had a chance to capture the boy again and lure Mouse into the web.

"I would have found her," he said quietly.

"How would you have found her?" Kitty asked.

"Somehow." He carefully pulled the Book of the Just out of his bag under the table.

"Come on, son, you think you could have taken that girl from her father? You couldn't take a lollipop from a baby," the Reverend said.

"I wouldn't have to take her. She would've come." Angelo flipped toward the back of the Book and glanced down quickly to find a spell.

"Don't you understand, Angelo?" Kitty said, her voice laced with pity. "She's with her father and her little brother. They're a family. And you're not part of it."

Angelo looked up as he heard another noise coming from the stairs. "You're planning to summon the boy again. And I'm here to do what?" But he knew already.

"Use the weapons God sent you to do what they're meant to—battle evil little monsters like your Mouse."

"I want her when you're done," the Reverend said to Kitty.

"I don't care what happens to her, as long as I get the boy."

Angelo tightened his grip around the rod of Aaron and slowly stood up. "I won't hurt Mouse."

"You'll do as you're told, son." The Reverend nodded to a guard who'd come halfway down the stairs.

"I'm not your son any more than I was the Bishop's." Angelo lifted the Book of the Just so he could read.

"I hear he made it through surgery but has a long recovery ahead." The Reverend shoved a big piece of bloody prime rib into his mouth, juices running down his chin.

"If you're trying to threaten me, it won't work. I will not hurt Mouse."

"Then I'm afraid you have a difficult choice to make," Kitty said.

"Our last guest has finally arrived." The Reverend looked to the stairs.

Two guards held Birhan by the arms and corralled him down the narrow steps. He had a gash across his cheek and his eye was swollen shut, his shirt torn and bloody underneath a black jacket that had been thrown over his shoulders. Angelo watched in silent rage as they pushed the boy across the room and down into the seat opposite him.

"I'm sorry, brother," Birhan said.

Angelo sank back into his chair. "It's not your fault. It's mine."

Only as he looked past Birhan, out the windows, did Angelo realize that the boat had pulled away from the dock and was heading out to sea.

CHAPTER TWENTY-EIGHT

Night had fallen when the Reverend and Kitty finished eating and invited Angelo and Birhan to join them on the upper deck. The handful of guards now flanking the table accepted the invitation on behalf of the two men, yanking Angelo and Birhan up from their seats when they refused to move and marshaling them up the stairs. One of the guards tried to take the rod from Angelo but snatched his hand back when fingers of charged energy sparked from the wood.

The sudden change from the frigid temperatures of the air-conditioned cabin to the warmer, salty air on the open deck made Angelo feel like he was moving between worlds. A brilliant blue circle, lit by the underwater lights, blossomed out from the yacht and merged with streaks of yellow and purple from the running lights, until they disappeared into the black of the sea. With a clear night, free of the obstructions of trees or mountains or buildings, the universe spilled out over the huge sky and reminded Angelo of the nights he and Mouse had lain under such a sky in the outback, making promises with their bodies and plans with their words. An explosion of longing seared his chest, and he saw the Cheshire moon just rising up from the horizon, mocking him.

He'd lost so much, given away so much—but no more, Angelo swore. No more.

"Let Birhan go," he said to Kitty. "I'll do whatever you want. You don't need him."

"The Reverend came up with this part of the plan—it's for him to say what happens to your boy, not me," Kitty answered as she stepped forward to the bow. She put her pretty white clutch on one of the pretty white lounge chairs and pulled out three vials of blood.

"We're lit up like a Christmas tree out here. Hey, Cap!" the Reverend hollered up to the wheelhouse.

Birhan jumped at the sudden noise.

The Reverend laughed and then called out again. "Cap, cut all the lights but the ones you need and a couple down here so we can see."

The boat and the water around it went suddenly dark, as if they'd been swallowed, then a couple of lights buzzed back to life, casting a thin glow over the deck where they stood. Kitty set to work. Angelo could hear her mumbling her spell as she poured blood onto the glossy golden deck wood.

"You don't need Mouse's brother anymore, Kitty. I've got Aaron's rod and the Book of the Just. Use them instead."

She popped the rubber stopper out of the second vial of blood. "I'm not a fool, Angelo, and you've taught me so much about how all this magic works. I saw what happened to the guard just now when he tried to touch it. I'd prefer not to get fried by the power in that thing. And I'm pretty sure the rod will only work for the person who holds the Book, maybe just for the person who found it."

"I'll use them for you."

"You're a bad liar, Angelo. I suppose some might say that makes you a good man, but I know it just makes you a fool." She shrugged. "And besides, I want to do this."

Angelo could hear the thrill of power in her voice. Crafting spells and forcing the world to obey her whim fed all of Kitty's desires.

"I think we're still just a bit too visible if there're any other folks out here," the Reverend said to no one in particular.

Angelo kept his focus on Kitty—she was his only hope. "He's just a little boy, Kitty."

"Like your Mouse is just a girl?" Kitty hissed. "He's the son of Satan. He deserves what he gets."

Angelo shivered as a chill ran through him and lingered.

"Alright, Angel-boy," the Reverend said as he slapped Angelo on the back. "What can that thing do?"

"Why don't you try it out?"

"I'll follow my wife's lead on this one. I'm not inclined to touch it myself. But I would like you to give me a demonstration, and I won't ask again."

"If I say no?"

The Reverend lurched forward, pulled a gun out of the holster of the nearest guard, aimed at Birhan and fired before Angelo could even register what was happening.

Kitty screamed, and there was a sound of breaking glass. "For heaven's sakes, Kevin! You made me drop it!" A fist-sized red blob burst like a sun outside the line of the spell she was crafting. Pieces of shattered glass jutted up like broken teeth.

Birhan dropped to his knees, clutching at his arm where a slow, thin waterfall of blood oozed out of a gash along his bicep. Angelo started to take a step toward him, but a guard grabbed him from behind.

"I just winged him," the Reverend said. "A warning for you. When I say I'm done asking, I'm done. You understand?"

"Yes."

"Yes, *sir*."

"Sir."

"That's enough, Kevin," Kitty barked. "Thanks to your pissing contest, I have to use my last vial of blood for this spell. You better hope it's enough." She bent back over her work.

"Are you okay, Birhan?" Angelo asked.

The teenager had pushed himself back to his feet, his hand pressing against the wound to stop the bleeding. "I am . . . fit as fiddler." He smiled weakly. "I say that right, brother?"

"Close enough."

"It's fit as a fiddle, boy. And you better hope your *brother* does what I've told him to do." The Reverend was starting to sweat in the warm air, little beads lining up in the creases of his forehead and catching bits of the light.

Angelo looked at Birhan a moment longer, saw the pain and fear in his eyes, and then he opened the Book of the Just. He searched for a spell that seemed least likely to go terribly wrong.

"Shroud us in the safety of your breath. Hide us from our enemies in a cloak of your making." As the words left his lips, Angelo felt the power build in the rod and stretch up and out and down to the sea. Gauzy wisps rose up from the water, shimmering a moment in the rising moonlight, until they billowed and grew thick like clouds and surrounded the boat, tendrils snaking around the deck, running between legs like cats.

The guards gasped and cursed. Kitty smiled. The Reverend's lips pressed together in a hard, unreadable line.

"Finished!" Kitty said through the fog. "I'm r—"

"Ready or not, here I come." The voice came from higher up, on the sundeck. Everyone turned to look. The thick mist obscured all but a dark silhouette looking down on them. But a dazzling joy ran through Angelo as if the sun had suddenly come out.

He knew that voice. He thought he'd never hear it again.

But Mouse had found him at last.

⚊✦⚊

Her father pulled the cloak back and Mouse stepped out into a murky grayness. She felt his absence in the next breath. She was alone.

She could see little through the thick fog, but she smelled the fishy water and the wax on the boat and the Reverend and Kitty's perfumes and someone's blood she did not know—and lots of Luc's blood. So Kitty *had* collected more. She must be crafting a spell with it even now. And then Mouse smelled Angelo.

But she needed to take care of business first.

She closed her eyes and counted—eighteen souls, plus Angelo's. Though still bright and full, there was something different about his that Mouse couldn't identify. Angrily, she shoved that away, too.

"Finished!" Kitty said through the fog. "I'm r—"

"Ready or not, here I come," Mouse said.

In the moment of stunned silence, Mouse pulled her hand up sharply as she spoke to the water on the starboard side: "Rise!" A rush of sea and foam raked over the rail and across the deck.

"No!" Kitty cried as she fought to keep standing against the wave and watched her blood-soaked spell wash away.

Bullets flew at Mouse. She dropped to a crouch, her ears sifting through the cacophony for the sounds of the guards reloading. She readied herself to make for the stairs, but the whizz and ping of bullets suddenly stopped. Cautiously, she eased up and looked out over the deck. There was a shimmer, like superheated air over a stretch of hot road. It ran the length of the sundeck, and the bullets hit and ricocheted off as if it were an invisible shield.

Her eyes searched for Angelo, but through the haze and dim light she could make out little more than the shape of his body and a long staff stretching up and out from it. The rod of Aaron. And Angelo was using it. But was the shield meant to protect her or to pin her down?

Mouse reached to the small of her back where she had sheathed the bone shard, but her fingers groped empty cloth and brushed her bare skin. Frantically, she scanned the deck around her, but the shard was gone. It must have slipped out and rolled overboard. Mouse would have to do what had to be done by her own hand. She jumped off the back of the deck, down to the landing behind the wheelhouse, and kicked in the doors, dodging a spray of bullets from one of two men in the room.

"Don't shoot!" she commanded. The man lowered his gun, his face blank and confused for a moment, and then he rushed her. Mouse was expecting it. She ducked as he swung the butt of the gun at her, swiped his legs out from under him, grabbed him by the throat as he fell, and slammed his head hard against the wood floor. "Stay down!" she whispered in his ear.

The other man had stayed beside the ship's console, his hands up. "I'm just the captain. I drive the boat. I don't want to hurt anyone."

"Stay in here." Mouse pulled back on the power, but she could still feel a trace of it behind her words. The captain nodded and sat down. "Stairs down to the next deck?" she asked.

He pointed to the far corner beside a low wall, but as she turned toward the stairs, something outside the wheelhouse window caught her eye. A pair of shadows in the heavy fog stood at the tip point of the bow on the main deck, one tall and one very short at his side—her father and Luc.

There was no way Kitty could have cast a summoning spell that quickly. Could she? And why was Mouse's father here? He surely wouldn't have followed his son into the mouth of danger. Unless he'd learned regret from abandoning Luc the first time.

Mouse took to the stairs, her plan shifting. She'd bypass the upper deck where Kitty, the Reverend, Angelo, and all the shooting guards were. She'd get Luc to safety and then come back.

Another gun went off. Angelo screamed and a hail of bullets shattered the windows of the wheelhouse. The shield was gone.

Mouse's stomach wrenched.

⊶━⊷

Angelo was already searching the Book of the Just for a spell before the guards regained their footing from the rush of water Mouse had called up. He didn't know if the Book and rod would work this way, but he had to try.

He found the spell as the first bullets pounded the sundeck where Mouse had been. But Angelo changed the words.

"Shield her from her enemies. Let no arrow nor spear nor lance nor any weapon pierce the righteousness of her cause." He felt the power course through the rod, feeding the air with energy and heat. It made a wall in front of Mouse. Angelo smiled at the shouted confusion among the guards—no bullet could penetrate the shield.

He got a glimpse of her face as she swung into the lighted wheelhouse and took out the gunman and spoke to the captain. She looked different. Her hair was short, her face hard and gaunt, her eyes dark. She looked like her father. Then she looked out past Angelo, toward something in the mist, and her eyes woke with worry and love. And he knew that Mouse was as she'd always ever been—good.

Angelo turned to see what she was looking at, and his fears came rushing back as he saw the silhouette—Mouse's father was here. Why would she bring him unless they were working together? For a moment, Angelo worried that Kitty and the Reverend had been right—that Mouse belonged now to the family she had always craved. Then Angelo saw a smaller silhouette beside the larger. The fog swirled and thinned for a moment, and he could see the boy's face more clearly. Angelo hadn't realized until that moment that he already loved this boy—loved him for who he was and for who he might become. He loved him all the more for having eyes just like his sister.

The gun went off so close to Angelo's head that his left eye flashed with light and his ear rang with a shrill squalling. The hulk of the Reverend moving up beside him blocked Angelo's view of the stairs. Where was Mouse?

His eyes pivoted to find Birhan's again. Angelo was going to signal for him to drop when Mouse made her move. But Birhan wasn't standing where he had been. Birhan was on the floor, completely still, a river of blood running from him.

Angelo screamed and pushed forward, but the Reverend caught his arm and spun him around. Rivulets of sweat oozed down the fat face pressed cheek to cheek with Angelo's. "He's not dead yet. He's got a bullet hole, clean shot, through his thigh." The Reverend's voice, moist and languid, filled Angelo's ear. "I might have nicked that big artery that runs through there. He'll bleed out unless someone gets some pressure on that wound. You got a chance to save him, but not your girl, too. Choose." His pale blue eyes looked empty and dead as he stared into Angelo's, which were full of fury and fear.

Defeated, Angelo lowered the rod, hoping he'd given Mouse an advantage. In the second he'd had to weigh an impossible choice, he knew that win or lose, Mouse would live, just as surely as Birhan would die if Angelo wasted any more time. The power snapped back with a jolt and bullets went flying as the shield disappeared.

"Good choice, son. Now take the girl down."

Mouse heard the clunk of footsteps lower on the stairs. She braced herself against the handrails and swung forward, feet out, slamming her boots into the chest of the first guard, who toppled back against a second man coming up behind him. A spurt of bullets bounced against the walls, and the first guard cried out as one dug into him.

"Don't shoot!" Mouse commanded them as she jammed her elbow into the throat of the second guard and climbed over him and out onto the deck.

Angelo stood beside the Reverend to Mouse's right about eight feet away. Two guards flanked the Reverend. There was a body on the floor in front of her. She held her breath a moment, listening. He was still alive, but not for long, unless someone stopped the bleeding. Instinctively, she moved toward him, but guards pulled around the starboard side and started shooting.

Her shoulder recoiled as a bullet bit into her collarbone, and she fell back, crouching on the port side of the deck. Clenching her teeth against the searing pain, she put her hands down on the wood flooring and started to sway, side to side.

"Rise up," she said to the sea.

High, rolling waves crashed against the side of the yacht. The boat swelled up over the water, leaning hard to port, and slid down the back side and up against the next mountainous wave. The Reverend fell to his knees with a loud thud. His two bodyguards tried to haul him up, but they were pitching back and forth so violently they couldn't touch him. Mouse heard the guards on the starboard side cry out, followed by two sharp slaps of water as they fell overboard. Angelo was the only one left standing.

With a quick scan of the deck, Mouse realized she'd lost track of Kitty, and a cold dread ran through her veins. But then Angelo called out for her.

"Mouse! He's sliding off! Help him!"

The body in front of her rolled hard to the left as another wave hit. Mouse lunged for it as it went over the side. The head lolled back, face up, as she knotted her fists into his shirt and waistband. She could see now that it was a young man, a boy really, about sixteen or seventeen years old. Blood was pouring out of a gaping hole in his thigh. His heartbeat was slow and faint. He would be dead soon.

Mouse could hear the bullet wedged into her broken collarbone grind and squeal as she tried to pull him up. He was too heavy. When another wave hit the starboard side, the boy's weight pulled her halfway overboard.

"Be still," she said through gritted teeth to the water, and the water went still like glass.

She looked over her shoulder toward Angelo. His face silenced all her doubts, and, even in the midst of the chaos and danger, she felt joy catch at her throat. Angelo looked at her with such faith—he still believed in her, body and soul. She'd found home again, at last.

The boat started rocking. Angelo leaned against his crutches and the rod, working to keep his balance. He looked up to see Birhan sliding overboard. Angelo couldn't get to him in time. But Mouse could.

"Mouse! He's sliding off! Help him!"

Mouse didn't know Birhan, didn't know if he was one of the Reverend's men. But it didn't matter. She lunged for him. She saved him. As Angelo knew she would.

"Take her now! She's vulnerable!" the Reverend yelled.

Angelo smiled down at him as he rolled on the deck. "You have no idea what she's capable of, but I do. If you have a way off this boat, I'd go now."

"I'll do it myself, then!" The Reverend lunged for Aaron's rod, his chunky fingers wrapping greedily around the smooth wood. Thick, radiant blue branches of light shot out from the rod and into the Reverend, who buckled backward, his eyes wide and slathers of foamy spit bubbling at the corners of his mouth. The crackles of lightning were gone as quickly as they came. The Reverend's men caught him as he pitched forward, but there was no point. Spinal fluid poured from his ears and nose as his guards dragged him down the port side, away from the shooting, his eyes fixed and staring blankly toward the heavens.

"Angelo!" Mouse cried.

His eyes snapped up to meet hers.

"I can't hold him. Help me!"

Angelo catapulted himself forward with his crutches and let go of the rod as he dropped to his knees and threw his torso over the side, clutching at Birhan's waistband. He swung his legs around to brace himself against the rail and pulled. Mouse rolled over into the same position, and together they hauled Birhan back up onto the deck.

Mouse balled up the edge of her cloak and pressed down against the wound to stop the bleeding. "We need something to make a tourniquet."

"There's no time, Mouse. He won't make it." Angelo put his hands on hers. "Be who you are. Command him to live." He was begging her.

"If I tell him to live, he might do it—forever. I won't do that to anyone, Angelo. That's a curse no one should have to bear."

"Choose different words then. You're a healer, Mouse. Just heal him. Please."

She bent to Birhan's ear and whispered for him alone. "Heal. Heal fast. Heal sure. Heal."

Blood bubbled out of the wound as the skin knit itself together. She could hear his heart, steady and strong. She looked up at Angelo, smiling, but the moment of relief melted away as Mouse saw the scene playing out over Angelo's shoulder at the far end of the bow on the main deck below them.

Kitty stood between Mouse's father and Luc. Luc wore the tattered cloak Mouse had left behind at the gardener's cottage. He wore the mask of the *kurdaitcha*. He looked like a smaller version of Mouse when she had gone hunting for vengeance.

And in his hand, Luc held the glowing shaft of the bone shard sent down from the Seven Sisters.

He was pointing it at Kitty.

CHAPTER TWENTY-NINE

Mouse shoved past Angelo and stumbled to the railing, looking down on the deck below.

"Luc! Put the bone down!" Her voice was shrill, panicked, pleading.

He startled and turned up to look at her. The *kurdaitcha* mask, almost as long as his whole body, jutted up into the thick fog and sent wisps spiraling out from him like pinwheel universes born in the moment.

"Think about what this woman did to you," their father said to Luc. "What she did to your sister. This woman is evil." He was quiet and calm, reassuring. He drew Luc's attention back to the disheveled, blank-faced Kitty, who stood in front of the boy.

Mouse wrestled her panic and shoved it down, deep inside, so when she spoke, she, too, was calm. "She has hurt you, Luc. And she deserves to be punished for it. She wants to make the world look just like her. She wants to make everyone act just the way she wants. She wants everyone following her rules. And she's willing to do anything to make that happen."

"Then I *should* kill her," Luc said through clenched teeth.

"Yes!" his father hissed.

"No. Because this isn't about her, sweetheart. It's about you. About the choices *you* want to make." Mouse started to climb the rail.

"Stay up there!" Luc cried.

"Okay, okay." She stepped back. "I'm not going to make you do anything. I just want you to think it through first. I have faith in you, Luc."

"Me, too," their father said.

"I know you'll make the right choice. And I'll love you regardless of what you choose to do. Okay?"

Luc half turned and nodded. Their father was silent.

"Do you remember how you felt after your nanny died?" Mouse asked.

"I didn't mean to do it, and I was sorry it happened." He sounded so small. "But this is different. I want to do this!" His voice surged with all the pain and fear he'd suffered; the bone shard glowed brighter.

"Part of you does, yes," Mouse answered.

"I didn't do anything to her. I didn't do anything and she . . ." His heart was pounding in his little chest. "It hurt. Everywhere. And she . . . she laughed as she cut me, laughed when I screamed. She said I deserved it." He cocked his head toward Mouse again. "Did I? Am I something bad, Mouse?"

"No!" Anguish burned against Mouse's throat and eyes, but she needed to walk through this with him—wherever the path might lead. She would not let him walk it alone. It was a broken, little-girl Mouse, the girl who had spent so much of her childhood asking the same question, who gave him his answer. "You are not bad, Luc, and you didn't deserve it. You didn't do anything wrong. What you are is a beautiful boy with a kind heart. There's *nothing* wrong with you."

"No, there's not." Their father took a step toward Luc and put a hand on his shoulder. "And yet this woman ripped you away from your own bed, made your skin bubble and boil so she could cage you like an animal, and then she—"

"Stop!" Luc cried as he leaned forward, the tip of the bone shard just inches from Kitty.

"Do it," their father said. He kicked Kitty at the back of the knee, driving her down onto the deck. She pulled up and was now face-to-face with Luc, who took a step back, his hands shaking.

"I know you want to make her pay for what she did," Mouse said.

"Just like you did, you hypocrite." Her father sneered. "You picked off the people who hurt you and yours. One by one, you hunted them in this same cloak, wearing this same mask, trying to hide from your true self. My son has the strength to accept who he is, to embrace it. To do what he was born to do." He flipped the *kurdaitcha* mask off Luc's face. It went spinning out into the dark sea.

Mouse's head hung down. "He's right that I was weak, Luc. But the weakness was giving in to my anger. I wanted revenge for what had been done to me and to Angelo. And he's right—" She couldn't hold back the tears. "I hunted those people down. I killed them—I didn't mean to, but I wanted them dead. And so it happened. I will carry the guilt of that the rest of my life. But that's not who I am. Surely not who I was raised to be." She looked up to the star-strewn sky. The fog was gone, but her sight was blurred with shame. "I made the wrong choice, Luc. Which is why I don't want you to do the same thing." She leaned against the rail, looking down on him again. "And you are stronger than I am."

Luc shook his head, his hair ruffled and knotted where the mask had been. "No, I'm not."

"You are. Do you know how I know?"

He turned to look at her. His eyes were wide with fear. He needed her to have the words to help him let go of his anger.

"When you . . . when Mercy died—"

"That was an accident." His eyes squeezed tight against the blur of tears.

"I know, I know. You did it because you were angry. You didn't mean to—just like I didn't mean to. We all make mistakes, Luc. Because we're human. So is Kitty. Look at her."

Luc turned back to face his tormentor.

343

"This woman *meant* to hurt you, and she was going to do it again, son," their father interjected. "You saw her pouring your blood all over this boat so she could play her sick game. And she'll do it again if we don't stop her. She's your enemy." He sounded more urgent, pressing.

Mouse kept her voice even, hopeful. "Think about that day with Mercy. I know it hurts to look back on something we did that we're ashamed of—but there's something far more important about that moment. She forgave you. You remember how that felt?"

A little light drove out some of the anger and fear in his eyes.

"This is how I know you're stronger than me. You let her forgive you, and you forgave yourself. You accepted her gift of mercy. I'm not very good at that. I hope you'll teach me."

His body started to relax.

"I know you can be as strong as Mercy. I know—"

Mouse's father pulled himself up. "This woman does not deserve your forgiveness, and she will not love you for it."

"It's not about her, Luc. It's about *you*. What choice do you want to make?"

Luc looked up at his father, his lips quivering. Mouse could see the boy shaking, but he held himself as if bracing for something. "I won't do it, Father. I won't kill anyone. Not now. Not ever."

Like her little brother, Mouse saw the blow coming. She was over the rail and grabbing her father's arm before he could backhand his son. He shook himself free of her and his human form at the same time, Mouse and the shreds of his humanity falling to the deck at his feet. He kicked out at her, his clawed foot slamming against her chest and throwing her back against a table. His other hand snaked out and plucked the Seven Sisters' bone shard from Luc.

"Why am I the only one willing to do the dirty work that must be done?" His voice was high, playful—a voice Mouse had learned to fear. It signaled that her father was at the peak of his fury, wild and unpredictable. He sighed and shrugged dramatically and tossed the bone into the air. He caught it as it fell just in front of Kitty's face. And then he slammed the point of it through the flesh of her bottom jaw, up through her palate, and out her left eye. Blood shot out of her like a fountain.

Luc screamed when the blood sprayed across his face. He wiped at it frantically as if it were burning him. Mouse scrambled over to him. He threw his arms around her neck, wiping his face side to side against her shoulder and then burying his head against her chest. She tried to pull him back so she could make sure he wasn't hurt and to clean away the blood, but he wouldn't let go.

Their father lifted Kitty up, his hand still gripping the bone shard under her chin, blood raining down, and he tossed her into the sea. The bone glowed brightly blue down into the dark, until it was a ghost, and then it was gone. He reached down and grabbed Luc by the collar and pulled, ripping the seams of his shirt. Mouse kicked at him and wrapped her arms more tightly around Luc, who was screaming something meant to be words but which Mouse couldn't understand. A boot slammed into her ribs and wedged between her and Luc, pushing her away.

She couldn't hold on. Luc couldn't hold on. He cried out as he was torn away from her: "Mouse. Mouse."

"Please!" she begged. "Leave him here. Let me take care of him. Please!"

Her father hammered his knee into her face and sent her flying onto her back across the deck. She saw the storm then, swirling, massive, lightning popping, and she twisted her head around to see Angelo standing on the upper deck, the rod of Aaron in his hand, the Book of the Just in his other, and Birhan by his side.

"Leave them alone or I will unleash God's own fury against you," Angelo said.

Her father held Luc by the waist. The boy was tearing at him, trying to get loose. "I don't care about her. But I am going to take my son home."

He started to pull his cloak around himself and Luc.

Mouse had crawled to them and wrapped her hand around his boot. "I'll go in his place. Let Angelo have Luc. I'll go with you. I won't fight. I'll do whatever . . . whatever you ask me to do." She was sobbing. "And

I can take care of myself. You don't have to . . . you don't have to look after me like you do him. You know you don't like it. Please."

Her father paused. "How do I know you'd keep your word?"

"Because I love him."

"No, Mouse," Luc whimpered. "I want to be with you."

Her father tossed his head side to side, considering. "You know, if I take him, I bet you'll come home on your own, wagging your tail behind you. So, I'll see you later—" A finger of lightning shot down from the sky and struck him in the back. He arched, howling, and let go of Luc, who sank to the deck and curled into a ball.

"I will not let you take Mouse or the boy," Angelo said.

"Who are you to stop me?" Mouse's father demanded.

The boat began to quake as the sea churned.

"I bear the Book of the Just and the rod of Aaron," Angelo replied.

"Meh, been there, done that." He shrugged. "Now I have legions at my command."

Mouse could see forms taking shape in the water. Thousands. Hundreds of thousands. Demons.

Luc put his hand in hers, his face full of the same desperate surety that had settled on Mouse. They had no choice.

"Angelo, don't." She said it quietly, but he heard all the same. "It's not worth the end of the world. Let us go."

Angelo shook his head and tightened his grip on the rod. "I can't lose you again. Not to him."

The creatures in the sea started to scramble on top of each other, breaking the surface of the water. Some were giant-like demons Mouse had seen so long ago in the pit at Houska. Some were smaller. All of them had faces that were achingly hungry, and Mouse knew what they craved—the light inside all the people, light that the demons had never had or had forfeited. They wanted to gorge themselves on souls and devour hope.

"I love you, Angelo. If you love me, if you've ever loved me, you'll stop." She stood and pulled Luc up into her arms. She could taste blood and the salt of her tears on her tongue. "Put the rod down. Please."

Angelo's face crumpled and he lowered the rod. Birhan put his arms around him, holding him up. The storm uncoiled and floated away like ships in the sky.

"I don't want to say good-bye." Angelo could barely get the words out.

"Me, either." Mouse clenched her hands into Luc's shirt. "*Miluji tě*," she whispered to Angelo, and then stepped toward her father.

Angelo fell to his knees, unable to speak, his face turned up to the sky.

The sea was still churning with demons, though they seemed to be waiting for something. Mouse looked to her father. His face was full of something she couldn't read. She'd never seen him look that way. His eyes were on something past her.

"I wondered when you'd show up," he said.

Mouse spun to look where he was looking. On the upper deck, framed by the stars and a sliver of moon, sat a man Mouse knew was not just a man. He wore a simple linen tunic that bunched against faded jeans rolled at the cuffs, his bare feet dangling out. He was covered in tattoos—symbols and letters Mouse knew from a book she'd read once seven centuries ago, a book that had nearly killed her. The Book of the Angels. The man's face was full of the same expression her father wore, shame and sadness and a terrible hope.

"Hello, brother," the man said. "It's been a while."

"You're a little late, Gabe. It's all over. Crisis averted and all that. You can head back to your angelic throne." Mouse's father twitched his head and the demon-filled sea went quiet and still. "No Armageddon today. See?"

"You can't take credit for that this time, Star of Morning."

"That's not my name anymore."

"It will always be the name waiting for you when you forgive yourself."

"Let's not rehash old arguments. It's been a long night already."

"I'm the Messenger." He shrugged. "I deliver the message I've been asked to give. And it's hard to catch you at home these days."

"Asked? Since when does the boss ask?"

"You're proof of the free will he offers. Your own children have tried to teach you—through great cost to themselves." Gabriel sat unnaturally still, but his eyes turned to meet Mouse's for a breath and a heartbeat before returning to gaze on her father. "You have the power to choose."

"Just deliver your message."

Mouse had never before seen her father nervous and unsure of himself.

"Are you ready to come home?" Gabriel asked, his voice soft and compelling.

Their father looked down on Mouse and Luc, his eyes soft for such a brief moment that Mouse wondered if she'd imagined it. And then he looked out at the sea. "I don't concede defeat. I'm not done here yet."

Gabriel sighed. "That wasn't the question."

"Well, it's my answer. Can we go now?"

"No."

Anger flashed in his eyes as he snapped his head up to look at Gabriel. "You have no power to command me."

"*You* are free to go, Star of Morning. But they are not. They have choices of their own to make."

"They're mine. They go with me."

Gabriel shook his head. "You helped to give them life, but they are part human and so under another's purview. Thus, they have free will, like the rest of humanity."

"They belong with their father," he spat.

"They are certainly free to go with you, if they wish."

"No," Luc and Mouse said together.

The hurt in their father's eyes stayed much longer than the softness had, and then he masked it with disdain. "Fine. Stay. You're both weak."

Mouse could hear the promise in his voice—this wasn't finished. He snatched his cloak around him and was gone. A rustle of wind floated down as if the stars and the sky and the sea all sighed.

CHAPTER THIRTY

The boat swayed gently. Mouse turned to find Angelo standing behind her. She leaned into his arms, his crutches gently tapping against her legs, with Luc, still clinging tightly to Mouse's neck, nestled between them.

Mouse closed her eyes, counting souls. "Where's the Reverend?"

"Dead." Angelo looked over his shoulder toward the back of the boat.

She nodded—everyone else was accounted for.

"What now?" Angelo asked as he pulled back.

Mouse was looking up at the man on the upper deck. "Let's ask him. Seems like he's been pulling the puppet strings."

"Do we know him?" Luc whispered at her ear.

"I think I do," Angelo answered. "Sort of. He came to me at a monastery where I was doing research. And he's been in my dreams." Angelo turned and asked the man, "Why?"

"It goes back further than that, doesn't it?" Mouse said. "You pulled Angelo out of the Thames."

The man lifted his hands and shrugged.

"Why?" Angelo asked again.

"Some among my kind study the tides of humanity. They can sometimes see how events might play out. They help us be more watchful."

"Watchful for what?" Luc asked.

At the same time, Mouse asked, "Us who?"

The man smiled. "I am—"

"Gabriel, the Messenger. I think we all had that figured out," Angelo said.

Gabriel leaned back, laughing. Mouse saw that he even had words inked on the soles of his feet—a messenger covered in messages, though the tattoos made him look more like a biker than an angel. He grabbed the railing, slid his feet under him, and pulled himself upright in a single, lithe motion, like a dancer at the barre.

"I won't be able to answer most of your questions—not in any way that will satisfy you. I'm not really supposed to be here." He glanced at the sky and then down at Mouse and Angelo and Luc.

Angelo had been searching for an answer to one question ever since he'd miraculously survived his suicide at the Thames all those years ago. "Why'd you save me?"

"And here's the first I can't answer—" He threw his hands up as Mouse and Angelo tensed, ready to object. "Not because I won't, but because I don't know. You'd suffered so much sorrow in your young life already. I wanted to give you another chance."

Luc's head snapped up. "Did you hear it, Mouse?"

"Yes, I did. There's more you're not telling."

Gabriel smiled at her, his eyes lit with surprise. "You *are* good. Most people only hear what I want them to hear—that's my gift. It's why I'm the chosen messenger."

"Well, I've had lots of practice listening for lies and half-truths."

"I bet you have!" He looked over to where her father had stood.

"You came down with my father and the others, didn't you?" Mouse wanted answers, not polite conversation, and she'd already pieced enough together to have suspicions.

Gabriel leaned against the railing. "I didn't stay long."

"Long enough to do what you wanted—you had a family, didn't you?"

The sadness washed over his face again like the tide.

Mouse looked at Angelo. "And he's one of yours, isn't he?"

"I'm what?" Angelo asked.

"A millennia-old descendant."

"You've kept track of your offspring over all this time?" Angelo asked incredulously.

A ghost of a smile, mingled with regret, pulled at Gabriel's lips. "No. But every so often, once in a generation maybe, someone's born that still bears the mark of my seed. It shines to me like a beacon among the billions. It fills me with joy. It haunts me."

Mouse took a step forward, closer to him. "I thought you killed them all," she said sharply.

"Killed who?" Luc asked against her neck.

"The children of the Watchers."

"Most of my kind had already gone back home before the Watchers started making their trouble. We couldn't handle the pain of loving such terribly fragile creatures. We left. But your father and some of the others stayed and let their grief make them bitter, and their bitterness corrupted the world." He ran his hands over his shaved head. "We had to fix it," Gabriel continued softly. "We had to restore balance so humanity could have the chance to make their own choices."

"How much blood did you shed?" she asked.

"A lot more than you." He looked hard into Mouse's face. She understood now the almost unbearable expression he wore because it mirrored her own.

"Father . . . he's a Watcher, isn't he?" Luc asked in a high voice. "What's going to happen to us?"

"I won't let anything happen to you," Mouse said as she pulled him tighter, her eyes fierce with defiance as she lifted her face to Gabriel again. "You've been pulling all the strings. Saving Angelo, sending him to the church at Santa Maria in Cosmedin to find me, making sure we—"

"No." Gabriel looked at her, understanding.

"Don't lie to me." Her voice started to crack. "We deserve to know if everything we've shared was just part of your game."

"What do you mean?" Angelo asked, his own voice filling with the same wariness.

Gabriel sighed. "A person in the right place at the right time sometimes just happens. But sometimes it is a gift of the angels—there are others among my kind who wish to pay penance for mistakes they made."

"So some angel pulled a thread and wove us together to make up for something they did an eon ago? Why?" Angelo said, his jaw clenching.

"We have watched Mouse with great interest, as you might imagine."

"Because I'm the child of the Corruptor."

"No," Gabriel said sharply. "Because you give us hope. One heartbreak after another, and you still choose to love. Tormented for who and what you are, yet you still sacrifice for others, for your own tormentors. We, who were not strong enough, who ran from this flawed and fragile humanity, stand in awe of you, Mouse."

She was shaking her head, tears rolling down her face. "I don't deserve that. I am not what you say I am. I have—"

"Made mistakes? Yes. And you've paid for them tenfold. Forgive yourself. Luc will help you." Gabriel turned back to Angelo, pleading for understanding. "She struggled alone for so long, and when we watched her sinking into the pit with no one to help her, we sent you. But we merely brought you to the right place at the right time. The two of you did the rest. The two of you wove your stories together. Your love is of your own doing and none of mine."

"Mouse was really sad when you died," Luc said to Angelo. "I saw her."

Angelo stepped close to her and kissed her on top of the head, but then he looked up at Gabriel again. "Did I die? Am I—"

"Immortal? No. You're as human—and as mortal—as Mouse's son was."

"Then in the outback, how did I—"

"My father's doing," Mouse answered.

Angelo nodded, but he had a final question. "Why come to me at the monastery?"

"To help you find the rod and the Book of the Just."

"Why be so cryptic, then? Why not just come on in and translate it for me?"

"I don't think he was supposed to help you. Right?" Mouse asked.

"The Book and the rod belong now to the ebb and flow of humanity—not to the divine. The choice to use them or not belongs to you. When it was clear that they would be revealed once more, I wanted to make sure they came to the right hands."

"To the hands of the Just," said Birhan, who had been standing silently at Angelo's side. "Because someone who is just will not wish to punish but to forgive. They will never use the rod and Book to bring the end of the world." He clapped Angelo on the shoulder. "Is like Indiana Jones and the Ark of the Covenant, yes, brother?"

Angelo held the rod and the Book up to Gabriel. "You should take them, then. I don't know where to find a big empty warehouse to lose them in, and we wouldn't want them to fall into the wrong hands."

Gabriel put his hands up. "I cannot take them. You are the Bearer now. You can choose to hide them away like Joachim before you. Or you can keep them with you."

"What about us, Mouse? Will we be safe now?" Luc asked.

Mouse would not lie to him. She shook her head. "I don't think our father's done with us. We'll have to try to hide. I've done it before. I'll teach you." The idea of running again weighed as heavily as if the whole of the sea were pressing down on her.

"There are other choices," Gabriel said. "The Book of the Just and the rod can help you."

"But he knows where they are—they'll make it easier for him to find us." A new truth slammed against Mouse's already tired mind, and her eyes shot over to meet Angelo's.

353

"I can draw him away from you," Angelo said. He'd figured it out, too. Mouse and Luc would go one way, and he would have to go the other.

"I don't think the Star of Morning will come so near the rod and Book again. He risks forfeit of the deal he was given." Gabriel closed his eyes a moment. "And he's not ready for the end."

"So as long as I'm with them, they're safe," Angelo said.

"From him, yes."

"But not from others like Kitty or the Reverend," Mouse said sadly.

"Not if they have the means and the knowledge to do you harm," Gabriel answered. "And your immortality will still make you wanderers."

"What other choice do Luc and I have?" Mouse asked.

"You can stay. Or you can come home."

Home, Mouse thought with a mixture of excitement and anguish. She'd never really had that kind of home or family—someplace where she could truly belong with people like her. She could stop running. She could rest and be at peace. She could share that with Luc. She could say good-bye to Angelo now in a quick, agonizing stroke, rather than waiting through the long days for it to come.

She found him looking at her, his eyes filled with tears like hers. He was reading her face, as he did so well. "It's okay for you to go," he said, more breath than words.

And her mind flooded with all the moments of joy she'd be giving up—the kisses and caresses, the jokes and banter, the adventures, all the places she'd yet to take him, the things they hadn't done. She might have a lifetime with him. She didn't know if she could let that go.

But it wasn't her decision to make alone.

"What do you want to do, Luc?"

Luc looked up at Gabriel, his face full of knowing. Going meant no more Kittys, no more suffering. He turned to Mouse and put his little hand against her cheek, wiping away a tear.

"You said the world was a beautiful place full of beautiful people." His voice cracked with hope. "I'd like to see it, Mouse."

EPILOGUE

At twilight, a man walked down the street of a quiet cul-de-sac in a sedate suburb at the edge of a modest city. He stopped in front of a little bungalow with a front porch teeming with herbs and flowers. He crossed the yard, dipped beneath a willow tree, and stood just inside its curtain of leaves, mostly hidden from the view of any inconvenient passersby.

He watched the pleasant scene unfolding on the other side of the picture window. It framed a living room that stretched into the kitchen at the back of the house. The front room was cluttered with photos and handmade art crafted by a child. A blanket and pillows lay disheveled on the couch. Stacks of books precariously perched in towers everywhere. Dog toys were scattered on the floor.

Warm, creamy light spilled out onto the spring grass. The windows were open, and he could hear the clink of plates and a strain of music plucked on a guitar, then a man's voice singing silly lyrics, followed by the high, bright laughter of a child and the happy bark of a dog.

The sounds drew the man closer to the house, closer to the people inside, closer to his family.

They are mine, he thought. *I want them.*

But then Mouse turned, carrying something from the oven to the table. She took his breath away. She'd always been beautiful—he expected no less from his daughter—but he'd never seen her shine with such joy. She looked like an angel.

"Birhan texted this afternoon," Angelo said as he dropped the guitar onto the couch and went back to the table, where Luc was laying out the silverware.

"Is he coming soon?" the boy asked.

"His mom's with him in Rome now, and they were planning to come when he's on school holiday in a couple of weeks."

"That's perfect! They'll be here for my gallery opening," Mouse said as she sat down between them, now facing the picture window.

Her father spun away from the glass, his body pressed against the house as a flare of jealousy drove out his tender moment of pride. Mouse had finally gotten what she'd always wanted—a family and a normal life. Her dream closed the door on him. What part could he have in such a life?

But in the corner of his eye, he saw the thin line of crusted blood and sparkle of salt that ran along the baseboard between the window and the door. Mouse was his daughter still.

With a flush of unaccustomed generosity, he decided that she deserved a respite. A snippet of old scripture came to mind—*To everything there is a season.* He would ensure Mouse and Luc a season of joy and peace, free of torment from him or anyone else.

There would be a time later to fulfill his own dreams. He could wait. He was good at waiting.

ACKNOWLEDGMENTS

It might seem a little odd to some for an author to dedicate a book to dogs, though I know I'm not the first. I imagine for most "dog people," such a dedication makes perfect sense. And it's not that I don't love cats, too. I currently have two adorable kitties (okay, one we actually call "Fat-bottom Obi," but that's not the point). Cats teach me a different lesson than dogs. Cats teach me fortitude and my place in the world. Dogs teach redemptive love.

I was a lonely kid, mostly by self-design. I lived in my books and on my bike. I didn't know how much I needed some living thing to love me without reserve and without condition until I met Koko. He was an abandoned, tiny pup who needed me. I needed him more. Koko taught me to overcome the boundaries of my own experience. He played me out of too much seriousness about myself and life. He gave me the courage to show boundless, crazy, exuberant love. And he taught me how to say good-bye.

The love we shared moves forward with me, and, even now, I find ways to give him a snuggle and a heartfelt "Good dog." What Bohdan does for Mouse in *Bohemian Gospel* and what Mercy gives to Luc in *Book of the Just* are my tribute to Koko and to the other dogs, mine and yours, who have redeemed us with their love.

And now I get to thank the people who walked with me through this last part of Mouse and Angelo's story—a story that is also about redemptive love.

My creative writing students rode the highs and lows with me this round, giving me an incredibly supportive community and hopefully getting a wonderful learning experience in return. My students, past and present, grow my heart and my horizons.

As always, my ever-constant early readers, Paige Crutcher and Leanne Smith, bolstered my courage. They empowered me to let the narrative go where it needed to go; they pulled me back when I wandered too far. But sometimes writers find themselves lost in the wilderness at the end of the journey. Andy Davidson read for me when I had a last, panicked throe, and gave me the confidence to keep moving forward. My sister, Beth Spencer Cummings, shone like my very own Pleaides and guided me back home—as she always does.

So many hands touch a book as it's being born. I am immensely grateful for all the folks at Pegasus: publisher Claiborne Hancock, interior designer Maria Fernandez, and cover designer Charles Brock of Faceout Studios. I hope they are as proud of the result as I am. I owe special thanks to my editor for this book, Katie McGuire, who challenged me in all the right places, keeping me honest in the storytelling and working magic to make my sentences better.

My agent, Susan Finesman, not only takes care of the tedious, wonky, and wary bits of the writing business for me, but she's also a kindred spirit and a friend who inspires me, dreams with me, and kicks me in the butt when I need it.

Some people seem to have all the answers you need just when you need them. Amy Kerr is that guru for me. She is always there when I ask for help, and she's always thoughtful and wise—even though she doesn't like *Star Wars*. (May the Force be with you, Amy.)

And at least I have my younger brother, Shane, who loves a good lightsaber duel and hours-long chat about galaxies far, far away. My fellow rebel and resister, he has always been in my corner, patching up life things and tech things with grace and speed.

I mention last the people who come first in my life.

My sweet boyo joyfully took up the job of gentle taskmaster and kept me on track. He insisted that I stop after only one round of Yoshi and chastised me when I started to slide onto the couch beside him for an episode of *Loud House*, telling me instead to go work on my book. He was waiting for me when I was done and fed me daily encouragement and snuggles, without which I would have surely foundered.

The girl kid fed me music and filled my well when it ran dry. I gave her sketchy descriptions of spoiler-free plot and a sense of the general tone, and she built me playlists that gave me inspiration and pulled out just the right emotional notes. She even found an obscure cover of "Let It Be" that saved a scene and made it soar.

Greg, my partner in everything, did everything. He gave me insight into Angelo when the dude frustrated me more than once. He freed up my time so I could write. He did the laundry, the grocery shopping, the homeschooling, the kid-carting. He read for me—again and again. He edited, line edited, copyedited. And then he did it all again when I asked. He was my shoulder to cry on, my punching bag when I was angry, my touchstone when I was lost. He is my everything.